Chesapeake
Mystery

***

Waters Ebb, Rocks Emerge

M·G·Lewis

Copyright © 2020 Michael Gene Lewis
All rights reserved.

ISBN-13: 9798662921696

Cover photo by author

This book is a work of fiction. Names, characters, places, and incidents are the product of the author's imagination or are used fictitiously. Any resemblance to actual events, locales, or persons, living or dead, is entirely coincidental.

Also by M.G. Lewis

Gabe Bergeron Mysteries
Death on Daugherty Creek
Foreseeable Harm
Beauty in Ashes
Deep is the Chesapeake
Mr. Boghossian Loses a Tenant
The Nuptials of Ezmeralda Gutierrez
Keypunchers & Other Villains
Bornheimer's Demise
On Farm Deadly
Waters Ebb, Rocks Emerge

Other
Rune's Riddle

Nesrady Clone Series
The Clone Who Loved to Bake Bread
The Clone Who Loved to Fight
The Clone Who Loved to Swim
The Clone Who Loved Voltaire

Friday
6:00 am

He was running just as hard as he could. He didn't dare look back because he could hear footsteps pounding on the road behind him.

It was dawn, and he was racing along Nassawango Road as if his life depended on it. If he could make it to Aunt Flo's lane, he thought he might be okay.

He summoned a burst of energy out of thin air and sprinted along the lane, the stones crunching under his shoes.

He crossed the parking lot, arms pumping like he was trying to get airborne, eyes locked onto Aunt Flo's giant oak tree.

He patted the trunk as he flashed past. He circled the greenhouse slowing to a jog.

Cory was lying on the grass beneath the oak. He was on his back and naked to the waist, glistening with sweat as the rising sun illuminated his glorious muscles.

His beloved was gorgeous, even if he was panting like a St. Bernard in the dog days of summer.

His beloved was also a loser, having just been trounced once again by Gabriel Henri Bergeron.

He smiled his very best smile at Cory.

"Don't say a word, Bergeron!" Cory glared and panted. "You're cheating. I don't know how you're doing it, but you are."

"Nope. I'm just fast, fleet, speedy. Gifted with Olympic quality legs and the lungs of a racehorse."

It had been Cory's idea that he take up running as part of his training. Who would have guessed that he would excel? He had avoided track and field in high school as he had all other sports.

Cory snorted and then ignored him as he pulled himself into a sitting position. "And don't gloat, Bergeron."

"Moi? I would never do that, Corentin. Just as I would never remind you that I've beaten you the last three races. Handily."

He looked down at his gorgeous, humbled beloved. "You still have one more chance when we race tomorrow. I could tie one hand behind my back?"

Which might have been one comment too far.

Cory was getting to his feet, and the tight, little smile did not bode well for Gabriel Henri Bergeron.

He ran.

Cory was still winded but now mad enough to chase him. He ran for the river with Cory two paces behind him. He veered right and led Cory through the family graveyard before circling back to the parking lot.

He gained on Cory but not enough to get into his Jeep and lock the doors.

Cory was still smiling. "Only a matter of time, Bergeron."

They played ring-around-the-yellow-Jeep for a while.

"Okay! I'm sorry. I did cheat. I have new running shoes. They're prototypes...from a Swiss-Japanese consortium...one of a kind...with atomic insoles. I could win the Boston Marathon in these shoes."

Cory was smiling at him.

He tried running toward the dock. He tripped over a sunbeam and fell on his face. He might be fleet but agile? Nimble? Not so much.

Cory grabbed him and tossed him over his shoulder. He was carrying him toward the dock where Special Agent Cory Poirier of the FBI would, no doubt, toss him into the river like one of those telephone pole thingees in the Highland Games. A caber?

He didn't want to be caber tossed. True, it was a fine day in June, and the river wasn't that cold, but still.

He might be draped across Cory's shoulders like one of

Bette Davis' mink stoles from a 1940's film, but he locked his arms around Cory's waist and squirmed his sweaty body until most of his weight was behind Cory.

Cory was only gripping his ankles now. He thrashed until Cory let go, and he tumbled onto remarkably hard ground. But he rolled and scrambled away, running full tilt for the kitchen door.

Ezmeralda happened to be crossing the parking lot heading for that same door. He may have hidden behind her.

She fixed him with a glare from her black, almond-shaped eyes. She was in her sixties and double his mass.

"What are you doing? You're sweaty. Get away from me, Gabriel."

"Right. Sure. Sorry." He stayed locked in an Ezmeralda-synchronous orbit.

She was Aunt Flo's boon companion and co-conspirator for the last fifty years. And as unlikely as it might seem, looking at them now...Aunt Flo was in her eighties...they were veterans of the Dirección de Inteligencia, the Cuban KGB.

Cory was coming fast but slowed to a walk as Ezmeralda pointed a finger at him and shook her head making her graying curls bounce.

"No! I have work to do. I am not a part of your silly games."

She smoothed the brown, cotton frock over her hips and marched into the kitchen without a backward look.

He gave Cory his very best smile.

Cory smiled back and shoved him against the door.

He was about ten seconds from being rent limb from limb when Cory's smile and the probable course of the morning changed. Dramatically.

Except that Ute was knocking on the door behind him and demanding egress.

So Cory had to step back. Which was unfortunate.

Ute came out the door. She was a robust woman in her forties. Her black hair was cut very short, barely covering the tops of her ears. She wore no makeup, and her lips were pale and prim. Her dark eyes looked out from behind black, square-framed glasses.

Looked out upon Cory's nearly naked body with every evidence of lust and carnal desire.

He felt the need to throw himself in front of Cory. So he did. Cory may have snickered.

Ute's usual dour face contorted into something like a smile. He wasn't sure but he thought Ute winked at him.

And Cory was definitely laughing now.

Ute said, "Supplies."

Ute's German accent was barely there, but her enunciation set her English apart.

She marched to the black van parked next to Aunt Flo's black Lincoln Continental. She grabbed a box of groceries and reversed course.

Ezmeralda was about to prepare breakfast for the guests at Aunt Flo's bed and breakfast, and Ute was aiding her.

He managed to hide Cory's nakedness from Ute until she got to the door. He gritted his teeth and even opened said door. Which was more than she deserved.

Cory was smiling at him, mightily amused. "Put your freaking shirt on, Poirier. And adjust yourself."

Cory spread his hands. "What did I do?"

"If you don't know...."

And then a red sports car purred up Aunt Flo's lane and braked hard, kicking up little clouds of dust.

He and Cory had been introduced to Mrs. Lévesque when they'd arrived yesterday, but he knew nothing about her.

Except that she gave off the pungent aroma of wealth, and she loved red in all its wavelengths.

She had on a red suit, crimson as opposed to the candy-apple red of her car. She was sixty at a guess.

She had brown hair, dark eyes, and lipstick that was a fair match for her dress. She had painted on a thick coat of makeup, but her face was still mottled and a bit puffy. And she had eyebrows like black boomerangs.

She exited her vehicle.

"Good morning, Mr. Poirier."

She was looking at Cory and ignoring him, but he smiled at her anyway. "Good morning, Mrs. Lévesque. Lovely day, isn't it? You're out early?"

She gave him side eye so as not to lose sight of Cory's magnificence. "I like the morning."

Cory was trying not to smile. He wasn't embarrassed even a little bit at being ogled. Again.

He may even have flexed a muscle or two.

She said, "Racing again, Mr. Poirier? With your...friend?"

She had forgotten his name.

Cory smiled. "With Mr. Bergeron, Mrs. Lévesque."

"Did you beat him?"

Cory smiled and shook his head. "Not in a distance race. Not yet."

She smiled. "I'm sure you will soon...an athletic, young man like yourself."

Cory smiled. "I'll keep trying."

She gave Cory one last, whole-body scan that would put a MRI to shame, and walked up the front steps into the house.

He shook his head at Cory and followed her.

Cory was behind him, snickering sotto voce again.

The front door hadn't been used for decades, but with the coming of the Barnes B&B, everything had changed.

He wasn't sure he liked the changes, but Aunt Flo seemed happy. Which was the important thing.

The place did look grand. Annika had polished the floors and woodwork to a splendid, antique gleam.

Ute Wetzig and Annika Graf had been partners in a residential cleaning business, and Aunt Flo had been one of their clients. So Ute and Annika had been able to scope out her enormous Victorian house on the banks of the Pocomoke River near Snow Hill, Maryland.

And one fine day, Ute had put down her mop and suggested to Aunt Flo that the Barnes House would make a most excellent B&B, and, after some deliberation, Aunt Flo and Ezmeralda had agreed.

He climbed the stairs to the third floor, to the turret room, which had been his since he'd come to live with Aunt Flo when he was a boy.

He stripped off his sweaty clothes. "At least, this is still my room." It was roughly hexagonal with a vaulted ceiling and must have been some carpenter's nightmare to frame, but he loved it.

Cory shook his head. "Stop whining, Bergeron. This is her house after all, and she seems happy. Right?"

He nodded. "She does. Okay, I'm going to do better and give this a real chance." He gave it two months before some disaster struck.

And then Cory's phone chimed.

"Poirier."

Cory sat on the bed and listened, glancing up at him. This was not good news. Cory tossed the phone on the bed.

"Danielle?" She was Cory's boss. Cory nodded. "So you have to leave? Today?"

Cory nodded again. "We need to get cleaned up. I need to be at the Salisbury airport ASAP."

Cory was part of the Art Crime Team of the FBI, and it was his job, along with his partner, Matt Bornheimer, to find the artworks and treasures purloined by the unscrupulous.

He'd known that Cory was going undercover soon, but Cory had promised him this weekend; the whole weekend.

"Right. I understand." Which was almost true. "And where are you going this time?"

"Albany. To start."

"Right. Okay."

He followed Cory to the bathroom on the second floor and into the shower. Which would have be a lot more fun if Cory wasn't in a rush.

He'd hoped to ask Cory about Monroe this weekend. Monroe was the weird guy who had accosted him twice about a job of some sort connected somehow to Aunt Flo's B&B.

That had been months ago, but he had spotted him in the 30th Street Amtrak Station yesterday. Well, it might have been him.

Cory was drying his hair. "What's going on inside that head?"

"Nothing!" He turned off the water and got out of the shower. "Well, quite a bit really. I was talking to Billy about String Theory the other day...."

Cory was drying his body which was very distracting. "Gabe?"

"What?" He grabbed a towel. He couldn't tell Cory that he was seeing Monroe. Well, he could, but Cory might have him examined. "I was just wondering if Danielle had located Monroe? Or found out who he works for?"

"No, Gabe, she hasn't."

"And you asked Brunetti?" Brunetti was Danielle's boss, and it wasn't really politic for Cory to speak to her directly.

"Months ago, Gabe." Cory pulled on his briefs.

"Right. And tell me what she said again?"

Cory pulled a knit shirt over his head so his face was hidden. "She said she'd look into it."

What else had Brunetti said to him? "And that was all she said, Poirier?"

Cory nodded and started brushing his red locks.

"I see. And was Danielle pissed? That you went to Brunetti?"

Cory smiled. "At first, but I told her you were driving me up the wall."

"Was not! And have you followed up with Brunetti?"

"No."

"Right. If she finds anything, she'll get back to you."

"She will."

He had his doubts. Nadia Brunetti probably had other, far larger, shinier fish to fry. "Maybe you could give her a gentle reminder?"

Cory said, "No, I can't, Gabe. It...." Cory stopped mid-sentence. "Bornheimer and I have checked and rechecked, and we can't run this guy to ground. And if he hasn't popped up by now, he's moved on to something else. Or he's dead."

Which was true. But Cory wasn't telling him everything.

And wasn't going to.

So he had driven Cory to the airport, hugged him with all

his strength, and watched him take off. He hated it when Cory went undercover. He sighed.

But it had been six months since he'd seen Monroe. He had rushed to tell Aunt Flo and Ezmeralda after his scary meeting with Monroe and his lover/accomplice, Penelope Black Stanko.

Aunt Flo and Ezmeralda and Ezmeralda's semi-new husband, Danilo Ochoa, hadn't been fazed. They had faced many other threats and took this in their stride.

And Monroe hadn't really threatened him or them; just offered some kind of job that would require him to be at the Barnes B&B. And he had asked about his grandfather, Andrew? Who had been dead for thirty years?

But maybe Monroe was just a nut; a harmless loon?

And maybe he had overreacted?

Cory was right. Monroe was off somewhere playing cryptic games with some other poor doofus and wasn't stalking him. He drove back to the Barnes B&B

Friday
4:00 pm

He was sitting in Aunt Flo's parlor; the new one, not the one on the second floor.

Aunt Flo was Florence Barnes and granddaughter of Elijah Barnes who had built the house in 1910. She was really his great-aunt.

She was tiny with white hair and eyes that could look teal or silver depending on the light. She had a birthday coming up in a few months, and he had no idea what to get her.

Aunt Flo smiled at him and scratched Juju's head; Juju was a big, orange cat, and he was pretty sure she didn't like the changes to the house any more than he did.

He and Aunt Flo were sitting across from one another on the matching, leather sofas that had been in her old parlor. All of her books and music had been relocated too.

He munched one of Ezmeralda's sugar cookies and sipped his coffee.

Aunt Flo said, "What do you think of my new space, Gabriel?"

They were on the first floor; her rooms on the second floor had been given over to guests.

This room had been her office. The room next to it had been a sort of TV room; that was now her bedroom. The room beyond that had always been a bathroom.

Doors had been installed to connect the three rooms into a suite; the superfluous doors that had accessed the main hall had been sealed.

"It's very nice." Which it was. "And you don't have to worry about the stairs up to the second floor. Convenient. I like it."

Aunt Flo smiled at him, not buying a single word. "What is it, Gabriel? The expense? Or Ute and Annika?"

"Not Annika." She seemed like a sweet lady.

Aunt Flo giggle-cackled. "I know it has cost more than we projected, but I can afford it. Really, Gabriel."

He nodded, but he didn't really know. Would she tell him if she was financially strapped? Not that he could lend her money. But still.

The projections, Ute's projections, had been wide of the mark. By roughly the width of the Chesapeake Bay; at the mouth.

First, there was the construction and plumbing on the second floor so that Aunt Flo's old bedroom and Ezmeralda's had ensuite bathrooms.

Ute said that they could charge more for the rooms. Which was true.

Okay. So with those and the old master bedroom, Aunt Flo's old parlor, and another spare bedroom, they had five guest rooms available.

But she hadn't figured on putting in a new septic system when the old one couldn't handle the load. Or upgrading the laundry room. And the well was problematic. Not to mention the new fire alarm system.

"And you don't like Ute?"

He wasn't sure. She was about as warm and outgoing as a dead flounder. But that didn't mean she was incompetent or was trying to hustle Aunt Flo.

She probably wasn't. "She's okay."

Aunt Flo said, "You don't trust her?"

"What do we know about her?"

Aunt Flo was getting pissed with him. "Ezmeralda and I know quite a bit about her and Annika, Gabriel. I'm not some senile old lady."

Shit. "No! Of course, you aren't."

"And you're watching the finances."

Like your proverbial hawk. Ute had wanted to handle the books herself. Like he was going to sit still for that.

"And Ezmeralda is in charge of the purchases for food and sundries, Gabriel."

Which was all true. And Ezmeralda wouldn't be shy about putting Ms. Wetzig in her place if it should be called for. Or about taking other measures of the extreme prejudice variety.

"I know. I just worry about you being here with all these...guests."

Aunt Flo laughed. "You make it sound like they're all thieves and cutthroats, Gabriel."

"I guess they're okay." Some of them maybe. He wasn't sure about Mrs. Lévesque. "Are you still happy about all this?"

"I am."

"Okay, then I am too. So Cory went to Albany."

She said, "And he's going undercover? Looking for what?"

"He wouldn't say, but he took his best suits so he isn't pretending to be some street hustler."

"He'll be fine, Gabriel. He loves his job."

"He does. Completely."

Aunt Flo said, "And how is the Barnes B&B doing? Financially?"

"Ah! Well, the corporation is making a profit even with the debt repayment. And the insurance. And the taxes."

He had insisted that they incorporate and insure the Hell out of this little venture.

She smiled. "I'm so glad, Gabriel."

"I am too, Aunt Flo." He ate the last sugar cookie. "I should get going."

"Be careful on the road, Dear."

And he left her stroking Juju; poor thing was traumatized by all the strangers.

He was a little traumatized himself or he would have stayed the weekend.

But he and Juju would adapt. He ran up to the third floor and snagged his overnight bag and was almost out the door when he heard Aunt Flo.

"Gabriel?"

He put on the brakes and skidded on the rug like a cartoon character.

"Aunt Flo?" He sprinted across the foyer to her new parlor.

Ute was sitting on the sofa in his spot looking as calm as an iceberg bobbing along in the Arctic Ocean. Juju had fled.

Aunt Flo said, "Please tell him, Ute."

Ute was looking at her phone. "We have a new reservation, Gabriel. For three rooms. For tomorrow." A tiny smile tugged at her features.

"Right? And?"

"A Mrs. Gibson made the reservation. By email."

He was going to strangle Ute Wetzig. Well, he was going to try. He put the fight odds at 60-40 in Ute's favor.

She aimed her phone at him. Her arm was cadaver pale juxtaposed with his.

Aunt Flo smiled before he could read the names. "One of the guests is named Bergeron, Gabriel."

He thought Ute was pissed that she didn't get to torture him longer, but he couldn't focus on that. "What? Any relation to my Bergerons?"

Ute shrugged her square shoulders. "The names are Lydia Gibson, Camille Rankin, and Phillip Bergeron. Do you know them?"

He shook his head.

Aunt Flo said, "Did she say anything else, Dear?"

Ute smiled at Aunt Flo. "Just that she would be doing research...." Ute glanced at him. "...genealogical research in the area."

Aunt Flo and Ute were staring at him. They seemed to be waiting for a reaction?

"Right." He got to his feet. "Interesting. Well, I'll be going now, Aunt Flo."

Aunt Flo and Ute continued to stare at him as he walked out into the foyer.

His bag was by the door; he grabbed it and ducked his head back into the parlor.

"Aunt Flo?"

"Yes, Gabriel?"

"I may stay another day."

Aunt Flo and Ute were grinning. Which in Ute's case was like witnessing a walrus whistling.

"Not that I'm curious about this Phillip Bergeron."

Aunt Flo was still smiling. "No, I understand. You're welcome to stay as long as you want. You know that, Dear."

"Good." He surrendered any pretense. "Because you couldn't get me out of the house with teargas and a SWAT team."

He spun around and lugged his bag back to the turret room.

He wasn't nosy. Nobody would leave and not investigate something like this. The chances of an unrelated Bergeron coming to the Barnes house were vanishingly slim.

And then he remembered Monroe and his question about Andrew Bergeron.

Just what had old Andrew gotten up to? And were the fruits of some ancient indiscretion about to check into the Barnes B&B?

And had they been sent by Monroe? For some fell purpose?

Saturday
11:00 am

His eyes popped open in the wee hours of the morning. He might have been a bit anxious, but everything still seemed fine at the Barnes B&B.

He woke later to hear the sound of Annika vacuuming from his bedroom. He may have stalked her on the balls of his feet like a jungle cat.

Not that she would have heard him coming over the vacuum's roar. When she shut off the thing, he said, "Annika?"

She wasn't as flighty as everybody said he was. She turned and smiled at him. "*Ja, Herr Bergeron?*"

"How are you, Annika?"

She was forty-something like Ute, and her hair was chopped off too, but hers was auburn. Her complexion was freckled and ruddy like she'd spent years outdoors. On a farm or on the water? Her eyes were more suggested than visible, but he was pretty sure they were blue.

She considered his question. "*Sehr gut, Herr Bergeron.* Good. Very good." She smiled at him. "And you are also?"

"I am well. We've never really chatted, Annika."

She looked at him, lips still curved in a sweet smile, but she didn't say anything.

"I live in Philadelphia. Where did you live before you came here?"

She pondered his question. "Live? In New York."

"You and Ute lived in New York City?"

"*Ja*. For three years." She held up three fingers.

"And before that?" Puzzled look. "Where did you and Ute live before you lived in New York City?"

"Ah. In Deutschland...Germany?"

"In Germany. I see. Where in Germany?"

"Where?"

"Yes, where in Germany? What city?"

"*Stadt?*"

He nodded, having no idea if *stadt* meant city.

Annika smiled some more. "We live in Niederkrüchten."

"And were you born there? In Needer Kruk Ten?" He omitted the throat clearing part of the pronunciation and mangled a vowel or two.

Annika giggled. "Yes, born in Niederkrüchten."

"And where is this city?" He wasn't ready to take a second run at the name.

A voice behind him said, "It is near Dortmund."

He may have spun around rapidly. Ute was glaring at him, looking pale and ticked off like a vampire risen from a hundred year nap and finding the blood bank bare.

She spoke to Annika in German, and they launched into a lively conversation with occasional nodding and pointing at him.

In the end, Annika smiled at him before hefting her vacuum like it was a feather duster and striding down the hall in her boots.

Leaving Ute glaring at him through her square, black glasses. "Annika's English isn't so good."

"She seemed to understand me okay."

"It upsets her that she can't understand."

He smiled his very best smile at Ute. "I'm sorry. I certainly didn't mean to upset her. So you were both born in this city near Dortmund?"

" Niederkrüchten. Yes, *warum*...why do you ask?"

"Just curious. And what did you do there? Before coming to New York?"

Ute stared at him for a long time. "We worked at a hotel there." She started to walk away, but she turned back. "In future, if you have questions, it would be better if you asked me, Herr

Bergeron."

And she stomped off.

He had upset Ute, and he wasn't sure why? But he needed to find Dortmund and this Needer place on a map. He pondered. Did Ute and Annika have families in Germany? Possible criminal records? Green cards?

Aunt Flo said she'd checked on them, but you could never be too cautious. Well, you could, but not in this case.

Of course, Cory would never run them through the FBI database of felons. Even if he begged.

He got breakfast and then wandered around.

But he was sitting on the front porch enjoying the shade when a blue Toyota Camry with a crumpled fender pulled into the lane.

He may have marked its passage.

He may have also scrutinized the guy who got out and began to climb the stairs. He was wearing mirrored sunglasses.

"Good morning."

The guy doffed the sunglasses and gave him side eye but ignored his greeting.

So he didn't ask if he was Phillip Bergeron.

He was probably forty. He had dark, arresting eyes and a mass of brown wavy hair long enough and wild enough to spill over his forehead and almost cover his ears. He had a perfect nose; maybe even better than Bornheimer's.

He was saved from being pretty by a strong jawline and a noble chin. He wasn't tall or muscular, but he had wide shoulders and carried himself like a prince to the purple born.

But he was wearing raggedy jeans and wasn't nearly as handsome as he thought he was. Well, he was actually. Handsome was hardly adequate to describe him.

The guy went inside, and he heard Ute greeting him. He identified himself as Phillip Bergeron.

He sat back in the porch chair. He hoped that Phillip wasn't a relative if he was a jerk, and he obviously was; a jerk, that is.

Or maybe he was just having a bad day?

He waited some more, and a silver Lincoln Navigator SUV

pulled in. No dented fenders on this baby.

Two ladies got out. They were wearing suits and were obviously sisters and probably about the same age as bad-day Phillip. They also looked a bit like him.

He said, "Good morning. May I give you a hand?"

Their overnight cases didn't look heavy, but he thought he should offer.

The darker one said, "Do you work here?"

"Not exactly." He smiled his very best smile.

The one with the blondish hair smiled back at him. "You aren't sure if you work here?"

"I'm the accountant for the business, but I'm not involved in the day-to-day toting and hauling."

They had managed to climb the stairs with their luggage all by themselves. The blondish one had an oval face and a nose every bit as perfect as Phillip's, but she had pale blue eyes. Ditto for the one with brown hair.

And yet the blondish one looked younger and much happier in a sort of ethereal way.

She held out her hand. "I'm Lydia Gibson, and this is my sister, Camille Rankin."

He shook her hand and went for it. "I'm Gabriel Bergeron."

Lydia smiled and looked at Camille.

Camille took a step closer and studied him like a specimen under a microscope. Her skin was almost as pale as her white blouse, and her eyebrows were barely suggested.

She finally nodded. "I suppose he looks a bit like the photos of grandfather."

Lydia smiled. "More than a bit, Camille."

"I do? Who is your grandfather?"

Camille glared at him for no apparent reason. "Who is yours?"

"Andrew Henri Bergeron. And David Sullivan, but I'm guessing you aren't interested in him?"

Lydia frowned at her sister. "Our grandfather was Samuel Nieves Bergeron, who was the brother of Andrew."

Camille was frowning back at her sister. "Why are we here,

Lydia?"

Lydia shook her head. "I'm here to research our family, Camille." She smiled at him. "And I'd say my mission is off to a wonderful start."

He smiled. "I'm always pleased to meet some new cousins. Is Phillip your brother?"

Lydia nodded. "He is. I see he's here." She frowned again. "Do we have other cousins, Mr. Bergeron?"

"Call me Gabe. Not that I know of? Except on my father's side of the family; the Sullivan side. I have scads of them...mostly in the Chicago area."

Camille said, "Sullivan? So who was your mother then?"

"Leanne Bergeron. Only child of Andrew and Natalie Barnes Bergeron."

Camille said, "And you go by her name?" She smirked. "Any reason for that?"

"Well, my parents never married. And I didn't know who my father was until five years ago."

Lydia was gazing at her sister. "Could you be more rude, Camille?"

The bluish, skim milk pallor on Camille's cheeks pinked up. "I was just curious...."

He said, "It must run in the Bergeron family." Ute was hovering on the other side of the door. "I'm sometimes curious myself, but you should go in and get settled."

Phillip was on the stairs. He wasn't looking one bit happier. He spun around without a word and preceded Ute and his sisters as they climbed the stairs.

He knocked on Aunt Flo's door. "Aunt Flo?"

"Come in, Gabriel."

She was smiling at him. "You met them?" The new parlor had windows that looked out on the front porch and the lane.

"I did."

"Are you going to tell me, Gabriel?"

"They're the grandchildren of Samuel Nieves Bergeron, the brother of Andrew Bergeron."

Aunt Flo said, "Your second cousins then. Do they seem

nice?"

He shrugged. "Lydia does. Camille is cranky, and Phillip is pouting. Have you heard of Samuel Nieves?"

"No, Dear, but I never met any of Andrew's family. I barely met him. I left for Cuba a week after he and Natalie got married."

"And they were married here?"

She smiled. "Yes, Gabriel. I told you. Natalie and Mother invited three hundred guests. There's the wedding photo."

She was pointing at a sepia group photo on the bookcase. He had seen it before, but he studied it more closely now. Andrew Bergeron didn't look all that happy.

His bride, Aunt Flo's older sister, was smiling shyly. "Natalie was beautiful."

Aunt Flo nodded with tears in her eyes. "She was."

Andrew and Natalie were standing in the center; her parents, Nathan and Sadie, were on the right. Aunt Flo was on the left, looking impossibly young.

"Aunt Flo?"

"Yes, Gabriel?"

"Who are the people standing next to you? The woman and the boy?"

Aunt Flo studied the pale ovals, even getting out a magnifying glass. She shook her head. "I'm sorry, Gabriel, but I don't remember."

"That's okay. It has been a few years."

"Over fifty years, Dear. But they must be relatives of Andrew. Perhaps the boy is Samuel?"

He nodded. "Maybe? But he looks an awful lot like Phillip Bergeron who is upstairs as we speak."

Saturday
2:00 pm

Aunt Flo had invited the Bergerons to tea in her parlor. He had fetched her favorite teapot. It was Meissen and shaped like a fat, white apple decorated with delicate, blue, stylized leaves and flowers.

Aunt Flo and Ezmeralda were on one sofa, and Lydia and Camille were on the other. He had a chair next to Aunt Flo.

She poured tea in one of the matching cups and handed it to him; somehow the tea always tasted better out of this pot.

Phillip had a chair next to Lydia, but he hadn't deigned to sit so far.

He was studying Aunt Flo's souvenirs from Cuba, which she had started to display in the last few years.

Lydia was looking at the wedding photo of Andrew and Natalie. "No, that's our father, Jonathan, and our grandmother, Ava. Dad went to live with Uncle Andrew after she passed."

Aunt Flo said, "And your grandfather, Samuel?"

Camille said, "He died when Dad was a baby, and Dad doesn't remember him at all. Great Uncle Andrew was like a father to him."

He washed a cookie down with a swig of tea. "You said that Jonathan went to live with Andrew? Natalie and Andrew lived here after they got married. So Jonathan lived here with them?"

Lydia and Camille looked at each other. "He must have." Lydia smiled. "Isn't that something? I'm so glad we came."

She glanced at her brother. "Isn't that something, Phillip?"

He shrugged. He grabbed a photo from the bookcase and held it out looking from it to Ezmeralda. "Is this you? With the rifle?"

She nodded. "Years ago. When I was in the Dirección de Inteligencia."

Aunt Flo said, "The Cuban intelligence service, Mr. Bergeron."

Phillip smiled at Aunt Flo and Ezmeralda. "Kill many men with that rifle, Mrs. Ochoa?"

Ezmeralda smiled at him. "Not as many as I wanted to but bullets were scarce."

Phillip started to laugh but cut it off as Ezmeralda stared at him.

Lydia said, "Why don't you sit down, Phillip."

Phillip wheeled and took his seat. He smiled a devilishly handsome smile. "I'm in for it now. That was Lydia's angry voice."

Lydia smiled at him. "You've never heard my angry voice, Phillip."

Camille said, "And you don't want to." She smiled at her sister.

Phillip stopped smiling. "So we came, and we met a long-lost cousin. What now?"

Phillip was looking at him like he was a one-eyed, stray cat with a bad case of mange.

Lydia said, "You didn't have to come, Phillip."

He smiled at her. "You said you'd pay. I can't afford to turn down anything free." He stretched. "I might ride over to Ocean City tonight and see what I can get up to."

Ten years earlier he had been a charmer without even trying.

Lydia said, "Don't expect me to bail you out." She looked at Aunt Flo. "I'm sorry, Mrs. Barnes."

Aunt Flo said, "Not at all, Dear. I had a husband who was just as charming as Phillip."

Phillip looked at her for the first time. "Do tell?"

"His name was Antonio José Cabrera, and he was a painter. And I loved him very deeply until I didn't...couldn't any longer."

21

Ezmeralda said, "He was lazy and thought the world owed him anything he wanted." She was glaring at Phillip.

Phillip put up his hands. "I don't think that Mrs. Ochoa. No, I've learned the error of my ways."

Camille said, "Phillip's upset because he was let go."

Phillip flushed scarlet; his dark eyes shining. "Don't make excuses for me. And I was kicked out, Camille! But at least I made some real money while I was there. Unlike you."

Camille said, "I'm very happy teaching."

Phillip sneered. "Sure you are." He shook his head. "Fired from Oxley freaking International after working like a dog for nineteen years."

He said, "I'm sorry, Phillip. What did you do there?"

Phillip glared at him. "I was middle management. I was the one who did the actual work that the bosses didn't want to be bothered with." He looked at the cold cup of tea in front of him. "Just when the company was about to make some real money. They had promised me stock options too. Bastards!"

"What does Oxley International do?"

Phillip ignored him.

Lydia said, "They're a biotech company. Whatever that means? Our father started working for them right out of college when they were Oxley Petrochemical."

He said, "So how did you discover the connection between your family and the Barnes B&B, Lydia?"

"I got an email from an acquaintance who said she had uncovered a link between the Barnes family and mine. And when I found that there was a Barnes Bed & Breakfast in the same area, I made reservations. I thought I'd check local records; I had no idea that you'd be here, Gabe."

He said, "So you didn't talk to your father, Jonathan?"

"No. I didn't want to bother him."

Camille said, "He's not well, Mr. Bergeron."

"Gabe, please."

Lydia said, "Do you know anything about Émile Jaubert Bergeron?"

He shook his head. "Sorry. Who was he?"

"He was Samuel and Andrew's father. I know he was born in 1890 in Quebec City, but that's all I know so far."

"So he would be your father's grandfather?"

Lydia nodded. "But Dad doesn't know anything about him."

Camille said, "He didn't get to know Samuel, you see."

"Right. Samuel died when your father was a baby."

Phillip was looking around the room. "Are we done, Lydia?"

Lydia said, "No one is making you stay, Phillip."

Phillip smiled and got to his feet.

He said, "I have one question. Have you met or heard of a guy named Monroe?"

The siblings shook their heads.

"How about Penelope Black? Or Penelope Stanko?"

Lydia and Camille had no idea, but Phillip's forehead and cheeks were splotched like someone had injected claret under the skin.

He was heading for the door. "Never heard of her."

Lydia said, "Who are those people?"

He smiled at Lydia. "Genealogists I ran into. But they aren't very reputable so I'd advise you to stay clear."

Lydia and Camille smiled, a bit at a loss as Phillip slammed the door behind him.

Lydia said, "I'm sorry about Phillip."

Aunt Flo said, "No apologies are necessary, Lydia."

He said, "Do you have any family pictures? Of Samuel and Andrew? Or Émile Jaubert by any chance?"

Lydia said, "We have one of Samuel and a few of Andrew taken with our father. Would you like copies?"

"I would. We don't have any photos of Andrew except for the wedding photo. But there is the family cemetery?"

Lydia said, "Andrew's buried there?" He nodded. "I'd love to see it...if you don't mind, Ms. Barnes?"

"Not at all, Dear."

Camille said, "And what about you, Mr. Bergeron? Are you married? Children?"

He smiled. "Not married. No kids. But I'm living with my

partner, Cory Poirier. He's a special agent with the FBI."

Camille shared a tiny, secret smile with Lydia.

He pulled out his phone and showed them a couple of photos of Cory.

Lydia said, "He's so handsome, Gabe!"

"He is. And what about you? Any family?"

Lydia had a wedding ring, but Camille didn't.

Lydia showed them photos of a tall, dark man and two dark children. "That's Reed, my husband. And Jack and Olivia."

Camille said, "Reed is a lawyer." She gazed at her sister. "And very successful. You may have heard of him?"

He shook his head.

Aunt Flo looked at Camille. "And you, Dear?"

Camille laughed. "I was married for a few years. I like to say that I have twenty children. I teach seventh grade math in Philadelphia."

She showed them a classroom photo with twenty smiling faces. She was really smiling now.

He said, "And you love it."

"I do, Mr. Bergeron."

"Call me, Gabe. Please. And what about Phillip?"

Lydia frowned, but Camille smiled again.

Lydia said, "Phillip has been married and divorced twice. He's currently in the wind."

Camille said, "But he has five wonderful children."

She offered photographic proof of her statement. Phillip was sitting flanked by a tall blonde woman and three sturdy teenage boys in the first. A chunky, dark haired woman, a preteen girl, and a boy who might be four or so were featured in the second.

Camille said, "He loves them very much, and they love him."

He said, "They look like him."

Lydia said, "And he seems to get along with Kelly and Christina. Better than I expected. Well, except for the child support he owes Christina."

Camille said, "He's doing the best he can, Lydia."

Lydia nodded. "I know he is. If only he hadn't gotten fired."

She looked at Aunt Flo and Ezmeralda. "I'm sorry to air all our dirty laundry."

Aunt Flo said, "All families have it, Dear."

Ezmeralda said, "He needs to find another job."

The sisters nodded. Camille said, "He's trying."

Aunt Flo said, "Did Mrs. Wetzig give you any recommendations for dinner?"

Lydia said, "She did. Very efficient woman." She got to her feet; Camille followed. "Well, it was wonderful to be able to talk to all of you. If Dad feels better, I'll tell him all about this."

Camille said, "That the house is still here. And that we found Uncle Andrew's sister-in-law." She smiled at Aunt Flo. "He'll be so pleased."

Aunt Flo said, "I hope he's feeling better soon. And I hope you enjoy your stay here."

He ushered his cousins out. He pulled out some business cards. "Here are my numbers; work and cell. I have an apartment in Philadelphia. Where do you live?"

Lydia said, "We're all in the Philadelphia area, Gabe. You work for Garst, Bauer & Hartmann?"

"For the last five years." He handed Camille two cards. "Maybe you could give one to Phillip?"

Camille nodded.

"And maybe we could all get together for lunch? Or dinner?"

Lydia smiled. "I'd like that, Gabe. Let me give you my number."

She dialed the cell number on his business card, and he added it to his list. She looked at Camille, but Camille just smiled a pale, wan smile and headed upstairs.

Lydia smiled at him again and followed her sister.

And he watched to make sure they didn't turn back before he darted back into the parlor and closed the door.

"So?"

Aunt Flo said, "Phillip knows this Stanko woman."

Ezmeralda said, "And she is a spy, Gabriel?"

"Of some sort. I think."

Aunt Flo said, "Well, Phillip certainly isn't."

Ezmeralda snorted. "Too stupid."

He wasn't sure Phillip was so much stupid as self-absorbed. "So this email that lured them here was bogus?"

Aunt Flo nodded. "Probably. But to what end?"

"An excellent question, Mrs. Barnes."

Ezmeralda said, "If they are who they say they are."

He raised an eyebrow at Mrs. Ochoa. "You think the whole Uncle Andrew thing is bogus?'

She shrugged. "Maybe yes, maybe no."

"Aunt Flo?"

She considered. "I tend to think they are who they say they are, but Phillip is hiding something."

Ezmeralda nodded. "And why was he fired from this job?"

"More excellent questions, Mrs. Ochoa."

He looked at Aunt Flo. "I'm going to call Jennifer and tell her as gently as possible that I won't be in...for an unspecified period."

Jennifer was his boss and absolute overlord of Garst, Bauer & Hartmann, the accounting firm which was lucky enough to employ him.

"No, Gabriel. That isn't necessary."

He shook his head. "Something is happening, and it involves the Bergerons and you and this bed and breakfast, and I can't leave you here..."

Ezmeralda smiled at him. "Leave us here alone and defenseless?" She gave him a fearsome scowl that would have shivered his timbers...if he had timbers.

"No! I know you aren't defenseless, but...."

Aunt Flo said, "No, we aren't, Gabriel."

"But I could stay as an extra layer of security...."

Aunt Flo glared at him. Her glare was less fearsome than Ezmeralda's, but smarted more. "And we aren't foolish either."

Ezmeralda said, "I called Danilo, and he's coming home."

Which was all well and good. Danilo had also been a spy and had been lethal in his day, but he was the same age as

Ezmeralda. And half her size.

She said, "He will call Mikhail and Kirill."

Which was a horse, a war horse, of a different color. Mikhail and Kirill were Danilo's sons and could handle almost anything, up to and including your basic terrorist attack.

"Well, okay. I guess it will be okay if they're here."

Aunt Flo and Ezmeralda smiled at him.

Mikhail and Kirill would hardly need his help in thwarting whatever might possibly happen at the B&B.

Especially with Aunt Flo to guide their actions.

Sunday
9:00 am

He was sitting at the kitchen table watching Ezmeralda make breakfast for the guests and thinking about Phillip.

She slammed a cast iron skillet down on the range like Thor smiting a giant.

"Something wrong?":

Without turning, she said, "You aren't a guest."

He put down his cup. "Meaning I could lend a hand? Right. What, exactly?"

She paused flipping eggs and pointed her turner at a tray. "Put that on the dumbwaiter."

The dumbwaiter had been built in 1910 along with the rest of the house. At some point in the following century it had been deemed unnecessary and immured with drywall.

But now that breakfast was once again being served in the formal dining room to the delight of the guests, it had been resurrected and electrified.

He loaded the tray and hit the button. It ascended with a pleasing whirring sound.

One flight above, Ute was no doubt serving the guests.

"Anything else?"

Ezmeralda inspected him. "Can you make toast?"

Which was a low blow.

He sniffed. "I make the best toast on the eastern seaboard, Mrs. Ochoa."

"Then make some."

From that self-same dining room had come a cornucopia of Edwardian gadgets; one of which happened to be a solid silver, toast rack.

He toasted and filled the rack and set it on a tray. Ezmeralda pointed in the general direction of an assortment of jams, jellies, and marmalades. He added them to the tray and sent it heavenward.

Ezmeralda was frying bacon like a fiend.

"Did you actually volunteer to do this?"

She snorted. "No one else cooks in my kitchen."

She spun around daring him to point out that it wasn't technically, legally, in point of fact, her kitchen.

He smiled at her. "I understand completely. I hate it when people use my computer at work."

She grunted and went back to work. "And it is money in my pocket."

She was drawing a salary as were Ute and Annika. The three of them owned shares of the corporation, but he had insisted that Aunt Flo possess fifty-one percent.

Did Ezmeralda need the money? Danilo's business was making a profit, but maybe she considered that as Danilo's money?

A timer dinged. She pointed at the oven. "Tray. Dumbwaiter."

He loaded a tray with pastries and croissant. He took in a lungful of the sublime aroma, but she was watching him. He smiled innocently and sent them on their way unmolested.

But he may have slipped up the stairs and popped into the dining room.

Mrs. Lévesque was there in a cerise blouse and black skirt along with a big guy who looked like he could head butt a mountain goat into submission. His name was Tuers.

He said, "Good morning."

He got a mumbled response as he took a seat across from Lydia and Camille. "Are you enjoying your stay so far?"

Lydia smiled; even Camille looked moderately pleased.

"We are, Gabriel. It's a lovely area."

"It is. Have you been to the river?" He wasn't sure they

were kayak people. "There are kayaks for rent?"

Lydia smiled. "I think I'll pass, but we walked down to the dock. The cypress trees are interesting."

"They are. Where's Phillip?"

Camille said, "He won't be up for hours yet."

He would lurk and tackle him when he crawled out of bed.

"So are you going to research Émile Bergeron?"

Camille smiled. "She's already planning on going to Quebec."

He smiled at them. "Would you like to see the graveyard?"

Lydia nodded, and they adjourned to the hallway and thence outside. They walked past Aunt Flo's greenhouse and came to the graveyard.

Lydia said, "It's so peaceful here, Gabe."

Camille hadn't been looking too enthusiastic, but she perked up at the sight of the river. "It is nice."

He pointed out the graves of his grandparents, Andrew and Natalie. He had gotten a small stone for his mother and interred her ashes next to them.

Lydia said, "May I take photos, Gabe?"

"Sure."

Camille was looking at his mother's stone. "She was so young, Mr. Bergeron."

"Only thirty."

Camille was looking at him, but he wasn't going to tell her about his mother being murdered. Lydia made a face at her, and she refrained from asking.

He said, "And these are my great-grandparents, Nathan and Sadie Barnes."

Camille said, "And Natalie was Ms. Barnes' sister?"

"She was."

He left them wandering along the river and went back to the dining room, but it was empty except for Ute who was clearing the table.

He helped.

Sunday Noon

It was high noon, and Phillip was still a no-show, but his car was still in the lot.

He was down by the river. He kicked off his sandals and dunked his feet in the tepid, brownish water.

Mr. Tuers was walking toward him; more of a march really by someone used to doing that and standing at attention.

Tuers joined him on the dock. He was a large, block-shaped man with a shaved, block-shaped head. The dome of that head towered above tiny, low-set ears.

He was probably imagining that Tuers' footfalls were making the dock shudder.

"May I join you, Mr. Bergeron?"

"Sure. Of course. Have a seat. I'm Gabe." He held out his hand and hoped for the best since Bruno had forearms as large as his calves, and his calves were nice.

Mr. Tuers shook his hand with non-bone crushing force. "Call me Bruno."

Bruno had tiny, pale blue eyes and a chisel-shaped chin.

Bruno said, "So you're Mrs. Barnes' nephew?"

"Great-nephew. Yes. I'm an accountant, and I'm trying to keep an eye on this for her."

Bruno smiled. "You don't think opening a bed and breakfast is a good idea, Gabe?"

"It can be, but I've witnessed the crashing and burning of too many small businesses."

Bruno nodded. "But I'd say your great-aunt is sharp, and Ms. Wetzig seems competent and energetic. As does the other lady?"

"Annika Graf. And they are competent." He sighed.

"But you worry about your aunt?"

"I do. I'm in Philadelphia. Or D.C. And I can't get down here every weekend."

Bruno nodded. "For what it's worth, I think they're going to be successful, Gabe. I've stayed in a lot of these, and this one is first rate."

"Really? Thanks. I hope so." He looked over at Bruno. "So what do you do?"

"U.S. Navy. Retired."

"Were you an officer? On a ship?"

Bruno smiled. "I was a commander, and I was all over, Gabe. All over the navy and the world."

"Did you like it?"

Bruno stared at him. "It had its moments."

They sat there listening to the birds and watching the river flow tranquilly to the Bay.

Bruno said, "Is that what I think it is?"

And then Bruno reached out a hand and flicked the hair around his ear. He was glad Cory wasn't present because he forgot all his training and froze.

Bruno smiled again. "Sorry, Gabe. Just curious about that notch in your ear. It looks like it was made by a bullet?"

He debated. He could pretend large men played with his hair all the time, or he could jump into the river and swim for his life.

"It was made by a bullet."

Bruno smiled some more. "Care to talk about it?"

He shrugged. "It was an accident, I guess."

"Not sure about that?"

"Not really. I happened to find myself in a parking garage where a killer named Julian used me as a shield while he and a FBI special agent had a spirited gun battle."

Bruno was staring again. "Is that bullshit, Gabe?"

"Nope."

"And the not accident part?"

"I've never decided if the special agent was actually concerned with missing me."

"Shit."

"Just so."

Bruno laughed. "I don't know if I believe you, Gabe."

"I know. It isn't very likely, is it? How about you? Have you been shot at?"

"More times than I can recall."

And he completely believed Bruno. "Not fun, is it?"

"Not so much."

They sat there side by side for a bit. He didn't feel threatened by Bruno, but there was all this power under the surface. It was like sitting next to a volcano. Or a killer robot with a winning personality.

Maybe he should say something. "There are kayaks to rent, Bruno."

Bruno nodded. "I might do that. Want to come with me?"

He sort of liked Bruno, but he didn't want to go paddling with him into a remote area with no witnesses. "Maybe another time."

Bruno nodded.

And then he spotted Phillip running down the front steps with a bag in his hand; mirrored sunglasses in place.

He spun around, found his sandals, and clopped toward him at best possible speed.

He waved. "Phillip!"

Phillip jumped into his blue Camry and roared down the lane. There was no way that Cousin Phillip hadn't seen him. He watched the dust settle on Nassawango Road.

Shit. He probably wouldn't have told him anything about Penelope and whatever the Hell was going on, but he would have liked to have questioned him.

Camille came out the front door.

He called to her. "Phillip just left. Is he coming back?"

"I don't know, Mr. Bergeron, but I doubt it. He said he had

something important to do in Philadelphia."

She was looking worried and unhappy; the unhappy part seemed to be her default state.

"Please call me Gabe."

"Sorry. I don't know what's going on. He'll usually tell me eventually, but not this time. It's almost like he's scared of something."

"Any idea of what?"

"I have no idea. And he's upset with Lydia."

"May I ask why?"

But she shook her head and went back inside.

Bruno said, "Gabe?"

Bruno was right behind him, and he hadn't heard a sound. He tried not to flail or shriek in an unmanly fashion.

Bruno said, "Anything wrong, Gabe? Can I help?"

He looked at Bruno. If he needed any trees uprooted or doors battered down, he knew who to call.

"No, thanks Bruno. It's probably nothing."

Bruno nodded. He looked at Commander Bruno and made a judgment call.

"But are you going to be here for a while?"

"A few days. I like it here. Peaceful. And I do want to go kayaking."

"Right." He gave Bruno one of his business cards. "So if you should spot a tall guy in his forties with silver hair, could you call me?"

It wouldn't hurt to have Bruno back up Mikhail and Kirill.

Bruno smiled at him. "Will do. But what's going on, Gabe?"

"I have no idea, Bruno."

Monday
2:00 pm

He had waited for Danilo to arrive and then Mikhail before driving back to Philadelphia, to his lonely, Cory-less apartment on Arch Street. And he had dutifully gone to work.

Not that anyone noticed.

His buddy and junior partner of the firm, Neal, was on vacation; he had taken his mother Clare on a trip to the Far East.

The other partners, Jennifer and Mr. Bauer, were at some kind of conference somewhere. He hadn't paid attention when Jennifer had talked about it.

He was sitting at his desk trying to calculate just how early he could leave and not so outrage his fellow cubicle dwellers that they would feel compelled to report him.

It was a tricky computation.

He looked over at Baldacci in the next cubicle. Harry was his closest friend except for Neal and wouldn't squeal on him.

Baldacci was his height but had a definite paunch. His egg-shaped head wasn't totally carpeted, but the remaining hair was jet black and as dense as Berber wall-to-wall.

And he had big, brown eyes and a grin that could melt hearts and make women putty in his hands.

Not that Baldacci was puttying around with anyone but Carla Wong-Baldacci since they had wed back in February, in the Year of the Rat. Which didn't sound auspicious no matter what she said.

Carla was working away across the aisle; black, frizzy head

bent to her task. He wasn't sure about Carla. He pondered.

Carla said, "Stop looking at me, Bergeron."

"Am not!"

She spun around and focused black eyes upon him. "Whatever you're going to ask, the answer is no, and that goes for Harry too."

Harry lay down on the floor and rolled over exposing his belly to be scratched while wagging his tail at Carla.

Well, he wasn't physically on the floor, but he smiled at her and nodded.

"I wasn't going to ask you to do anything, Mrs. Wong-Baldacci or you either Harry."

She snorted and smoothed the jacket of her charcoal suit over her bosoms. "And don't think about sneaking out early."

He drew himself up and tried to stare her down. "I would never take advantage of Jennifer's absence in such a fashion."

A wave of laughter swept over the cubicles.

Carla shook her head as she returned to work. "Bergeron, Bergeron, Bergeron."

Baldacci said, "Anyway, Dana was told to take names."

Dana was the receptionist. She was a known informer and quisling, and she was giving him an appraising look over the top of a fashion magazine.

It was June, and she had draped her slender form with a walnut brown sweater over a tan, knit top, an ankle length skirt made of pumpkin-colored Naugahyde, and sheepskin-lined clogs.

He tried to project innocence, but she knew him too well.

And then his cellphone chimed.

It was Vonda.

"Shit."

Baldacci, ever alert, rolled his chair over and peered at the screen of his cellphone. "Shit."

Carla rolled over. Chatterjee leaped to his feet and darted close.

Carla and Baldacci were smiling at one another.

Chatterjee said, "Is Vonda the detective?"

Carla said, "Detective Golczewski of the Philadelphia

Police."

Baldacci said, "What did you do, Bergeron?"

People often asked him that. It was totally uncalled for. Most of the time.

"Hello, Vonda? How are you this lovely summer day?" Vonda, or someone, expelled a deep breath. "Vonda?"

Vonda said, "So you aren't dead."

"Excuse me? I am the picture of health. Wait. What do you know? You have to tell me...."

"Shut up, Bergeron. I can't talk now. Are you at work?"

"Of course...."

"Good. Stay there. Do not move without calling me first."

Carla, Baldacci, and Chatterjee, who wanted to be called Dhruva, pulled their collective heads back like wide-eyed turtles.

Baldacci said, "Shit, Gabe."

Carla said, "Why did she think you might be dead?"

"No idea." He really couldn't imagine.

He called Cory. And got his voicemail. "Call me just as soon as you get this."

And then he called Aunt Flo.

A voice said, "*Ja*? Sorry. Hello?"

"Annika? This is Gabriel. Is everything okay? Is Aunt Flo okay? And Ezmeralda? And you and Ute? Annika?"

"*Bitte*, hold on. Yes?"

And Annika left him hanging there.

The entire office staff had collapsed into a dense ball of humanity around him.

"Annika! Hello! Somebody pick up the freaking phone!"

A clear, calm voice with crisp, almost mechanical enunciation said, "Gabriel?"

"Ute! Just tell me this! Is Aunt Flo okay?"

"Of course."

"And Ezmeralda? And you and Annika? And the house?"

"*Natürlich*."

Ute put the phone down.

"Ute? Are you there?"

He was going to stomp on his phone until it was reduced to

shards embedded in the gray, threadbare, commercial carpeting.

Carla wrestled the phone out of his hand. "Hello? Hello? Mrs. Barnes? This is Carla Wong. In Gabe's office? How are you? You're fine. I'm glad to hear that. Gabe wants to talk to you."

She handed him the phone.

"Aunt Flo?"

"Yes, Dear? Is something wrong?"

He would never be able to express how relieved he was to hear her voice. "Maybe yes, maybe no. I got a strange call from Vonda, and I may have freaked out a tiny bit."

Carla snorted, but he ignored her.

Aunt Flo said, "You managed to upset Ute which is something I didn't think was possible. Take a deep breath and tell me everything, Gabriel."

And he did with the entire office listening in.

Aunt Flo said, "I can see why you were upset, Gabriel, but we are all fine here."

"And Mikhail and Kirill are there?"

"They are."

"You might want to put them on high alert until I talk to Vonda again."

She laughed. "I will, Gabriel. Call me back as soon as you know anything."

"Will do."

He ended the call and leaned back in his chair and took a deep breath. He should call Cory's boss, but before he could his phone rang again.

He looked at the screen.

Baldacci said, "It's Vonda!"

"I can see that."

Dhruva smiled. "We need popcorn."

He may have made several obscene hand gestures directed at young Dhruva before he answered the call.

"Yes, Vonda?"

"Get here, Bergeron!"

He took another breath. "Where exactly?"

She gave him an address in Port Richmond.

"And why do you need me there?"

"Because they called me in on my day off."

Which didn't explain anything really, but she was gone.

"And Port Richmond is not Vonda's beat...not even close."

Carla said, "You won't find out sitting here, Bergeron."

Baldacci said, "Do you want a wing man?"

Carla Wong-Baldacci shook her head.

Baldacci said, "Why not?"

"Because you have no idea what this is, and it may be something you shouldn't get involved in."

He would have liked Harry's company, but Carla was right. "I'll call you and let you know what's up, Harry."

"Promise?"

"Sure."

Carla said, "Good luck."

The cubicle dwellers waved good-bye to him smiling en masse like the *Tricoteuses* loitering around the ole guillotine.

Monday
4:00 pm

He had gotten to the Savin Street address as fast as he could, but none of the officers on the scene seemed to have any idea who he was or even who Detective Vonda Golczewski was.

Savin was one way. The row houses were two-story and narrow. There were no yards, trees, or greenery. The sidewalk sprouted a row of metal pipes which might have been topped with parking meters at some point. A few weeds were barely surviving in the sidewalk cracks.

A/C units hung out of a scattering of windows; a satellite dish clung to a wall. It was neat enough but kind of urban bleak.

He was sitting in his car at the intersection of Savin and East Allegheny Avenue. The center of the action appeared to be a tiny, brick house wedged into the middle of a row of nearly-identical houses.

He tried calling Vonda again and got her voicemail. Again.

"Vonda. I'm here. Where are you?"

He sat and pondered. He was hungry and tired, and he wanted to go home.

His phone chimed. "Vonda?"

"Where are you?"

"Down the block."

"You're still driving that yellow Jeep? I see you."

And he spotted Vonda waving at him from the sidewalk in front of the brick house. She met him at the crime scene tape and allowed him to duck under.

She was wearing camel colored jeans and a short-sleeve, brown knit blouse. Her black hair wasn't constricted into a tight bun and floated freely for once.

The casual clothes made her look slender and almost fragile. Her badge hung on a lanyard around her neck.

"Come with me." And she stepped inside the row house.

"What is it, Vonda?" He wasn't sure he wanted to follow her until he knew what was inside. The house was only wide enough for a series of single rooms, front to back.

"Get in here, Bergeron." She looked at him not glaring this time. "It isn't pretty."

The front room had a sofa and a TV and smelled like dirty socks and something even more unpleasant. The sofa was brownish and looked like the dust mite colonies were the only thing holding it together. The walls were a sickly green.

But the TV was a flat screen and looked newish.

"Golczewski? This your guy?"

Vonda nodded. "Detective Czerwinski, this is Gabriel Bergeron."

He held out his hand. The detective didn't want to take it, but a glance at Vonda changed his mind.

He was in his early twenties or maybe a little older. He was slender with bony shoulders, and he was wearing a rumpled, gray suit that was one stain shy of being shabby. His red tie was only half knotted and faded.

But he had a mop of lustrous, black, curly hair hanging down to his brown eyes. He had an oval face and wasn't ugly even though his right eye was definitely lower than his left and larger. His right ear was lower too but wasn't so noticeable.

Czerwinski gave him an asymmetrical smirk. "And what can you tell me about Phillip Bergeron?"

"Phillip? Right. Well, I met him for the first time Saturday...two days ago. I think he's my second cousin."

Czerwinski shook his head; something about the novel arrangement of his features made him look perpetually skeptical. "You think?"

"He and his sisters came to stay at the Barnes Bed and

Breakfast in Snow Hill, Maryland. That's my great-aunt Florence Barnes' house. Phillip's older sister, Lydia, said that my grandfather, Andrew, and her grandfather, Samuel, were brothers, but I don't actually know if that's true."

The detective looked at Vonda and back to him. "Any reason to doubt it?"

"Not so far. So why am I here?"

Czerwinski said, "And that's all you know about this Phillip?"

"No. He was recently fired from Oxley International...from a job in middle management. He's been married twice and has three sons from the first marriage and a boy and a girl from the second. His other sister, Camille, says he gets along well with his ex-wives. He drives a beat up, blue Toyota Camry with Pennsylvania plates."

Czerwinski was taking notes.

"And he's behind on his child support payments to the second wife. Being out of work."

Czerwinski studied him. "Okay. Come with me."

He looked at Vonda, but he couldn't read the expression on her face.

They went through the next room, which had been a dining room, and then came to a hall with a set of steep stairs.

The bathroom stench hit him first. Phillip was hanging from the second floor banister; a thick cord of knotted, white fabric around his neck. A chair was lying on the floor beneath the body.

Phillip's face was contorted and grotesque but still recognizable.

He ran back outside the house and threw up on Savin Street until there was nothing left inside.

Monday
4:30 pm

He wiped the phlegm off his mouth with a handkerchief as he fought back a fresh bout of gagging.

Vonda said, "Are you okay, Gabe?"

He spun around. "No, I'm not okay! Shit, Vonda, you couldn't have warned me? No, strike that! Why did I have to see him at all?"

Vonda looked upset. He couldn't imagine her crying, but if she did, he would feel really crappy. He liked Vonda.

Czerwinski was standing beside her. "My case, Bergeron. I wanted you to see the body."

"Why?"

"To see how you'd react."

"Did it live up to your expectations, Detective? I could throw up some more?"

"Shut up!"

Punching Czerwinski was a very bad idea. So why did it feel so right? Czerwinski stuck out his chin. "Go ahead. Take a shot, Bergeron."

Vonda said, "He isn't going to do anything that stupid. Are you, Gabe?" Vonda's eyes were shiny.

He shook his head.

Czerwinski snorted derisively. He grabbed the detective and slammed him against the brick row house before two uniformed officers could pull him off.

Czerwinski straightened his suit; not that it made any

noticeable difference. "I'm going to throw your ass into a cell, Bergeron." He combed his hair with his fingers.

Vonda sighed, probably at the stupidity of all men. "Gabe, where were you around 10:00 am?"

"Today?" She nodded. "At work. Oh. Is that when he...died? Twenty people can vouch for me, Vonda. You know how the office is laid out."

Czerwinski looked disappointed and skeptical, but he couldn't help looking skeptical.

"Wait. He didn't commit suicide?"

Vonda and Czerwinski put on their cop faces which said no comment without a word being uttered.

Czerwinski said, "With me, Bergeron."

He wasn't going back inside the row house. "No! I'm not going back in there."

Czerwinski pointed at two, large individuals in blue uniforms, either one of whom could pick him up by the scruff of the neck like a kitten.

"In. Now."

He followed Czerwinski, but he wasn't going to look at Phillip. But Czerwinski didn't stop at the body.

He went into a kitchen. The wall were the same green except where the black mold was growing next to the sink. The floor was linoleum. There was a table, a refrigerator, a range, and one cabinet.

The appliances had been white at one time but now they were rusty and grimy and looked generally unclean.

The table was maple but was gouged, scarred, and water-marked. Czerwinski was pointing at it.

His business card shared pride of place in the center with an empty bottle of whiskey and a single glass. A wallet and a set of keys lurked behind the bottle.

He could see a bed through an open door. He spotted Phillip's mirrored sunglasses on the floor. He took a deep breath, determined not to get choked up in front of Czerwinski.

The mattress was leaning off the frame. A chenille bedspread faded to gray was wadded in a bunch on the floor. There were no sheets.

"Shit!"

Czerwinski said, "What?"

"Nothing."

Vonda said, "Gabe."

"It's nothing. I just realized why there aren't any sheets on the bed." At least one of them was knotted around Phillip's throat.

Czerwinski smiled at him. He so wanted to punch him.

Czerwinski said, "Have you been here before?"

"No."

Moderately skeptical face. "We're dusting for prints. We'll know."

"I haven't been here. Ever."

"Who else might have been here?"

"I don't know, Detective. I just met the guy."

Czerwinski said, "So you said. Do you know of anybody who might have wanted to hurt this guy?"

"Nope." He could tell him about Monroe and Penelope, but Czerwinski would think he was a loon, and he didn't even know if Phillip had been murdered.

But Vonda was looking at him. He put on his own no comment face.

"Can I go?"

Czerwinski looked at Vonda. "Detective Golczewski says you're okay." He smiled at Vonda. "She's also told me a few things about you, Bergeron."

Czerwinski got into his face and poked him in the chest with an index finger with a torn nail. "This is my case, and if you try to mess around in any way at all, I will charge you with obstruction. No hesitation. One time and your ass is in jail. Clear?"

"Totally. Can I go?"

Czerwinski waved him away.

He walked out of the house heading for his Jeep.

Vonda followed and got in with him. "Bergeron, you know something you didn't tell Czerwinski."

"Nope. And even if I did, he would think I'm paranoid or something. And this is a suicide. Right?"

She didn't say a word.

"So you don't think it is. Wait. Why did you think I might be dead?"

She flexed her lips into a tight, little grimace that might have been a smile. "There was a mix-up in communications, and the first report was that it was Gabriel Bergeron who was dead in a row house in Port Richmond."

"And they called you?"

"Someone pulled your file...which is extensive, and my name is on every freaking page. So they called me even though I was off duty. And told me you were dead."

"Sorry, Vonda. I guess you were upset?"

She punched his shoulder. "Of course, I was upset. You are a total pain in the ass...."

"But you like me?"

She nodded. "I do. I'm not sure why." She glared at him. "Okay, you've had a shock so I'm letting you go, but you will call Czerwinski and tell him whatever the Hell it is you're holding back tomorrow morning, or I will throw you into a cell myself."

"Yes, Vonda." He wanted to talk to Aunt Flo first. "Or I could call you instead?"

"No! This is Czerwinski's case, and you will talk to him." She got out of the Jeep. "And you won't get involved, Gabe. No matter what happens."

"I promise. I learned my lesson with Oscuro."

Detective Oscuro had punched him in the stomach and had wanted to do much worse to him.

"Good. Czerwinski is okay."

He thought Vonda was fibbing and didn't know the first thing about young Detective Czerwinski.

He watched her walk back to the crime scene.

He called Aunt Flo.

Annika answered. "Hello?"

"Annika, it's Gabriel Bergeron. May I speak to Aunt Flo?"

Annika just put the phone down.

But Aunt Flo was there ten seconds later. "Gabriel?"

"I'm fine, but I have bad news. I guess shocking news is

more like it since we didn't really know him and probably would never...."

"Gabriel. Focus. What news?"

"Right. Sorry. Phillip Bergeron was found hanging in a row house in Port Richmond...which is an area of Philadelphia...it has a large Polish-American population...."

Aunt Flo said, "He's dead?"

"Very."

"You saw the body?"

"I'll never forget it, Aunt Flo. I threw up. Repeatedly and with great vigor."

"I'm sorry, Gabriel. A hanging victim isn't pleasant."

"You've seen somebody hanged?"

"Afterwards."

Of course, she had.

"Gabriel, do they think it was suicide?"

"Nope. They're being really cagey about it, but something has set off their homicide detectors."

"Do they suspect you?"

"Nope. Well, they might have, but I have a rock solid alibi."

Aunt Flo said, "Good. Tell me the rest. Try to organize your thoughts."

He tried.

She said, "And you don't know if Phillip was living in this row house?"

"Nope."

"Or how they found the body?"

"Again, that's a negatory."

"And you haven't told them about Monroe and Penelope."

"But Vonda knows that I'm holding something back. Should I just tell Czerwinski the story and let him make of it what he will?"

"Yes, Gabriel. Phillip obviously knew Penelope, and if she's involved and you never mentioned her...."

"It wouldn't be good."

"No, Dear."

Tuesday
9:00 am

He was sitting in his cubicle when Cory called.
"Hi there, Special Agent."
"Hi yourself. What's up? You sounded weird?"
He had forgotten about the call to Cory. "Weird? I am never weird." He cast his eyes around the office and spotted a photo of Rook's new puppy pinned to her cubicle wall. "Want to get a puppy?"
"What?"
"A puppy. The larval form of a dog, Canis familiaris?"
"Gabe."
"No, I'm serious. I would take care of it."
Cory sighed. "Is that really why you called me, Bergeron?"
"Yes. Well, and also to ask how the case is going?"
"It's going. Anything else?"
"Nope."
"Bye, Gabe."
He guessed that was a hard no to the idea of getting a puppy?
He wanted a cup of coffee, but his stomach was not quite coffee-ready just yet. After Monday's unpleasantness.
Maybe a cup of tea would stay down? And plain crackers? The breakroom was barren of victuals. Who might have a personal cache of tea? Chatterjee? He had been seen quaffing a golden brown beverage on occasion.
He was sauntering over to Chatterjee's cubicle when

Detective Czerwinski bounded out of the elevator.

He sighed. It was to be expected. He looked at Jennifer sitting all unaware in her office. She had just arrived. He could have warned her but where was the fun in that?

Dana took one look at the badge. "You want Bergeron, right?"

Czerwinski nodded, looking surprised and skeptical.

Dana invited Czerwinski to do his damnedest with a carefree wave in his direction.

But Jennifer popped out of her office. "Dana?"

Dana snuggled down within her sweater. "Police. For Bergeron."

The cubicle dwellers gave a baying cry like excited hounds. Jennifer gave them a scathing look; the more timid sank behind their cubicle walls.

Jennifer advanced upon Czerwinski with her large, mannish hand outstretched. "I'm Jennifer Garst Boltukaev. I'm in charge here. And you are?"

Czerwinski shook her hand. He was wearing another wrinkled, gray suit or the same one? The tie was different, but it was red and three-quarters tied.

"Detective Czerwinski, 24th District, PPD." He flashed his badge again. "I need to speak to Mr. Bergeron, but I can start with you, Ms. Boltukaev."

And then Czerwinski flashed his smile. Which was as shiny as his badge and transformative; in a good way.

Jennifer was wearing a new, cream colored suit which molded to her body, highlighting her curves to the evident delight of Czerwinski.

She twisted a lock of her long, brown hair and made a spectacle of herself by simpering at the detective. "Please come into my office, Detective."

And she flounced into said office.

He covered his eyes in vicarious shame.

But then he perused Czerwinski again. He wasn't ugly, and if you ignored the shoulders, his body wasn't that bad. The smile was quite something. Altogether, he might be more than the sum of his parts.

Baldacci rolled over. "That the guy who made you look at the body?"

Baldacci had called him after he'd talked to Aunt Flo, and he'd told him what had happened; well, what little he knew.

"That's him."

Carla said, "He's hot."

Baldacci said, "No, he's not."

She looked at her husband. "And how would you know?"

Baldacci flushed from chin to receding hairline. "I wouldn't! Obviously. But Gabe doesn't think he's hot. Right, Gabe?"

He shrugged. "He's asymmetric."

Baldacci said, "What?"

"Never mind."

Jennifer popped out of her office and led Czerwinski to the conference room. When she was absolutely sure, he was comfy, she spun around and pointed a finger of doom at one Gabriel Bergeron.

He smiled his second best smile at her. "I am totally innocent of all wrongdoing, Jennifer."

She shook her head, rolled her eyes, and snarled at him in an impressive triple feat. "That's what you always say." She whispered, "But you were here yesterday? All day?"

"Of course, Jennifer."

She nodded and shifted the glare to Baldacci. "The detective wants to talk to you first."

Baldacci nodded. He was in the conference room for scant minutes before he was ejected, and Carla was summoned.

Carla went in as stony faced as ever, but was soon smiling. True, this wasn't a unique event...more like a total eclipse of the sun. She lingered in the conference room as long as she could smiling at Czerwinski; probably to torture Baldacci.

Czerwinski was looking extra skeptical after he talked to Hearne; probably because Hearne hardly knew where he was on most days.

But after Matthews, Rook, and Chatterjee, he gave up

trying to break his alibi.

Chatterjee came out. "He wants you, Gabe."

He entered. He tried smiling at Czerwinski, but it was wasted effort.

"Plant your ass, Bergeron."

"Yes, Sir."

Czerwinski said, "It looks like your alibi is solid."

He kept his mouth shut and his lips flaccid.

Czerwinski said, "Is there anything else you can tell me?"

The detective looked very young saying that, and a bit at sea. Of course, he might be faking it. Still, he had promised Vonda.

"There is one thing. Well, it's more than one, but it's all connected...somehow."

He paused. Czerwinski was glaring at him.

"Right. So there are two people who might know something about what happened to Phillip."

Czerwinski readied his notebook.

"Penelope Black Stanko and Monroe. Now, Monroe could be his real name, but I doubt it."

Czerwinski had graduated to looking moderately skeptical already.

"Penelope is the mother of Billy Stanko and partner with him in the coffee shop, CoffeeXtra, which is down the block. Billy's my client, and I've known about her for over a year, but she was always traveling, and I had never met her until the end of last year."

He was losing Czerwinski.

"So last October, she came in pretending to want accounting services. She said she was a doctor and called herself Svetlana Kutuzov."

Czerwinski looked up. "Russian?"

"*Da.* I mean, yes."

"And?"

"I have no idea what she really wanted, but she split when she saw that I wasn't buying the Russian doctor gambit."

"And?"

"Okay. So I met Monroe a year ago at the FBI headquarters

in D.C. Well, outside the building. They wouldn't let me in, but somebody thought it was okay to let him inside. Go figure."

Czerwinski was staring out the window.

"He said he might have a job for me."

"A stranger comes out of the Hoover Building and says he might have a job for you?" Heavy duty skepticism.

"Yes. And then six months ago, Penelope and Monroe accosted me together at the 30th Street Amtrak Station about a possible job again. But she admitted that she was Penelope Black Stanko this time."

And he tried to tell Czerwinski exactly what they had said and about Aunt Flo's B&B and about his grandfather, Andrew, and about Phillip reacting when he mentioned Penelope's name, but Czerwinski was maxed out on skepticism.

The detective was shaking his head.

"Look, I know how it sounds...."

"The Hell you do."

"Right. But Chatterjee talked to the fake Dr. Svetlana Kutuzov, and you can call the FBI about Monroe."

Czerwinski was undecided.

"Call Vonda. She'll tell you that I'm not crazy."

Czerwinski said, "Send this Chatterjee in here."

So he did.

Of course, Chatterjee didn't know that Dr. Kutuzov was Penelope. Chatterjee came out. Czerwinski sat in the conference room for a while just shaking his head.

And then he got to his feet and headed for the elevator.

He may have followed him.

"Detective?"

Czerwinski punched the elevator button like it had made a nasty comment about his mother.

"You can call the FBI." Czerwinski was ignoring him. "They know about Monroe. Well, they claim they don't, but Cory has talked to his boss, Danielle Elkins, and even to her boss, Nadia Brunetti, about him...do you know who Cory is?"

Czerwinski nodded. "Special Agent Cory Poirier, Art Theft Division; Golczewski told me."

"So you'll talk to them?"

"I have other leads I'm going to check out first, Bergeron."

"Like?"

"Like the ex-wives. And his former boss. And this is none of your business."

"I know. I just wanted to help."

Czerwinski glared at him and boarded the elevator. "Keep out, Bergeron. I'm not going to warn you again."

"Right. Will do. Honest." Czerwinski was holding the elevator door which was interesting. "Is there something else?"

Czerwinski gritted his teeth as he came to a decision. "Think you'd recognize this Penelope's voice?"

"Why? Sorry. Maybe yes, maybe no." He looked hopefully at Czerwinski.

"We have a recording I want you to listen to."

"Of Penelope?"

Czerwinski patted his face as he let go of the elevator door. "That's what you'll tell us. If she isn't all in your head."

He grabbed the door this time. "A recording?"

Czerwinski sighed, drawing a breath from the soles of his scuffed boots. "A recording of a female with a heavy, Russian accent letting us know that we'd find a body in that row house on Savin."

And Czerwinski slapped his hand from the elevator door.

Tuesday
1:00 pm

So he had driven to Whitaker Avenue and parked across the street from an Egyptian mortuary temple with steps grand enough for your budget, pharaonic funeral procession..

Which noble edifice was the headquarters of the 24th District; and also of the 25th District.

He had gone inside, and in the fullness of time, someone had collected him and let him listen to the recording.

He had been very glad that Czerwinski hadn't been there, because he couldn't swear it was Penelope. He thought it was, and he had told the bored lady that, but he couldn't be sure.

But he was sure that the woman on the recording was genuinely upset and in tears. Which was understandable given the condition of the body.

But would Penelope have reacted like that? He didn't know.

And then the bored lady, who said she was Agnes, took him to another bored lady who declined to give her name.

And she had tried to produce sketches of Monroe and Penelope. In the end, Billy wouldn't have recognized the woman in the drawing as his mother. The sketch of Monroe was better, but lacked his silvery, seductive charm.

But if Czerwinski really wanted a likeness of Penelope, he could go ask Billy for one.

So he had driven back to South 16th Street, and he was now sitting in CoffeeXtra and eating banana bread.

The place was located on a corner and had floor-to-ceiling

glass walls on the front and one side and was flooded with light.

The ceiling was high and cluttered with girders and duct work, all painted black. The floor had been a rich, walnut when a former owner had installed it, but it was showing its age now.

He sipped his coffee and continued to stare at Billy who was the current owner along with Penelope. He wasn't going to ask for a photo. How would he ever explain why he wanted one?

Billy was in his mid-twenties, and skinny, tall, and gangly. A modest head with an oval face and big, brown, typically-sad eyes sat atop a Sauropod neck.

Billy looked up. "What, Dude? You need something?"

"Nope. I'm fine."

Billy went back to filling orders, apparently on his own. Where was Martin, his chief assistant?

When he had first met Billy before the bloody, violent deaths of Garth and Iona, the former owners of CoffeeXtra, Billy had been a simple barista and had worn shorts and tank tops.

Some time after Billy had mysteriously come to own the place, he had graduated to gorgeous, big-boy suits; some of which had probably cost more than the entire wardrobe of Gabriel Bergeron.

But today, sadly, Billy was back in shorts and a tank top. Which wasn't a good look for him.

Mostly because Billy was as furry as a grizzly bear; arms, legs, shoulders, back and, it could only be assumed, everywhere else.

Billy looked up again and caught him staring. "What the Hell, Dude?"

Billy was swamped with orders and a bit cranky. "I'm sorry."

And then Martin walked in with one of his girlfriends; the blonde one. Martin smiled at Billy like a salamander that had been born without a brain, but he took over. He was more capable than he looked, but then he'd have to be.

Billy stomped over to his table and sat; a sheen of sweat on his brow and shoulders.

"You want something, Dude?"

He wanted to know where Penelope Black was.

"It's nothing, Billy. How's business?"

Billy was actually Dr. Vilim Stanko with a doctoral degree in mathematics, specializing in something so esoteric that only three people in the world understood it.

"Fine. But you should know, Dude. You do the books. What's up?"

"Not a thing." He should just finish his coffee and go. "I have some paperwork that will need your mother's signature...if she's around?"

Billy considered. "She didn't call you again, did she? She's been upset about something, but I didn't think it was you?"

Billy was looking concerned. And sad, but it was ever thus with Vilim.

"No, I haven't heard from her. So she is in Philly?"

"Why, Dude? You can tell me."

Billy leaned closer. Billy had nice eyes. Billy also might still have a bit of a crush on him.

He casually leaned back in his chair. "Is she in Philly?"

Billy shook his head, but said, "She was."

"And do you know where she is, right now?"

"You're freaking me out, Dude. Is something wrong? Is she in some kind of danger?"

"What? No. I'm sure she isn't, Billy." He had no idea, but he wouldn't be surprised. "Why do you think she might be in danger?"

Billy wrapped his long, hairy arms around his head like a spider being pelted with rain drops. "She was upset when she called me this morning."

"And?"

"She doesn't get upset. She seemed okay on Saturday except for her boyfriend. She said she was going to dump him." Billy looked at him. "I thought she really liked this one."

"Who's the boyfriend?"

"She wouldn't tell me his name. Why do you want to know, Gabe?"

"Just curious. Have you ever seen him?"

"Not really. He picked her up once, but the car had tinted windows. What's going on, Dude?"

"Where does she live? When she's in town?"

Billy shook his head. "She has a house."

Ah, the lair. He aimed his very best smile at Vilim. "And where might that be?"

"No way, Dude."

"Come on, Billy. I'm trustworthy." He smiled some more and even patted a hairy shoulder.

Billy looked shocked but recovered quickly and smiled back at him. "Where's Cory?"

"He's on a...it doesn't matter where Cory is, Vilim." Billy stopped smiling. "Where is your mother's house?"

"Tell me why you want to know?"

There was no way he could tell Billy the whole story, but a half-truth might work. "She and a friend of hers, maybe the boyfriend you didn't see in the car, said they had a job for me, and I just wanted details...."

Billy stood up. "Told you not to do that, Dude. I warned you!"

"I know you did."

Billy was waving his arms. "No freaking way, Dude, can you get involved in whatever...."

He stood up and actually hugged Billy. "I won't. I promise. I'm sorry I upset you."

Billy hugged him back. "Don't do it, Gabe."

"I won't. Okay, I have to go."

Billy continued to stare into his eyes.

"Billy?"

"Yeah, Gabe?"

"Let go of me."

"Right. Sure, Dude." Billy stepped back. "You'd tell me if you knew something abut Mom...something serious?"

"I don't know anything, Billy."

And he got out of the shop as fast as his feet would carry him.

He didn't know anything really. And even if Phillip had

known Penelope that didn't mean that she had killed him, or that she was in danger herself.

And he didn't think that Czerwinski was looking for Penelope so there was no point in mentioning that to Billy either.

He marched back to Garst, Bauer & Hartmann and focused his keen intellect upon accounting stuff. He had promised Czerwinski that he would stay out of this mess, and by gosh and by golly, he was going to do just that.

Friday
2:00 pm
10 Days Later

He had called Lydia and told her how sorry he was about Phillip, which was the least he could do. Well, he had arranged for flowers too.

And Phillip had receded from his thoughts except for one doozy of a nightmare that featured Czerwinski chasing him up an endless flight of stairs.

So he had felt really bad when Lydia had called and invited him to the graveside funeral for just the family.

The cemetery was near Berwyn. He parked beside a church that looked like it had been hewn from the local bedrock. The cemetery itself had a wall built of granite blocks, topped with shards of granite for a crenelated look.

He spotted a knot of people and walked down the gravel drive with the June sun beating down on his head. He was sweating already, but Lydia was his cousin, and maybe Phillip wouldn't have been so bad if they had gotten to know each other.

So he was going to forget about how hot he was in his best, dark suit and be sympathetic and supportive.

This area of the cemetery was old enough to have the above-ground vaults; some were flat, some gently arched. Most of the vaults had dark stains or orange patches of lichen.

He stepped off the gravel drive onto a path that threaded its way between the graves. He glanced over at the group of mourners and almost ran into a granite angel looking down at him from her plinth. Her naked feet peeked out from beneath her flowing robe;

the nose and chin were lichen free. Her face was crudely carved, and her eyes were shadowed, but she seemed to be staring at him.

The inscription read, "Pauline, beloved wife of...." The rest was lost to time and the elements.

Lydia spotted him and waved him over. He saw Camille, but the rest of the group were strangers; relatives maybe, but strangers.

Lydia's hair was swept back emphasizing the perfect oval of her face. She was wearing the proverbial, little black dress, and he was willing to wager that it had cost the earth.

He made this assessment not because he knew anything about dresses, but because the guy next to her, whose arm she was locked onto, was wearing a suit that had cost at least the GDP of Sri Lanka.

"Gabe, thank you for coming." She squeezed his hand. "This is my husband, Reed."

Reed was tall and thick-bodied. He had black hair, blue eyes, and a wide forehead that implied a massive brain was chugging along behind those layers of skin and bone.

Reed executed a perfect handshake; correct strength, duration, skin dryness, and grip position. "Glad to meet you, Gabe. Lydia has been talking about you non-stop since you met. She says I have to come with her to your aunt's B&B."

"You'd be very welcome, Reed. It's a beautiful location."

Reed's cold eyes had been analyzing everything about him since he'd approached Lydia. Gabriel Bergeron had been assigned to one of the lower rungs of the social hierarchy; a lightning analysis ranked him low for both risk and benefit potential.

Lydia gave her husband a look that was less than loving. "Gabe, I'd like you to meet my son, Jack, and my daughter, Olivia."

They had black hair and blue eyes like their father. Jack was about fifteen and a virtual clone of his father. He was too young to hide his indifference as they shook hands.

Olivia was younger; a preteen? Her eyes weren't as non-mammalian as her father's or her brother's. She gave him a fleeting, unhappy smile.

He made eye contact with Camille and nodded. He wasn't sure she knew who he was. She had a handkerchief clutched in her hand, and of the dozen people present, she seemed the most sorrowful.

He looked at Lydia. Maybe he was being unfair, and Lydia would grieve in her own way in her own time.

A tall, blonde woman was checking him out. She was fortyish; her hair was parted in the middle and flowed silkily to her shoulders. Her black dress was a bit too sparkly to be funeral wear.

She could be one of Phillips' ex-wives? Three, blond, young men were flanking her; they looked like Phillip. The eldest might be twenty. He was distinguished from his siblings by the width of his fullback shoulders, but they would catch up with him given a few years and high-protein diets.

She walked over. "Hello. I'm Kelly Lovett, Phillip's first wife, and who are you?"

"I'm Gabriel Bergeron."

"Bergeron? A relative?"

"I'm Phillip's second cousin. Lydia discovered the connection. My grandfather, Andrew...."

She said, "When was this?"

"Two weeks ago. At my aunt's B&B?" He didn't know why but Kelly's fullback sons were glaring at him.

"So that's what that trip was about?" A short woman with black hair, who had troweled on the mascara and eye liner, poked him in the shoulder. "Phillip told me he wasn't going."

Blonde Kelly smirked. "Maybe he didn't tell you everything, Christina."

Christina put a hand tipped with scarlet nails on her pneumatic assets which were popping out of her dress. "I'm Christina Guidry, the second wife. The younger, prettier one."

Christina smirked back at Kelly.

He looked from Kelly to Christina. "I'm very sorry for your loss. I had only just met Phillip, but I'm sure you all loved him."

The ladies made faces, but before they could deny loving Phillip, the eldest of the fullbacks said, "We did. Dad was the best."

His voice rumbled from a solid frame. Phillip's sons were trying to be stoic and manly about it, but they were close to tears.

He held out his hand. "I'm Gabe Bergeron. I'm sorry about your father. I can imagine how hard this must be."

The middle son said, "No, you can't!"

He said, "I lost my mother when I was ten." Which wasn't something he usually shared.

The youngest said, "Don't mind Jacob. He's upset."

Jacob looked at his younger brother. "And you aren't?"

"Of course, I am."

Kelly said, "Boys! Keep your voices down. The minister is going to start."

And he did. He was short and round and gray, but he had a rich, baritone voice. He talked about life and death and life everlasting, and he spoke of Phillip and his family.

And then he read some nice verses from the Bible.

The minister finished with a verse that included: "*...for the trumpet shall sound, and the dead shall be raised incorruptible, and we shall be changed.*"

And he heard the trumpet and the baritone performing Handel's sublime setting of this Bible text, he felt a chill run up his spine to the back of his head in the bright, June sun.

He opened his eyes.

Reed was shaking the minister's hand, and he and Lydia were walking with him toward the church. Camille and Christina were behind them.

The rest of the group were ambling away, but Phillip's sons were still standing next to the casket set above the grave.

He didn't know them, or what to say to them. And Kelly was with them. She was crying as she hugged them, She coaxed them toward the exit and the cars beyond.

A guy about his age was walking more or less beside him. He nodded.

The guy said, "I thought I knew all of Phil's friends?"

"I'm Gabriel Bergeron; Phillip's second cousin." He was starting to feel a little weird saying it; it was like he was claiming some relationship that he wasn't entitled to.

But the guy smiled at him and extended this hand. "I'm Luke Shaffer. Phil and I have been buddies since college."

"I'm sorry for your loss, Luke. I just met Phillip two weeks ago."

"Yeah? Oh, this must be part of Lydia's genealogy thing?"

"Yes, it was. She found me. Phillip told you about that?"

Luke nodded. He was about his age and size. He had black hair, a square face, and big, bushy eyebrows that even beat out Mr. Boghossian's, his former landlord.

Luke said, "I can't get over it."

"I know it must be a shock."

"Sure, but I will never believe that Phil killed himself. He had a few problems, but he would have solved them. Phil didn't sweat the small stuff." He smiled. "Or the big stuff too much."

He kept his mouth shut. When Czerwinski wanted Luke or anybody else to know that Phillip had been murdered, he would so inform them.

Luke pointed at a red Lexus. "That's me."

"Right. Nice meeting you, Luke."

Lydia and Reed were on the steps to the church; the minister had gone. Lydia was talking to Reed, and he was looking across the cemetery. She stopped, shook her head, and glared at her husband for a bit.

And then she turned and waved. "Gabe? May I speak to you?"

He ambled over trying to figure out what Lydia was going to say to him. Reed was still communing with the spirits of the dead and had no time for the quick.

"It was a very nice service, Lydia."

She smiled. "Thank you, Gabe, and thank you for coming."

She hesitated and looked at Reed who was as animated as the late Pauline's granite angel.

"Gabe, would you be free to talk with us...tomorrow? Or Sunday?"

"Sure, I guess." Cory was in New York. Or Turkmenistan. "Tomorrow is fine. Where?"

"At our home."

Reed was not a happy husband, but he handed over a card with an address and other contact info. He smiled.

Why wasn't there a word for a lip flexion that looked like a smile but obviously wasn't? Not a grimace or a grin.

Reed said, "Would 2:00 pm suit you, Gabe?"

"Sure. That's fine."

"Do you know where this is?"

"Near Berwyn? I can find it. I've been out that way before." He looked from Reed to Lydia. "May I ask what this is about?"

Reed let his lips rest, and he looked exhausted for just an instant. "It's better if we talk about it tomorrow."

And Reed took Lydia's arm and urged her to stride away from Gabriel Bergeron.

He may have stood there shaking his head before heading for his yellow Jeep again.

All the cars were gone except for a metallic blue Mercedes sedan which was idling. The windows were tinted, and, in the bright sunshine, looked almost black.

He kept walking toward his Jeep, but he had the feeling he was being watched.

Which was silly. It was just one of the mourners taking a call or something before pulling off.

He got in his Jeep and looked in the rearview mirror. The Mercedes was still there, dozing like a shiny beetle in the sun.

Saturday
2:00 pm

So he was motoring along on Route 30 again. He passed the exits for Merion, Bryn Mawr, Villanova, and sundry other of the Main Line suburbs before taking the Berwyn exit.

Cory's house, which his grandmother had left to him and his siblings, Judd and Diane, was past Berwyn.

After getting home from the funeral, he had called Max Nagy. Max was a lawyer and had gotten him out of jail on more than one occasion.

Max had tried to maintain an air of nonchalance, but he had obviously been impressed that he, Gabriel Bergeron, CPA, but of peasant stock, had been invited to visit the abode of the gods.

"Reed James Farley Gibson, III invited you to his house, Bergeron? Are you sure about that?"

"Yes, Max." He hated name droppers. "His wife...."

"The beautiful Lydia."

"Yes, Max. Lydia is my second cousin...on my mother's side."

"Bullshit!"

"Nope. True. So what can you tell me about RJFG3?"

"He's the senior partner in Vance & Gibson."

"Okay. Should I be impressed, Max?"

"Damn straight. If you want Heaven and Earth moved or the Constitution amended, you call V&G; not that they would take your call. Or mine."

So he was prepared to be impressed by the Gibson pied-àterre as he turned onto the drive.

Not prepared enough.

Well, it wasn't Schönbrunn Palace. It didn't have fourteen hundred rooms like the Hapsburg palace, but he didn't want the job of counting the rooms it did have.

He parked. His Jeep looked tacky next to the house. He climbed the stairs and rapped on the door with the lion's head knocker.

A uniformed maid opened the door. "Hello, I'm Gabriel Bergeron. I'm here to see Mrs. Gibson."

She was Nordic blonde. And tall. She gave him an icy stare straight from a frozen fjord, but she nodded and waved him into the entrance hall.

"Please wait here, Sir."

The room was chilly even in June, being mostly marble and vast and empty. The 30th Street Amtrak Station was homier.

He stood and waited.

The maid came back to retrieve him. He followed her up a flight of stairs, down a hall, and then down another hall. She pointed at the door before them and slipped away.

He knocked.

"Enter."

Reed was sitting on a brocaded sofa set upon an oriental rug floating all, all alone in the center of the room. Lydia was sitting on the same sofa but a couple of yards from Reed.

A matching sofa anchored the other side of the carpet. A small table was between them.

Lydia said, "Welcome, Gabe. I'm so glad you came."

Reed smiled and rose. "Yes, welcome to our home, Gabe."

They shook hands, and Reed indicated he should park it on the other sofa. He did so. He surveyed the shelves of books. They matched. So Reed had gotten his books rebound to fit the décor? Or they were just a show piece purchased for their looks?

"Nice place you have. Roomy."

Lydia may have smiled. Reed made a face like he was having a gas attack.

The closest window looked out on the gardens which were

a riot of color. "Roses?"

Lydia said, "Yes, Reed grows them."

Reed looked faintly embarrassed. Because he soiled his hands with Mother Earth?

"So does Aunt Flo. She loves yellow roses."

There was a knock on the door, and the maid entered after Reed gave her leave. She had a tea service with an array of petits fours.

The maid retired, and Lydia served them tea. He popped a white cube topped with an orange icing flower into his mouth.

Lydia looked at Reed, and he aimed a hand at her, palm up.

She said, "I asked you here, Gabe, because I'm not satisfied with the progress being made by the Philadelphia police in solving Phillip's murder."

Reed said, "Or the lack thereof."

"I'm sure Detective Czerwinski is doing his best."

Reed had another gas attack but didn't comment.

Lydia said, "Reed has been looking into the case...he has friends in the city government and the police department." She smiled at her husband. "And everywhere really."

Reed smiled demurely.

Lydia said, "The detective has no suspects...after two weeks. He has no idea why Phillip was killed."

"I'm sorry to hear that."

Reed said, "I also found out some things about you, Gabe."

Lydia said, "He didn't intend to pry into your life."

"No, I didn't. I asked for all the information they had collected, and someone included your file." Reed was smiling at him. "But once I had it, I couldn't put it down."

"I don't know what to say to that, Reed. I never mean to get involved in things. It just happens."

Lydia said, "How did you solve those cases, Gabe?"

"Dumb luck. Well, I have been told I'm nosy."

Reed smiled at Lydia. "Several of the comments in your file mention that, Gabe."

He was afraid he knew where this was going. "Why am I here?"

Lydia said, "I'd like you to work with Detective Czerwinski and find out who killed Phillip."

Reed said, "Do you think this mystery man, Monroe, is involved?"

"I don't know."

Lydia said, "Would you mind telling us what happened with Monroe? And this Penelope Black?"

"No. I guess not."

And he told them everything he remembered about the encounters. He may have fortified himself with more of the petits fours.

Lydia said, "And he asked you what you knew about your grandfather, Andrew Bergeron?"

"He did."

She nodded. "So you think Phillip and Camille and I were maneuvered into going to your aunt's B&B?"

"I don't know. What do you think?"

She shook her head. "I talked to my friend, and she said she found the reference online."

Reed said, "Which could have been planted."

Lydia nodded.

He said, "You saw Phillip's face when I asked about Penelope? I think he knew her."

She nodded. "Phillip was terrible at lying. I think he knew her too, but Czerwinski hasn't been able to find her."

Reed said, "I don't think he's looked, Lydia. But I've looked for her and for this Monroe person."

"And?"

Reed said, "I think I'm being stonewalled, Gabe, by people who should know better." He looked at his wife. "I haven't given up."

He was gazing at the last petit four. He couldn't scarf it up. Well, he could, but it wouldn't be polite. He sighed. They were very good, and he was about to be ejected never to return. Maybe Ezmeralda could make them if he described them?

Lydia said, "Will you do it, Gabe? Work with Czerwinski?"

"He'll never agree to that, Lydia."

She said, "He will. But if you sense that he isn't cooperating completely, give me a call." She smiled at her husband. "And Reed will take care of it."

And fire and damnation would rain down upon poor Czerwinski's curly head.

"I don't think so. I'm sorry, but I'm not sure I want to get involved in this. I'm very sorry about Phillip, and I understand how you feel about finding his killer...."

Lydia said, "Did you find your mother's killer, Gabe?"

He froze up as she continued to stare at him.

She said, "There are a few cryptic notes by this other detective...."

Reed said, "Golczewski."

"You were working on it, digging into the details?"

He hadn't told Vonda or any law enforcement officer about Nancy. Well, except for Cory, and even he didn't know what had happened to her. He wasn't going to share with Lydia.

"I'd rather not talk about that."

Lydia said, "I think you did find the killer, Gabe."

He sat there and didn't say a word.

Lydia closed her eyes, trying to hold back the tears. He felt bad, but he couldn't. If he did, not knowing anything about Monroe or Penelope or who they really were, or how dangerous they were, he could be putting Aunt Flo and Ezmeralda into danger. Not to mention himself.

Reed said, "If he doesn't want to do it, Lydia, we can't force him." And Master Reed looked just a smidgen relieved.

But Lydia said, "Will you think about it, Gabe?"

He nodded. "I guess I can do that."

He left the Gibson estate and merged onto the highway. He wasn't paying too much attention to the other cars until a metallic blue Mercedes blew past him.

It wasn't the car from Phillip's funeral. Why would it be? There were probably hundreds of blue Mercedes in the area.

Monday
Noon

He had thought about what Lydia wanted him to do for two days. He wanted to help her, but he couldn't. He had just called her and told her the answer was no.

Which was hard because he knew how she felt.

She had said, "Reed will be relieved."

And she had hung up before he could ask why exactly.

He was standing in line at CoffeeXtra waiting for his order.

The place was packed with warm bodies. The shades hadn't been lowered, and the June sun was irradiating the place. Every reflective surface glinted dazzlingly.

The barista seemed unaware that his customers were being fried alive. He was focused on filling orders; neither accurately nor quickly.

Where were Billy and Martin?

The new guy was almost as tall as Billy. His head and beard had been trimmed to a quarter inch stubble. His concentration was evident by the three horizontal creases across his forehead and the pair of vertical gashes bracketing the bridge of a generous nose with nostrils like hanger bays.

The guy handed him a dampish, miscellaneous object wrapped in white paper and a cup filled to the rim with a tan liquid.

He looked at the guy.

But he was totally oblivious and working on the next order.

He shook his head and grabbed a table. He unwrapped the

dampish object; it was a pastry that had fought the good fight and lost. The red stuff squishing out smelled like something a chemist might think smelled like strawberry.

He glared at the tan liquid. He should dump it and take his business elsewhere. He sighed and tried calling Cory.

"Hi, Gabe."

He was so taken aback he almost dropped his phone. "You answered?'

Cory said, "I always answer when I can."

"Right. I know that. I'm at CoffeeXtra. Some new barista has given me coffee that looks like weak tea and smells funny."

"Take it back."

"Right." He wasn't really comfortable doing that. "I will." Cory knew he wouldn't. "So how are you? And Bornheimer? And where are you?"

"We're fine. We're in Newburyport, Massachusetts."

"Why?"

Cory sighed. "I'm asking myself that. A lead which is leading nowhere. So what's new with you?"

Cory didn't need to know about his second cousin being murdered. "Nothing at all. I miss you. Work is boring."

"Boring can be good, Bergeron. Are you staying out of trouble?"

"I am." Which was absolutely true since he had just finished refusing Lydia's request.

"Gabe."

"I am trouble-free. So when are you coming home?"

"Unclear."

"Shit, Poirier. Sorry. I shouldn't have said that."

"It's okay. I have to go. Bornheimer is waving at me."

And he was gone. He sat there staring at his phone until he realized the sun was frying the back of his neck. Enough was enough. He got up and started lowering the shades.

The patrons started clapping; he lowered the last shade and turned to acknowledge the applause.

Billy had appeared from somewhere and was navigating his way among the tables. He slipped behind the bar and began filling orders.

He reclaimed his table and sipped his "coffee." It tasted funny, but he masked the taste with a bite of the pastry, which also tasted funny, but in an artificial fruity way.

He glared at the anonymous barista and at Billy as he drank more tan stuff. It tasted vaguely like coffee but was obviously not what he'd ordered.

He should get back to work, but the lunch rush was over, and Billy was heading his way.

Billy sat down. Billy was pissed with him. "What?"

"Dude!"

"Sorry, I need more, Stanko."

"A detective came to see me about Mom. Twice."

Shit. "And you're telling me because?"

Billy shook his head. "He asked about you too. You told him something about Mom, didn't you?"

He smiled his best smile at Billy. "I had to, Billy, but I didn't think Detective Czerwinski paid any attention to me."

"What did you tell him?"

"Nothing really. Just that she and Monroe had this job for me which was connected in some way with Andrew Bergeron."

Billy was a good four inches away. "Who's that?"

"My grandfather."

Billy was cogitating. "Monroe had the job. Not Mom. She just told him about you."

"You know Monroe?"

"No, but I've seen him. Once or twice. But, Dude, this Czerwinski threatened to arrest me if I didn't tell him how to find Mom."

"I'm sorry, Billy. But he didn't?"

"I told him I haven't seen her and don't know how to reach her, and I guess he believed me. He searched her house. She's going to be so pissed."

"And you don't know where she might have gone?"

Billy shook his head. "No, Dude!" His big, brown eyes were shiny with tears. "I'm worried about her. This Czerwinski is a homicide detective. What's going on?"

He didn't want to get into Phillip's murder, but he didn't see how he could avoid telling Billy something.

But Billy was looking at the counter; the new barista was being swamped again.

"Shit. I have to help Calvin. Can you stick around, Gabe? Please. I have to know what's going on?"

"Okay. I guess."

Billy said, "Wait for me in the office, Dude. I won't be long."

He swayed as he got to his feet. He shook his head and went to the Men's Room. He splashed water on his face, and then went to Billy's office and sat down to wait.

Billy's desk was very neat. He thought about checking to see if Billy had changed the password on his computer.

He couldn't be too late getting back to work. Jennifer had some kind of project for him.

His stomach wasn't feeling just right. He was going to punch the new barista in the face. He should get up, but he couldn't remember what he had been going to do.

He sat there.

The letters on Billy's white board were blurry.

Billy said, "Gabe! Are you okay, Dude!"

He tried to tell Billy that he was fine, but the words didn't come out right. "Uhhhmfffff...."

He thought Billy was slapping his face hard, but it didn't seem to hurt. And then he threw up on Billy's brown and orange carpet.

And he seemed to be on the floor, and Billy was yelling, and then it was just a cascade of white blobs that might have been faces?

Someone was peeling his eyelids back and shining a bright light into his eyes. He wanted them to stop.

It took an incredible amount of effort to say, "Stop."

Well, it was a faint whisper.

"Mr. Bergeron? Can you hear me?"

"Yes."

"Do you know where you are?"

He opened his right eye. A woman in cranberry scrubs was staring at him.

"Hospital?"

She smiled. "Yes, sir. I'm Dr. Uccellini, and you're at Hahnemann University Hospital."

"Right. Threw up."

"Yes, and that was a good thing, Mr. Bergeron." She stared at him, dark eyes boring in. "Have you been taking a sleep medication, Sir?"

"Nope." He thought he should ask why, but he was much too tired. He closed his eyes.

Tuesday Noon

He didn't feel great, but he didn't want to be in the bed if the doctor should appear. He wanted to look ready to go home.

He had tried to put his clothes back on, but the nurse had gotten cranky over that. Maybe because he was messing up the IV?

Anyway, he was still in the gown.

He couldn't find his briefs. He wasn't sure he wanted to ask the nurse what had happened to them.

So he had wrapped the gown around him so his bare ass wasn't on the vinyl chair seat. He was pretty sure his ass was clean, but still.

And then Jennifer walked in.

He may have hugged her.

She looked him over. "Are you all right, Gabe?"

"Moi? Fine as frog's hair. Never better. Can you find the doctor? I want this IV out of my arm." He tried to remember. "I don't know the name, but the nurse can tell you. Ask the nice one with short, black hair; not the cranky one. I think she was a woman? The doctor. The nurses are women; even the cranky one. Probably."

Jennifer crossed her arms, rolled her eyes, and shook her head in a medal-worthy feat of muscle control. "You should be in bed, Bergeron."

"Should not."

Jennifer pushed him against the bed, and he fell back powerless to resist. She grabbed his feet and tossed his nether regions onto the bed. She checked that the IV tube wasn't kinked, and she was covering him with the sheet when Baldacci and Carla walked in.

Baldacci checked him out. "Are you okay?"

"I am. Hale and hardy. Able to leap tall buildings in a single bound. I need you to get me out of here, Harry."

Baldacci smiled at him.

Carla said, "So who tried to kill you this time?"

He looked from one quizzical face to the other. "Wait. Somebody tried to kill me?"

Jennifer said, "What did you think happened, Bergeron?" She was giving him a how-dumb-are-you look? Which was really mean...especially if someone had tried to kill him.

"I thought...maybe food poisoning? And I was planning on suing Billy and Penelope for every last penny they have. And giving CoffeeXtra a bad review on every app I can find."

Jennifer said, "Haven't you talked to the doctor?"

He drew himself up. "I would if I could find her. If it is a her...I think I remember a woman in scrubs standing over me, but it's a bit blurry."

Jennifer said, "You were drugged."

"At CoffeeXtra?" She gave him an ambivalent nod/shrug. "How do you know that?"

Jennifer looked at the open door. She lowered her voice. "I told the nurse I was your sister."

"Right. Okay." He wasn't sure he wanted Jennifer to be privy to his medical records. "Shit! Has anybody told Cory or Aunt Flo?"

Jennifer said, "We didn't know how to reach Cory, but I called Mrs. Barnes last night...after you were out of danger."

"Shit! Wait. I was in danger? Of dying?" He waved his mortality aside. "Find my phone! Harry, look in that wardrobe. My clothes are in there."

Baldacci retrieved his phone. He dialed.

Annika said, "Hello?"

"Hi, Annika. This is Gabriel...." He stopped talking due to the clunking noise as Annika dropped the phone. Aunt Flo was going to need a new phone if Annika didn't learn to chill.

He smiled at his friends and waited. He would circle back to that out of danger bit.

"Gabriel?"

"Yes, Aunt Flo. I'm fine. Well, I'm in a bed in the hospital, and I'm wearing a gown with no behind, and I haven't eaten anything, not that I really want anything...."

"Gabriel!"

He paused. "Yes, Aunt Flo?"

"Are you sure you're okay?"

"I feel okay." He handed the phone to Jennifer. "Tell her I'm okay."

Jennifer said, "Mrs. Barnes. Yes, he seems fine. No, we haven't talked to the doctor yet."

He waved at Jennifer and took the phone. "Aunt Flo, I'm sorry if you were worried, but I'm fine."

He heard Ezmeralda say, "What happened to him?"

He said, "Tell Ezmeralda that I don't know, but I'll call you as soon as I talk to the doctor."

Aunt Flo said, "What is the doctor's name, Gabriel?"

"No idea. But I'll call you as soon as I know anything. Bye for now."

"Bye, Gabriel."

"Shit!" He gave Jennifer his fiercest glare. It didn't appear to strike terror into her heart. "Did you tell her that somebody tried to kill me?"

"No. We didn't know what had happened when I called her."

"To let her know I was out of danger? You didn't say it like that, did you?"

Jennifer matched his glare and doubled it. "Give me some credit, Bergeron."

"Okay. Good. Thanks."

And then a woman in a long, white coat entered. The name on her coat read, "N. Uccellini." She looked vaguely familiar.

She looked at his company and smiled. "And who are these people, Mr. Bergeron?"

"Friends. You can say anything you need to say in front of them. What happened to me?"

Dr. Uccellini said, "You ingested a large dose of a sleeping medication...one of the benzodiazepine family. Are you taking that drug, Mr. Bergeron?"

"Never."

She nodded. "And you weren't trying to...end your life?"

He snorted. "I was not! I like my life. I'd like it even better if I could lose this IV?"

She smiled at him.

"So somebody did this. How long between ingesting and passing out, Doctor?" She frowned. "An hour? Six hours? A day?"

She shook her head. "Less than an hour."

"Shit. So it was in that awful coffee! Or that pastry! I will get the most blood-thirsty lawyer in Philadelphia and sue Billy Stanko. And I'll testify against him when he's tried for attempted murder!"

Doctor Uccellini said, "That's a matter for the police, Mr. Bergeron."

"Right. Of course. So this was a lethal dose?"

She frowned and started backing out of the room. "I don't think I should comment on that."

He had freaked her out by mentioning lawyers and suing. "So can I go home?"

She took another step back. "I think the police would like to talk to you first."

And Detective Czerwinski was in his doorway, giving him a skeptical look.

Tuesday
1:00 pm

Czerwinski was in a navy, rumpled suit. He had another red tie, loosely knotted around an unbuttoned, frayed collar. The detective looked at Jennifer and Baldacci and Carla. "I need the room."

Jennifer nodded and headed for the door.

Carla was staring at the floor under his bed. She pulled out a pen and crouched.

Baldacci said, "What is it?"

Carla stood up with his briefs dangling from her pen like the flag of the Titanic. If the flag of the White Star Line had been a black field stuffed with orange, bird-of-paradise flowers.

She gazed at him and shook her head. "Care to explain, Bergeron?"

Baldacci started laughing and couldn't stop.

He grabbed his briefs and stuffed them under the sheet. Carla smiled and winked at him. She hustled Baldacci out of the room before he wet himself laughing.

For half a millisecond, he thought Czerwinski was going to smile, but he managed to twist it into a grimace. "You didn't take the drugs?"

"No! I did not!"

And then Vonda walked in. She looked pissed. "I didn't do anything, Vonda. I didn't investigate or ask a single question. Honest!"

Vonda was in a ecru suit with a brown cravat. Czerwinski

looked extra slovenly next to her. "Tell me what happened yesterday, Bergeron." She held up a slender hand, big, brown eyes boring into him. "Organize your thoughts. Do not tell me every last thing that happened."

He still had the briefs in his hand. He suddenly had a wisp of a memory of running down a hallway? With a nurse chasing him? And he was pretty sure he'd been naked as a jay bird.

He could feel his face getting hot. Czerwinski and Vonda were staring at him.

"Bergeron? Are you okay?"

"Never better, Vonda. Well, I have been better, much better...."

She held up the hand again.

"Right." So he told her and Czerwinski everything he could remember about his lunch at CoffeeXtra.

Vonda said, "And you left your coffee unattended while you lowered the shades?"

He nodded. "That's when he did it."

She said, "Do you have any idea who he is?"

"No. I didn't see anybody. It was crowded and people were at the tables around mine. Anybody could have just reached over and poured something into my coffee."

Czerwinski was looking extremely skeptical; his lower right eye was squinting at him. "And it didn't taste funny?"

"It did, but there was a new barista, and he messed up my order...my coffee was tan when he handed it to me. I just thought it was bad coffee."

Vonda said, "Name?"

"Of the barista? Calvin. I think."

Czerwinski said, "And was this Billy Stanko there?"

Shit. "He was." He wasn't going to tell them that Billy had passed by his table.

Czerwinski and Vonda exchanged a look. "Did you see this Penelope?"

"No, I didn't."

Vonda said, "Gabe, do you think Billy drugged you?"

"No! Billy is a friend."

Vonda said, "Why were you in his office?"

"He was worried about his mother and wanted to talk to me. Czerwinski had spooked him by asking about Penelope."

"And his mother is connected to this Monroe?"

"Yes. But I don't know that Monroe has any connection to Phillip's death." He looked at Vonda. "So was I given a lethal dose?"

"Probably not. But certainly enough to disorient you and knock you out in short order."

"So what was the point?"

Vonda was glaring at him. "Could have been to make it easy to grab you."

"Shit, Vonda. So what? He or they would have snatched me off the street as I walked back to the Mahr Building?"

Vonda said, "It's a possibility."

"But Billy asked me to wait?"

Czerwinski said, "Or Billy wanted you to pass out in his office so he could haul you out the back door of the coffee shop."

"But he dialed 911?"

Vonda said, "Maybe he had to. Maybe somebody saw you before he could get you out the back."

Which was possible.

"But why? You think this is connected to Phillip? I haven't done anything."

Czerwinski was glaring at him; upper and lower eyes squinted, eyebrows flexed, and his rosebud mouth pursed. "You talked to Reed Gibson."

Vonda was back to looking pissed.

"Mostly to Lydia. But not to ask them questions. They invited me to their house on Saturday. Lydia asked me to look into Phillip's death." He wasn't going to mention that they thought Czerwinski was a piss-poor detective. "But I told them no. I called her on Monday."

Vonda said, "But somebody knew that you had talked to them. And knew about your connection to Phillip."

Czerwinski said, "And they knew that Reed was sticking his well-connected nose into my case."

"How would they know that?"

Czerwinski said, "Don't know. But they did."

He looked at Vonda, but it wasn't her case. Why were they so sure there was a connection?

"So how did Phillip really die?"

Vonda looked at Czerwinski. "Detective?"

Czerwinski frowned. "Shit. Why not? Everybody else has looked at the file. He was drugged before somebody dragged him to the stairs and strung him up like a cattle rustler in an old Western."

Vonda said, "The techs found traces in his glass. But not in the bottle."

"Traces of what?"

Czerwinski said, "Probably the same shit that was put into your coffee."

Vonda said, "They're running a comparison, but they think it's an exact match. It's a prescription med; Mirelzepam. Prescribed for severe insomnia."

"Shit."

Vonda nodded. "So what are you going to do, Gabe?"

Czerwinski looked at her. "He's going to stay out of this! That's what he's going to do!"

And he walked out.

Vonda watched him leave and turned back. A smile flickered across her face. "He doesn't know you very well, does he?"

Tuesday
2:00 pm

Vonda shook her head. "But you really should stay out of this, Gabe."

"But somebody thinks I'm already in it!"

"I know. Where's Cory?"

"Massachusetts. On a case. Undercover."

She shook her head again. "Can you call him? I'd rather you weren't on your own for a while."

He would like not to be on his own too. "I'll think about calling him. Or I might go stay with Aunt Flo."

Vonda smiled. "Do that. Mrs. Boltukaev won't mind. She likes you, Gabe. She called me to let me know you'd been drugged."

"Jennifer called you?" He'd have to think of some way to thank Jennifer, or at least not irritate her for a while. "Thanks for coming, Vonda. I appreciate it."

She smiled. "I like having you around. Czerwinski is okay. Once you get to know him."

"Is that so? Right. Thanks again, Vonda."

And she had gone. And in the fullness of time, Dr. Uccellini had returned and told the nurse to unhook the IV.

"Does this mean I can go home?"

"I don't see why not, Mr. Bergeron. I'll get the paperwork started."

It had been fifty-seven minutes already. According to the timer app on his cellphone. Plenty of time to dress, pace, and now call Aunt Flo.

"I'm fine, Aunt Flo. Dr. Uccellini is releasing me, and I'm going straight home."

"Tell me what happened, Gabriel, and don't leave anything out."

He heard Ezmeralda in the background. "I say we go there. The Lincoln has a full tank."

And the trunk was probably stocked with enough fire power to overthrow the government of Bolivia.

"Tell Ezmeralda that you don't have to drive to Philly. I'll be okay. In fact, when I'm feeling a little better, I thought I'd come to stay with you...for a few days."

Aunt Flo said, "What happened, Gabriel?"

He had stalled as long as he could so he told her the whole story. There was a silence after he finished.

"Aunt Flo?"

"I'm here, Dear. So the drug that was used to incapacitate Phillip was used on you."

"Probably."

"Can you stay with your friend Baldacci for a few days?"

He wasn't sure that Carla would allow that, and he didn't want to ask and put Harry in an awkward position. "That's not necessary, Aunt Flo. Really."

"Jennifer then?"

"You want me to ask Jennifer if I can stay with her for a few days? I don't think so, Aunt Flo. I'll be fine. I'll take a taxi home, and I'll call you when I get there."

There was some muttering from Ezmeralda, but Aunt Flo said, "All right, Dear."

He walked out to the nurses' station and gave them a hopeful but pitiable look. The good nurse, the one with short, black hair, smiled at him.

"You're all set, Mr. Bergeron. Just sign everywhere there's an X."

He should probably read the three pages of small type to see just what he was agreeing to, but he didn't feel that good, and his magnifying glass was at home.

He smiled at the nurse. "Is that it?"

She smiled back. "Are you a runner, Mr. Bergeron?"

"What? Yes, I am. I took it up a while back. Why?"

"Nothing, Sir."

"Really?"

She and Cranky Nurse smiled. "It's just that we didn't think we were going to catch you."

He folded his copy of the paperwork and slunk out of the hospital.

He got a cab as he had promised Aunt Flo he would, and he arrived home safe and sound.

He hadn't realized how weak he was until he climbed the stairs to his apartment on the fourth floor.

He sat on his sofa and caught his breath.

He called Aunt Flo. "I'm home. No problems."

"I'm glad to hear that, Gabriel."

And he stretched out on his sofa and closed his eyes.

It was dark when the pounding on his door started. He may have run down the hall and grabbed the Glock from the gun safe.

He stood against the wall. "Who is it?"

"Kirill. Open the door, Bergeron."

So he did.

Kirill strode in, but he halted when he saw the Glock.

"Hand it over, Bergeron."

"No."

Kirill glared at him. "I can take it. If I want to."

He ignored the challenge. "Why are you here?"

Kirill threw himself on the sofa. "You're welcome."

He slammed the door and glared back at Kirill.

Mr. Kirill Ochoa was the younger son of Danilo Ochoa and Valentina Kutuzova. And now he was Ezmeralda's stepson.

He and Kirill were the same age, but Kirill had spent his years in riotous living. Still he was strong, with a neck as thick has his head, and rough, powerful hands.

He was also white-blond, blue-eyed, and blessed with killer Slavic cheekbones.

But he had shaved the hair on the sides and back of his

head to achieve what he thought was called a Faux Hawk? It looked like he'd affixed a blond scrub brush to the top of his head. That, a three-day scruff, and a scar beneath his right eye upped his bad-boy creds to the max.

Except he was looking a little doughy.

"Kirill, why are you here?"

"To protect you." He smirked at a guy so weak he couldn't protect himself.

He could shoot Kirill...in the leg. Everybody would believe it was an accident. Well, Cory might not because Cory had been training him assiduously.

Kirill laughed. "Is that loaded?"

"Full clip." Kirill stank of alcohol, and a shower couldn't come too soon.

More smirking. "Have you ever fired it?"

"Thousands of rounds."

Kirill frowned. "But not at anybody?"

"Only once. With this particular weapon."

"Bullshit?"

"Nope. His name was Yuri Corzo, and he was a Cuban spy. And a murderer. This was before you and I met, Kirill." He smiled. "I shot him in the leg."

Kirill didn't need to know that his eyes had been closed when he'd emptied the clip in Yuri's general direction.

Wednesday
10:00 am

But he hadn't shot Kirill as much as he'd wanted to. He had called Aunt Flo instead, and she had requested that he come to stay with her. To which end, she had dispatched Kirill to transport him to Snow Hill. Or stay with him if he wouldn't come.

Kirill had arrived in an old, blue Ford, Econoline Van. It seemed to run okay, but it was older than its owner.

Kirill was supposed to drive, but it had become clear that Kirill was not quite up to the task.

And he had driven from Philly feeling shitty, but not so bad as he would have if Kirill had been at the wheel.

He had pulled into Aunt Flo's lane and helped Kirill into the house since he had finished off a bottle during the trip.

He had tossed Kirill into the first available bed. Danilo had not been pleased with his son.

He had told Aunt Flo he was fine but really tired, and he had crashed. But now he was lying in his bed in the turret room and feeling better; even a bit peckish.

He tried calling Cory and got his voicemail. He left a message just asking for a call back.

He showered and dressed and went looking for Aunt Flo. She and Ezmeralda were in the kitchen.

He hugged them both. "I'm fine."

Ezmeralda said, "You're pale. Even paler than usual. You need to eat something."

"I am hungry. Maybe we start out with toast?"

Ezmeralda nodded. She sliced a couple of slabs from a loaf of homemade bread and dropped them into a restaurant-sized toaster; another thing Aunt Flo had bought for this B&B.

Aunt Flo was looking at him. "Tell me what happened again, Gabriel."

And he did.

She said, "And you didn't see anyone?"

He sighed. "That's the problem. I saw lots of customers all around my table, but I didn't see anybody do the deed."

Ezmeralda handed him the toast. "Why did you drink the coffee?"

"I thought it was just bad coffee. Calvin did not inspire confidence."

Aunt Flo smiled. "Who is Calvin, Dear?"

"New barista. Just hired by Billy. Looks marginally brighter than Martin but isn't."

He looked at Aunt Flo and Ezmeralda. "You don't think that Billy was involved?"

"In drugging you?" He nodded. "We don't know enough, Dear. From what you've said, Billy likes you, but we don't know what he'd do for his mother. We don't even know if she's involved. All of the actors in this...whatever this is...are unknown to us as are their motivations."

"It's a mystery. I know. Poor Phillip. I didn't like him very much, but I can't think he deserved what happened to him."

Ezmeralda said, "Hanging can be very quick...or not so quick."

"But he was drugged so he didn't know what was happening."

She nodded. "He was fortunate."

There was a knock on the door, and debonair Danilo entered. He crossed the kitchen and kissed Ezmeralda. She smiled at him.

He was getting used to the smiling and exchanges of affection, but it was hard. She had been a tower of glower throughout his teenage years, but then she had found love.

With Danilo Ochoa. What were the odds?

Danilo was wearing his gray tweed, flat cap, his red bow tie, and his gray suit. Danilo needed to update his wardrobe.

Mr. Ochoa adjusted his rimless glasses and peered at him. "How are you feeling, Gabriel?"

"Better." He munched on toast. He wanted coffee, but he thought it was too soon.

And then Kirill clomped down the kitchen stairs. He cast a bleary, blood-shot eye on the occupants and kept walking.

Danilo and Ezmeralda glared at him but didn't say anything.

Aunt Flo said, "I'm so glad you're here, Gabriel."

"Me too. Shit! Sorry, Aunt Flo. I have to call Jennifer."

Aunt Flo smiled. "I called her, Dear. She's fine with you taking as long as you need."

"Thanks, but you know I can't hide here?" He certainly didn't want to draw the killer here. "I'll stay a few days until I'm feeling better."

Aunt Flo said, "Can Cory come home?"

"I don't know. I called and left a message for him to call me, but it could be a few days...or a week before I hear back."

He looked at Aunt Flo. "I didn't want to get into this because I thought I might put you in danger, but now...."

Ezmeralda said, "Now, you are the one in danger."

Aunt Flo said, "We've had the security system updated and installed more of the motion activated cameras. We're quite secure. So if you want to find out what is going on, you shouldn't worry about us."

"I'm glad to hear that. Did I tell you about Lydia Gibson's husband, Reed?"

Aunt Flo smiled. "No, Dear?"

And he told them all about Lydia's request and the fact that Detective Czerwinski would have to cooperate.

Aunt Flo said, "So he has a great deal of influence."

"And a mansion that dwarfs Buckingham Palace. I have the feeling Czerwinski will be lump of clay in my hands; resentful but malleable all the same."

"It's up to you, Dear."

He thought Ezmeralda wanted to tell him to go for it, but she just looked at Danilo and didn't say anything.

He finished his toast and had a half cup of coffee. He went outside and lay down on a chaise-lounge under the oak tree. He had brought the Glock and the shoulder holster, but he would feel funny wearing it here.

Mikhail drove up and went into the kitchen, and then he and Danilo came out and headed for Kirill who was sitting on the dock.

He couldn't quite hear what they were saying and a lot of it wasn't in English, but they weren't happy with Kirill.

It ended with Danilo and Mikhail marching back to the kitchen. Kirill wandered toward him and took the other chaise-lounge without a word. He was wearing an old faded, t-shirt with red Cyrillic lettering. Kirill had told him that the word meant "assassin" a while back.

They lay there with the June breeze wafting over them. He was about to doze off when Kirill cleared his throat.

"Sorry."

"What?"

Kirill was glaring at him; his sculptural cheekbones were red, his scar was white. "I'm sorry, Gabriel."

"That's okay. No harm done."

Kirill relaxed back onto the chaise-lounge, and they lapsed into silence again.

He was on the cusp of nap time again when Kirill said, "I lost my job."

He shook himself. "I'm sorry to hear that. But you'll get another one."

Kirill was staring at his scuffed boots. "Not so easy."

Kirill had been a longshoreman on the docks in Philadelphia. "So you were laid off?"

Kirill made a short, bitter sound that wasn't much of a laugh.

Shit. "So you won't be getting a reference from your former employer?"

Kirill got up and walked away.

He looked at the oak tree. "I'll take that as a no." The oak tree agreed with him, and then he did fall asleep.

Somebody was kicking the chaise-lounge. "What?"

Kirill said, "I won't screw up again, Gabe."

"Right. Good to know." The sun had set, and he was hungry. "I'm starving. How about you?"

Kirill smiled. "I could eat."

And they went to the kitchen. He couldn't help noticing that Kirill smelled of alcohol as they made sandwiches.

But maybe that was from the night before? He hoped that was the case.

Friday
10:00 am

He was sitting on Aunt Flo's dock with his feet in the water. He should get off his ass and go home. It was time to take charge of his life and find out who had drugged him.

And murdered his cousin. Well, second cousin.

He marched toward the house. Aunt Flo was sitting on a chaise lounge beneath the oak.

"Are you heading back, Gabriel?"

"Yes. I feel good, and I want to talk to Czerwinski and see what he's found out."

She nodded.

"I'll be careful, Aunt Flo."

"I hope so, Gabriel. Mikhail has agreed to go with you."

Mikhail was older, quieter, and a lot more dependable than his younger brother. "But doesn't he need to get back to Ochoa Imports?"

"Anna is filling in for him, Dear."

Anna was Mikhail and Kirill's older sister. She wouldn't be his first choice to run Danilo's import business.

"Right."

Aunt Flo smiled. "She'll do fine temporarily, Gabriel."

"I don't doubt it for a second." He smiled at Aunt Flo. "Did I tell you I read an article about Betelgeuse going supernova in the near future."

She smiled. "No, Dear."

"Well, I did. And it's a red, super-giant star...as you

know...and when it goes boom, it will shine as bright as the full Moon. Almost. And it will be bright enough to cast shadows at night."

"I know, Gabriel. I've been reading the articles about its dimming and what that may portend." She sighed. "I would like to see it."

"Of course you would, and so would I. It's going to be soon. Any day now, Aunt Flo."

She said, "Soon in astronomical terms isn't soon in human terms."

"I have a good feeling, Aunt Flo."

"I hope you're right."

He got to his feet.

"Call me when you get home, Dear."

"I will." He wanted to tell her not to worry, but that was just dumb. "Aunt Flo?"

"Yes, Dear?"

"I don't suppose I could talk you into closing the bed and breakfast? Just temporarily?" She was shaking her head. "Until whatever is going on is resolved?"

"No, Gabriel. I understand how you feel, but Ezmeralda and I check out the potential guests...especially now, and we know what we're doing."

He nodded. "Of course. I know. Okay. I'll be back soon...probably next weekend."

He went looking for Mikhail and found him cleaning the kitchen after Ezmeralda had prepared breakfast for the guests.

Ute appeared to be supervising though she was well aware that the kitchen and food prep were Ezmeralda's domain.

Mikhail was unloading the dishwasher.

Annika came down the kitchen stairs. She spotted Ute and then Mikhail. She said something in German to Ute with a twinkle in her eye. Ute glared at her and stomped out. Annika followed her laughing.

He thought Ute liked looking at Mikhail. He leaned against the counter.

"So how is Marta?" Mikhail gave him a big grin. "That

good? I'm happy for you. And her."

Mikhail said, "I love her, Gabriel."

Mikhail Ochoa, son of Danilo and Valentina was a smidgen taller than his brother but they were both big, Russian bears and looked like they had won more than their share of bar fights.

Mikhail's face was a bit longer. He had the Slavic cheekbones, but his cheeks were a bit more concave than Kirill's. He also had more blond hair since Kirill had shaved most of his head, and he had a cauliflower ear.

But the biggest difference between the brothers was that Mikhail was quiet. When he had first met the brothers, he had thought Kirill was sharper, but he had been wrong.

Mikhail pulled out his phone. "Look."

Marta was making a face at the camera; she was Cuban-American and dark and pretty. She looked a bit younger than Mikhail who had to be pushing forty.

"She's beautiful, Mikhail."

And Mikhail shared a photo gallery of Marta Padilla Ochoa, including the wedding photos.

He smiled and made suitable comments. Mikhail just beamed. Inner Mikhail was as tender as outer Mikhail was tough. He hoped Marta was being kind to him, because he deserved it, but mostly because his mother, Valentina, would kill her and bury her body in a shallow grave if she hurt him.

Mikhail and Marta had gotten hitched back in October when he had been on a farm in Loudoun County, Virginia, with Cory's parents, trying to avoid pickled okra and discovering bodies.

Mikhail put his phone away still smiling. "Are you ready to get on the road, Gabe?"

"I am. Where's Kirill?"

Mikhail said, "First floor. The back bedroom. Why?"

"I'm going to ask him to come back with me."

"Because?"

"Because I'd like you to be here."

Mikhail smiled at him. "Mrs. Barnes won't like that."

"But I'll be gone before she finds out...unless you squeal on me. That is, if Kirill will go?"

Mikhail said, "He will."

"I don't want anybody to force him."

Mikhail shrugged.

"You know he lost his job?"

Mikhail snorted. "He didn't lose it. He threw it away. And stomped on it."

"What happened?" But Mikhail just shook his head. "Okay. So maybe you could hire him at Ochoa Imports?"

"We tried that. He can't stand taking orders from me."

"Right. A brother thing? Okay. I'm going to ask him. Please don't tell Aunt Flo."

Mikhail went back to work on those dishes.

He ran up to the turret room and got his bag, and then he knocked on the back bedroom door and got no response. He opened the door a crack; the shades were drawn, and it was dark.

"Kirill? Kirill!"

"What?"

"I'm going back to Philly."

He could just make out Kirill's body on the bed. "So?"

"So I'd like you to come with me. To back me up."

Kirill lay there.

"Is that something you might be willing to do?"

More silence.

"You'll pay for food? And gas? And I stay in your apartment?"

"Sure. Of course. Is that a yes?"

Kirill got out of bed. "What about Mikhail?"

"Mikhail's going to stay here."

"Yeah?"

"Yeah."

"And you want me?"

"I do. I could handle it by myself, but having a little back-up might not be a bad idea."

Kirill snorted. "When do we go?"

"As soon as you can get ready."

"Okay. Fifteen minutes."

He backed out of the bedroom and headed down the kitchen stairs.

Mikhail looked up. "He's coming with me."

Mikhail nodded.

He walked out with his bag. Aunt Flo had disappeared which was good. He dropped his bag beside Kirill's blue, Ford Van. He circled it. He hadn't felt like checking it out before.

The tires had tread, no pieces were dragging on the ground, and it wasn't leaking vital fluids.

It looked road-worthy to him.

He wanted to get on the road before Aunt Flo found out about the Ochoa brother switcheroo.

And then Bruno Tuers pulled into the lot. He got out and smiled. "Hi, Gabe."

"Hi, Bruno. Back again?"

Bruno smiled. "I like it here."

And Ute opened the front door as if she'd been watching for Bruno. She waved and pursed her lips in a smile-like fashion.

Bruno said, "See you later, Gabe."

"No...well, I'm leaving now, but I'll be back really soon."

Bruno nodded and marched over. He ascended the stairs, and Ute ushered him into the house.

He had thought Bruno was okay. He probably was. He was just a satisfied customer. That was it.

Shit.

Kirill popped out of the kitchen door. "Ready?"

He could stay another day?

Kirill got in and started the engine and glared at him. "Waiting for me to open the door for you, Bergeron?"

"No! I am not."

Kirill said, "We need gas."

"Okay?" The gauge was reading three-quarters full.

Kirill smiled. "The gauge doesn't work." He raced the engine and pulled out of the lane. "We should stop in Snow Hill."

"Okay."

"And I'm hungry." Kirill smiled like a wolf, and he, or his wallet at least, was playing the role of Little Red Riding Hood.

"Not a problem. I need some coffee anyway."

And he needed to call Mikhail. What was the point of having a security system with cameras and stuff if you let the enemy into the gate...as guests.

He didn't think that Commander Bruno was actually a Trojan Horse or a Greek within said horse, but he was going to tell Mikhail to watch him. And tell Danilo. And Ezmeralda.

Or he could take a breath and not freak out.

After he called them.

Friday
4:00 pm

He had called Lydia before he left Aunt Flo's house and told her that he wanted to investigate Phillip's death.

And she had called Reed.

And Reed had called Czerwinski. Well, it was more likely he'd called Czerwinski's captain or the police commissioner. Or the mayor.

In any case, Czerwinski had called him before Kirill had gotten them to Philly.

"Think you're hot stuff, don't you, Bergeron?"

"No, Detective."

"I should resign this freaking job!"

"No, you shouldn't. Please don't do anything until we can talk."

Silence.

"I'll be in Philly soon. I just want to help. Can we meet somewhere?"

"Not here!"

"Right. Where is here?"

Silence.

"Detective?"

"Whitaker Avenue. Headquarters."

"Right. Well, I can meet you anywhere you'd like."

"Your apartment. One hour."

"Okay, I should be there...."

But Czerwinski was already gone.

Kirill smiled. "Not happy?"

"Not so much."

Kirill parked in front of the apartment building. He grabbed a faded duffel bag from the back of the van which was stuffed with bags and boxes and junk.

"Come on, Bergeron."

Kirill seemed to be in a hurry so he followed along, but Kirill slowed as they climbed and was puffing by the third floor. Which was pissing him off.

So he let Kirill get to the fourth floor first.

Kirill dropped a bag on the floor beside the sofa. "A/C?"

"Yes, I'll turn it on."

"Bathroom?"

"End of the hall. You can't miss it."

Kirill plodded down the hall.

He cranked the A/C to the max and opened the curtains. The sun was blasting into the three, tall windows. He lowered the shades. He liked south facing windows in the winter.

Kirill sauntered back and threw himself on the sofa. He grabbed the TV remote and ran through the channels until he found a MMA bout. Two guys were punching and kicking each other. Kirill smiled.

"I'm going to see if I have any mail." Kirill shrugged.

A strange guy was outside of Mrs. Bruska's door; she had the small apartment at the back of the building. Her place had a couple of windows in the back but was otherwise as window-shy as his apartment.

He should call the building manager or owner, and ask about putting in a skylight? Not that he had ever talked to the guy. The name on the lease was "F. X. Foley."

The stranger was wearing a gray coverall; a new, leather tool belt was riding low on some ample hips. A gray Phillies cap with a maroon and white "P" was pulled down almost to his eyebrows.

"Hello." The guy ignored him. "Excuse me?" The guy looked his way. "Mrs. Bruska is out."

Actually, she was somewhere in New Jersey visiting a

daughter, but this guy, whoever he was, didn't need to know that.

"Can I help you?"

The guy left his ladder leaning against the wall and waddled toward him looking at the light fixtures overhead. He had a round, plump face and sandy hair. "Cordrey, electrician. Had any electrical problems?

"Not that I know of, but I've been gone for three days. There was another guy here a month ago?"

He had come home from work and discovered he had no power, and the candles that he thought he had were no where to be found.

Cordrey shrugged. "I got the call."

"So what's wrong this time."

"Circuit breaker blew."

"Right. And what caused that?"

Cordrey shrugged. "I'm still checking it out." And he turned and started down the stairs.

He followed, and Cordrey looked back at him. "I'm picking up my mail."

Cordrey nodded and kept his head down until they got to the third floor. Cordrey went down the hall.

He got his mail, but he didn't spot Cordrey on the way back.

Kirill was into the match, but he mumbled something about food. "Sorry. I think the cupboard is bare. But I can make coffee."

Which he did as he pondered how he was going to win Detective Czerwinski over?

He may have jumped when a fist started beating on his metal door. Kirill smiled again.

Having Kirill in his apartment was getting old. And it had only been thirty-seven minutes.

He put his eye to the peephole; Czerwinski.

He threw open the door, and Czerwinski stomped in. He stopped when he spotted Kirill and looked at him.

He wasn't sure how Czerwinski had thought this meeting/confrontation was going to go down, but Kirill had thrown a wrench into the machinery.

He said, "Hi, Detective."

Czerwinski pointed a thumb at Kirill. "This isn't Poirier."

Kirill snorted and got to his feet. "Kirill Ochoa."

"Detective Czerwinski, PPD." He flashed his badge, but neither extended the hand of friendship.

He circled his kitchenette island and held out his hand to Czerwinski. "I'm glad you came, Detective. This is my friend. Well, he's also an in-law. Sort of. His father, Danilo Ochoa, married Ezmeralda Gutierrez, and she...."

Czerwinski ignored his hand and his explanation. "I don't care what he is to you, Bergeron. I don't care if he's the freaking tooth fairy."

Which was the wrong thing to say; the fairy part.

He threw himself between Kirill and Czerwinski. He put his hands on Kirill's shoulders and pushed as hard as he could, but he was sliding across the floor toward the detective.

"He didn't mean anything!"

Kirill was unconvinced and tried to go around him to get at Czerwinski. He let Kirill get past him just far enough to kick his legs out from under him. He jumped on Kirill's broad, sweaty back and twisted his arm hard.

Kirill was momentarily shocked. And then, he yelled, "Get the Hell off me! I'm going to rip your head off!"

"Calm down. If you get arrested, I'm not bailing you out!" Czerwinski was standing there looking at him.

Kirill was making a renewed effort to get to his feet so the head ripping could commence before Czerwinski put a knee on his back and brought out his cuffs. Together they subdued Kirill.

A bound Kirill was not a happy Kirill. But it seemed that Russian was a better language to cuss in so he and Czerwinski couldn't appreciate the finer points of Kirill's oration.

He rolled on his back and managed to get to his feet, shoulder muscles practically jumping out as he strained to get free.

Czerwinski may have smirked at him. Which didn't help. Kirill was almost frothing at the mouth.

Czerwinski looked skeptical and perplexed. "What's his problem?"

He got in front of Kirill. "He didn't mean that you're gay." He looked at Czerwinski. "Did you, detective?"

Kirill's face was white; the veins and arteries in his neck and on his temple were distended and throbbing. If he didn't have a stroke, it would be a miracle.

Czerwinski said, "What? Is that what set him off?" He got in Kirill's face. "I didn't mean you're gay...not that I care one way or the other."

Kirill took a deep breath. And then another. "Bastards! Both of you! I can take both of you."

He nodded. "Of course, you can. I just took you by surprise. Sorry, but I didn't want to lose you." He smiled.

Actually, he was deeply regretting that he'd intervened...or at least so soon. Was Kirill in jail for assaulting an officer really such a bad thing?

Kirill was calming down so that he only looked moderately apoplectic now. He was still glaring at them both.

"All right."

Czerwinski said, "All right, what?"

"Take the cuffs off."

Czerwinski said, "And why would I do that?"

"Because...." Kirill's face was getting red again.

He said, "Because Kirill is sorry that he overreacted. And he's calm now. Right, Kirill?"

Kirill made a slight head bob.

"Isn't that right, Kirill?"

"Yeah."

Czerwinski looked at Kirill. He had probably dealt with hundreds of combative guys. He shrugged. "Turn around."

He uncuffed Kirill and jumped back with his hand on his gun.

But Kirill was tuckered out. And still hung over. He flopped onto the sofa and stared at his boots as his breathing gradually slowed.

He and Czerwinski watched him.

He said, "Maybe you'd like to take a shower, Kirill?" Kirill raised his head enough to give him a blood-thirsty look. It was in the eyes, but the bared teeth also helped convey the message. "Not that you're in any way offensive or need a shower."

Kirill got to his feet. He grabbed his bag and slouched down the hall. They heard the bathroom door slam.

Czerwinski took a deep breath. "That's one scary 'friend' you've got."

The emphasis on "friend" pissed him off. "He's not gay."

"Who cares?"

He glared at Czerwinski.

Czerwinski said, "I'm sorry about the tooth fairy...it just popped out."

"Right. Sure."

"No, really! My niece is four, and my sister told her that she'd get a dollar coin when her tooth came out. From the freaking tooth fairy."

"Is that true?"

Czerwinski held up his right hand and put his left over his heart. "I went to the bank to get one."

And then he smiled. Not that he was going to let a smile win him over. Even if it was a very nice smile.

He said, "He would have broken your arms off at the shoulders." Czerwinski looked skeptical. Or he tried to. "The next time I'll let you handle two hundred fifty pounds of enraged Russian. Well, Cuban-Russian. Which might be worse?"

Czerwinski smiled again. "He does have a temper."

"He does. So you're here, and I'm here?"

Czerwinski lost the smile and yanked today's red tie off. He pulled out his phone and stared at it. "I hate doing this."

"Right. Take a seat at the table."

And Czerwinski shared everything that he had learned in the eighteen days since Phillip had been hanged.

It wasn't an impressive haul. Which Czerwinski knew.

Which made him cranky.

His black, curly hair was in his eyes, and he pawed at it. "So what are you supposed to do that I haven't, Bergeron?"

"An excellent question, Detective."

Czerwinski ramped his skeptical look up to the top of the

scale. "You have no freaking idea."

"Not true." Actually, it was, but he looked over the reports and crime scene photos. "So no fingerprints except Phillip's. The place had been wiped down. And nobody saw anybody else going into the row house?"

Czerwinski nodded.

"And Phillip was living there?"

"Yeah. He was broke. After he got fired."

"Did you talk to his former employer?"

He nodded. "Yeah." He stretched. "They were a little too slick."

"Why did they say he was let go?"

"Restructuring."

"And you think that was bullshit?"

"Brahma bull grade."

"Right. So why was Phillip living there? Specifically there? Any reason?"

Czerwinski said, "His buddy...from college...owns the block and let him stay there rent free."

"And the buddy is? Wait. Luke Shaffer?" Czerwinski looked at him. "I met him at the funeral."

"And?"

"Nothing. So far. But I want to talk to him again. And the ex-wives. And his sisters. And the people at Oxley International."

Czerwinski shook his head. "I've done all that."

"I know you have."

Czerwinski was looking at his phone.

"Is there anything else, Detective?" Czerwinski shrugged and tried to look innocent but it was hard with his face. "What?"

"So you just met Reed Gibson?"

"As I told you."

"So why did he call in a bunch of favors for you?"

"For his wife, Lydia." He thought Czerwinski was stalling. "There's something you haven't told me."

Czerwinski tried the smile again, but he wasn't in the market for any bootless charm. He pulled out his phone and found Reed Gibson in his contact list. He may have let Czerwinski see the name.

Czerwinski glared at him. "Go ahead. I don't give a shit."

But he did. He got up and paced across the living room.

"Want some coffee, Detective?" He left his phone on the table. "Are you hungry? I don't know what I have."

He examined the contents of his refrigerator; it was arctic tundra bleak. He gave Czerwinski his best smile. "I could order pizza?"

"I don't want any freaking pizza, Bergeron!"

"Suit yourself." He went down the hall. Kirill was in his bedroom just sitting on the bed. He smelled like Cory, but Cory's shower gel was in the bathroom, and Kirill traveled light.

"Hi. I was thinking about ordering pizza, but I can get something else?"

He noticed his digital clock wasn't flashing. So his apartment hadn't lost power?

Kirill shrugged. "Pizza's good. He still out there?"

Kirill knew that he was. "He is. Why don't you come out? There's probably some boxing or MMA on the TV?"

Kirill shrugged again but followed him to the living room. He and Czerwinski exchanged wary looks as Kirill flopped on the sofa and grabbed the remote.

Czerwinski said, "Are we done?"

"Nope. I'm sorry if you hate this, but I'm only trying to help, and I promise to share anything I learn...no matter how small. And you can take the credit if I get lucky."

Kirill was watching Czerwinski. He snorted. Which was an elliptical comment on Czerwinski's abilities?

Czerwinski shook his head.

"I don't want to call Reed, but I will. So tell me now, or come Monday, allowing for the weekend, somebody new will tell me. And neither of us wants that. Right?"

Kirill smiled and flicked the remote. The MMA program was still going, but two women were currently beating the crap out of each other. Kirill smiled again.

Czerwinski said, "Walk with me."

So he followed the detective down the stairs to his car. He

leaned against it and finally made up his mind.

"One thing."

He leaned against the car beside Czerwinski. "And that is?"

"It seems Phillip had some fun his last night."

"What kind of fun?" Czerwinski smirked at him. "Oh, that kind of fun. So you found evidence of a female presence?"

"Semen and vaginal secretions."

"On the bed?"

He shook his head. "On the sheet that was used to hang him."

Did that have some twisted, symbolic meaning? "Did you get DNA from the...female contribution?"

"Yeah."

"But she wasn't in any database?"

"No."

"So is that it?"

Czerwinski nodded. He threw his jacket and tie onto the passenger seat and got into his car. He was pulling away.

He ran after him and beat on the passenger side window.

Czerwinski braked and stared at him with his lips moving. Luckily, he couldn't read lips. Czerwinski rolled down the window.

"Did you see if Billy Stanko matches the DNA? A familial match?"

Czerwinski's face tightened up like his skin was shrinking, or his skull was expanding. But then he laughed through gritted teeth. "Not this Penelope woman again?"

"Yes."

Czerwinski sat there.

"You could rule her out, Detective. And make me look useless and a little bit insane?"

Which thought brightened the detective's day no end, but he said, "If I can find Billy Stanko."

Saturday
10:00 am

He had slept soundly in his own bed, secure in the knowledge that any attacker would have to go through Kirill, who was sprawled on the air mattress in the living room.

Which was a good thing.

The bad thing was that Kirill slept in the nude. He had made sure that Kirill was covered with a sheet before he had gone into the kitchenette to make coffee; he himself was fully clothed.

Kirill grunted. "What time is it?"

"Ten. Time to get up and get rolling."

Another grunt. Kirill glared at him, and then rolled off the air mattress, taking the sheet with him.

He padded down the hall semi-toga style and went into the bathroom. If yesterday was any indicator, there would be a wet towel left on the bathroom floor.

Kirill came back partially draped again. He flopped on the air mattress and pulled on briefs and shorts before tossing the sheet. He took a stool at the kitchenette island.

Kirill said, "What's for breakfast?"

"I have bread for toast. There's some grape jam. There's cereal, but no milk."

"Eggs? Bacon?"

"Nope."

"You need to get groceries." Kirill had a cross tattooed on each pec. The crosses had three horizontal crossbeams; the lowest one was slanted. And he had a double-headed eagle in the center of his chest.

"A Romanov eagle?"

Kirill shook his head. "A Russian eagle." And he flexed his pecs and biceps in a little display. He had muscles but they were overlaid with an obvious layer of fat. Kirill had a dad bod compared to Cory.

"Whose weights?"

"Cory's"

Kirill smirked and loaded the bar with a lot of weight. He started doing bench presses.

"You should have a spotter for that."

Kirill gave him a don't-tell-me-what-to-do glare, but after a few reps, he said, "Are you offering?"

"Sure." He spotted Cory all the time. Kirill was strong but not Cory strong. Which made him happy.

Kirill was gazing up at him. "How much does Poirier bench?"

He was pretty sure that Kirill would kill himself trying to best Cory. "I've never really noticed...." He looked at the weights like he'd never seen them before. "What you're using now."

Kirill hopped off the bench and added ten pounds and proceeded to bench "more" than Cory. If it made Mr. Ochoa less grumpy, a little lie was totally justified.

Kirill was lying on the bench panting with cheeks as red as Old St. Nick's.

He sat up. The asshole may have slapped his biceps and smiled. "I'll take some toast."

"Okay. There's the toaster." Kirill looked at him. "Fix your own or starve."

Kirill stopped smiling and flexing. "Not very hospitable."

"Maybe not." He took his toast to the table and munched away.

Kirill said, "Shit. I'm going out to get breakfast."

He pulled a t-shirt on and held out his hand.

"And you want what exactly?"

"Money. For breakfast. You said you'd pay..." More smiling. "...for my protection."

Which was seeming less and less like it was worth it.

He extracted a ten from his wallet. Kirill snorted, but he could snort all he wanted; he wasn't getting another penny.

Kirill marched out of the apartment.

He sighed and consulted the contact information that Czerwinski had turned over.

He called Luke Shaffer. Luke answered on the second ring. "Hello, this is Gabe Bergeron. We met at Phillip's funeral?"

Luke processed. "Sure. I remember you. What can I do for you?"

"I'm looking into Phillip's death...for Lydia, and I was wondering if I could ask you a few questions?"

"What? So Phil didn't kill himself?"

"No, he didn't."

"I knew it. But why you? Are you a cop?"

"No, but I've investigated other crimes...unofficially, and Lydia asked me to look into this."

Luke did some more processing. "I don't know, Mr. Bergeron. I'm really busy currently."

"You were letting Phillip stay in your property rent free?"

"How do you know that?'

He didn't want to say that Czerwinski had told him. He wasn't sure how public his access to the case was supposed to be. "Maybe you could check with Lydia and call me back?"

"I guess I could do that."

And he was gone. He finished his toast. He should have asked Kirill to bring some food back.

He paced the apartment waiting for Luke or Kirill. Luke called back first.

"Mr. Bergeron?"

"Yes?"

"I can meet with you today."

"Excellent. Around noon?"

Luke said, "Sure. I'm going to be near Rittenhouse Square?"

"Great. Do you know CoffeeXtra? On South 16th Street?"

"I do. I'll see you there."

And Luke was gone again. Now he had to get to CoffeeXtra. He paced some more and was just about to search Kirill's bag for the van keys when he banged on the door.

"Great. We have to get going. Have you got your keys?"

Kirill nodded. "Where are we going?"

"To South 16th Street. To meet Luke Shaffer."

Kirill shrugged and then he looked a bit closer. "Are you packing, Bergeron?"

He had on a sports coat which didn't disguise the shoulder holster as well as it might.

"Yes."

Kirill's smile faded. "Okay." He rooted through his bag and brought out a pistol and shoulder holster of his own.

"I thought you had a Glock?"

Kirill frowned. "Sold it. This is a Makarov...a Russian pistol. It was my grandfather's."

Kirill smiled.

"Very nice." It was a bit shorter than his Glock and had a star embossed into the grip. "Right. But you can't wear that without a jacket to hide it."

Kirill shook his head. "Don't have one."

He had an attache case, but nobody would ever believe that Kirill would carry one. And then he remembered a back pack that Cory used for undercover work.

"How about putting the Makarov in this? And just carrying it on your shoulder?"

Kirill frowned.

"It's just a backpack."

"Okay. But I need a key...to the apartment."

He really didn't want to give Kirill a key, but he couldn't refuse. Kirill was doing him a favor. Well, he was doing it for Danilo. Or maybe, Ezmeralda.

He gave him the spare. "Don't lose it."

Kirill snorted. They ran down the stairs; Kirill burnt rubber down Arch Street for no particular reason.

He couldn't remember the last time he'd been in CoffeeXtra on a Saturday. He did a quick walk-thru looking for Luke Shaffer.

Or Billy.

No joy.

But Martin was behind the counter. He may have glared at the guy when Martin smiled at him. "Hi, Gabe."

"Where's Billy?"

Martin just smiled harder. "No idea, Gabe."

Martin was tiny and slender and had black hair waxed and spiked on top with the sides shaved close. He had brown eyes, and a smile that seemed wider than his actual face, like some kind of topological joke.

He didn't really think Billy had drugged him, but he might be able to direct him to his mother, and he wanted to talk to Penelope. Bad.

Kirill was looking around, underwhelmed by the ambiance and the clientele. He focused his displeasure onto little Martin. "Is this the guy?"

"No. Luke Shaffer was Phillip's best friend. He isn't here yet."

Martin tried the smile on Kirill but gave up, proving Martin wasn't as dumb as he looked. Which he knew.

Martin said, "The usual, Gabe?"

"Sure. Hold the sleeping pills this time."

Martin looked unhappy for once. "Sorry that happened to you, Gabe. Are you okay?"

Kirill focused. "This is where they tried to kill you?"

Kirill reached out and grabbed the front of Martin's shirt, lifting him off the floor effortlessly. Martin was nose-to-nose with Kirill before he realized what was happening.

Martin grabbed Kirill's mitts for all the good that did him. "I didn't do anything, Dude! Honest."

"Kirill?" Kirill shook Martin. If Kirill punched him, he feared Martin would disintegrate like a pinata. "He's not the one, Kirill!"

"No?"

"No. Some guy named Calvin served me...but I don't think he had anything to do with it either. Please put Martin down before you break him, and the police put you in prison for a very, long time."

Kirill thought about it and finally dropped Martin.

Martin's legs were unequal to the task of supporting even his weight, and Martin flowed to the floor like warm taffy.

He went around the counter and helped Martin stand up. "Are you okay?"

Kirill was shocked that a life-form as fragile as Martin existed. "I didn't hurt him."

"No, I know. Martin, is Billy here? In the office? Or hiding in the kitchen?"

He peeped through the little windows in the swinging doors, but he didn't spot Billy in the kitchen.

Martin shook his head. "No, Gabe, he isn't here. He's very sorry about what happened to you."

"Right. Okay." He looked at Kirill. "What do you want?"

Kirill surveyed the signage and the chalkboard. "No beer?"

"Nope."

Disgust writ large.

"How about coffee and a sandwich?"

Kirill shrugged. Martin nodded without making eye contact.

He grabbed a table toward the front and waited. Martin brought their order over, making sure to stay well out of Kirill's reach.

Kirill smiled. "Going to drink that?"

He smiled back. "Sure. You're here to avenge my death. Right?"

Kirill nodded. "I would do it, Gabriel, but Ezmeralda has claimed that honor...she has a list."

Shit. "A list?"

"The women who came to the house; this Monroe and Penelope. Some others. A guy named Oscuro?"

Growing up, he had thought that Ezmeralda could barely tolerate him, but he had come to think that she liked him...but maybe she loved him? Nothing said love like planning a Klingon blood feud upon his death.

Saturday
1:00 pm

But his coffee was good and so was the banana bread, and he wasn't feeling any ill effects by the time Luke Shaffer finally arrived.

They shook hands, and he introduced Kirill who got to his feet and glared at Luke as they shook.

Luke got coffee and came back to the table. He looked at his watch which was glowing warmly in the sun as gold does. "So I can't stay long, but what can I do to help, Gabe?"

"When did you last see Phillip?"

Luke said, "It's been a while...over a month at least."

"But you were his best friend?"

Luke's bushy, black eyebrows climbed up his forehead. "Yeah, but I've been busy. I'm in real estate...."

Kirill made a derogatory noise; an expressive blending of a snort and a grunt.

Luke glanced at Kirill and then away. "...and things have been super busy."

"Right. I understand. How long had Phillip been living in the row house on Savin Street?"

"Three months."

"Rent free?"

"The least I could do for a buddy."

"Right. Was he looking for a job?"

"Sure he was, but it was hard...after he got fired from Oxley."

Kirill had been staring out the window at female passersby, but he focused on Luke. "I got fired."

Luke gave Kirill a glance. "Yeah. Phil was really upset about it. Said it was unfair."

Kirill grunted agreement.

"What happened?"

Luke looked at him, eyebrows on the move again. "What does that have to do with his death?"

"Maybe nothing. I'm just gathering information, Luke."

"I see. Well, I can't really help you. Phil didn't want to talk about it beyond saying that he got fired just as he was about to receive some stock options."

"Right. I heard about that. So, anything else you can tell me about what was going on in his life before he died?"

Luke shook his head and made a show of looking at his watch. "No. Nothing."

"What about a girlfriend?"

Luke smiled. "Well, Phil was a handsome guy, and he had someone, but I don't have a name or anything."

"You don't know anything about her?"

"No. Like I said, I hadn't seen Phil in a while." Luke got to his feet and paused. "He did say she was smart."

"Just that?"

"Yeah. He said she was smart.... Maybe clever was the word he used? And hot. Way hot."

He shook Luke's hand and watched him depart. Kirill had gotten bored and wandered away.

He finished his coffee. He thought that Luke knew more about why Phillip lost his job, but he wasn't going to share. He didn't want to blacken his friend's name?

The only thing that had the ring of truth was the "way hot" comment about Phillip's girlfriend.

Which wasn't helpful in finding her.

He consulted the contact information Czerwinski had given him. He wanted to talk to the ex-wives. He came to Christina's name first and called her. "Hello. This is Gabe Bergeron. We met at Phillip's funeral?"

Christina said, "I remember you?"

"Lydia has asked me to look into Phillip's death." Christina didn't respond. "Christina?"

"I'm here. Are you a detective, Gabe?"

"I've had some experience...not necessarily because I wanted to. I'd like to talk to you. Would that be possible?"

"I guess so. When?"

"Today?"

She laughed. "I don't know, Gabe."

"You could call Lydia and verify that she asked me to do this."

"No, I won't be calling Lydia. What the Hell. I'm going to be home all afternoon. Not that there's anything I can tell you."

"Then I'll see you soon. And thanks, Christina."

Martin was watching him. He strolled to the Men's Room and then ducked down the hall to Billy's office. The door was locked, and nobody answered his knock.

He had never tried kicking a door or ramming one with his shoulder. He didn't think it was as easy as it looked on TV.

He walked out, stopping by the counter. "Tell Billy to call me, Martin. I need to talk to him."

Martin nodded and tried out a smile. "Okay, Gabe. He really hasn't been in today."

"Okay. I'm sorry about Kirill."

Martin nodded.

Saturday
3:00 pm

He had found Kirill and given him the address before retrieving his Jeep from the parking garage where it had been since he'd been drugged.

He proceeded to west Philly, not far from Mr. Boghossian's apartment building which had been home not so long ago.

Kirill had arrived before him, and he was pacing on the sidewalk looking like a thunderhead. Well, a blond one wearing a red, sleeveless t-shirt and ragged, gray shorts. He draped a beefy arm over the roof of the Jeep, the blond, peach fuzz on his forearm gleaming in the sun.

"How long?"

"I don't know. Not long." Unless Christina knew more than she was letting on. "You don't have to come in, Kirill."

Kirill stretched his arms over his head. He locked his hands together and pulled one against the other until his muscles popped.

He shrugged and leaned against the Jeep. Which was fine. He didn't need Kirill's help to ask questions.

The house was tiny but still occupied most of the lot. Fences separated Christina's property from her neighbors'; there was barely room to squeeze between fence and house.

He got out and headed for the door. Kirill didn't move. It was just too bad if he was cutting into his drinking time.

Christina opened the door. She peered past him. "Who's tall, blond, and scary?"

Kirill was still propped against the Jeep studying the cracks in the street.

"A friend."

She smiled as she looked at Kirill. She was wearing a tight black t-shirt and even tighter black jeans. She adjusted her bosoms about as self-consciously as a cat attending to the grooming of its nether regions. The nails were still scarlet, and the mascara and eye liner were just as thick.

"Is he coming in?"

"Doubt it."

"Okay. Have a seat, Gabe. I'll be right back."

He sat.

He waited. Christina had disappeared through a door that led into the kitchen, but he heard the pattering of tiny feet on the stairs behind him.

A girl who looked school worthy, and a little boy who was not, jumped off the last step and ran over to him.

They stared. They had brown hair and looked like Phillip.

"Hi, there. Who are you?" He had been told their names, but he had totally lost track of Phillip's progeny at this point.

The little girl had long pigtails and big, dark, widely spaced eyes. "My name is Hallie, and I'm eight years old."

She grabbed the arm of her little brother and held him out like he was a rag doll. "This is Timothy. Not Tim." She scowled at him ferociously. "He's only four."

Timothy wore a crown of brown curls. He had the same dark eyes as his sister...as his father.

"I'm Gabe Bergeron."

Hallie shook her head whipping her pigtails back and forth. "No!"

"Am too!"

"No, that's our name!" She beat on her shield maiden's chest. "Bergeron is our name and not yours!"

Timothy was ambivalent about the whole matter as he was focused on picking his nose.

Christina popped back with a tray. "Hallie, inside voice. And he's Daddy's cousin. So he's also a Bergeron."

She sat the tray on the coffee table and took a seat. "Coffee,

Gabe?"

Hallie was dubious. "But I've never heard of him before. Daddy never said."

Christina smiled at her scowling daughter who was beginning to remind him of Ezmeralda; well, more in spirit than form.

"Daddy just found out about him. Your granddaddy, Jonathan, lost track of that side of his family."

Hallie wasn't buying it.

Christina sighed. "Would you like to go outside and play for a while?"

Hallie nodded.

"You have to take Timothy, and you have to watch him and not let him eat anything he picks up."

Hallie looked at her little brother with an evil gleam in her dark eyes. "Okay, Mommy."

He feared for Timothy, but Christina seemed perfectly relaxed as her daughter led her son into the backyard; a valley of deadly plant toxins...and bugs...and dirt. And worms.

Christina said, "She's in school now, but there were times I thought I might not last long enough to see her enrolled."

"Parenthood must be so rewarding."

She snorted and giggled. "For a masochist." She smiled. "I do love them both."

Sure she did.

"So what do you want to know, Gabe?"

"Anything about Phillip that might help me figure out why he was killed."

"I can't help with that. What does the Ice Queen think happened to Phil?"

He smiled at Christina. "And by Ice Queen, you mean Lydia?"

"Got it on the first try."

"She has no idea. I don't think that Phillip would have confided in her."

Christina laughed. "Not in a million years! And that husband! What a pair. I got inside the mansion exactly one time.

Just after Phil and I were first married."

She shook her head and brushed the bangs out of her eyes. "And I didn't see much of Phil the last month or so."

"No?"

She frowned. "Phil didn't have the cash for child support so he was avoiding me, Gabe. I wasn't a total bitch about it; I knew he was flat broke. He'd sold his condo, but the money from that had run out. But I needed the cash...for Hallie and Timothy."

"Sure. So he was fired from Oxley International? How did that happen?"

She frowned. "I don't know. He came around a few times after it happened. He'd usually had a few, but one time he was plastered. I let him sleep it off on the couch."

"And?"

"Well, he got up during the night and tried to crawl into my bed, and I kicked his ass out, but he was mumbling." She looked at him. "Something about 'proprietary information' and that they owed him. He wasn't making a lot of sense."

"Anything else?"

"Well, Phil told me he didn't get a severance package. Which I didn't buy, Gabe. He'd been there nineteen years."

"So you called Oxley?"

She snorted. "And got nowhere. So I went to the home office in Wilmington. They tried stone-walling me, but I made a scene, and I told them my lawyer would be calling them, and eventually I got to talk to some VP in the legal department...Scanlon was his name."

"And?"

"And Mr. Scanlon let me know that good ole Phil was lucky the company had 'taken no action beyond termination.' He told me to leave the premises and not return or that would change. He implied that Phil should have gone to jail."

"So Phillip stole something from Oxley?"

She shrugged. "You hear about industrial espionage."

"Was Phillip capable of that?"

"Stealing from Oxley?" She shrugged again and adjusted her bosoms. "He wasn't happy there. He was always saying they weren't treating him right, but I don't know."

He looked at Christina. "That's interesting. Thanks." He wanted to ask her about Phillip's friends, specifically those of the female persuasion.

She smiled at him. "Ask whatever it is, Gabe. No need to be shy."

"Did he have a girlfriend?"

"Phil was a good-looking bastard, and he could hide the bastard part for a while. He had lots of girlfriends, before and after we divorced."

"Anybody around the time he got fired?"

She nodded. "But I never knew her name."

"You never saw her?"

She laughed. "Even Phil wouldn't have brought one of his skanks here."

The level of noise from the backyard was rising; an almost ultrasonic squealing was penetrating the french doors.

Christina got up and looked out. She smiled and turned. "I never saw her, but I think Hallie did. She said that Daddy's new friend had blond hair, and she was old. But to Hallie anybody past puberty is old. So who knows?"

Christina picked up her purse. She fished out a lipstick and proceeded to paint her lips as scarlet as her nails.

She went back to the French doors. "Gabe?"

He joined her. Kirill was in the backyard. And he appeared to be playing with Hallie and Timothy, and they all appeared to be having a grand time.

"Does your friend have a name?"

"That's Kirill. He's more of a step in-law than a friend. He's a longshoreman."

She perused Kirill like she was doing a study for a life-size sculpture. "He can unload my crates any time."

And she sallied forth into the backyard.

Hallie and Timothy were hanging onto Kirill's arms as he spun like a top. They were shrieking with delight.

Kirill spotted Christina and slowed to a stop. Hallie and Timothy fell to the ground drunk from the G-force.

Christina was looking at Kirill, and Kirill was definitely looking back.

He said, "Christina, this is Kirill."

Kirill struck an untamed savage pose and gave her his bedroom eyes. "Kirill Ochoa."

And they smiled at each other. He could hear the electricity crackling between them. Well, he couldn't really, but only because Hallie and Timothy were yanking on Kirill's hands and screeching.

"Again! Spin us again!"

He checked to see if he was bleeding from the ears as the shrieking intensified.

Christina said, "Hallie! Stop that yelling right this minute!"

Hallie faltered mid-wail. Timothy wrapped himself around Kirill's leg and hid his face.

"But he wants to play with us! And you never do! And it was fun." She smiled up at Kirill. "Do it again."

Christina said, "No! You go back inside! And take Timothy!"

Hallie stomped her foot. "You never let us have any fun. Daddy did. I want Daddy."

Christina looked stricken for a second. "You go up to your room...and...and I'll read you a story."

Hallie looked at Kirill who shook his head. "Sorry, Sweetheart."

Hallie fixed her mother with a rebellious glare. "Two stories."

"Maybe. Now scoot! Let go of the man's leg, Timothy."

But Hallie had to peel her brother from Kirill's calf, and then she pulled him into the house with much wailing and sniffling.

Which left Christina and Kirill. And Gabe Bergeron.

He smiled at them, not that they noticed him. "Thanks, Christina. You've been a big help."

She waved a hand at him. "Sure, Gabe."

He said, "I'll be in the Jeep."

And he went. Gabe Bergeron didn't stick around where he wasn't wanted. No sir.

After fifteen minutes, he headed for Arch Street. Christina and Kirill were consenting adults, and he was tired of Kirill anyway.

He arrived home and decided to call it a day. He watched TV and thought about Phillip and what he'd been up to. Which didn't take long since he had no idea.

Not yet.

He didn't exactly wait up for Kirill, but he fell asleep on the sofa. When he woke up, Ochoa still wasn't home, and he went to bed.

Kirill would show up at some point so he didn't put the chain on.

Sunday
2:00 am

He opened his eyes. His bedroom had no windows so it was completely dark except for the light from the clock and the pale outline of the doorway into the hall.

There had been a noise? Or something to rouse him?

A voice, three inches from his left ear, said, "Kirill?"

He didn't shriek or flail.

He did leap out of the bed and switch on the light. He may have almost shot himself fumbling for his Glock.

It was a woman. With red hair. All over.

He knew this because she was profoundly naked

And she was crouching on his bed.

Her breath was flammable. She peered at him; her eyes didn't seem to be focusing. Which might be due to her blood alcohol level.

And then a moue of disappointment passed over her slack face. "You aren't Kirill."

"Out! Get out of my bedroom!"

She got up. She gave him side eye and sniffed. "Chill, Dude. I was just looking for the bathroom."

And she walked out of his bedroom.

She didn't grab a sheet to cover herself; she just sauntered out. He stood there amazed.

True, he was aware that finding a naked woman in the bedroom of a healthy, young male was not a remarkable occurrence, but it had never happened to him.

And he had relied upon the fact that it never would. Ever.

He sat on his bed. Having Kirill as a roommate was not working out.

He heard the toilet flush and saw a form run past his doorway. And then there was a lot of giggling and hearty, bass laughter.

He didn't care what Kirill did. Except that he was doing it in his apartment. If it was Kirill?

It had to be, but he felt justified in finding out for sure. He didn't creep down the hallway; it was his apartment after all.

Before he reached the living room, the laughing had segued into a subtle harmony of grunts and squeals.

He peered into the living room. He had left a low wattage light on over the range in the kitchenette.

It was Kirill. Which was something.

Naked Kirill and the naked woman were on Cory's weight bench. Well, the naked woman was on Kirill, and Kirill was lying on the bench. She was bouncing as Kirill did bench presses.

They were both having a splendid time; judging by the vocalizations.

He didn't know how he'd explain what had been going on to the paramedics or the police if there was a barbell accident?

He wheeled about and went back to his room.

And Kirill's partner wasn't Christina. Which was another something.

With rest breaks, the Bacchanalia went on for an hour and a half. And then things got quiet, and he fell asleep.

Until he heard someone being violently sick in his bathroom. It was 6:47 am. The retching continued until he was pretty sure he'd find a dead body slumped over the toilet when he went to investigate. He wasn't sure he would be sad about that.

But a form limped past his doorway.

And after a few minutes, he heard the apartment door open, but he didn't hear the door close.

He sighed and went down the hall again.

The dawn light of a lovely June day was pouring in the windows.

The apartment door was open. Kirill's friend was gone. Kirill was face up, spread-eagled on the air mattress.

Kirill was also profoundly naked. Which was much less traumatic, but he threw a sheet over him anyway.

He locked and chained his door.

He glared at Kirill; he resisted the urge to kick him. Kirill's presence might deter someone who wanted Gabe Bergeron dead, but only when he was conscious. And sober.

He wasn't sure what he was going to do. Well, he was going back to bed and try to get back to sleep.

He sighed and looked at Cory's bench. After breakfast, he was going to wash it down with bleach. And never tell Cory what had happened on it.

And then he went into the bathroom.

The woman had neglected to flush. Her aim had also been poor. He went into the bedroom, but he knew he'd never sleep knowing what was in the room next door.

He found a mop and rubber gloves. And bleach. He wanted a face mask, but he knew he didn't have one.

And he scrubbed every inch of his bathroom until it looked and smelled pristine. Almost. He thought he could still smell puke.

Which was probably coming from his t-shirt and maybe his hair?

He took a long, hot shower, and then he went back to bed. He surprised himself by falling asleep, and it was almost 10:00 am when he woke up again.

He stomped down the hallway. He glared at Kirill who didn't appear to have moved a muscle.

There was a limit to the amount of noise that could be produced by making coffee and toast. Kirill still lay there. He raised the shades, letting in the sunlight, but Kirill didn't react. Was he okay?

So he may have been standing over Kirill when his eyes popped open.

"Get away from me, Bergeron!"

He took a couple of steps back. "I thought you were dead, and I was wondering if it's a crime to toss a dead body out a window. Since I knew I wasn't carrying you down all those stairs."

Kirill sat up. "Where's...Gina? Jenny? Nina?"

"They all left...after puking all over the bathroom."

Kirill smiled. And then he may have started for him.

Kirill leaped to his feet, holding the sheet in front of him. "Hey, take it easy, Bergeron! I didn't do anything!"

"You brought her here! After getting her drunk!"

Kirill was trying not to smile. "I didn't get her drunk. She got me drunk; she was buying." He smiled again. "I think we had a real good time too."

Kirill was big, but he had let himself get out of shape as evidenced by the love handles and the beer belly. And he was hungover. Again. He could take him.

Kirill said, "Don't try it, Bergeron. I can see you're pissed, but I didn't do anything."

"You could have asked before you brought her back here."

Kirill was picking up his clothes that were scattered over the living room. "You'd have said no."

Which was true.

Kirill said, "Got anything for a headache?"

"Bathroom."

Kirill winked at him and sauntered down the hall.

He had calmed down a little by the time Kirill had showered and gotten dressed.

"Don't bring anybody else back here."

Kirill glared at him. "No promises, Bergeron." He smiled. "I have needs. You'd understand if you had a sex drive."

"I have a sex drive, and it's first rate! I'm a wild man in bed."

Kirill just smiled at him.

Monday
11:00 am

He and Kirill had coexisted peacefully Sunday until Kirill had wheedled gas money out of him mid-afternoon. He had taken the money and disappeared for the rest of the day.

Which had helped the peaceful coexistence.

Kirill had been drinking but wasn't drunk when he showed up around midnight.

And Kirill had been alone.

He didn't think he needed backup to go to work, which was just as well, since he hadn't been able to rouse Kirill and had left him on the air mattress.

Jennifer had summoned him before he'd even reached his cubicle, but he had told her he was fine. She had looked as skeptical as Czerwinski.

But it was true, and he was sitting at his desk setting up a new client, minding his own business.

Baldacci was looking at him. "What?"

"Nothing."

Carla didn't turn from her work. "We just don't believe you aren't investigating your cousin's death."

Baldacci nodded and rolled over until their chairs collided.

"Personal space, Baldacci."

Baldacci was behind him, three inches from his ear. "Cranky. But I guess I'd be cranky too if somebody put me in the hospital."

He spun around. "Baldacci, go away."

Instead, Carla rolled across the aisle.

Baldacci suddenly smiled at him. "Shit, Gabe! I don't think Jennifer is going to like it if she finds out you're packing heat."

Carla said, "Me either, Bergeron. Is it loaded?"

He had thought this jacket hid the bulge of the Glock. "Of course not. I would never carry a loaded firearm."

Carla and Baldacci looked at each other.

Baldacci said, "What the Hell, Gabe. Do you know how to use it?"

"Yes." Carla was glaring at him. "Cory has been training me for the past eight months. I can clip a butterfly's antenna at five hundred paces. While the butterfly is in mid-flutter."

Carla shook her head. "Jennifer should know."

"No!" Hearne was heading for the breakroom so he lowered his voice. "He really has trained me."

Baldacci said, "Is that the truth, Gabe?"

"Yes, Harry. You and Carla can come with me to the gun range, and I'll show you."

Baldacci looked at his doubting inamorata and nodded.

Carla said, "So you're expecting somebody to come in here guns blazing?"

She looked more excited than frightened.

"No! Of course not. But I have to walk to my Jeep. And there's the parking garage."

She nodded. She smiled. "So let's see it."

"No."

Baldacci said, "Come on, Gabe?"

"No. It isn't a toy. Now, go away."

"Come into the breakroom. Nobody will see."

He gave them his scariest look. He tried to remember how he'd felt when he'd been ready to kick Kirill's ass.

They smiled at him.

And then he sensed Dana slithering behind him and whirled.

Dana took a little hop back. "You have clients, Bergeron."

"Do not!"

But then he spotted Lydia floating sedately by Dana's

receptionist desk. Well, she wasn't actually floating. Maybe because she had Reed at her side anchoring her to this mortal realm.

He trotted over and escorted them into the conference room double time, but he glanced at Baldacci as he shut the door; Harry's eyes were twice normal size. Shit.

He smiled Lydia and Reed. "Please sit down. Would you like coffee?"

Lydia shook her head. Her blonde hair was perfectly coiffed; her oval face as serene as a Renaissance Madonna. Except for the eyes.

Reed executed another perfect handshake. He unbuttoned his jacket and took possession of a chair; his suit was navy and hand stitched; the fabric was hand woven from the output of hand-fed silkworms. His underwear was probably hand washed.

"Yes, Gabriel. That would be nice." He massaged his noble temples. "It's been quite a day actually."

He fetched and served.

Lydia said, "I was so happy when you called Friday and said you'd changed your mind, Gabe."

"Right?" Was he being fired already?

"And then I found out that you were attacked. I didn't know anything about that when you called."

She aimed a pair of icy blue eyes at Reed. He waved a hand. "As I told you, Lydia, I only just found out. I do have other matters to deal with. And Gabe survived."

"I did."

Lydia said, "Tell me what happened. Please?"

"I drank what I thought was just a very bad cup of coffee."

Reed sipped at the cup in front of him and smirked. "At this CoffeeXtra place."

"Yes. Which is run by Billy Stanko, the son of Penelope."

Reed sighed. "I told you all this, Lydia."

She ignored Reed. "Go on, Gabe."

"It was the same drug that Phillip was given." Reed was tapping his fingers on the table.

"We think the idea was to incapacitate me and grab me as I

walked back here."

Lydia said, "We?"

"Detective Golczewski. She came to see me in the hospital. And Czerwinski too."

Lydia said, "I'm so glad nothing more serious happened to you, Gabe. I'm sorry I asked you to get involved."

And she shoved a tan slip of paper across the table. It was imprinted with the name of a prestigious financial institution as well as "Lydia Bergeron Gibson." And, in a little white box, a two followed by four zeros had been written; well six if you included the cents. With blue ink.

He maintained an air of nonchalance. Well, one eyebrow may have escaped voluntary control and shot up. "Wait. Does this mean I'm being fired?"

Lydia looked at him. "No, Gabe."

Reed said, "We just assumed that you wouldn't be willing to continue?"

He smiled at Reed. "Did you really read my file?"

Reed gave him a furious look; he got to his feet and went to the window.

He said, "I'm going to continue, Lydia, and you don't have to pay me...but I guess I could stop if you have a really good reason for me to do that?"

Reed didn't turn around. "So an attempted abduction doesn't count?"

"Nope."

Reed looked at Lydia.

She said, "What kind of reason could I have, Gabe?"

He wanted to pat her hand, but he didn't think she'd like that. And a hug was so verboten. "I think that Phillip may possibly have been engaged in activities which might not redound to his credit."

Reed laughed; Lydia's lips fumbled for a smile.

"I knew my brother, Gabe. I don't think I'll be shocked if you find something...."

Reed was still smiling. "Discreditable, Dear?"

She stared at Reed. "Always so helpful." She continued,

"He was what he was, Gabe, but it you do find something, you might keep it to yourself. If possible."

"Of course." He nudged the tan slip of paper back to her. "You don't have to do this."

But Reed said, "Of course, we do. Keep it. For expenses, Gabe."

Reed was moving toward the door with a man-of-action stride. "I really do have to go, Lydia."

"I know." She smiled at Reed for the first time.

He said, "One thing. Could you call Kelly and ask her if I could stop by to see her?"

Lydia nodded. "Of course, Gabe."

And he escorted them out and went back to his cubicle. Baldacci and Carla rolled over.

Carla said, "Spill, Bergeron."

"Just a potential client. No biggie."

Baldacci snorted. "That was Reed Gibson, of Vance & Gibson."

"Reed James Farley Gibson, III. I know."

Carla was focused on him. "Who was the woman?"

"Her? No idea. He never introduced her."

But Baldacci said, "Nice try, Bergeron. I looked him up, and that was Lydia Gibson, his wife."

Carla smiled. "Of course. She's your cousin."

Baldacci grinned at him. "And Phillip's sister."

Monday
4:00 pm

He had fended off Carla and Baldacci mostly by showing them his Glock in the breakroom. He had ejected the magazine and double-checked that the chamber was empty before letting them play with it. They were like ten year-olds.

Hearne had drifted by during play time. If he noticed the Glock, he didn't say anything.

He had tried calling Kirill and gotten his voicemail, and now he was outside CoffeeXtra, glaring through the window at Martin.

He marched in. Martin said, "I haven't seen him, Gabe."

He pointed a finger at Martin and made come-hither motions. Martin left the counter in Calvin's incapable hands.

"What, Dude?"

He grabbed Martin's arm and urged him along. "Show me the office."

"He's not there." Martin shrugged and unlocked the door.

The office was tiny and offered no hiding places. He opened the door into the room that Billy had converted into a bedroom. It was empty too, and the bed was made.

He turned and glared at Martin. "Stockroom."

Martin nodded. It was empty. Well, it was full of supplies but not Mr. Stanko. He looked into the kitchen.

He left Martin and checked the Men's Room; every stall. He was eyeing the Ladies Room when Martin rejoined him. "He isn't in there, Dude. Honest."

"When did you last see him?"

"A week ago." Martin was studying the dark, hardwood floor.

"The day I was drugged?"

Martin nodded. "But he's called a couple of times."

"Did you tell him I want to see him?"

"Sure, Dude. And the detective."

"Czerwinski?"

Martin nodded like a bobble-headed doll. "Yeah. He was here again this morning."

"So you called Billy today?"

"No, he calls me." Martin looked around them. "I think Billy's scared, Gabe."

"Of what?"

Martin shrugged. "He won't say which usually means it's Penelope stuff."

"Okay. Thanks, Martin. How are you doing? Running the place?"

Martin smiled his mile-wide smile. "I'm fine, Gabe."

"Good."

And he walked out and stood on the sidewalk. He called Kirill again, and Kirill picked up.

"What?"

"I'm going to see the other ex-wife."

"So?"

"So you could come along?" Silence. "Kirill?"

"I'm here. What's the address?"

He gave it to Kirill and headed for his Jeep. He was striding toward it when it occurred to him that maybe he should exercise some caution.

His Jeep was yellow. And obvious.

He exercised a bunch of caution. Which took time since a parking garage was just chock full of shadowed hiding places for villains and waylayers.

He looked under the hood. The engine was there and looked much as he remembered it. He snapped some photos for future reference. He took off his jacket and looked underneath the

Jeep; no suspicious boxes with flashing lights were in evidence.

And then, and only then, had he set course for Kelly's house. So he had expected to see Kirill's van parked in front.

He called Kirill again. Voicemail.

He sighed. Bodyguards weren't what they used to be.

Kelly's house was a ranch style home on a medium-sized lot which was being mowed by the middle son, whose name he couldn't recall. The middle son gave him a nasty look.

The house was stucco that had been painted apple green; the roof was sage. The trim was a deep ruby red.

Kelly opened the door and looked at him; eye to eye since they were the same height. She was wearing a tank top and shorts; both pristine white. "So you're a detective, Gabe? I would never have suspected."

"People never do." He smiled at her. "Actually, I'm an accountant really."

"But you're looking into Phillip's death? For Lydia?"

"Yes."

Kelly said, "Oh, come in, Gabe. Where are my manners?"

"Thanks."

Kelly led him into the kitchen which was black and white and all the shades of gray in between. The counters were granite.

She poured coffee that was as pellucid as coal tar.

She joined him on a stool. The light from the sliding, glass doors highlighted a few wrinkles, but she looked good to have a son in college. She had minimal makeup on; blonde hair and blue eyes presented without artifice.

"So, Gabe, why you? If you're an accountant?"

"Because I've had experience."

"In solving murders?"

"Yes. Not that I wanted to."

She nodded and when he didn't amplify, she said, "So what can I tell you?"

"Anything about Phillip that you think might help? Anything out of the ordinary?"

She shook her head. "I've thought about it of course, but I didn't see Phillip that much the last few weeks before...."

"Before he was murdered. So he didn't come around here?"

"No. Hardly ever. He didn't like running into Haruki."

He smiled at her. "And Haruki is?"

Big happy smile. "Haruki Ihara. My husband...or soon will be."

"And Phillip didn't like Haruki? Or Haruki didn't like Phillip?"

She shrugged. "I think it was mutual. Men can be such children. Even Haruki. Who is usually chill and very evolved."

He wanted to ask what species Haruki had become after leaving Homo sapiens behind, but he thought better of it. "So they avoided one another?"

She smiled. "Haruki didn't hurt Phillip."

"No. Right. So did Phillip have a girlfriend?"

"I'm sure he did."

"But you don't know a name or anything?"

She smiled all placid and laid back. "No."

"Did Phillip see his sons?"

She nodded. "Sure. He had joint custody." She frowned. "He really loved them and would do anything for them."

Which seemed to upset her for some reason.

"Sorry I can't help you." She smiled and got off the stool and put her long legs to good use by sauntering to the door.

She opened the ruby portal and urged him out. "I hope you find out what happened to Phillip."

"I'll do my best."

She smiled and closed the door.

He stood there. He wasn't sure what had been going on among Phillip and Kelly and Haruki, but things were not as chill as Kelly would have him believe.

He wandered toward his Jeep.

And almost bumped into a large object dressed in a t-shirt and shorts. He let his eyes travel upward.

The largest, oldest, and blondest of Phillip and Kelly's progeny was standing foursquare in his path. "Hi, there. You're Phillip Junior?"

"Yeah." Junior was crushing a football in his hand.

"Is there something I can do for you?"

He looked at the house. He wouldn't mind talking to the sons, but he wasn't sure how Kelly would feel about that. And more importantly, he wasn't sure how the sons would feel about that.

The second son had put away the lawn mower, and he joined Junior in glaring at him.

He smiled. "I'm sorry, but I don't remember your name?"

"Jacob."

"Hi, Jacob. The lawn looks nice." There were flowering shrubs scattered here and there in a naturalistic way. "The flowers are pretty too. Do you take care of them?"

Jacob shook his head while glaring at him so hard that he was in danger of crushing his own eyeballs. "No!"

Junior said, "Dad planted them."

Jacob said, "And took care of them."

"Well, they're beautiful."

Jacob said, "You should go."

"Okay."

When Junior didn't move, he started to circumnavigate him. But Junior said, "No."

And then Jacob punched his brother in the arm. Which, from the tender expressions on their faces, would have led to battle and bloodshed, if the youngest brother hadn't come jogging out of the garage.

He got between his brothers. Which seemed ill-advised. "Come on, Guys! No fighting. Jacob, I want to talk to him."

Jacob shook his head but didn't say anything.

The youngest one said, "I'm Zack. Can we talk, Mr. Bergeron? In your Jeep?"

"Sure, Zack."

Junior waited until Zack was moving away before delivering a massive blow to Jacob's arm. They stood toe-to-toe, but neither seemed ready to start hostilities.

Zack shook his head as he got into the Jeep. "I try to keep peace between them."

"Do they fight a lot?"

"Not really. Mostly because Junior is a chill guy."

Jacob was walking away when Junior hurled the football at his head. Jacob ducked and then retrieved it. He hurled it back, and they played a spirited game of spear your brother in the front lawn.

He smiled at Zack. "So what can I do for you, Zack? How old are you, by the way?"

"I'm 15." He looked at his brothers. "Jacob will be a senior this fall. And Junior is 20. He's in college."

He didn't say anything, but Junior did not seem like college material.

Zack was looking at him. "Junior's really good at math and spatial relationships."

Which Junior demonstrated by threading the football between Jacob's hands and striking him in the groin. Jacob went down. Junior smiled.

"I see."

Zack looked very like his brothers; same nose, mouth, and chin. But his face was squarer, and his hair was a darker blond. And his blue eyes were bigger.

"I have to ask you something, Mr. Bergeron."

"Call me Gabe. We're cousins, Zack."

Zack nodded. "What happened to Dad, Gabe?"

He wasn't sure what he should say? What had Kelly told her sons?

"I know he didn't kill himself." Zack's voice was barely louder than a whisper, but the words were expelled with fervor.

"No, he didn't." Why hadn't Kelly told them that much? Didn't she know? He was sure Czerwinski had told her.

Zack said, "You know that for sure?"

"I do."

His body seemed to relax and meld with the Jeep's seat. His brothers had stopped trying to impale each other; they were watching Zack, vigilant and semi-hostile. Well, Jacob was all hostile and Junior wasn't.

"So somebody killed him?"

"Yes, Zack. They put a sedative in his glass. He was unconscious when...when he died. He never knew what was happening."

Zack faced him. "Is that the truth? Or some bullshit to make the kiddies feel better?"

He smiled at Zack. "People do that, Zack. All the time. They think they're being kind. But in this case, it's the truth. If you don't believe me, you and your brothers can go see Detective Czerwinski. He isn't a sugar-coating kind of guy."

Zack nodded. "No, I believe you."

He sat there not saying a word.

"Is there something else, Zack?"

"Yeah."

They sat some more. The Jeep was getting hot even with the windows rolled down.

Zack said, "He did something, didn't he?"

"I don't know what you mean?"

Zack frowned. "He came by the house before...he died. Haruki wasn't around. He took me out into the backyard, and told me I would go to college just like Junior. And Jacob too. He told me not to worry; that there would be money. He said he was going to make sure of that."

"And?"

"I told him that I had a job, and I could get a student loan. I asked him if he had a new job, and he said he didn't. Not yet. So I asked where this money was coming from." Zack faced him. "He said he had found a rich uncle, and I didn't have to worry."

"Did he explain what he meant?"

"No, he just laughed and hugged me and took off. Do you know?"

"No, but I'll find out."

"And you'll tell me when you do? No matter what it is?"

"I promise." He looked at Zack. "So do you and your brothers like Haruki?"

"Pretty much. Jacob's gotten used to him. Mom is happier than she's been in a long time. They're getting married soon."

He didn't look very happy about that.

"So that's a good thing, right?"

He nodded. "Sure, but she and Haruki want to move to

California. He has a job lined up."

"Right."

"They were both born there, and Mom has always talked about going 'home' so it wasn't a real shock."

"And you and Jacob would go with her?"

He had no idea how joint custody worked, but he thought Phillip would have had to agree to that?

"Yeah."

"But you didn't want to go? And your Dad didn't want you to go?"

"Dad knew I didn't want to change schools."

"And Jacob?"

"Jacob said he was okay with it, but Jacob likes to pretend he's tough...tougher than he is."

"And Junior?"

"Junior has been living here to save money. Dad said that he would help Junior find a place or maybe Junior could live with him, but I don't know."

"And now you and Jacob have to go with your mother and Haruki?"

He nodded without a word.

"California is beautiful, Zack. And you'll like it after you get settled in and make some friends."

Another nod. And then he got out of the Jeep.

Thanks, Gabe. You'll call me? When you know something?"

"I will." He handed Zack a business card. "But you can call me if you want."

He had no idea what he would say to the boy.

Zack was walking away. "When are you leaving for California?"

Zack shrugged but didn't turn back.

He started the Jeep and pulled away from the curb. He remembered when Aunt Flo had come to get him after his mother had died.

He had hated leaving Philadelphia and his friends, but it had turned out to be the best thing that had ever happened to him.

He should have told Zack that California might be that for him too.

He wondered what Kelly would have done if Phillip had tried to keep the boys in Philadelphia? How laid back would she have been then?

Tuesday
2:00 am

He had arrived home after 6:00 pm.

No Kirill; no blue van.

He didn't wait up for Kirill, and he put the chain on. Just in case.

He opened his eyes. Someone was banging on his door and yelling. He was pretty sure it was Kirill so he took his time getting out of bed.

The door was open as far as the chain would allow, and Kirill's head was wedged in the gap.

"Gabriel! Where the Hell are you! Unchain the freaking door and let me in!"

All this was roared with gusto; it would carry for miles across the Serengeti.

He would have been worried about his neighbors, but the other front apartment was empty, and Mrs. Bruska was still at her daughter's house.

"Is that you, Kirill?"

"Who else! Let me in, Gabriel, or I'll break the door down!"

"Are you alone?"

Kirill laughed. "Sure."

There was a treble giggling which indicated that he was fibbing. "No, you aren't. Go away."

"Let me in!"

"You can huff and puff all you like, but the chain stays on. And if you break my door down, I'll shoot you. I'll tell the police that I thought it was a home invasion."

Silence.

"You wouldn't shoot me. You need me, you stupid, little shit!"

Kirill was slurring his words due to the level of intoxication and fury. "I need somebody I can rely on. Which isn't you. Go away, or I'm calling the police."

The treble voice said, "Come on, Kirill. I can't get arrested. Greg would find out and kill me...kill both of us."

"No! I'm going to break the door down."

He threw himself against the steel clad door. The door and the heavy-duty chain laughed at his puny effort. Still, Kirill was large and dense and pissed and might eventually snap the chain.

"I'm calling the police."

The treble voice said, "I'm out of here."

And the determined clicking of high heels could be heard heading for the stairs.

Kirill said, "Where are you going, Gina?"

The treble voice said, "My name is Nina! Asshole!"

Naked Nina of the Red Hair; he ran the multiplication tables trying to keep haunting images at bay.

Kirill's heavy tread could be heard on the stairs.

He shut the door and unchained. He peered out. No Kirill in sight. He relocked the door, fastened the chain, and engaged the second deadbolt for which Kirill had no key.

He peeped out the window; Kirill's van was in front of the building with the back doors open. He didn't see Kirill, but Naked Nina was standing on the sidewalk with her hands on her hips; not that she was naked at the moment.

He watched as she got into the van, and the doors closed.

He went back to bed and slept soundly.

Tuesday
8:00 am

He awoke at the appointed hour and dressed for work.
Kirill's van was still out front.
He had locked both deadbolts so Kirill wasn't getting back into the apartment. He was going to just walk past the van, but he wondered if Kirill was inside? With Naked Nina?
The back windows were filthy, and he couldn't see anything. They also didn't open. So even with the driver and passenger windows open, it must be stifling inside?
He may have peered in the passenger window, but if Kirill and Nina were onboard, they were in the back shielded from view by the mounds of Kirill's junk.
Which was probably everything he owned?
Which was kind of sad, but he hardened his heart and went to work.
He called Camille's cellphone before lunch. It went to voicemail. He left a message for her to call him back.
It was mid-afternoon, and he still hadn't heard anything. Czerwinski had given him her work number too.
"Bala Cynwyd Catholic High School?"
"Hi, I'd like to speak to Camille Bergeron Rankin."
"Hold on just a moment, Sir."
And he did.
Camille said, "Camille Rankin."
"Hi. It's Gabe...Gabe Bergeron. I'd like to talk to you."
He got background noise for a moment; two women were

chatting about a student who have loved not wisely but too well.

"Camille?"

"Lydia hired you to investigate Phillip's death."

He couldn't keep the money if he didn't find out who had killed Phillip, but he had deposited Lydia's check so it was accurate to say that he'd been hired. "Yes, she did."

"Why?"

"I could explain it to you better in person."

Silence.

"Camille, I want to find out what happened to Phillip, and I think you want to know too?"

"I suppose. I mean I want to know what happened. Of course, I do."

"Okay. Where do you want to meet?"

"There's a bagel shop on Montgomery Avenue."

"In Bala Cynwyd?"

"Yes." And she gave him the number.

He looked up, and Jennifer seemed occupied. "Okay, I can be there by 4:00 pm?"

"All right."

And she was gone.

He sighed. "Harry?"

Baldacci's head went up, eyes alert, nostrils distended. "What?"

"Put my stuff in my desk and turn my computer off before you leave."

Harry raised one eyebrow and smiled. "And why would I do that."

"You're my best friend in all the world, Harry, and I would be eternally grateful?"

"Tell me where you're going."

"I have to speak to Camille Rankin."

Carla's ears swiveled toward her beloved.

Baldacci said, "Phillip's other sister?"

He sighed. "Yes."

Baldacci said, "I have a better idea. I'll go with you, and Carla can cover for both of us."

Carla didn't turn around. "No."

Harry, who should have known better, said, "You aren't the boss of me."

When the gales of laughter from the cubicle dwellers had ebbed, Carla said, "You aren't going with Bergeron."

"It will be okay. Where are you going, Gabe?"

"A bagel shop in Bala Cynwyd."

Baldacci rolled over to Carla and whispered in her ear. "See? What could happen in a bagel shop in Bala Cynwyd?"

Carla spun about. "You ingest a lethal dose of cyanide. You are shot a dozen times in a drive by. You and Bergeron are abducted...and I never see you again."

"Never happen."

Carla said, "Are you armed, Bergeron?"

He had to nod.

Carla kissed Baldacci on the forehead and went back to work.

Harry said, "I guess I'm not going, Gabe."

"I never thought you were."

He slipped out of his chair and began crawling, ninja-like, toward the stairs. Carla said, "Be careful, Doofus."

He halted mid-crawl to hug her. "Thanks, Carla."

He made it out of Garst, Bauer & Hartmann totally undetected. Well, except for every person on the 11th floor except for Jennifer, and he wasn't even sure about her.

He found the bagel shop.

Camille was not present. He had a blueberry muffin and a cup of decent coffee.

He had a second cup of coffee.

Camille came through the door. She gazed at the patrons and found him. The discovery did not fill her with joy.

She was wearing a pale yellow, linen dress. She walked over and stood looking down at him; pale blue eyes just this side of hostile.

"Please sit down, Camille. The blueberry muffins are good."

She sat and pushed her long, brown hair behind her ears.

"No thank you. I won't be staying that long, Mr. Bergeron."

"Camille, please call me Gabe. Or Gabriel."

She'd lost weight which she could ill afford. She shrugged. "All right. Gabriel." She stared at him. "So why does Lydia think you're qualified to investigate...what happened to Phillip?"

"Because her husband had me checked out. I think he was really trying to find something so Lydia wouldn't hire me."

She smiled. "Good ole Reed. Well, you must be a saint if Reed couldn't find some dirt."

She had put a little makeup on her cheeks, but the color only made her look paler.

"You don't like Reed?"

"No."

He smiled at her. "I like decisive women. Well, I tend to avoid crossing them. So what was Phillip up to that would have brought in enough cash to ensure Jacob and Zack's college educations?"

"My brother wasn't up to anything! Who told you that?"

"He talked to Zack and told him not to worry about college. He said it would be taken care of by a rich uncle?"

She shook her head. "You stay away from Zack."

"I went to see Kelly, and Zack wanted to talk to me."

"Stay away from him. He's just a boy no matter how bright he is. And I don't know anything about any uncles. Did Phillip really say that to Zack?"

"According to Zack."

She shook her head. "Well, I have no idea what he meant."

"What do you know about his job and why he was fired?"

"Nothing. Well, I know he hated it. He said he was being cheated by the company."

"And he did something about that?"

"I don't know what you mean?"

"Did he have access to company secrets?"

She shook her head, but she looked down at the table. "I think I will have a muffin. And some tea."

She seemed to defer to him so he ordered; he got another muffin for himself. She consumed her muffin like she hadn't eaten in days. She took a swig of tea and prepared to leave.

"One last question. Please." She settled back into her seat. "Did Phillip have a girlfriend?"

She smiled. "He did. He liked women, Mr. Bergeron. Sorry, Gabriel. He wasn't exactly faithful to Kelly. Or Christina. I didn't approve of that, but he was my brother."

"Of course. So do you know anything about his latest girlfriend?"

"Not really."

"Anything at all?"

"He wouldn't tell me her name, but he really liked her. I could tell by the way he talked about her. But he said she wasn't the kind of girlfriend you brought home to meet the family."

"Did he explain what he meant by that?"

"No." She was studying the dregs of her tea. "He was proud, Gabe."

"Proud?"

She frowned. "He thought he was a lady's man, and I got the feeling that he thought this woman had seduced him...or taken advantage of him...in some way. It wasn't something he would have shared with me. Or anyone. He would have been too embarrassed."

She got to her feet. "Lydia feels guilty. That's why she's doing this."

"Why does she feel guilty, Camille?"

"Because Phillip went to her, and she turned him down."

He nodded. "He asked her for money."

Camille said, "For a loan, Gabe. Not a gift. Do you have any idea how wealthy Reed is?"

"I saw the house."

Camille stopped. "You were granted an audience?"

"I was summoned to Berwyn and had tea in the library. I was allowed a peek at Reed's roses."

"Lucky you." She smiled. "I sound like a real bitch."

"No, you don't."

She frowned at him. "I do love Lydia. I just wish she hadn't married Reed. But she did, and he could put Jacob and Zack through college and grad school for what he spends on fertilizer for those stupid roses."

    And she walked out of the bagel shop. And he followed her after buying a dozen blueberry muffins and a dozen bagels.

Tuesday
6:00 pm

He had stopped at the market and gotten a few groceries before motoring back to Arch Street. Kirill's van was still parked in front, but it was empty.

He climbed the stairs. Kirill was sitting on the floor leaning against his door.

Kirill said, "About freaking time, Bergeron. Open up."

"No."

Kirill looked and smelled like he'd been on a bender for days and had slept in a van. Which was the case. So his brain wasn't functioning at anything like optimal capacity.

"What?"

"I mean I'm going to open my door, but you aren't coming in."

Kirill tried to look scary, but his eyes were bloodshot and weren't focusing all that well. "You can't keep me out! I'll crush you like a bug! Smirking bastard."

He set his groceries down. He was pretty sure he could toss Kirill around like a rag doll; a chunky rag doll.

Kirill got to his feet and smiled at him. It was the smile that decided it. So when Kirill did a sort of staggering lunge at him, he grabbed Kirill's arm, twisted, and threw Mr. Ochoa over his shoulder.

The throw was called *ippon seoi naga*.

He did it fast and lifted Kirill as high in the air as he could to maximize the impact with the tile floor. Kirill made a satisfying splat sound when he landed. He lay there.

Sensei Travis would be proud of him.

He had used the throw on Ben, his old sparring partner at the dojo, and on Matt Bornheimer, Cory's FBI partner. But this throw was the best.

Kirill was still lying there, but he was groaning.

Which was good. He didn't want to really hurt the guy.

He went inside and dropped his groceries on the island. He locked and chained and settled on his sofa, safe in Fortress Bergeron.

After a little bit, there was a knocking on his door.

Kirill said, "Gabriel?"

He should just ignore him, but he opened the door as far as the chain would allow. "What?"

"Let me in. Please."

"Nope."

"Please. I don't have any money, and I think the van is running on empty. I don't have anywhere to go."

He looked at Kirill. "Why should I let you in?"

"I know I've been drinking too much...but I promise I'll do better."

He shook his head. "No. I just want you to go. Go stay with Valentina or Mikhail."

"You don't want me here?"

"No." But he was looking so hang dog and pitiful. "Look, you can stay the night, and I'll give you money for gas. If you promise to leave in the morning?"

"All right."

"Okay." He unchained, and Kirill dragged himself in. He made it as far as the air mattress before collapsing.

"Kirill?"

His eyes were closed. "In the morning, Gabriel. I promise."

And Kirill was down for the count.

He took Kirill's boots off and covered him with a sheet. He would have taken his belt and pants off, but Kirill might have gotten the wrong idea.

Wednesday
7:00 am

He was looking down at Kirill; he didn't appear to have moved during the night, but his chest was moving up and down.

"Kirill? Kirill?"

His eyes popped open; still bloodshot but better. "Is it time for me to go?"

"You could take a shower first...if you want. And have breakfast?"

Kirill nodded. "Thanks, Gabriel."

He headed to the bathroom and came back looking and smelling a whole lot better.

"Do you want some breakfast? I have bacon and eggs and bagels?"

Kirill nodded and sat on a stool at the island. Kirill was looking at him. "So judo?"

"Yes. At the dojo of Sensei Travis for over three years now. I'm his star pupil. Well, I'm not the worst...maybe second from the bottom?"

Kirill smiled. "No, you're better than that. From what I remember."

He started to say he was sorry, but he wasn't.

"Are you hungry?"

Kirill nodded so he slid a lot of bacon and half a dozen eggs onto a plate and poured coffee.

Kirill said, "Thanks."

He took a stool, and they ate in silence. Kirill had used

Cory's shower gel again, and he smelled good.

Kirill said, "So you really want me to go?"

"Yes."

Kirill nodded. And they ate in silence.

Kirill said, "Are you going to tell them I screwed up?"

"Danilo and Ezmeralda?"

"And Mrs. Barnes."

"I won't if you don't want me to."

Kirill nodded. "Okay. I should get going."

He pulled out his wallet. Kirill had been with him for five days, but he'd been missing or unconscious for much of that time. He gave him four hundred. Which was all he had on him.

Kirill said, "Thanks, Gabriel."

"Sure."

Kirill stuffed his dirty clothes into his duffel bag. He could offer to let him use the washer, but he had to get to work.

"So where are you going?"

"I lost my apartment." Kirill shrugged.

He couldn't imagine being homeless which Kirill was. "Valentina will take you in. Or Mikhail."

He smiled. "Mom would, but she would yell at me. Maybe, Mikhail. For a while." He smiled. "Or Nina."

"Naked Nina of the Red Hair?"

Kirill smiled some more.

"What about Greg?"

Kirill said, "Who's Greg?"

"No idea, but he's why she really didn't want to get arrested. She said he'd kill both of you."

Kirill smiled. "Shit. So I should find out where Greg is before I drop in on Nina?"

"Might be a good idea."

"Stay safe, Gabriel."

"That is the plan."

Kirill had his duffel bag on his shoulder standing in the doorway. "So are you going to catch the bastard who killed Phillip?"

He looked at Kirill. "I'll do my best."

Kirill nodded. "I hope so. She misses her daddy."
"Who?"
"Hallie. Christina's girl."
He nodded. "I'm sure she does."
Kirill nodded and walked out.

Wednesday
3:00 pm

He had solved the problem of slipping out of GB&H without anybody noticing by taking a late lunch and just not going back.

He felt sure that Jennifer was tallying his missed time, and the retribution would be swift and merciless. She was surely sharpening her terrible swift sword like a distaff Jehovah.

But for the moment, he was safe in Wilmington, seated in the lobby of the main office of Oxley International.

The building appeared to be six stories, and the glass-fronted lobby rose the full height. It was like a giant blade had sliced open the building, exposing the floors to the lobby.

Stairs were slung here and there connecting the floors. They appeared suspended in mid-air and unsafe.

A grouping of four sofas, gray and unyielding as the walls around them, were placed just inside the doors, and he was perched on one of them; quite alone.

He was being slowly parboiled as the sun shone upon him, as merciless as Jennifer. There were shades that could be lowered, but no one seemed eager to do that.

Set just outside the solar death ray area was a circular bank of counters and desks.

Reception and Security occupied this area. They were looking upon Gabriel Bergeron with a wary distaste better suited to Nazi war criminals.

He had asked to speak to Mr. Scanlon, the guy who had

made vague threats against Phillip when Christina had visited here.

Reception had sniffed and been doubtful that he would ever see Mr. Scanlon. Security had fastened all of their gimlet eyes upon this interloper.

But he wasn't going anywhere. Unless he expired from heat stroke, and paramedics were summoned to cart his lifeless body away.

He was just about ready to use Reed's name in vain and to suggest that Vance & Gibson had been retained in the Phillip Bergeron affair, when he spotted a guy in a navy suit descending.

Reception trotted to the stairs to make sure Suit Guy didn't trip or lose his way. Security rose to their collective feet; a lot of loin girding was going on. Well, metaphorically.

Suit Guy nodded as Reception whispered in his ear. Suit Guy was heading for him with Security at his back.

Suit Guy turned ever so slightly and gazed at them. They froze in place as Suit Guy continued.

His suit was obviously bespoke; the fabric was on the cusp of sumptuous. His white shirt gleamed like Arctic snow, but the tie was a letdown; blue and black diagonal stripes. He was of average height and solid. He was about fifty.

Suit Guy said, "Mr. Bergeron?"

He looked around, and he was still the only person on the sofas. "Yes, I'm Gabriel Bergeron."

"I'm Richard Scanlon. I understand you wish to speak to me about Phillip Bergeron."

They shook hands; Scanlon had a firm grip.

Scanlon sat across from him. The sun was in his eyes for only as long as it took Security to rush to the windows and lower the shades.

Scanlon made a finger motion, and Security rushed back to their bunker even faster.

He smiled at Scanlon. "I'm Phillip's second cousin."

Scanlon nodded. His ruddy cheeks were puffy and were threatening to overwhelm tiny features clumped in the center of his face. His hair was silver and black and brushed back. His lips were almost non-existent, and his little eyes were of an indeterminate color.

"I'm sorry for your loss, Mr. Bergeron."

"So you know that Phillip is dead?"

"I do. A colleague spoke with a detective a month ago."

"That would have been Detective Czerwinski."

Scanlon shrugged. "I wouldn't know."

"So what do you think happened to my cousin, Mr. Scanlon?"

Another shrug. "Suicide. But the information I received was second hand."

"Well, let me update you. He was murdered. Drugged and then hanged. He was probably unconscious for the hanging part."

Scanlon's little eyes were riveted on him now. "That's terrible. I'm truly sorry to hear that."

"So I understand that you're a VP in the legal department here, but you knew Phillip."

"Barely. I spoke with him at his exit interview."

He smiled his very best smile. "And that's why I'm here. To find out about his exit. He'd been here nineteen years. And he was summarily fired."

Scanlon's face was as gray and emotional as the sofa on which he sat. "I've spoken to his wife...."

"Christina. Yes, I know."

"Just what is your interest, Mr. Bergeron?"

"Phillip's sister, Lydia Gibson, has asked me to look into his murder. She wants to know who killed her brother as does her husband, Reed Gibson."

But Scanlon already knew about Phillip's connection to Reed and the law firm of Vance & Gibson. "I see. And she chose you?"

"She did."

"But you're an accountant, Mr. Bergeron."

So that was why he had been left to parboil. "You checked me out, Mr. Scanlon?"

"Of course."

"What did Phillip steal from Oxley?"

He thought Scanlon was smiling but it was hard to tell with

lips as narrow as kite string. "He didn't steal anything, Mr. Bergeron."

"But he tried. And got caught."

Scanlon shook his head. "No, that isn't...."

"But for some reason, it was too embarrassing to have him arrested. Your security wasn't very good?"

Scanlon clammed up and looked about ready to bolt.

"I don't care about any of that, Mr. Scanlon."

Scanlon was trying to determine just how venomous a creature he was.

"And I'm not interested in any kind of payout."

"Then what do you want?"

"First, I'd like to know how you caught him, and if you know if Phillip had a partner; outside or inside the company?"

He grunted. "No one inside. I can tell you that."

"So outside?"

Scanlon nodded. Well, his head moved a millimeter or so.

"And have you identified this person?"

"We have a name, but it was fake."

"Anything else?"

Scanlon said, "We're sure that we weren't the first biotech company she tried to penetrate."

He tried very hard not to smile at Scanlon. "She?"

Scanlon nodded again but the movement was now in the micron range. He got to his feet. "We're done, Mr. Bergeron."

"Did you get a description of her? Around forty, probably blonde, dark eyes, square face, voluptuous?"

Scanlon smiled a string-smile as he repeated, "Voluptuous." And then his lips relaxed, and he nodded.

"Thank you, Mr. Scanlon. Just as a sort of pro forma thing, Oxley didn't have Phillip murdered? In a fit of pique?"

Scanlon looked at Security and pointed at the door, and they, who had been straining against the leash for too long, bayed and rushed him en masse. Well, they didn't actually bay.

They did toss him out the door gleefully, but it was probably boring sitting at the bottom of that glass fishbowl of a lobby all day.

Thursday
5:00 pm

He was sitting in his cubicle working hard after everyone else had gone home. Well, Chatterjee was doing something on his computer, but it didn't look like work.

Jennifer hadn't mentioned his absenteeism. Which was nice of her, but it made him feel guilty enough to stay late.

His phone rang: Czerwinski. "Hello, Detective?"

"Where are you?"

"At work."

"Stay there."

And Czerwinski was gone. He should leave. He could go to Cory's condo in DC and not answer Czerwinski's calls. So there.

But he could imagine how he'd feel if Jennifer came to him and told him that a detective was taking over the account for Ochoa Imports.

So he went into the breakroom and made coffee.

There was nothing to eat; well, there were some ketchup packets. He went back to his cubicle.

"Dhruva?"

Chatterjee spun around with a guilty look on his face. "What?"

"Got any snacks? Cookies, crackers, anything?"

Chatterjee said, "Bring your own, Bergeron."

"I do. Usually. When I remember."

Chatterjee shook his head. "You're a mooch, Bergeron."

"Am not!"

Chatterjee said, "Go home. You never work late?"

"Do to. But why are you still here?"

Chatterjee looked death row guilty. "I'm catching up on work."

"No, you aren't. If you're downloading porn, they will find out."

"I'm not! Don't tell anybody that, Gabe!"

"All right. Sorry. I won't."

Chatterjee turned off his computer and was heading out.

"Here." And dear, sweet Dhruva dropped a whole bag of double chocolate chip cookies on his desk. "I expect you to replace these, Bergeron."

"I will. Without fail. Tomorrow. No, I'm off tomorrow. Monday. Monday morning. As my word is my bond."

Chatterjee stomped to the elevator.

He sat in the empty office. It was kind of creepy being in the office alone. Creepy and quiet.

He was glad he had the Glock.

Where the Hell was Czerwinski? He had more work that he wanted to get finished, but he couldn't focus knowing Czerwinski was coming.

He had eaten six cookies and was drumming his fingers on his desk when the elevator dinged. He may have dropped to the floor until he was sure it was the detective.

"Bergeron?"

"Here."

"What are you doing on the floor. No. Don't tell me."

He smiled at Czerwinski who was in a gray suit that looked like it had been wadded in a ball for a month and then run over by a forklift. The knit, red tie was painfully narrow.

"Want some coffee?"

Czerwinski nodded. He grabbed Carla's chair and rolled it over to his cubicle.

"Cookie?"

Czerwinski looked at him skeptically. Which he couldn't help given his physiognomy. Did having unevenly placed eyes affect his vision?

Czerwinski said, "Stop staring at me."

"Sorry. Do you wear glasses? Or contacts?"

"No. Why would you ask that?" He held up a hand in Vonda-fashion. "Have you learned anything?"

"About Phillip's murder?" Czerwinski was looking murderously skeptical. "A few things."

And he told him everything he'd learned and surmised and suspected. Czerwinski was looking carefully blank.

"So you think Phillip tried to steal some biotech secret from Oxley and got caught. And he was put up to it by Penelope. And after that fell through, he was blackmailing some 'rich uncle' for college money for his kids. Is that it?"

"Yeah."

Czerwinski sipped his coffee and ate a whole cookie. He sipped more coffee.

"Detective?"

"So you think this Penelope is an industrial spy?"

"A freelance one who'll do pretty much anything for a buck."

Czerwinski smiled. "You don't like her much."

"So what do you think of my ideas?"

"It isn't the most unlikely pile of bullshit I've ever stepped in."

He smiled back. "High praise indeed."

Czerwinski said, "I still haven't tracked down that son, Billy Stanko. Which makes me believe that his mother is a lawbreaker. That and the fact that her work history is sketchy and probably bogus, and she travels outside the country a lot. Anyway, I have more now than just your gut feeling."

"Did you go to her house?"

"Yeah. It was obvious nobody's been there for weeks or maybe months. Not a single piece of paper; not even junk mail."

"Have you talked to Martin?"

"The weird barista guy? Yes." He opened a notebook. "And Martin Abraham Van Buren swears he hasn't seen Billy in over a week."

"Wait. Martin's name is Martin Van Buren."

"Yeah?"

"Nothing. I just never knew. So can you triangulate on Billy's phone or loose a fleet of sniffer drones to home in on Billy's DNA?"

"No! I took Martin's phone, and the calls from Stanko were made on burner phones. A different one each time. So he's obviously hiding. But I checked him out, and he really is a mathematician."

"Right. I know that. He did a paper last year: 'An Analysis of Geometric Structures on Differentiable Manifolds.' I have no idea what that means but I remember the title. So Billy is hiding so you can't find him?"

Czerwinski shrugged and polished off the last cookie.

"He's afraid he'll have to give up info about Penelope."

"Maybe." Czerwinski was staring at him. "So any ideas about finding her or this 'rich uncle' or even Billy Stanko?"

"Nope. Not yet."

Czerwinski continued to stare. "Got a license for that?"

He smiled his very best smile. "For what?"

"For the bulge under your jacket?"

"Yes." Well, he had a license for the gun but not a license to carry.

Czerwinski shook his head, but he didn't say anything or disarm him then and there.

He said, "There is one thing." Czerwinski raised an eyebrow. "Could you check on some people?"

"I could."

"Right. Well, they may have nothing to do with Phillip's murder or they could."

Czerwinski looked skeptical and long suffering. "Names."

"Ute Wetzig and Annika Graf. They may have been born in Niederkrüchten, Germany." He had found Dortmund on a map and searched the environs until he found a town that looked like it might be Needer Kruk Ten. He spelled the city name. "And the 'u' has two dots which is called an umlaut. It's on the border with the Netherlands."

"And why am I doing this?"

"A hunch." Well, it was. "And while you're checking: Bruno Tuers, U.S. Navy commander, retired."

Czerwinski shook his head, but he wrote down the information. "Okay. I could rattle Oxley's cage again? Demand whatever they have on Phillip and his accomplice. Who might be Penelope."

"It couldn't hurt."

Czerwinski got to his feet and smiled. He really wasn't unattractive.

"There's one other mystery."

"And what is that, Detective?"

"I can't figure out why I'm still on the case. I know I'm working hard at this and following every lead...no matter how bizarre...but that shouldn't matter to a shark like Gibson."

He shook his head, and Czerwinski slouched to the elevator.

He turned off his computer, brushed cookie crumbs off his desk, and put Carla's chair back precisely where it had been.

Why hadn't Reed insisted on somebody more senior?

He rode down to the lobby in time to spot Chatterjee walking out to a car and talking to the driver, who happened to be a pretty girl with blonde hair.

Chatterjee saw him looking. He leaped into the car, and they shot off before he could get near.

What was young Dhruva up too?

He would replace his cookies and grill him on Monday.

He went home.

Friday
8:00 am

He wanted to check on Aunt Flo, but he decided that he should go to work for a few hours first.

On a Friday.

He usually worked four, 10 hour days, more or less, and his Fridays were sacrosanct. But that was when Cory was home, and they would be spending the weekend in Cory's condo in D.C.

Jennifer had walked by his cubicle and checked to see what he was working on. She had fixed him with a perplexed glare but made no comment.

So he was working away, and Baldacci and Carla were late as was Chatterjee.

The elevator dinged, and Chatterjee stomped out in boots that weighed half as much as he did. He froze for a second when he spotted Gabe Bergeron at his desk.

He smiled. He held up a bag of cookies which Chatterjee snagged as he walked past.

He let him get to his cubicle. "Who was the blonde?"

The cubicle dwellers turned toward young Dhruva like they were flowers, and he was the life-giving sun.

Young Dhruva ignored him. Which was always a mistake.

But before he could follow up, Baldacci and Carla entered.

Baldacci smiled. "Okay, who are you and what have you done with my buddy Gabe?"

"It's the end of the quarter."

"So?"

"I have work to do."

"On a Friday?"

Carla said, "Cory's off on some undercover mission."

Harry said, "Right. So you won't be going to the condo."

"No."

He went back to work, ignoring Baldacci and Chatterjee. He wanted to get out of the office before Jennifer gave him another project.

His phone chortled; Lydia Gibson. "Shit!"

Baldacci lunged and grabbed his phone and shared the screen with Carla. She said, "Lydia Gibson." She arched an eyebrow.

"Phone."

He had half a mind to toss Harry across the floor. Which might have been reflected in his face since Harry yielded the phone without comment.

"Gabe Bergeron."

Lydia said, "Hello, Gabe. May I come to see you?"

He made a fearsome face and shook a fist at heaven much to the cubicle dwellers delight. He was never going to get on the road at this rate.

"Of course, Lydia."

"I could stop by your office? If that would be convenient?"

He rolled his eyes. "When were you thinking?"

"A half hour? I'm sorry to be such a bother, Gabe."

Which made him feel really bad since her brother had been murdered most foully.

"No, you aren't a bother at all. I'll be here."

He put his phone back into his pocket. He marched down to Chatterjee's cubicle and tore the cookies from his feeble grasp.

Carla said, "Something wrong?"

"It's the end of the quarter, and I need to get out of here."

Baldacci waved the accounting piffle aside. "Do you know who did it yet?"

"No."

Carla said, "Have you found out anything? Have you talked to the ex-wives?"

He may have glared at her before he thought better of it. "I don't want to talk about it."

Baldacci said, "Do you at least have a suspect?"

"No."

They shook their heads at his abject failure.

Baldacci said, "So is Cousin Lydia paying you?"

He counted to ten. And then he counted to twenty. He smiled. "I don't want to talk about it, but if you leave me alone, Harry, I'll tell you when I do know something."

Baldacci patted him on the back. "Okay, Gabe. But you better hurry up, or she's going to fire your sorry ass."

He didn't get a chance to reply because Lydia arrived. She stepped out of the elevator, blonde hair, blue eyes, oval face all as perfect as perfect could get. And she was wearing a white linen suit belted at the waist. Her bag and shoes were a matching pale yellow. Which color the sisters appeared to favor.

Dana escorted her to the conference room unbidden; Dana would have vacuumed the chairs and polished the table if she'd had time.

Dana exited the conference room backwards still smiling at Lydia. Dana was wearing an ankle length skirt, a blouse, a sweater, and a scarf, all in shades of a bilious green. She was thus attired in July because she claimed the air conditioning was too cold.

Dana whispered to him. "Don't lose this one, Bergeron. She's loaded." Which showed more judgment than he thought Dana possessed.

He got coffee from the breakroom to serve with Chatterjee's cookies and joined Lydia.

She smiled at him. "Is this a bad time, Gabe?"

"Not at all."

"I don't want to pressure you, Gabe...."

"No, I understand. You want to know what happened to Phillip."

And he told her what he had been told and the castles he had built from such insubstantial bricks.

"A rich uncle? But there is no one, Gabe. Dad was an only child."

"I know. I think Phillip was making some kind of joke, but I don't get it."

She shook her head. "No, I never got his jokes." She sipped her coffee.

He had talked to most of the people in Phillip's life except for his father, Jonathan. He knew Jonathan was ill, but he didn't know more than that.

"Would your father know what Phillip meant?"

Lydia shook her head. "I'm sure he wouldn't, and I'd rather you didn't bother him. He was so upset when I told him about Phillip's death."

"Right. I understand."

Lydia said, "But what about this woman? This Penelope?"

"I haven't found her yet, but I will."

"Camille thought she took advantage of Phillip? I'm surprised he didn't tell her more. They were always close."

Lydia sat there for a moment. "Is there anything I can do? Or Reed?"

"No. Well, there is one thing. Does he have any contacts at the FBI?"

"I'm sure he does."

"I'd like to find Monroe."

"And you think the FBI knows who he is?"

"I think they know more than they're telling me. Or Cory."

"Then I'll ask Reed to try again. He's in Boston, but I'll call him."

"And you think he'll talk to his contacts?"

"I'm sure he will...after I make it clear how important it is to me."

She looked just as serene as ever, but he was pretty sure she suspected that her husband was only pretending to help her find out what had happened to Phillip.

He had been thinking about Czerwinski's comment. And it seemed that a lack of commitment to finding Phillip's killer was the most obvious reason that the all-powerful Reed Gibson Esquire hadn't gotten junior detective Czerwinski replaced.

But why was the effort half-hearted? Because he wanted to

protect Lydia?

Or because he was involved in some way with Phillip's death? Not that he had strung up poor Phillip himself. But had he arranged for it to be done?

It was a puzzlement.

He realized Lydia was staring at him. "Sorry. I was lost in thought."

She smiled. "I want to know what happened, Gabe. No matter who was behind it."

So she suspected Reed? Just a tiny bit?

She rose to her feet and departed.

He came out of the conference room making a beeline for his cubicle; he might still manage to leave before noon. Hearne was just standing there with a slight smile on his face, and he had to circle round him.

He was on the road bound for Snow Hill when he thought of calling Max Nagy. Max could be persuaded to give him more data about Reed.

But Max was gone for the day.

Monday. He would call him first thing Monday.

Friday
3:00 pm

He had crossed the entire length of Delaware, reached the Salisbury Bypass, and turned onto MD Route 12. The turnoff onto Nassawango Road was just ahead.

But he spotted Ute's black van coming from Aunt Flo's house, and she made a right. He may have followed her.

He wasn't sure why, or what he expected to learn. There was one car between them, but it was a big SUV so maybe she wouldn't spot his very yellow Jeep behind her.

He crossed the bridge over the Pocomoke River and entered Snow Hill. The city could claim that it had two thousand souls and was the county seat of Worcester County, Maryland, but neither fact was a good excuse for this visit.

Ute's van made a right onto West Market Street heading past the courthouse. The SUV went straight.

He pulled over and counted to ten before making the right. He looked at the courthouse where Danilo had gotten his marriage license and had just escaped being run down promptly thereafter. Escaped because he had been at Danilo's side, and his reflexes were cat-like. Sometimes. Ah, sweet memories.

He saw Ute's van ahead. She made a left.

He poked along until he came to the intersection. No Ute in sight. He turned left.

This part of Snow Hill was laid out in a slightly irregular grid pattern and was all residential. He cruised along at a robust fifteen mph on the narrow, tree-lined streets.

He went through a couple of intersections before he spotted Ute's van parked on a cross street. He continued through the intersection and managed to do a u-turn.

Ute was parked in front of a small house on Poplar Street. He couldn't drive by since there was no earthly reason for him to be on Poplar Street. Well, he could claim he'd gotten lost. His sense of direction was renown in a negative way; infamous? But still.

He stopped at a grocery store and bought a bag of licorice sticks just to have an excuse for detouring into Snow Hill.

And then he noticed he needed gas.

So he took care of that.

And then he drove to Aunt Flo's. He parked and strode toward the front door like a man who had not been spying on a couple of women who might have souls totally immaculate.

The grounds were thick with strangers. They were sitting under his oak tree and lolling on his dock and generally taking up his space. Well, it was Aunt Flo's space. And they were paying for the privilege. But still.

And not all of them were strangers; he spotted Bruno Tuers under his oak tree. Why was he back? Or had he never left?

He glowered at them all and entered the house.

"Aunt Flo?"

The door to her new parlor was open. "In here, Gabriel."

He bounced in. "Hi! How are you?"

She smiled at him. Juju had been stretched out beside her having a nice nap, but she was girding herself to run and hide.

He sat next to Aunt Flo. Juju was still trying to decide who he was. She was not the sharpest cat in the litter and would need lessons on batting a ball of yarn.

"It's me, Juju." He rubbed her and scratched her eye ridges. She relaxed, and the purring commenced.

Aunt Flo was looking at him. "I'm fine, Gabriel. Is anything wrong?"

He smiled his very best, non-sneaky smile. "Nope. Everything's excellent. Well, I haven't heard from Cory for over two weeks, and I have no idea what Phillip was up to before he was killed. But other than that. How's business?"

Aunt Flo was still looking at him funny. "Business is booming." She smiled. "Ute is quite happy."

"How can you tell?"

"She isn't as dour as you make her out to be, Dear."

She was. "If you say so."

"So Cory doesn't know you were drugged?"

He frowned. "Cory doesn't know anything. Not even that a Phillip Bergeron existed."

"He won't be happy with you, Gabriel."

"I know. I could call Danielle, but if Cory knew, he might want to come home."

Aunt Flo nodded. "And Kirill?"

He smiled at her. "Right, Kirill. I need some coffee. Do you want some? Or some tea? Has Ezmeralda baked any cookies? I'll just run down to the kitchen and see."

Aunt Flo smiled at him but didn't say a word.

He made tea and found a whole container of shortbread cookies that, upon sampling, melted in the mouth.

He returned to the parlor with a tray.

"Thank you, Gabriel." Aunt Flo had her phone in her hand. "I've just spoken to Valentina."

"I can explain."

Aunt Flo said, "I'm glad to hear it, Dear. Why is Kirill at his mother's house?"

"Well, he lost his job and his apartment...."

He stopped; Aunt Flo was not amused.

"Okay. He was with me for five days...one hundred twenty hours. He was drunk, hungover, unconscious, or cavorting with Naked Nina of the Red Hair for at least a hundred of those hours...maybe a hundred and ten."

"Gabriel."

"No, he was, Aunt Flo. I'm not exaggerating. He went with me to talk to Christina, and that was the only time he actually had my back."

"Christina, Dear?"

"Phillip's most recent ex-wife."

Aunt Flo smiled. "And Naked Nina?"

170

"Kirill found her, or she found him in a bar. Kirill brought her to my apartment. They had sex on Cory's weight bench! In my living room! But before that, she mistook me for Kirill...it was dark...and climbed into my bed!"

"Naked?"

"Hence the name."

She giggle-cackled. "Let me call Ezmeralda."

And in the fullness of time...well, he finished a cup of tea and three shortbread cookies...Ezmeralda joined them in the parlor.

She looked him over. "How are you, Gabriel?"

"Fine. Never better."

She hugged him. Which wasn't a first, but he could count the times on the digits of a three-toed sloth.

Aunt Flo said, "Tell Ezmeralda about Nina."

It occurred to him that he had promised that he wouldn't tell about Kirill's non-performance as a bodyguard. Shit. He had a big mouth.

"Go ahead, Gabriel. She knows that Kirill is at his mother's house."

So he told her about the debauchery of one Kirill Ochoa while downplaying the drunkenness and bodyguard ineptitude.

He had expected outrage, but it appeared she was trying to contain the giggles rather than righteous fury.

"And she climbed into my bed, Ezmeralda. And I'm not a prude, but I had to ban her from my apartment."

Ezmeralda nodded, face as red as your proverbial beet.

"And even if I could have dealt with her, I was afraid Greg would show up."

Aunt Flo said, "Greg?"

"The husband or paramour of Naked Nina. Kirill didn't seem worried, but still."

And they gave up pretending to be proper old ladies and laughed and laughed.

Which was good. They couldn't be worried about him while rolling on the floor...or on the sofa in this case. Juju looked put out and jumped down.

But when decorum had been somewhat restored, he

repeated everything he had been told about Phillip and outlined his working hypotheses.

Ezmeralda said, "So this 'rich uncle' didn't like being blackmailed? But you have no idea who that might be?"

"In a nutshell."

Aunt Flo said, "And Czerwinski can't find Penelope? Or Monroe?"

"Nope and nope."

She nodded. "I would make two suggestions, Gabriel. If you're going to continue this?"

"I am."

"Then find Billy. He should be easier to locate than Penelope. Talk to Martin. And I think you told me that Billy had a boyfriend?"

"Yeah. Snow White. He came to Uwe Bornheimer's funeral with Billy. I haven't spotted him since then, but he might still be around. And the second suggestion, Ms. Barnes?"

"Monroe specifically mentioned Andrew Bergeron. I don't think you'll find Monroe unless he wants to be found, but there's someone else who might know about Andrew: Jonathan Bergeron."

"Right. I've been wanting to meet him, but he's ill."

Aunt Flo said, "Yes, Camille said he wasn't well, but what does that mean? You could press Lydia or Camille about seeing Jonathan." She finished her tea. "I wouldn't mind talking to him myself."

"About Andrew and Natalie?"

"And my mother. About anything he might remember, Gabriel."

"Of course. I'll let you know if I am allowed to see him."

Ezmeralda said, "What about Kirill?"

He made a face; he really didn't want Kirill back at his apartment.

Ezmeralda said, "Danilo could talk to him?"

"No, I don't think that would help. He needs a job if he's going to stop unraveling."

Ezmeralda nodded.

And they left the matter of having someone to stay with him up in the air.

He ran up the stairs. The second floor was crawling with strangers. A couple, giddy with joie de vivre and bonhomie, came out of the master bedroom.

They smiled at him, and he smiled back, but in his heart of hearts, he knew that the master bedroom was not for them.

And he blamed Ute. Well, Annika too, but not so much. Ute was the mistress of his discontent.

He trudged up to the third floor and dropped his bag in the turret bedroom. He threw himself on the bed and tried to forget about all the "guests."

He was in that twilight stage between waking and sleep when his phone chimed.

He couldn't identify the sound for a while, and then he managed to grab his phone.

"Bergeron."

"I did it, but I don't see how it's connected to this stupid, freaking case."

"Czerwinski?"

"Who else? Do you want to hear this or not?"

"Sure." He had no idea.

"Ralph Bruno Tuers. Fifty-two years old. Retired from the navy two years ago. Has a house in Norfolk, Virginia. Spotless record. In the navy and out. Divorced. One kid."

"Right. Good."

"And the two Germans...German-Americans. Came to the U.S. almost six years ago. Lived in New York City for three years. Naturalized citizens. One is forty-three and the other's forty-two. No indication of spouses or children. Address in Snow Hill, Maryland."

"Poplar Street? For both of them?"

"Yeah."

"Okay. Anything hinky?"

Czerwinski made a snorting sound. "Hinky? Everything's been hinky since I met you, Bergeron."

"This is not my fault, Czerwinski. Not even a little bit. So don't go there."

Czerwinski said, "Whatever. There's one thing."

He counted to ten really fast. "Which is?"

"They weren't born in this Needer Kruk Ten place."

"No? So where? Dortmund?"

"No. Some place called Chemnitz. Wherever the Hell that is. So is that everything I can do for you, Bergeron?"

"Thank you, Detective."

"Because if there's something else I can put my weekend on hold and jump on it double quick."

"No, that won't be necessary, Detective Czerwinski. What is your first name by the way?"

But all he got was the sound of one hand clapping in the ether.

So Bruno was who he said he was. If this guy was Bruno? He should have asked Czerwinski for a photo. Maybe when he was in a better mood?

And how had Ute and Annika gotten from New York City to Snow Hill, Maryland? Was that suspicious?

He sighed and got out of bed. He went downstairs and invited Aunt Flo and Ezmeralda out to dinner at the nearby Cypress Inn.

It held fond memories since he had introduced himself to Cory there. Cory had been wearing a yellow bandanna to corral his red locks. Of course, he had claimed to be a solar panel installer, and was pursuing Aunt Flo in the belief that she was an art thief.

Which she wasn't.

But he and Special Agent Cory Poirier had worked out those little misunderstandings in due course.

Where the Hell was Cory? He would call and leave another message.

He smiled at Aunt Flo and Ezmeralda, and they set off. Danilo had gone off somewhere. Which was okay. Danilo was a dish best served infrequently.

Saturday
10:00 am

He had helped Ezmeralda with breakfast for the "guests." Well, he'd helped deliver it to them. All of them sitting in the formal dining room at the antique table. Smiling.

He hated them all. Well, he didn't really.

Ezmeralda was looking at him. "What's wrong with you?"

"Nothing! What could be wrong?"

She shook her head. She pointed at the dishes piled high which he had collected from the greedy rabble upstairs.

"You want me to wash those?"

She nodded with an aggressive head shake. "Mikhail is with his wife, Marta. For a few days."

"Right. Have you met her?"

She nodded. "Nice."

Which wasn't exactly a ringing endorsement. "What's wrong with her?"

But Ezmeralda was marching for the door. She may have been smiling when she exited.

He loaded the dishwasher. He was bored. He pulled out his phone and looked up Chemnitz.

It seemed that Ute and Annika had not been born near the Dutch border at all but on the Czech border; in what was then called Karl-Marx-Stadt in the *Deutsche Demokratische Republik*.

Which was East Germany.

And the city of Karl-Marx-Stadt had only reverted to its original name of Chemnitz in 1990 after the reunification of

Germany.

So why had Annika fibbed to him? Or had she just not understood?

He did the math, and Ute and Annika had barely been teenagers at reunification, but their parents had been communists? Or just people who had survived as best they could under a communist regime?

Did Aunt Flo know about their past? Which she probably wouldn't mind having been sort of a communist herself for a part of her youth. Or a socialist.

He couldn't ask her. She would want to know why he was investigating her business partners. Shit.

He stopped. He was putting dirty dishes away sans washing. He focused on the task at hand and then went outside. Annika was talking to Bruno Tuers. It looked like they were flirting, but that could be a cover for their nefarious intentions.

He took a deep breath. He was freaking out over nothing.

He needed more data.

It was the Fourth of July, and Ute had organized a picnic for the "guests" with light refreshments and a few fireworks.

But this meant that Ute and Annika would be present at the Barnes B&B all day. And their dark abode would be unguarded.

He looked at his sunflower yellow Jeep. He loved it, but it was not a stealth vehicle.

But Poplar Street was not that far, and Gabe Bergeron was a running fool. Or a foolish runner. In any case, he could jog to their house and see what he could see.

He got his running shoes and jogged down Nassawango Road and across the little bridge. He passed beneath the antique clock on its fancy, cast iron column and into Snow Hill like the wind. Or like one of the Furies bent on vengeance. Not that he had wings or was female. And he had no idea if Ute and Annika had done anything wrong.

He ran easily. He had been shocked to find that he liked running when Cory had first dragooned him into it.

He ran down Market Street and closed in on Ute's house.

He didn't see anyone in the neighborhood as he approached

as swift and silent as a jungle cat.

Ute's house was white clapboard with a simple green, gabled roof. It had two windows on the first floor bracketing a black door. The second story had three identical windows; all had green shutters. A brick chimney popped out of the center of the house.

The small front yard was filled with shrubs and flowers. There was a privacy fence between Ute's yard and the house on the left.

He didn't see any people or cars on the narrow street.

He slowed and ever so casually sprinted across Ute's yard and crouched beside the fence to get a view of the back of the house.

The windows were closed against the heat and humidity; an air conditioner was purring softly from a second story window.

He tried the back door; locked.

He had his wallet, but he wasn't tearing up a credit card trying to finagle the lock. He thought he understood the principle involved, but the door had a second lock which looked more robust than the original one.

He sighed. This was the point when he was supposed to whip out his lock picking tools and gain entry in seconds.

He tried the nearest window which was also locked. He could see the latch mechanism; not that seeing it helped.

But there was a brick on the ground.

He shook his head. He wasn't smashing Ute's window without more to go on. And he didn't have a glass cutter nor had he ever used one. But there was probably a video online.

He peeped into each window trying to stay out of sight of anyone in the surrounding houses.

He didn't see much. Well, furniture. And a kitchen.

But the house was a fortress to an intruder like Gabe Bergeron. He sighed again.

The last window he peeped into was in the living room. Photos and memorabilia were aligned with Prussian precision in columns and rows on a table next to the window.

He saw a slightly faded photo of a dark-haired, young

woman in a pink, ruffled and beaded, skating costume. She was wearing a pair of white skates and a tiara, and gliding across the ice with an out-of-focus crowd behind her.

Next to it, a posed photo of the same young woman in the same costume had a signature in blue ink.

A third photo of the same woman had her smiling and displaying a medal hanging around her neck.

There were other framed medals and stuff he couldn't quite make out. He snapped photos of everything and then returned to the street and jogged away at a steady, non-suspicious pace.

He took an indirect route away from Poplar Street. He passed Snow Hill High School which he'd attended after Aunt Flo had taken him in.

He had mostly good memories of the place. He hadn't gone to the tenth year reunion, but the twentieth was on the horizon. He should probably go?

He was across the bridge to Nassawango Road and was almost home. With any luck, no one had seen him or reported him to the police. He had just been jogging. That was his story, and he was sticking to it.

He ran upstairs, showered, and then may have taken a nap before creeping downstairs. Aunt Flo was outside mingling with the "guests" and her parlor was empty. Her computer was on.

He transferred the photos to her computer.

And thanks to Ute's, or probably Annika's spotless windows, he could see lots of details. He couldn't make out the signature on the photo of the skater, but he could read the medals.

Well, he couldn't but not because they were blurry. The shiny gold one with the red ribbon was inscribed with "*Kinder und Jugendspartakiaden Karl-Marx-Stadt*" and had a shield with a lion and vertical stripes.

The other medal was aquamarine with gold trim and lettering. A rectangle with "Karl-Marx-Stadt" and "1980" was linked to a circle with "*DELV*" in the center and "*DDR Meisterschaft Im Eiskunstlauf*" in a circle.

It was not immediately apparent what the Hell he had photographed.

He consulted the Internet. The *"Kinder"* one was a medal from a children and youth sport's event in Karl-Marx-Stadt. It appeared that a *"Spartakiade"* event had been created to compete with the Olympics by the Russians and adopted by East Germany.

The *"DDR Meisterschaft"* was a championship medal awarded at an East German Ice Skating competition in Karl-Marx-Stadt in 1980.

It took the better part of an hour to figure out that the *"DELV"* was an acronym for the *Deutsche Eislaufverband* or the East German Ice Skating Association.

He sat at Aunt Flo's computer and stared at the screen. What had he learned? That somebody, probably a parent or a sibling of Ute or Annika, had won some ice skating competitions; probably Ute because the young woman in the photos looked a bit like her.

This was hardly a smoking gun which he could take to Aunt Flo. He sighed.

He enlarged the rest of the photos and peered at them. There was a black and white photo of two men standing together in front of a building. They were wearing uniforms. One had his arm over the other's shoulder. They were smiling.

The uniforms had been gray, or maybe green? They had dress shirts and ties and belts with shiny buckles. He couldn't see the shoulder patches.

He had no idea who they were or what organization they'd belonged to, but the East German army was a possibility. Or the police in Karl-Marx-Stadt?

He erased everything off Aunt Flo's computer and went outside. She was reclining on a chaise-lounge beneath the oak tree. A "guest" was chatting with her and sitting on the other chaise-lounge.

He wandered around until the "guest" took herself off and then claimed his place on his chaise-lounge.

Aunt Flo smiled at him. "And what have you been up to, Gabriel?"

He had often wondered if Aunt Flo was psychic. "Nothing. I went for a run...to no place in particular. And then I took a shower. So when are the fireworks?"

Aunt Flo was looking at him funny.

She said, "As soon as it gets a bit darker, Dear. Bruno volunteered to set them off. Maybe, you could help him?"

"Sure." Bruno and Annika were sitting on the grass and smiling at one another. Annika looked very happy, over and above the usual smiling.

Bruno's block shape made him look like an Easter Island megalith planted in Aunt Flo's lawn; only happier.

"So does Annika like Bruno?"

Aunt Flo nodded. "And vice-versa. Ezmeralda thinks he's going to pop the question."

"Really?" And how would Ute take that? "Right. I'll go see if Bruno wants some help. With the fireworks."

Aunt Flo smiled.

Bruno was polite enough to give him some menial tasks; tasks which wouldn't allow him to blow off his fingers no matter how much he screwed up. He thought Bruno had used larger and far more deadly fireworks in his day.

And he didn't ask Bruno if he was going to propose to Annika. He wasn't that nosy.

And the fireworks were nice, and he forgot to be suspicious of the immediate world in the rockets' red glare.

Sunday
10:00 am

He had gotten up, showered, and dressed in time to help Ezmeralda with breakfast.

He finished a waffle and started on the dishes without being asked, but he could feel her eyes on him.

"What?"

"Nothing."

He looked over his shoulder. "No, something's up?"

She said, "You know that Florence loves having the house filled with people again?"

"She does?"

Ezmeralda nodded and marched out the door.

She was a woman of few words. He loaded the dishwasher, and then sat and waited for it to finish.

He was being selfish and self-centered and a piss-poor nephew. But he could do better. He would do better.

He marched to the parlor and knocked on the door. "Aunt Flo?"

"Come in, Gabriel."

She was reading; she put a marker in her book.

"I just wanted to say that I'm happy about the bed and breakfast. I think it's a wonderful idea, and I'm sure it's going to be a rousing success, financially and in every other way."

Aunt Flo was staring at him. "Are you sure, Dear?"

"Very. Absolutely." He gave her his very best, most sincere smile. "I may have been slow to get onboard, but I am now. One hundred percent."

"I'm glad to hear that, Dear." Her silver eyes were focused on him. "Did you use my computer, Gabriel?"

Shit. "I did. I hope that's okay?"

"Of course, Dear."

She kept staring at him, but he was going to be strong and not break. He could do this. He had faced down contract killers and psychopaths, and he had erased everything.

"What do you know about Ute's past, Aunt Flo?"

Aunt Flo smiled. "Ute is a very private person, Gabriel, and she wouldn't want me telling tales."

"So you do know something?"

"If you have questions, you should ask her, Dear."

"Okay. What about Annika?"

"The answer is the same."

"Right." He sat there, and Juju got into his lap, turned three times and settled in for a nap. He rubbed her until the purring commenced.

"Are you lonely, Aunt Flo?"

"Sometimes, Dear."

"Right. I have to go back to Philly."

She took his hand and patted it. "Of course, you do. Don't give that a thought, Gabriel. You have your own life there with Cory."

"When he's around." He smiled at her. "But I could come more often?"

"I'm always happy to see you, Gabriel."

"Right. And I'm happy to be here." He would come more often, and Cory would come with him. Cory owed him for the days he'd spent at his parent's farm finding all those dead bodies.

"So I'm going to get on the road."

She smiled. "Be safe, and call me when you get there."

"Of course."

"Mikhail will go with you, Gabriel, if you like?"

He shook his head. "I appreciate that, but I'd feel better if he stays here. He is staying here, right?"

"He is."

"Good." He moved Juju off his lap, and hugged Aunt Flo. He got home in good time.

The place smelled funny. Well, not funny so much as funky from Kirill's lack of hygiene and alcohol consumption. And maybe a noxious lingering of Naked Nina's perfume?

He opened the windows even though it was ninety in the shade and cleaned the place until it smelled like a bleach factory operating deep in a pine forest.

Monday
10:00 am

He called Max Nagy.

"Hi, Max."

"Bergeron? I'm too busy to talk. Unless you're in jail?"

He laughed. "No, Max, I'm not in jail. Not even close to being arrested and locked away...I even made a new friend on the police force...well, Czerwinski isn't a friend yet, but I have high...."

"Bergeron."

"Right. You may recall that we spoke about Reed Gibson?"

Max paused. "Where is this going, Bergeron?"

"I was just wondering if you've heard anything about Reed?"

"Like what?"

"That he's having difficulties? Or that he hated his brother-in-law? I thought with you being a lawyer and all like Reed."

"Saying that I'm a lawyer like Reed is like saying that you're an accountant like the chairman of the Federal Reserve."

"Right, but you have your ear to the ground, and your finger on the pulse...."

"I don't know why I take your calls. What kind of difficulties?"

"Any kind. Financial? Legal? Spiritual? Ethical? Epistemological?"

"Do you know something?"

"Nope. But I suspect a great many things."

Max laughed. "I'm hanging up now. Don't call me back."

"But you'll call me if you hear something?"

"Maybe."

And Max was gone. Carla was looking at him. "What?"

She shook her head. "Have you ever had a head CT? Or a MRI?"

"I don't know? Probably?"

She turned back to her work. "I bet you broke the machine."

"Did not."

He went to visit with Jennifer. "Hi, there. That's a ravishing pants suit; crimson is your color."

She was twirling a lock of brown hair round and round her finger as she made stabbing motions at her keyboard. "It isn't crimson, Bergeron. What do you want?"

"I'm going to be out of the office until after lunch."

"And you're telling me instead of sneaking out because?"

"I'm hurt, Jennifer, and this is legit. I need to check up on CoffeeXtra. Billy Stanko is AWOL, Martin Van Buren is in charge, and I fear for the solvency of the enterprise."

Jennifer was still focused on her computer screen, but she smiled. "Who the Hell is Martin Van Buren? And do not tell me he was president of the United States."

"Well, he was; the eighth. I looked him up. But I digress. This Martin is a barista with the brain power of a fungus, albeit a crafty fungus."

She finally looked up at him. "Okay. I guess."

She kept staring. If she had detected the bulge of the Glock under his jacket, he was going to lie and run. Or run and lie later.

"Are you okay?"

"Sure. Excellent."

She shook her head. "Is Cory back yet?"

"Nope."

"Are you planning on doing anything incredibly stupid?"

"I am not." He smiled. "I should go."

"Go. But come back in one piece."

"Yes, Jennifer."

So he walked into CoffeeXtra with his briefcase in hand

and fixed Martin with a terrible glare.

Well, Martin failed to notice the terrible glare and gave him a double-wide smile. "Hi, Gabe. The usual?"

"No. I'm here on business. Is the office unlocked?"

Martin shook his head, smiled again, and came around the counter. He had a ring of keys attached to a wide leather belt that was long enough to almost wrap twice around his wasp waist.

Martin unlocked the door and waved him in. "Billy will be relieved that you're checking things."

He smiled at Martin. "If you talk to him, tell him I have some papers for him to sign."

But Martin didn't even hesitate. "He calls me. I don't have his number."

"Right." Martin was indeed crafty.

He had been sick over Billy's carpet, but somebody had cleaned up. He turned on Billy's computer and logged in and began to look things over. "Any invoices or payments that haven't been entered?"

Martin shook his head. "No, I've been keeping up with those, but could you look at the taxes?"

"Sure. No problem. So how was Billy the last time he called you?"

"Tired. And worried about Penelope. And worried about you, Dude. About you being drugged."

"Tell him I'm fine."

Martin nodded. "But it's freaking crazy. And Billy wants to come home."

"Why doesn't he?"

Martin stopped smiling. "Because the detective will arrest him, Dude!"

"No, Czerwinski won't arrest him. Billy just has to cooperate and tell the detective where Penelope is."

"But he doesn't know, Dude. Honest."

"How do you know that, Martin?"

"Because Billy's a good guy, and I believe him."

And then Martin's girlfriends, Selena and Astrid came out of the kitchen.

The tall one had black spiky hair like Martin's. "Ask him about the taxes."

Martin smiled at her. "I did."

The blonde looked just as dim as Martin, but in her case, appearances weren't deceiving. She smiled coyly. "Do you want me to take over the counter, Martin?"

He knew that one of them was Astrid and one was Selena. He looked at Martin. "Are they 'working' here now?"

Martin nodded. Black Spiky glared at him. Coy Blonde smiled looking oblivious.

He shook his head. "Did they fill out the paperwork?"

"Sure, Gabe. It's in the desk drawer."

"Does Billy know they're 'working' here?" He may have emphasized the "working" a bit more.

Black Spiky growled; Coy Blonde was still looking blank but the vacuity was tinged with sadness now.

Martin turned and ushered his inamoratas back into the kitchen and closed the door.

Martin said, "They're hard workers, Gabe. Really. And I need them...with Billy gone."

He tried not to snort. "Okay, Give me an hour to check things."

"Sure, Gabe."

And Martin brought him coffee and banana bread unbidden. He smelled the coffee carefully before sipping but it seemed fine. He should get Coy Blonde to taste it, but that would be like abusing a hamster.

It didn't take long, because everything was organized, and all the entries were correct. He hated to admit it, but Martin was doing a good job; probably better than Billy himself.

He was finishing a revised tax payment schedule when Martin popped in. He smiled at Martin. "Everything looks good. You're doing an excellent job."

"Thanks, Gabe. I'm trying to hold it together for Billy."

"Well, you're doing fine."

He leaned back in Billy's chair. "So is Billy still seeing that guy? I can't remember his name but he had snow-white hair?"

Martin smiled but for a second the smile wasn't so cheerful. "No. I think they broke up."

Right. Sure they did. "Well, thanks, Martin. And tell Billy, whenever he contacts you that I have some forms for him to sign. Pronto."

Martin smiled. "Roger that. Pronto."

He left Billy's office and sauntered past the counter where Coy Blonde was standing there staring out the windows.

He stood in front of her until her eyes focused. "Hi, there. You know who I am? Right?"

"Sure! Gabe Bergeron. The accountant." She leaned over and whispered, "Astrid doesn't like you."

So, assuming she knew her own name, this had to be Selena. She wasn't very tall, and her boobs were polishing the counter.

"I'm sorry to hear that. I think she's swell."

Selena smiled the smile of the perpetually unaware. "I do too!"

"So, Selena, remember Billy's boyfriend? The young guy with the white hair?"

"Sure! Jannik is a cutie."

"Right, Jannik. So what was Jannik's last name? It's on the tip of my tongue."

Selena nodded. "I hate when I can't remember stuff." She smiled and stood there.

"So what was his last name?"

"Jannick's?"

"Yes." He was going to fracture his jaw if he gritted his teeth any harder.

She pondered. "I don't know. Let me ask Astrid."

And she disappeared into the kitchen. He figured that Martin or Astrid would realize he was fishing and come out to send him on his way, but Selena popped back.

She smiled. "Engel. Astrid says it means 'angel' in German."

"Thank you, Selena! You've been super helpful."

She was still beaming as he walked out.

Monday
3:00 pm

You would think that it would be easy to find a guy with a name like Jannik Engel.

It was beyond the abilities of Gabe Bergeron.

He had tried Yannik and Yannick and Engle. No such person in Pennsylvania. Or Delaware. Or New Jersey.

He was about to call Czerwinski and beg him to find the guy when his phone rang.

It was CoffeeXtra. Martin said, "Hi, Gabe."

"Martin."

"About those papers that need Billy's signature."

"I have them right here." Well, he could manufacture some easily enough.

"So why don't I come get them so they'll be here when Billy comes back?"

"Fine."

"Really? Okay, I'll be right there."

And he scrambled to make photocopies of documents which Billy had already signed but with his signature artfully covered.

And Martin trotted out of the elevator and headed for him.

He handed over the ersatz documents. "No big hurry, Martin, but in the next few weeks."

Martin was smiling at Carla, and Carla was smiling back.

He studied Martin from the spiky tips of his hair to his hollow chest to his scrawny legs to the soles of his worn jogging shoes. He didn't see it.

Baldacci was glaring at Martin now.

"Thanks for coming, Martin."

More smiling at Carla. He could see her resistance melting away. Soon it would be Selena and Astrid and Carla following Martin around.

Baldacci got to his feet, and as Martin scurried away, the glow slowly faded from Carla's face.

Baldacci said, "Carla!"

She turned and focused. "What's your problem, Baldacci?"

"I don't have a problem! What's with the smiling at the shrimp?"

"Smiling?" She glared at poor Harry. "I wasn't smiling."

Martin's power was so overwhelming that the victim didn't even realize it was happening.

He stopped marveling and called Czerwinski from the breakroom.

He got a grunt. "Detective?"

"What now, Bergeron? I'm busy."

"I have another name."

"Not happening."

"Jannik Engel."

"Another German. You got some kind of vendetta against Germans?"

"Not at all. I love Germans. Well, not Ute, but all the rest of them."

"Go away, and don't call me again."

"I thought you might react like this so I have an alternative."

Czerwinski was silent so long he was sure he'd lost the connection. "Tell me. In ten words or less."

"Billy Stanko is coming to CoffeeXtra tonight."

"Sure about that?"

"Mostly. And you can stake out the place and catch him. And then you can get DNA and prove that his mother was doing the nasty with Phillip. And probably find her too."

"No."

"Why not?"

"There's no way I'd get authorization for the overtime, Bergeron. And don't even think about asking me to do it on my own time, because I'm up to my eyeballs in crime here."

"Right. I'm sorry to hear that you're overworked."

"Is that sarcasm I hear?"

"Absolutely not!" Well, it was. "Not really."

"Don't call me again." Czerwinski sighed. "Unless you actually find this Stanko woman."

He put his phone in his pocket and looked up. Baldacci was smiling at him.

"What?"

"You and me, Bergeron."

He shook his head on general principles. "You and me what?"

"We stake out CoffeeXtra."

He shook his head some more. "No. And Carla won't let you do it anyway."

Which was as close to an absolute certainty as it got in this life.

But Carla had listened to Harry and said, "Only if I come along." She was excited.

"What?"

"Somebody has to keep you two from getting arrested or shot or kidnapped."

He wanted to point out that he had the Glock, and it was his case. He wasn't sure he wanted to stake out CoffeeXtra, but the idea seemed to have taken on a life of it's own.

Carla said, "We can't use your Jeep, Gabe."

"Right. It does stand out, but I don't know if I want...."

Carla looked at Baldacci. "And my car is in the shop."

Baldacci shook his head. "We aren't using my baby."

"It's just a car, Harry."

He looked from Harry to Carla. "Why doesn't he want to use his car?"

Carla just frowned as she turned around. "Chatterjee! Front and center."

Chatterjee trotted over looking apprehensive. "What is it, Carla?"

"We need you to go to CoffeeXtra. Stay there until it closes. Call if you see Billy Stanko."

"No way! I have plans."

He smiled at Chatterjee. "Do these plans have anything to do with the blonde?"

Chatterjee shook his head. "No, and that's none of your business, Bergeron. No. I can't do it. Sorry."

And he stomped off.

Carla was amazed that Chatterjee dared thwart her authority but before she could wreak havoc, Hearne raised his hand.

Carla said, "What?"

"I could do it. If you're buying?"

Hearne looked like nothing so much as a gray, fuzzy teddy bear. With vacant, blue glass eyes.

Carla considered. "Bergeron?"

"I don't know? Hearne, do you even know who Billy Stanko is?"

Hearne nodded happily. "Sure. He owns the place. Tall, skinny, hairy. Nice suits. Sometimes."

He looked back at Carla. She shrugged. "Okay. All you have to do is camp out at one of the tables so you can see down the hall past the bathrooms to the office door. Can you do that?"

"Sure." He held out a pudgy hand.

He fished a ten out of his wallet, but Hearne shook his fuzzy head slowly. He selected a twenty.

Hearne grabbed the twenty and the ten and smiled.

"Okay. If you see Billy Stanko, you call me. Right away. You do have a cellphone?"

Hearne pulled an antique flip phone out of the pocket of his baggy gray pants. He gave Hearne his number.

Carla got in Hearne's face. "You sit. You call Gabe if you see Billy Stanko. Got it?"

Hearne nodded with a trace of a smile on his gray, wrinkled face. "Sure, Carla."

He said, "Do you know why we want you to do this,

Hearne?"

"Something about the detective who was here? Doesn't matter."

And Hearne slouched off.

Carla said, "Not my first choice for a spy."

"Nope. But on the plus side, who would ever suspect him? So the place closes at 9:30...."

Carla said, "We'll pick you up at your place, Bergeron, before that."

"Right. Okay."

So he left and headed for his Jeep. He may have slipped past CoffeeXtra and peered through the glass. .

Hearne was positioned correctly and had settled in with a muffin and a book and was looking as suspicious as a throw pillow.

He drove home. He knew nothing about Hearne; not even his first name. And they had worked in the same office for five years. He felt bad about that for a bit.

He would engage Hearne in conversation at his earliest convenience.

Monday
9:00 pm

He was at his window when he got Carla's call.
"We're outside. Get down here, Bergeron."
"Yes, Carla."

So he ran down the stairs and shot out into the humid, night air. A black Mustang was idling throatily before him. It was the sound that Juju might make if she were the size of a Brontosaurus.

Baldacci rolled down the window. "Get in, Bergeron."

He smiled. "How long have you had this, Harry?"

Baldacci glanced nervously at Carla. "A while."

He could do a better inspection in full sunlight, but he did his best.

It was midnight black, Stygian black, but with a red outline around the front grille, a red slash over the windshield, a red air foil, and wheels with five, red double-spokes.

And lastly, a red artistic splash across the driver's door with "BOSS 302" printed in black. It was a little less obvious than his yellow Jeep but not by much.

He smiled at Baldacci again and leaned in. "Very nice. Very powerful...vigorous...one might even say manly."

"Get the Hell in the car or I'm leaving your ass, Bergeron."

So he did. Well, Carla had to get out and let him slip into the backseat. The front bucket seats appeared luxurious and comfy; the back seat not so much.

But he ignored his claustrophobia and leaned over Baldacci's shoulder. "So this is nice. What happened to the red

Lexus?"

Baldacci engaged the warp drive, and they shot down Arch Street as if they were being sucked into a Black Hole.

He was flung back, but he grabbed Baldacci's seat and pulled himself forward.

He took note of the instrument panel which had way more gauges than could possibly be necessary, and a gear shift with reverse and six forward gears. He used two in his Jeep, but Baldacci's right hand was moving like he was knitting a sweater.

"Six gears. Very nice."

"Stop breathing in my ear, Bergeron."

"Sure, Harry." He grabbed hold of Carla's seat. "So when did he get this?"

He thought she was going to ignore him. "Before we got married."

"Right. I see." And he did. "So, Harry, why haven't I seen this vehicle in the parking garage on South 16th?"

"I don't drive this to work."

Carla said, "He takes the bus when I can't lug him around."

"I see. So how fast will it go? Ninety?"

Baldacci snorted. "For your information, the engine has 444 hp and 380 lb·ft of torque."

Which sounded impressive. Well, except for the torque thing which meant nothing to him.

"So car make big vroom-vroom? And is capable of speeds which you will never dare to attempt?"

Baldacci shook his head. "Sit back and don't say another word."

"Yes, Harry. Sorry. It's very pretty."

And it was. "So what year is it?"

"2012. Shut it, Bergeron."

So he did until they got close to CoffeeXtra. "Where are we going to park?"

Carla said, "I found a spot on South 17th Street. It's dark and has a view of the alley behind the place and the side door."

He frowned. He wasn't sure he liked Carla taking over.

Baldacci parked as if he were driving a carton of eggs, and

when he was satisfied that nothing was within a yard of his baby, he shut off the engine.

He said, "I'm going to get out and reconnoiter."

And then Carla opened her door.

And came within a millimeter of raking the door across some rebar sticking out of broken concrete. Carla looked at Baldacci, but he was unaware. She took a deep breath and gave him a sickly smile as he wriggled out of the back seat with the door half open.

He strolled around to Baldacci's window. "You might want to pull up a few feet, Harry."

"Why?"

"It will give us a better view of the place."

CoffeeXtra was just closing, and Hearne was ushered out the side door and started ambling away.

"Hearne. Hearne! Over here."

Hearne ambled his way. "Hi, Gabe."

Which made him feel bad about not knowing Hearne's first name again. "Any sightings?"

"Sightings? Oh, you mean Billy Stanko? Nope."

"Right. Well, thanks. For a job well done."

Hearne held out a twenty. "I wasn't very hungry."

"No. Keep that. You've been here for hours. Wait. Why weren't you hungry?"

Hearne just patted his paunch.

"Okay. I hope you feel better."

Hearne resumed ambling but paused again. "I think Martin got a call from Billy." He held up a little notebook to catch the light. "At 9:12 pm."

"How do you know?"

"Well, Martin said, 'Hi, Billy' and told him about some forms that needed to be signed."

He almost hugged Hearne. "Well done...you."

Hearne smiled and walked away.

He slipped back to the car like a ninja. "So Hearne heard Martin telling Billy about the bogus paperwork he needs to sign."

He could make out Carla's smile. "So the trap is baited."

"Yep. So what is Hearne's first name? And is he sick or something? Is he married?"

Baldacci and Carla turned in their seats to glare at him. Well, he felt sure they were glaring, but their faces were in shadow.

Carla said, "His name is Paul."

Baldacci said, "He has an ulcer. His wife died two years ago."

Carla said, "Her name was Annie, and she was a very nice lady."

Shit. "How did I not know about his wife dying? I'm not that self-centered, Guys. Really."

Baldacci said, "You were at the wedding."

Carla said, "Mrs. Gutierrez...Ezmeralda. And then Garth and Iona were murdered."

"Right. Okay." That made him feel a little better.

They settled in. They had a view of the side door and since the walls were glass, they could even see if anybody came in the front.

But he was betting on the alley.

After six hours scrunched up in the back seat of a Mustang, he didn't care about Billy or Penelope or anybody. Baldacci had run off somewhere and gotten coffee and snacks a few hours ago.

But the coffee only made him have to go to the bathroom.

"I have to get out, Carla."

"Again? You need to have your prostate checked, Bergeron."

Baldacci snickered.

"I do not. Open the door."

She handed him a super size drink cup. "Use this."

"Nope! Not happening."

Baldacci said, "Damn right it's not. What if his aim is off?"

Carla said, "Then you clean the car. As you're going to do as soon as we get home anyway."

Baldacci was shaking his head. "He's already gotten crumbs everywhere, but I draw the line at this."

He gave Carla her cup back. "You don't have to worry, Harry. I'm not going in a cup."

He didn't think he could even in extremis. Not with Carla right there. Or even Baldacci. He had a shy bladder.

"Open the door."

She said, "This is the last time, Bergeron. So make it count."

He went into the alley and did his business; as thoroughly as he could. It would be funny if Billy returned at this particular moment.

He sighed. Martin and Astrid and Selena had left at 10:00 pm, and the traffic had died away. It was almost 4:00 am, and he was done.

He walked back to the Mustang. "I say we call it."

Carla muttered something which sounded like "wimp," but he didn't care.

Baldacci said, "We should stay until dawn?"

"Nope."

And he crawled into the Mustang for the last time.

And crawled out in front of his apartment building. He leaned over. "Thanks, Harry. Thanks, Carla."

Carla said, "I thought he'd come."

"Yeah. I did too." He smiled at Baldacci. "If you want, I'll vacuum your car, Harry?"

"No. Thanks, Gabe, but I'll do it."

And he roared off secure in his masculinity.

Tuesday
5:00 pm

He hadn't mentioned staking out CoffeeXtra again for the entire day, and neither had Carla or Baldacci. They had avoided him as much as was possible, given that they were six feet away.

And now he watched them run for the elevator. A stake-out was no fun at all.

But he wanted to find Penelope Stanko.

He was mulling his options when he felt a presence behind him. "Dana?"

Hearne laughed.

He spun. "Hi, Paul. How's it going? How's the ulcer?"

Hearne sat in Baldacci's chair and scooted over. "I'm okay, Gabe. So you want me at CoffeeXtra?"

"Are you willing to do that? Again?"

Hearne smiled. "Sure. It was fun. I finished my book, but I have a new one. So?"

"I guess so. Yeah, sure. If you're up for it?"

Hearne nodded.

He grabbed his wallet and pulled out a fifty. "Here."

"I'll bring you the change."

"No, you keep whatever you don't spend on coffee."

"No coffee, Gabe." He patted his stomach. "Tea is okay. Sometimes."

"Right."

Hearne got out of the chair. How old was he? Fifty? Sixty?

"So I should be there when they close, but if not, you can

call me. Okay, Paul?"

Hearne nodded. "Will do." And he went back to his cubicle, which was at the far end of the second row but next to a window. Hearne had plants on the sill.

He watched Hearne shuffle out with a book in hand; a thick tome.

He felt funny calling him Paul, but he was getting used to it. He looked up, and Jennifer was staring at him. He smiled and waved. She made a face and went back to work.

And then he called Stan.

Stan was his mechanic, and they had been through a lot together. Stan had kept a yellow Fiesta and a black VW Jetta running until bad men had made that impossible.

He was currently keeping his Jeep purring.

"Stan, it's Gabe. I need to rent a car."

Stan laughed. "What did you do to the Jeep, Bergeron? Is there enough left to fill a teacup?"

"My Jeep is fine."

"Okay?"

"I just need something a little less obtrusive."

Stan was momentarily overcome with hilarity. "There's a story behind this. When do you need it?"

"Tonight?" Stan sometimes worked late. "Is that possible?"

"Get over here right now."

And so he did.

Stan was beneath a pickup. Or so a pair of legs sticking out indicated; legs very like those of the Wicked Witch of the East.

"Stan?"

"Bergeron? Hold on."

Stan was in shorts due to the heat. He rolled out and got to his feet. He was tall and lean. He wiped his face and looked at the Jeep. "Amazing."

"I told you it was fine."

"Yeah, I know. So why do you need to rent a vehicle?"

"My Jeep is yellow, Stan."

"I know that. And you want something that doesn't scream Bergeron?"

"I do."

"But you aren't going to tell me why that is? Okay. I have a 2016 Kia Forte that I might let you have. If it's totaled while in your hands, you've bought it. Are we clear on that?"

"Absolutely. Only fair."

"All right. It's over there."

Stan's greasy finger was pointing at a small, gray, two-door car that whispered anonymity.

"I don't know, Stan. How much?"

"I'm running a special...today only...just for you."

"Right. Does it run okay?"

"It does." Stan smiled. "And it's all I have."

Vehicles of various ages and types packed the lot around Stan's garage. None faded into the background better.

"Okay. I'll take it. Can I leave my Jeep here?"

"Sure, Gabe."

Stan got the keys. "Gabe?"

"Yes, Stan?"

"Take care of yourself."

"I will."

Stan was staring at him. "Are you packing?"

"Nope."

Stan smiled and shook his head. "You do know which end the bullets come out of?"

"I'll have you know that I am now a skilled marksman."

Stan shook his head. "How long do you need the Kia?"

"A couple of days. Maybe a week."

Stan patted his shoulder. "Call me...if you get into something?"

"Right. Thanks, Stan. But I won't."

Stan watched him drive away; Stan was not optimistic about the chances of seeing Gabe Bergeron or the Kia ever again.

Thursday
9:00 pm

He parked the Kia in his spot. Well, it wasn't his, but it felt like it after three nights. He rested his head on the steering wheel and almost fell asleep.

He shook himself. He needed coffee. He peered through the glass walls at the patrons of CoffeeXtra.

Hearne was sitting at the same table as always, just as antsy as a statue of Buddha. He was reading a book. He should ask Hearne what he was reading.

He tried to get comfortable and rolled down the windows. It had cooled off some, but it was too hot to wear a jacket to hide the shoulder holster. He had the Glock on the seat next to him under a newspaper.

He had come to respect the officers who had to stake out a location. The only way he had made himself drive the Kia to South 17th Street again was the knowledge that he could sleep all day Friday.

He watched as CoffeeXtra closed. Astrid held the door for Hearne. They were laughing and joking as he walked out and headed down South 16th Street toward the parking garage.

Hearne had made a friend. Of Astrid. He could understand Selena or Martin.

He sat there in a fugue state, eyes not quite focusing.

He may have jumped six inches straight up when somebody knocked on the roof.

"Shit!"

Hearne smiled at him. "Did I scare you?"

Hearne had circled round the block and come up behind him. Hearne was actually good at this undercover, surveillance shit.

"A little bit." He smiled wearily at Hearne. "So how goes it, Paul? Anything to report?"

Hearne considered as he leaned against the Kia. It was best to let him tell whatever he had to tell at his own pace.

"Martin got a call."

"From Billy?" A definite head shake. He took a deep breath and calmed himself.

"No."

He sucked air into his lungs until they wouldn't hold any more, held it for a ten count, and expelled it

"About Billy?"

Hearne nodded. "Sounded like it. Martin seemed upset...no....more undecided. He took Astrid and Selena into the office and closed the door." Hearne smiled at him. "Not for that."

He smiled at Hearne. "That what, Paul?"

"Well, they don't seem to have threesomes. When one of the girls wants coitus, she grabs Martin, and it's one on one. In the office."

"And you know this how?"

"I have good hearing. For a man of my age."

He shook his head. "So no group coitus? Then what?"

"I got as close to the door as I could."

And Hearne took time out to study the stars...not that you could see stars with the streetlights.

"And Martin was asking them what to do...about something to do with Billy. But that's all I got, Gabe. Sorry."

"No! You are a wonder, Paul. Okay I've got it from here. Are you heading home?"

Hearne nodded and did so.

He stopped to wonder if Hearne had always been an accountant?

He shook himself. He felt like he had to stay awake after Paul had done his job so well and without whining.

He had his eyes on the empty alley, but he wasn't sure that he'd notice a rogue elephant on a nocturnal stroll at this point.

It was the banging that finally caught his attention.

A guy, as tall as Billy but not Billy, was banging on the side door of CoffeeXtra. Martin and Astrid and Selena were arrayed on the other side of the door staring at the banger.

Thursday
10:00 pm

He shoved the Glock in the back of his jeans. He rolled out of the Kia and hoofed it toward the action.

Tall guy said, "Let me in, Martin. I need to speak to Billy."

Martin was rent with indecision. "He isn't here, Mr. Stanko."

His heartbeat may have become syncopated.

Astrid spotted him and pointed. He slowed to a halt as this Mr. Stanko turned.

"Hi, Mr. Stanko, you don't know me, but I'm Gabriel Bergeron..."

Mr. Stanko took a second and then smiled. "Of course. Billy's talked about you. He's had a terrible crush on you for years."

He tried smiling as Mr. Stanko looked him over. "I like him too, Sir...as a friend. I need to speak to him."

Martin was shaking his head.

Mr. Stanko was shaped like Billy and had the same brown eyes and dark hairy arms, but the hair on his head was white and combed back on the sides and top, with a puff in the front.. He was in tan chino pants and a short-sleeved, white dress shirt. He had brown loafers with tassels.

And he was wearing glasses with black frames.

"It's something to do with Penelope, isn't it?"

"Yes, Sir, it is."

Mr. Stanko smiled. "Call me Joe. And I'll call you Gabe?"

"Sure. Is that your real name?"

More smiling. "It's Jozef, but everyone calls me Joe."

And Joe turned and stared at Martin, who looked right and left at Astrid and Selena. Astrid nodded, and Martin unbarred the door.

Joe smiled at Martin, and Martin smiled back. "Hi, Martin."

He smiled at Astrid and Selena. "Are you still with Martin? Girls, you can do better. Just look at him."

Blond Selena looked deeply shocked. Little red spots blossomed on her pale cheeks. "Martin is wonderful. We love Martin...."

Astrid smiled at Joe. "Selena. Selena! He's joking."

Joe smiled at Selena and hugged her. "It was a joke, Selena dear. A bad joke."

Selena blinked back tears with her translucent eyelashes. "A joke?"

"Yes, Dear. Martin is a fine specimen of manhood."

Selena nodded. "He is, Mr. Stanko. He really is."

Astrid shook her head. "Come in. Are you hungry, Mr. Stanko?" She ignored the other person in the room.

"Astrid, please call me Joe." Astrid nodded. "If there's any coffee left?"

Joe put his long limbs to good use and was in the back room with the overstuffed, black leather sofas in two strides.

He sat and patted the seat next to him. "Join me, Gabe. You look tired."

"I am."

Selena and Martin perched on the facing sofa.

Astrid came back with a single cup of coffee and put it in front of Joe before sitting on the other side of Martin.

Joe said, "Thank you, Astrid. I've been on the road for twelve hours."

He sipped his coffee and relaxed against the sofa. He ran his hand through his white locks. He smiled; his big, brown eyes casting loving looks on the assembled company. "So tell me what Billy has been up to. Martin, you go first."

Martin was smiling at Joe. "Gabe came here and got Billy

worried about Penelope...asked where her house was, and if she was in Philly..."

Astrid said, "A month ago."

Martin nodded. "And this detective came and threatened Billy if he didn't tell where Penelope was...."

Astrid said, "Detective Tad Czerwinski."

He said, "Wait. His name is Tad?" But Astrid ignored him.

Martin said, "Because Gabe had told Czerwinski that Penelope knew this murdered guy. And then somebody tried to kill Gabe."

Astrid said, "Two weeks ago."

Martin smiled at Astrid. "So Billy's been in hiding since then."

Joe nodded. He gave Martin and Astrid a beatific smile; he even included Selena even though she hadn't said a word.

"I see. Well, I need to speak to Billy at once."

Selena, tickled to have something to contribute, said, "Martin has a burner phone to call Billy. It's untraceable."

Crafty, fungal Martin had been lying to him.

Joe said, "Thank you, Selena." He looked at Martin.

Martin tried to resist, but he folded under a fresh smile offensive and handed over the phone.

And Joe called. "Billy? Yes, it's me. I'm here at your shop, and I need to speak to you."

Joe listened. "No, Billy. I want you to come here right now."

More listening. "You don't have to worry about that, Billy. Now, Billy."

Joe smiled at everyone again. "Martin, if you want to finish your work, don't let me hold you up."

Martin smiled, and he and his girlfriends went back to work.

Joe said, "Martin has a perfect Duchenne smile." Joe focused on him. "And how are you, Gabe? And how is Cory?"

"Fine. We're both fine. How do you know about him?"

"Billy."

"Right. But Billy's never mentioned you?"

Joe was still smiling, but the smile was starting to wear on him. "Billy doesn't share easily. He had an interesting childhood...growing up with Penelope for a mother."

"You weren't around?"

Joe said, "Not as much as I would have liked."

"So I've only met her twice. Once she was pretending to be a Russian doctor...." Joe grinned at him but said nothing. "She seems a bit secretive."

Joe gave two barks of laughter and went back to smiling. "A bit? But with her job, I suppose it's to be expected."

"And what job would that be, Joe?"

"I don't think I should say anything further about that, Gabe. Let sleeping dogs and all that."

"Right. So she's a spy. And what do you do?"

Joe said, "I'm a psychologist."

"And may I ask who you work for?"

"You may ask." Two more barks of laughter like a seal who thought he was funny.

"So you work for the CIA or some other alphabet agency. That is if you're on the American team?"

Joe smiled. "I think we can assume that and move on, Gabe. So why don't you tell me what's going on? What has dear Penelope been doing in my absence?"

"Okay. Do you know a guy named Monroe?" Joe nodded eyes locked onto him. The glasses seem to make his eyes larger. "What do you know about him?"

Joe just shook his head.

"Right. Well, he and Penelope approached me about a job six months ago. Monroe asked about my grandfather, Andrew Bergeron, and about a bed and breakfast my great-aunt has opened."

Joe nodded.

"But he wouldn't explain anything more. And I never saw him again. And then three, long-lost second cousins showed up at Aunt Flo's B&B: Lydia Gibson, Camille Rankin, and Phillip Bergeron."

He wasn't sure, but he thought there was a slight eye flicker at Phillip's name, but he was trying not to look directly into Joe's big, brown eyes. There was something vaguely disturbing, vaguely hypnotic about them

"Did you know him?"

"'Did'?"

"Yes, he was murdered four weeks ago."

Joe turned his head away and was staring at his shiny loafers which were size fourteen or so.

"You knew him."

A nod. "Of him." He took off his glasses and rubbed his nose.

"And he was Penelope's lover and/or mark."

Joe smiled at his loafers. "From what Billy's told me, more the former than the latter."

"Did she kill him?"

"I wouldn't think so."

"No? Does she know who killed him?"

Joe looked back at him. "I wouldn't know. Penelope and I don't communicate. Except as it concerns Billy. And this seems to be one of those times when it will be necessary."

"I think it might be, Joe."

And they sat there with a murmur of voices coming from the kitchen. And he may have fallen asleep.

Thursday
11:00 pm

Somebody was touching him. It wasn't Cory because Cory was in Massachusetts. His eyes popped open, and Billy was kneeling beside him running a hand underneath his body.

He sat up, drew his legs in, and kicked Billy hard.

Billy fell back and landed on the facing sofa before tumbling to the floor. He pulled out the Glock that Billy had been reaching for, and pointed it at Billy and Joe.

Joe was helping his son to his feet, but he put up hands the size of dinner plates. "Easy, Gabe! Everything is okay. There's no threat. It's just the three of us."

"Then what was Billy doing?" Joe smiled. "Stop smiling! No more smiling!" He had the Glock pointed at the bridge of Joe's nose.

Joe said, "It was my idea. I thought that our discussion might go more smoothly if you weren't armed, Gabe. We weren't going to hurt you."

Billy said, "Chill out, Dude! Dad wouldn't hurt anybody, and I would never hurt you. You know that, right?"

He relaxed a smidgen. "Yeah. I guess." He lowered the gun, but he didn't put it away."

Joe almost smiled at him before he thought better of it. "Billy thought that you weren't very...skilled with firearms...."

Billy said, "Yeah. So we thought maybe you shouldn't have one."

"I'm very skilled. Cory's been training me."

Billy said, "Cory is the FBI agent, Dad."

Joe patted Billy's face. "I know that." Joe looked at him. "So can we sit down and have a civilized discussion?"

"Sure. I'm very civilized. As long as people keep their hands to themselves."

Billy said, "Sorry, Dude."

He shook his head. "No, I'm sorry too, Billy. I haven't had much sleep lately."

Joe said, "So we want you to know that we don't know where Penelope is."

"Then why has Billy been hiding out?"

Billy said, "Because of the detective, Dude. I had to tell him about Mom's house, and I know she'll be pissed about that, and I didn't know what else he might want to know about if he came back. And Mom said that...."

And Billy trailed off.

He said, "What did Mom say, Billy?"

But Billy shook his head and scrunched his big, sad eyes shut.

Joe patted Billy on the shoulder. "It's all right, Billy. Penelope won't be angry with you. She loves you. Fiercely."

He said, "Did she tell you that you might be in danger, Billy?"

Billy shook his head at first.

Joe said, "Did she, Billy?"

And Billy nodded.

Joe smiled but his face was so white that it looked frosty, and his lips might shatter if touched. "Did she tell you who might come after you?"

Billy shook his head.

He said, "But she knows, doesn't she?"

"Maybe. She said she was sorry and that it wasn't her fault."

Joe said, "It never is."

"No, Dad! Really. She said that it was his fault."

"Who? The boyfriend?" Joe snorted. "That's very convenient, Billy, since he's dead."

"No, Dad!"

He said, "Joe? I think Penelope may be telling the truth. In this one isolated instance."

Father and son looked to him for enlightenment.

"We are talking about Phillip Bergeron?"

They nodded.

"Well, I think Phillip was blackmailing someone...."

Joe said, "Someone? That doesn't narrow the field much, Gabe."

He didn't really like Joe Stanko, and he didn't blame Penelope for dumping him. Not one bit. "I realize that, but I'm working on it."

Billy looked hopeful; Joe looked skeptical.

"But I need to speak to Penelope."

Billy shook his head. "Gabe, Dude, I really, really don't know where she is, and I haven't heard from her since the day after somebody spiked your coffee. Honest."

He looked at Joe. "Don't look at me. Penelope hasn't contacted me in over a year."

"But you two know her better than anybody else on the planet, right? You must have some idea how to find her?"

Joe snorted again. "I don't think I ever really knew her at all. I wonder why I tried."

Which wasn't something a son liked to hear his father say.

"But you loved her? In the beginning?"

Joe glanced at Billy and nodded. "Yes, I did, Gabe." He hugged Billy.

"One of you must have some idea where she might go? Things she likes to do? She can't spend twenty-four hours a day hiding in a bunker somewhere? She has to come out. Some place she'd feel comfortable?"

They sat there like two tall, hairy lumps on a log. Or a black, leather sofa in this case.

And then Billy had a thought.

"What, Billy?"

But Billy glanced at Joe and shook his head.

Joe smiled again. The man could not help himself. "Go

ahead and tell him, Billy. Whatever it is, I'm fine with it."

But Billy clammed up.

Joe smiled some more just because his lips were bored and then got to his feet. "I'm starving. Is anyone else hungry?"

He held up his hand.

Joe said, "I'll raid the kitchen then, shall I?"

Billy nodded. "Sure, Dad."

As soon as Joe was out of sight, he shot to Billy's side. He may have put an arm around Billy's shoulder.

Billy was in a tank top and shorts, so it was like hugging a slender Saint Bernard. "I'm sorry I kicked you, Billy. Are you okay?"

"Sure, Gabe. It was Dad's idea about the gun."

"So you thought of some place where Penelope likes to go?" Billy shook his head. "Yes, you did, Dude, and you have to tell me. For your sake as well as mine. If you leave Martin in charge any longer, Astrid will take over, and you'll never be the boss again."

Billy smiled. "Astrid has a strong personality."

"Lucretia Borgia with a toothache."

Billy said, "But I don't want Dad to know."

"Okay. Fine. Where?"

"There's a bar. A Russian bar, but I'm not sure where it is, Dude."

Joe's head popped out around a corner. "Is she still going there?" He smiled at Billy. "Don't worry. I've known about her...outings there since you were in diapers."

"You have?"

"Yes, Billy." Joe sat on the sofa, and he was being pressed between two Stankos like a flower in a book; a hairy book.

Joe said, "She loves that bar, Gabe. She is Russian, you know? Oh, she was born here, but her heart was forged in Mother Russia."

"I didn't know that. So where is this bar?"

Joe said, "And her name isn't Black. Not really. Her name is Chernova."

"Right. And the bar?"

Joe was staring into his eyes. "If I help you, I expect you to forget that you've seen Billy. You won't tell the police or anyone else. I don't want him to be collateral damage from this...mess that her greed...her miscalculation has created."

"Okay. I can do that." Actually, he didn't think Czerwinski would come to question Billy if he sent the detective an engraved invitation and a limousine.

"So?"

Joe said, "It's down by the docks, Gabe."

"Right. So when did she use to go there?"

Joe nodded. "On the weekend. If she's in Philadelphia and alone, she'll turn up." Joe smiled at him. "But you can't go in there."

"Why not?"

Joe smiled but this one might be real. He'd seen Billy smile just like that. "You wouldn't last two minutes."

He glared at Joe. "Would to." Joe was unimpressed. "Why not?"

"Because it caters to a rough crowd. The place is called Pavel's Bar, and the clientele is predominantly Russian. I really don't see you fitting in. I wouldn't feel comfortable myself."

Was Joe implying that he was more masculine? He was way more masculine than Joe. Or Billy.

"Right." He smiled at Joe. "Let me worry about that, but I need a photo of Penelope? As recent as you have?"

Joe said, "She won't let anybody take her picture." He smiled as he played with his phone. "But she doesn't know I took this...it's a few years old, but it's a good likeness."

And an image of Penelope Chernova popped up on Joe's phone. "Perfect. Send that to me? And thank you, Joe." He shook Joe's hand.

Joe said, "So if that's it, I'll unlock the door for you."

"Sure. Thanks again."

And he stepped outside. Billy waved at him, and he waved back.

Joe turned and said something to Billy.

Billy nodded, and they walked toward the office.

He got in the Kia. All he had to do now was get home without falling asleep at the wheel.

Friday
2:00 pm

He didn't remember climbing the stairs to his apartment, but when his eyes had finally opened, he had been in his bed, fully clothed. With a plan fully formed in his head.

And now after a shower and a gallon of coffee and a toaster pastry or three, he was in the gray Kia motoring along on I-95 heading for Wilmington.

He was trying to be positive. He was lucky really. But he wasn't sure that his luck was going to hold, and this drive might be for naught.

But he was soon traversing North Pine Street. He didn't remember the number of Valentina's little brick house, but he found it. He parked and sat. The neighborhood looked much the same; small, neat houses with a few commercial buildings.

The trees were shading the brick sidewalk; Valentina had planted some annuals in a tiny bed wedged against the foundation; zinnias, he thought.

A wall of gray clouds was forming in the west, and the wind was picking up.

He got out and walked manfully up to the door. He could do this. He knocked. Nobody came to the door. He tried knocking again.

Valentina's home was half of a double house. A pair of eyes set above a nose that could probably smell when rain was coming protruded from the door of the other half.

"She's not home."

"Do you know where Mrs. Kutuzova went?"

The disembodied head rotated from side to side. "No. Don't know when she'll be back either."

"Well, thank you."

"But he's here."

"He? Kirill?"

She nodded. "Yeah. The loud one. He's round back making a racket like always."

"Thanks."

And he steeled himself and followed the black-topped lane toward a garage in the back. There was no yard; just an expanse of more sticky black top. A chain link fence separated Valentina's property from a parking lot of uncertain function.

He didn't see Kirill, but his van was here. He wondered what Mrs. Nose meant by making a racket? Was Kirill drunk and rowdy? If so, he feared for the success of his mission.

A mighty voice from above said, "Gabriel?"

He closed his eyes for a second, not sure he wanted to be wafted up into Heaven at this particular moment. He would need to say good-bye to Cory and Aunt Flo. And Ezmeralda. And set his affairs....

"Up here."

And then he saw the ladder, and Kirill standing on the roof, shirtless and sweaty and sun burnt.

"Hi, Kirill. What are you doing?"

"Repairing the roof and replacing some shingles for Mom."

The house began at the street with a one-story, enclosed porch, followed by a three-story, central block that transitioned into a two-story bump, and ending in another one-story addition.

Kirill was on the hindmost, one-story addition, but there were ladders reaching up to the top of the house.

Kirill smiled at him. "Grab those shingles for me, Gabriel?"

He smiled back. "Sure. Glad to."

He had never lifted a bundle of asphalt shingles. They were a lot heavier than he expected, but Kirill was still smiling, and he would carry them up the ladder or die trying.

"Put the bundle over your shoulder, Gabriel."

"Right."

He started climbing the antique, wooden ladder. It wasn't so bad. He could do this. But when he was half way up, the ladder started to bounce and sway with each step.

"Is this ladder safe?"

Kirill wasn't in sight. "Sure. It held me."

"Right. Wait. Were you carrying shingles?"

Kirill's head popped into view; little smile. "You worry too much."

He did a rapid calculation, and he reckoned that his weight with shingles was greater than Kirill's weight without shingles.

But he kept going.

And when he was at the top, the shingles were lifted off his shoulder.

Kirill smiled at him again. "That ladder's crap, but it's all I've got."

Kirill offered him a hand, which he wanted to ignore.

He was on the one-story addition. It wasn't high at all, and he wasn't bothered by the precipitous edge and the unforgiving, black top below or that the clouds had blocked the sun, and the wind had begun to howl around the building.

Kirill grabbed the bundle of shingles and started up a second ladder. This one was aluminum, but it seemed a little warped and had a dent about midway.

"I want to talk to you, Kirill."

"What?" Kirill climbed to the top of the ladder as carefree as a squirrel with a nut in its cheek pouch. Kirill looked down at him. "Come on up, Gabriel."

This ladder wasn't so bad. It wasn't going to snap at that dent. He climbed staring at the side of the house.

The second-story roof was pitched, but it wasn't slippery at all, and he wasn't going to slide off and fall on the aforementioned, unforgiving black top which was now even farther below.

The wind was blowing harder, and the sky was no longer a spring-shower-gray but blackening steadily.

Kirill smiled at him and started climbing a third ladder. This one looked structurally sound, but he didn't like the way it was braced. One hard jiggle, and it would toboggan across the sloped roof.

"Kirill! I just need a minute."

Well, it would probably take longer, but he wasn't telling Kirill that.

"Come on, Gabriel."

He knew better, but he had come this far, and he didn't like the idea of going down much more than he liked the idea of following Kirill.

He climbed one rung at a time, barely breathing, as the wind gusted around him.

He pulled himself onto the topmost roof, which was also gently pitched. He flattened out like a jellyfish tossed onto more of that hot black top.

"Kirill! What the Hell are you doing?"

Kirill dropped the bundle of shingles on top of three more bundles. "You brought those up here?"

Kirill smiled and nodded. "The ladders are fine, Gabriel" He pointed at a section of roof which was bare plywood and looked new. "I have to finish this before the rain comes, Gabriel."

Which was only sensible.

But then he saw a flash of lightning in the distance.

"Shit!"

Kirill just smiled. He decided that he hated Kirill's smile even more than Joe's.

"We can get down faster if you help."

Which was also sensible but might involve moving.

"Open the bundle of shingles." Kirill tossed him a knife.

He didn't catch it, but he trapped it with his body.

Kirill was unrolling black stuff across the bare roof; tar paper? He seemed to remember that from somewhere and somewhen.

Kirill nailed the tar paper down. "Shingle, Gabriel."

And he fed Kirill shingles as requested. Kirill started at the very edge of the roof and seemed perfectly fine with half his body hanging in midair.

The wind was blowing harder, and the sky was deadly

black, and Kirill was hammering shingles like a bare-chested Siegfried forging his sword, Nothung, in the cave of the Nibelungen.

Well, he wasn't singing "Hoho! Hohei!" with a mighty voice. But still.

He handed Kirill the last shingle and watched as he fussed around with the finishing touches.

"Can we go down now?"

Kirill smiled and winked at him. "Scared?"

"No, I like it up here."

He was terrified, but on the bright side, he might be killed by a lightning strike and wouldn't know anything about falling to smush like a watermelon. On that unforgiving black top so far below.

Kirill stood tall. He held his hand out to see if he could catch a drop of rain. He shook his head. "It's going to pass over, Gabriel."

He was a huddled mass. "It is?"

"Yeah. Let's get down, and you can tell me why you're here."

"Right."

He couldn't do it. He was going to stay on this roof until his emaciated body had been picked clean by crows, and his bones scattered by the wind.

But Kirill went first. "Come on, Gabriel. Put your foot on the rung."

His legs were shaking too hard for him to try. But Kirill took pity on him and guided each foot to a rung.

Until they were on the lowest roof. And he had to do that ladder on his own.

He collapsed into a gelatinous puddle on the back steps much like the aforementioned jellyfish. He sat there until Kirill got bored with laughing at him and hauled him to his feet.

And dragged him into Valentina's kitchen.

And offered him coffee.

"Thanks for saving my life, Kirill." Kirill grinned at him. "Aren't you afraid of anything?"

"Snakes."

"Really?"

Kirill laughed. "No."

"Spiders?"

"No, Gabriel." But then he stopped laughing. "Of being homeless."

"That will never happen. You're going to find a job."

Kirill shook his head. "I've tried, Gabriel."

"So you keep trying. I'll help you find something. Would working for Mikhail at Ochoa Imports be so bad?"

He shook his head. "I told Mikhail I'd never work for him again. I yelled an him. I punched him, and he punched me back, and we almost got into it."

"Pish posh. Is that all? I'm sure Mikhail's forgotten all about that."

"No, he hasn't. And even if he might take me back, I can't call him. I can't do it, Gabriel."

He smiled at Kirill and got out his phone.

"What the Hell, Gabriel?"

"Mikhail? Gabe here. Kirill is sorry that he lost his temper, and he would like to work at Ochoa Imports again."

Mikhail said, "Okay."

"Good. So when can he start?"

"Monday."

"Excellent. Want to speak to him?"

"No."

But Mikhail didn't hang up so he waited and pondered if Valentina had cookies stashed anywhere.

Mikhail said, "Tell him I love him."

And Mikhail was gone.

Kirill was staring at him. "What did he say?"

"Well, he said you can start Monday, and then he said something terrible."

Kirill's face tightened up. "What?"

"He said that he loves you."

Kirill left the kitchen. He poured himself a second cup of coffee and casually open cupboard doors, but no cookies were obvious. He found flour and chocolate chips, but he didn't feel like baking.

He sighed and waited.

Kirill returned and paced a bit and then poured himself a cup of coffee and drank it down.

And then he said, "Thanks, Gabriel."

"Sure. Do your best not to make him or yourself crazy at work. Okay?" Kirill nodded. "And now about why I'm here."

Kirill looked up.

If it were done, t'were best done quickly. He didn't think he had the quote right, but the sentiment was on target.

"I'd like you to come back to Philly, go to a Russian bar, find a dangerous woman, smite her with your devilish charm, and bring her back to my apartment."

Kirill took a moment.

And then he laughed and laughed. He didn't actually roll on the floor, but tears came to his eyes.

Kirill wiped his eyes. "No."

"No? I'll pay you? Five hundred? For one evening. You don't even have to sleep with her...unless you want to. And she is kind of hot...or so I've been given to believe."

"No."

"Okay. I understand I kicked you out for almost the same thing..."

"Not almost."

"You're right. For exactly the same thing. But this is different."

"No."

"Okay, my last offer: a thousand dollars and a lifetime supply of vodka....no scratch that. I could never afford that."

"So I drink too much?"

"Not at all. Well, a little moderation might be in order..."

And then the front door opened.

Valentina said, "Kirill? Did you finish the roof? Who's here? In the gray car?"

And Valentina Kutuzova, who had married Danilo Ochoa and given him three children in fair Cuba many years ago, walked into her kitchen.

She arched her stenciled eyebrows. "Gabriel?"

She was in her sixties, about Ezmeralda's age, but she had so far declined to let the gray show. Her hair was brown, permed, and nearly as bouffant as Lady Bird Johnson's had been.

"Hi, Valentina. Kirill finished the roof."

Kirill nodded, but then he got up and hugged his mother lifting her briefly off the floor.

"Gabriel wants me to help him again. And Mikhail will take me back! On Monday!"

She smiled at her son. "Let go, Kirill Danilovitch." She patted his face. "What does Gabriel want you to do?"

"Wait. Are you coming with me, Kirill?"

Kirill nodded and smiled. "He wants me to go to a bar; a Russian bar. And pick up...invite...a nice lady to come home with me. To Gabriel's apartment."

Valentina didn't say anything, but she kissed Kirill on the cheek.

"I have to get my stuff together, Mom."

And he ran out the kitchen door heading for his blue van.

Valentina looked at him. "Sit down, Gabriel."

He smiled his very best smile at her.

"Will Kirill be in danger?"

He shook his head. "I don't think so."

"Think?"

"No, he won't. I mean Penelope isn't violent. Just crafty and sneaky. And Kirill is only going into a bar."

"And is she Russian?"

"So I'm told. Her name, her real name, is supposed to be Penelope Chernova. But all Kirill has to do is get her to come to my apartment and then he can go to work on Monday at Ochoa Imports."

Valentina snorted.

"Are you thinking that Kirill and Mikhail working together won't last?"

"It never has."

"Right. I sort of suspected that. But while he's there, we can be trying to find him another job. Right?"

She nodded. "He's running out of things to fix around here."

"Right. Okay, well, I'm going to see if Kirill is ready to roll."

She pointed a finger at him, a finger tipped with a lethal looking pink nail embedded with possibly radioactive, sparkly bits. "Don't let him get hurt."

"I'll do my best to keep him safe."

"Gabriel."

"He won't." Which he was almost sure of. Unless Penelope had murdered Phillip and then the odds got much worse for Kirill. And for him.

Saturday
10:00 pm

Kirill had gone to the bar Friday night and gotten very drunk on his dime, but Penelope had not graced Pavel's.

He had loaded Kirill into the gray Kia. It had been a tight fit getting all of his limbs inside, but he had driven him home and virtually carried him to the fourth floor.

He had to give Mr. Ochoa points: when he took on a role as a rowdy, boisterous, hard-drinking dockworker, he put heart and soul into it. Except this was type casting.

He had peeped into Pavel's once during the long evening of waiting for Penelope to show, and Kirill had been perfectly at home playing pool. He had expected at least one bar fight, but it had been a low testosterone night at Pavel's.

He was now parked down the street from Pavel's again. Kirill was leaning into his window. "I won't drink so much tonight, Gabriel."

"Okay. Do your best. You're sure you'll know Penelope?"

Kirill nodded. "Yeah."

"Because it would be very bad if you brought home a miscellaneous blonde woman, Kirill Danilovitch. Very bad."

Kirill smiled at him and swaggered down the street to Pavel's. He thought Kirill got an ovation upon entering the bar.

He sat in the Kia. It was hot, and he had to keep the windows down or smother. He tried to slump down in the seat but there wasn't much slumping room.

The hours dragged by. Well, actually only one hour dragged

by before he saw a woman with dark brown hair whose superstructure bore a striking resemblance to Penelope's.

She strutted into Pavel's, hips swinging like twin scythes, ready to reap Russian men.

He was pretty sure it was her.

The question was would Kirill recognize her? If Kirill wasn't already too drunk to recognize anyone?

He pondered slipping over to Pavel's dirty window and peering in. He didn't think that was a good idea; especially if this woman was Penelope, and she spotted him.

He stared into the darkness; the streetlight nearest to the Kia was hanging limp and shattered.

He tried listening to music with earbuds. He got out of the car and did deep knee bends. He got back into the car.

Pavel's was rocking now; the thump of the bass was making the car throb and putting his teeth on edge.

And then somebody was thrown out of Pavel's.

He had never actually seen someone tossed out of a bar. It looked like it hurt, but the guy, who looked like a Kodiak bear with tattoos, picked himself up and charged back inside.

And was tossed out again. He wasn't sure, but he thought that Kirill might have been the tosser.

The tossee got up eventually and staggered off bleeding. He was not going into Pavel's no matter what happened.

But after two more hours with no Kirill and no brown haired woman. he was reconsidering.

Pavel's probably had a back door, and the woman was long gone, and Kirill was sleeping on the floor beneath a pool table.

He sighed.

He could peep in the window.

He wasn't sure what he'd do if he saw Kirill on the floor. He had promised Valentina to take care of him. Maybe nobody would notice him if he slipped in? He could drag Kirill if he was truly unconscious.

He owed it to Valentina to check on her son.

So he was almost to Pavel's entrance, drifting soundlessly through the night like a shadow, when Kirill and Miss Buxom

Brown Hair stumbled out of Pavel's arm in arm.

They were singing a song in Russian or so he assumed. They were loud and oblivious. Which was good since he was close enough to touch them.

He stayed motionless scrunched against the concrete block wall. Pavel needed to repaint. Well, he needed to disinfect first. The wall had an aroma; the top note was urine.

He watched as Kirill steered Miss Buxom Brown Hair to his blue van. She kissed him like a octopus trying to pry open a clam and suck the flesh out.

He reciprocated. They appeared ready to ravish one another on the street, but Kirill picked her up and threw her over his shoulder.

She was laughing. She yelled at him and punched him in the back. Which made him laugh and spank her generous behind. It was obviously a match made in heaven.

She grabbed the passenger door and pulled it open hitting Kirill in the head. He yelled something in Russian.

And then they both laughed, and he tossed her into the van. Kirill pulled off. If he were one quarter as drunk as he appeared, he would never make it to the apartment.

He followed the van, ever hopeful.

Kirill drove like a little, old lady. Well, not like Ezmeralda who was an old lady but didn't drive like one.

Kirill parked in front of the building, and he and Ms. Buxom staggered inside.

He parked and followed. The tracking was easy thanks to the bellowing of Russian folk songs.

He let them get inside.

He pulled out his Glock and tried the door. It was locked, but he had a key. The door opened as far as the chain would allow.

Shit. Kirill was deviating from the plan.

He stuck his face into the crack, but he couldn't see anybody. He heard giggling which seemed to be moving away.

They were going down the hall.

He whispered, "Kirill."

He heard distant laughing and squealing.

Shit.

"Kirill!"

He heard a door slam. He didn't want to think that it was his bedroom door.

"Kirill!"

Sunday
8:00 am

He had slept in Kirill's van.

It had been that or the tiny backseat of the Kia or on the sidewalk. Kirill's van was more comfy, but he hadn't done laundry in a long time, and it was like sleeping in a sweat lodge.

So he had arisen early.

He had tried opening the apartment door and calling softly for Kirill. He hadn't screamed and kicked on the door mostly because he was not one hundred percent sure that the woman who had spent the night with Kirill was in fact Penelope.

So he may have been sitting on the floor leaning against the door when he heard the chain being undone. And he may have been a bit cranky.

He leaped to his feet.

And Penelope Black Chernova Stanko found herself staring into the business end of a Glock 22 when she threw wide the door.

She was in her bra and panties. Which was something. The rest of her clothes were bundled in her arms.

He smiled his very best smile. "Going somewhere, Ms. Chernova?"

She snarled at him. "Get the Hell out of my way, Bergeron!"

He would never know if he would have shot her...in the leg or shoulder or some place not usually fatal...because Kirill grabbed her.

Kirill handcuffed her to Cory's weight bench which had

been the plan for last night. Kirill smiled at him, and sauntered down the hall naked as a jay bird.

He and Penelope watched him until he disappeared into the bathroom.

"Let me go!" She tried dragging the weight bench, but he locked the deadbolt and sat on the sofa.

"Let me go or I'll scream the place down!"

"Go ahead." She looked at him. "Scream until the neighbors call the police. It will save me a call. There's a Detective Czerwinski who really wants to talk to you."

"Bastard."

He frowned at her and tossed the clothes she'd dropped by the door. "Get dressed."

She glared at him. "Let me go, Bergeron. I haven't done anything to you." She couldn't put on her knit top because of the cuffs, but she shimmied into a skirt four sizes too small. "And I have no idea why any detective would want to talk to me."

"That would be because of your involvement in the grotesque murder of Phillip Bergeron."

She was hungover and exhausted from a night spent partying with Kirill, so she was a little off her game. Her face blanched, and he thought tears formed in her dark eyes.

"Who?"

He laughed. "Oh, please. Even I could do better than that, and I'm terrible at lying. Phillip Bergeron, your lover. The guy you got fired from Oxley International by seducing him into stealing company secrets. The guy in whose bed you left your DNA."

She looked shocked for a millisecond or so. "I don't know what you're talking about. You're insane. I told Monroe you were."

"Yes, good ole Monroe. How does he fit into all this? But I'm more interested in the blackmail scheme. Was that your idea too?"

She shook her head. "I have no idea what you're babbling on about."

Kirill came padding back still naked. He grabbed up clothes he'd shed the night before and got dressed. "Want coffee, Gabriel?'

"Yes, please."

Kirill smiled at Penelope.

She said, "So who is he really?"

"Him? That's Kirill. A friend."

She snorted. "He's no friend of yours. He's a real man."

Kirill smiled and bowed to her. "I had fun too."

She looked at Kirill and cranked up the lust. "Let me go, and tonight will be even better than last night, Lover."

Kirill shook his head. "That's up to Gabriel.

"Asshole." Penelope forgot about Kirill. "How did you find me, Bergeron?"

"A new friend told me that you liked Pavel's."

"What new friend? Not my Billy? No, he wouldn't. Shit. You met Dr. Jozef Stanko, the bastard."

"I have no idea who you're talking about."

She shook her head. "Tall, white-haired skunk. A real snake in the grass. Always smiling."

"Never had the pleasure. About the blackmail?"

"I don't know anything about blackmail."

"You do. Phillip liked to brag, didn't he? And he told you a secret while you were climbing all over each other."

"Phillip?"

"Phillip Bergeron, my second cousin. Who was too handsome, stupid, and arrogant for his own good. And who was a thief at heart."

Penelope was giving him the death glare, but she didn't say a word.

"The guy who was drugged and then strung up with the sheets from the bed you'd shared and left there to strangle slowly."

She turned away.

"The guy who was the father of five kids who loved him. You know or can guess who murdered him, Penelope. Help me...or help Czerwinski catch the guy? Please?"

"I'm not saying another word, Bergeron."

"That's okay. A few days in jail will change your mind."

She laughed at him. "I'll be out in a few hours."

"And you'll disappear like smoke."

She just smiled at him.

"You'd better hope you're good at hiding, because the guy who killed Phillip is looking for you too." He had no idea but it might be true.

She pretended to be bored.

Kirill said, "So what now, Gabriel?"

"Now, you watch her while I take a shower, and then we'll take her to the police."

And he showered and then checked out his bedroom.

It was bad.

Oh, he could burn the sheets, but what would he do about the mattress? He didn't think flipping it over was going to work for him.

He got dressed. He called Czerwinski and got his voicemail, but it was Sunday.

"Detective, I have Penelope Black Stanko, and I'm bringing her to headquarters. She knows who killed Phillip. She doesn't want to tell me, but you can crack her like a boiled peanut. Which aren't half bad. Anyway, call me when you get this?"

And with Kirill holding onto Penelope, they went down the stairs heading for Kirill's van.

Sunday
9:00 am

They stepped out into the sunshine. It was warm, but not as muggy and oppressive as it would be by the afternoon.

A big, black SUV was cruising toward them. The driver was looking at them. His face looked funny, and there was a guy in the back seat who looked funny too.

And as the windows rolled down, he realized they were wearing stockings over their faces.

And then the shooting started.

His reaction time was not great, but there was nothing wrong with Penelope's or Kirill's, and he was shoved to the pavement. They scuttled to Kirill's van like three blue crabs dumped on a deck.

Lots and lots of bullets were ripping through the van walls like they were tissue paper.

Kirill grunted and went down; a flash of red blossomed on his head.

He had the Glock in his hand. It seemed like he should do something with it.

Penelope screamed, "Shoot the bastards! Shoot, you hopeless idiot!"

Which was unkind, but he took her point. He crawled under the van and started firing. He emptied the clip. The SUV swerved and crashed into a parked car.

He reloaded and started firing again. The two guys exited and ran. He crawled out from under the van. He set himself.

They were probably out of range, but he squeezed off the remaining rounds carefully.

One of the guys went down.

He was out of bullets. Shit. Note to self: carry more ammo.

Kirill was lying on the sidewalk. Bleeding.

Penelope was running down Arch Street.

He knelt beside Kirill. "Shit! Kirill! Talk to me!"

Kirill smiled at him. "I'm fine. This is nothing."

He had his hand pressed to the side of his head just above his ear. Blood was oozing between his fingers and coating his neck and shoulder. "You're bleeding out!"

Kirill said, "No, I'm not. Got a handkerchief or something?"

He didn't have anything. He took off his shirt. Kirill grabbed it and applied pressure against the wound.

Kirill said, "Thanks, Gabriel. You should go after Penelope."

"Really? You aren't dying?"

Kirill laughed. "No. Go. Don't let her get away!"

So he took off against his better judgment.

Penelope had run toward North 2nd Street. She had a head start, but he thought he knew where she was going. He rounded the corner of Arch and North 2nd, and he could see her far ahead.

He ran, passing a theater company and then Christ Church.

He was gaining with every stride. Because he was younger and a better runner. Well, he also had much better shoes.

He was flying along the brick sidewalk whipping past the black, wrought iron fence of the church yard.

He was close now.

He skidded around the corner onto Market Street as Penelope ducked into the little glass and brick subway entrance. He could hear her running down the stairs.

"Stop!"

A police officer was pointing a gun at him.

"Put the gun down! Do it now!" Another officer was behind him.

"But it's empty."

"Put the freaking gun down or I'll shoot your ass!"

Which was clear enough. He carefully put the Glock on the sidewalk.

"Now kick it away!"

He did that. The officer behind him cuffed his hands behind his back.

"But she's getting away."

The officer in front of him holstered his gun; his name tag read "Goff". "Who? The wife? Is this a domestic?"

"What? No. I'm not married and certainly not to Penelope Black. And I haven't done anything wrong."

The officer behind him spun him around. "Of course not. You're just running around shirtless, covered in blood, with a Glock in your hand." He examined the Glock. "A recently fired Glock."

Officer Madden winked at Officer Goff, and they both had a little chuckle.

Officer Goff said, "You involved in the shooting on Arch?"

"Yes."

Officer Goff shook his head at the stupidity of the criminal class. "Hear that, Madden?"

"I did. I suppose you didn't do anything wrong there either?"

"Nope. I was defending myself. Look, I know how this must look...."

Goff and Madden had another chuckle fit.

"But call Detective Czerwinski at the 24th. He'll tell you that I'm not a criminal. Really. Look I have his number in my cellphone. Or call Detective Golczewski. I know Vonda will vouch for me."

"Golczewski?" Goff looked at Madden.

Madden shook his head. "So he's heard her name. Doesn't mean anything."

"Officers, I have her home number in my phone. In my pocket."

But Goff grabbed his phone. "She's in here, Madden."

Goff called.

He could hear Vonda say, "What? This had better be important, Bergeron."

Officer Goff cleared his throat. "Who is this?"

Vonda's voice cut through the traffic noise. "This is Detective Golczewski of the Philadelphia Police. Who is this and why have you got Bergeron's phone?"

"This is Officer Goff, PPD. I'm sorry to bother you, Detective, but there's a guy here...shirtless and covered in blood who was chasing a woman...."

Madden leaned in. "And he was waving a Glock around and we cuffed him."

Vonda said, "Let me speak to him, Officer."

"Hi, Vonda."

"Bergeron. Don't tell me that this wasn't your fault. Where are you?"

"On the corner of North 2nd and Market Street. I was chasing Penelope, but she got away, because these officers stopped me. Of course, I can see how it looked to them. You remember about Penelope, Vonda? She's Billy Stanko's mother...."

Vonda said, "Shut up, Bergeron. Have you called Czerwinski?"

"I left him a message, but that was before the guys in the black SUV tried to shoot us and Penelope escaped, so he's not exactly au courant with the situation...."

"What black SUV? No, where did this happen and when?"

"On Arch Street in front of my apartment. About twenty minutes ago. I really need to get back there to see if Kirill is okay."

"Stop talking. Let me speak to Goff."

He looked at Goff. "She wants you now."

And Goff put the phone to his ear. He listened. "Yes, Detective. Sure I can do that, but... Yes, Detective, I understand."

Goff ended the call.

He looked at Madden and shrugged. Goff grabbed his arm and marched him in the direction of Arch Street.

Sunday
10:00 am

Goff and Madden surveyed the scene; they pulled out their weapons. Kirill was still there with the shirt pressed against his head. Goff disarmed him too.

"Kirill, are you okay?"

Kirill smiled. "I'm fine, Gabriel. I have a headache." Kirill looked unhappy. "I'm sorry, Gabriel."

"For what?"

"I didn't get off one freaking shot."

"No? Well, that's okay. You got hit."

Goff and Madden were looking at them and at the van. Goff said, "What the Hell happened here?"

Kirill said, "Two guys in a black SUV tried to take us out with automatic weapons."

He said, "That SUV over there. The one that smashed into the parked car."

Goff said, "Why?"

Kirill shook his head and winced. "Shit. I shouldn't do that. Ask Gabriel."

Goff looked at him. "I don't know for sure, but I think it has to do with the murder of Phillip Bergeron a month ago. Detective Czerwinski knows all about it. Did you call him?"

Goff shook his head. "Above my pay grade. Golczewski will call anybody who needs to be called."

And Officer Goff handcuffed him and Kirill to the van and wandered off with Madden in the direction of the SUV.

"Wait. Hey! Has anybody called an ambulance? For Kirill! Goff!"

Kirill said, "Some nice lady called. I think she's a neighbor of yours."

"Right. Good." He sat on the pavement and took the sun while he waited.

The ambulance arrived first. Kirill was loaded into the back still smiling and giving him a thumbs up.

Kirill was okay. He was tough and would be out of the hospital in hours. He hoped. Was there any way he could keep Valentina from finding out that he had let her baby get shot?"

He was pondering that when Vonda arrived.

She stood looking down at him shaking her head. She put out her hand for silence when he started to speak.

She looked around. "Where's Officer Goff?"

Goff held up a meaty arm. "Here, Detective."

"Uncuff Bergeron." Goff looked at her. "Do it. But keep an eye on him. I want him right here when Czerwinski rolls up."

Goff nodded and freed him from his shackles. He gave Goff and Vonda his very best smile.

"Thanks, Vonda."

"Don't move, Bergeron."

The crime scene techs arrived next and started snapping photos and collecting shell casings. They were all over Kirill's van and the black SUV.

Down the street, one of them waved for Vonda. She went to inspect the area and came back.

"There's a blood pool, Bergeron."

"Right. I shot one of the gunmen; the slow one. He was borderline obese. He went down, but I guess he got up."

She nodded as she inspected the van and walked over to the SUV again.

She was wearing off-white slacks and a silky, black blouse; her hair was pulled back but the bun at the base of her head wasn't quite centered. Her badge was on a lanyard around her neck.

Vonda came back and put her hands on her hips.

"So tell me what happened here in the street. Nothing

before or after. Nothing from your childhood. And not one damn word about this great-aunt. Go."

Goff and Madden were trying to look useful while staying in earshot.

"Okay. We came downstairs with Penelope Black Stanko whose real name is Chernova. By we, I mean Kirill and me...."

Vonda said, "Kirill?"

"Right. Kirill Danilovitch Ochoa. He's a friend and the stepson of Ezmeralda Gutierrez...."

Vonda held up her hand. "Part of the Cuban Mafia you run with. Go on."

"I wouldn't say that, Vonda. Anyway. We came down. Two guys wearing stockings opened fire with automatic weapons from that black SUV. We ducked behind the van...which wasn't exactly bullet-proof...as you can see. Kirill got hit. I started returning fire."

Madden held up an evidence bag with his Glock.

Vonda glared at Madden who may have cowered slightly behind Goff.

And then Detective Czerwinski showed up. He was wearing a snug pair of blue plaid shorts and a red tank top.

He had shapely, hairy calves but he needed to go to the gym and work on his shoulders and arms.

Czerwinski nodded to Vonda. "Do I want to know what the Hell happened here?"

Vonda nodded. "Start over, Bergeron."

So he did.

Czerwinski said, "This Penelope is real? But her name is Chernova?"

"Yes, Detective. Kirill will tell you how real. He has what you might call intimate knowledge of Ms. Chernova."

Czerwinski said, "Just go on."

"Okay. So I took out the front tire of the SUV, and the windows, and the driver crashed into the parked car. And then they ran, and I winged one of them. The large one. And then I tried to help Kirill, but he said he was fine so I chased Penelope to the subway entrance on Market Street. And Officers Goff and Madden arrested me. And let Penelope escape."

Goff said, "He was covered in blood and had a Glock in his hand, Detectives."

Vonda said, "We know, Goff."

Czerwinski said, "You found this Penelope, Bergeron?" The detective pushed him against the van. "So why didn't you call me?"

"I did. You didn't pick up."

Czerwinski checked his phone and glared at him some more. "So did she give you anything?"

"No. But she knows who killed Phillip."

Czerwinski shook his head looking super-skeptical. "And how do you know that? Intuition?"

"More or less. She loved Phillip, but I think she's scared of whoever killed him."

"So you have nothing. We don't know anything more than we knew a month ago."

Vonda said, "We know somebody is worried enough to order a hit in broad daylight, Detective."

Czerwinski nodded.

Vonda said, "Who were they trying to take out, Gabe? You or this Penelope?"

Which was an excellent question. "Penelope." He had no idea.

Czerwinski looked hyper-skeptical.

Vonda said, "But how did they know you'd found her? And how did you find her?"

Czerwinski said, "Yeah?"

So he told them about Dr. Jozef Stanko and Pavel's Bar and Kirill's fatal charms.

Czerwinski shook his head. He looked at Vonda. "Look, I know you're right about this attempted hit meaning somebody is freaking out, but how does this help us?"

Vonda looked at him. "Gabe?"

"Well. Maybe you can find the shooters and trace them back to whoever hired them?"

Czerwinski looked glum. "Maybe."

"But if not, then there's my apartment. You can pull

Penelope's DNA from my sheets...."

Vonda smiled.

"Don't even think it, Vonda. Kirill was in bed with her. But as I was saying, you can also get her fingerprints. They have to be all over my apartment. And you didn't have those before."

Czerwinski nodded. "Yeah. The house on Savin had been wiped down. Okay."

"Shit. I have a picture of her." And he pulled out his phone and flashed the photo Joe had given him.

Czerwinski said, "So this is her?"

Goff was leaning over Czerwinski's bony shoulder. "Yeah, that's the woman he was chasing. Except she had brown hair."

Czerwinski glared at Goff until he backed off. And then he sent the crime scene guys up to his apartment.

While they worked, Vonda made Madden get them coffee and donuts. They were sitting in her car.

"Are you okay, Gabe?"

He drained his coffee. "Excellent. Well, I'm pissed that Penelope got away, and I need to see how Kirill is doing, and tomorrow is a work day, and I have a client coming in...."

Vonda smiled at him.

"I should shut up?"

"No, it's okay." She sighed. "Could you just drop this now? Czerwinski has some physical evidence and some new leads to follow?"

"Right. Maybe." He looked at her. "Thanks for the coffee. Shouldn't you be going home? To Sylvie and David?"

She snorted. "Not likely. I have to try to track down your shooters."

"So this is your case?"

She focused big, brown, accusatory eyes on him. "Anything to do with Gabriel Bergeron is my case. No other detective will touch this. Czerwinski just didn't know any better when he caught Phillip's homicide."

"Really? Shit. I'm sorry, Vonda, for messing up your Sunday."

She said, "Czerwinski wants you."

He got out of her car, and she drove off, but he thought she smiled at him.

Czerwinski hadn't smiled, but he hadn't yelled or screamed either. He had answered all of Czerwinski's questions and then and only then had he been released to climb all those stairs to his apartment.

Which had been a disaster area. Crime scene guys and gals were a messy lot.

But he had showered and driven to Hahnemann University Hospital on North Broad Street and found Kirill's doctor.

She had been of the opinion that Kirill was stable and baring complications might be released on the morrow.

Kirill was in a room, in a bed, in a hospital gown, with an IV, and was unhappy with every part of that.

"Gabriel! Get me out of here!"

"Calm down. Please. How is your head? The doctor says you have a concussion."

"I know. But I'm fine."

"Kirill Danilovitch."

"I am, Gabriel. They just want to keep me for observation."

"So? Let them. Lie back. Eat green gelatin. Ogle the nurses."

Kirill shook his head. He had a thick bandage strapped to his head by yards of gauze. "I can't stay, Gabriel."

"Why? Wait. No insurance?"

Kirill nodded.

"Right. Well, I'll pay." He had the money from Lydia.

"You will? You have the money?"

"I do. And I owe you."

"But Penelope got away?"

"Not your fault. You performed your assignment admirably."

Well, he'd chained the door so he and Penelope could have a carnal romp in his bed, but still. Kirill was Kirill.

The guy was smiling at him.

"So have you called Valentina?"

Kirill laughed. "No way. Later or maybe never."

"Good. Okay. Do you need anything?"

"No. Except clothes. I think they tossed my shirt."

"Right. I can take care of that."

No, he couldn't. Shit. They had towed Kirill's van for some reason, and he had no idea how long they'd keep it?

But Kirill was smiling again. "Think I'll have a scar?"

"Maybe. Would that be a good thing?"

Kirill nodded grinning.

A new battle scar to brandish.

Monday
7:00 am

He had slept like a rock and not your crumbly sedimentary rock either but like basalt, like a chunk of the Earth's mantle.

But something was chirping near him.

He opened an eye; his phone.

"Hello?"

"Gabe?"

He sat up on the air mattress. "Cory? How are you? Where are you? How is Bornheimer? How is the case? Are you coming home soon?"

"Whoa, partner. I miss you too."

"Right. So?"

"I'm in Halifax, Nova Scotia."

"Right. Wait. Did we annex Canada overnight?"

Cory sighed. "No, Henri. Bornheimer and I are here as guests of the Royal Canadian Mounted Police."

"Really? Well, that's cool. Wait. Is 'guests' a Canadian euphemism for 'prisoner'?"

"No, Henri. They are helping out with our investigation. So what are you up to?"

He had been anticipating that very question. "Oh, nothing much. Baldacci's got himself a black Mustang with red trim and red wheels; a Boss 302 model?" Which meant nothing to him. "It has a thousand horsepower or thereabouts."

"Good for him. And Carla let him get it?"

"Ah, you know Carla. Harry bought it before the wedding."

"Anything else? How is Ms. Barnes?"

"Aunt Flo is fine. I've decided I've been acting like a spoiled child about the bed and breakfast thing, and I have turned over a new leaf. I intend to embrace the concept."

"Because it makes her happy?"

"Just so."

"Good for you. So I should be home on Friday. Or Saturday."

"Great. Excellent. You've been gone a long time."

"I know. But the case has finally turned a corner."

"Also great. Can you share any details?"

"Sorry, Gabe. On Friday. Or Saturday."

"Okay. So I'll meet you at the condo?"

"Sounds like a plan. Bye, Gabe."

"Bye."

He rolled off the air mattress and visited the bathroom. He had four days, maybe five, to solve Phillip's murder. Well, he could always tell Cory what had been going on, but a better, less stressful plan would be to catch the bad guy before Cory got home.

And then he could maybe tell Cory the bare minimum in a month or so.

He wandered back to the living room. A car horn was breaking the dawn stillness. He looked out the window.

A taxi had pulled up in front of his building. A blond guy with his head bandaged was standing beside the taxi.

He grabbed some shorts and ran down.

"Kirill! What are you doing here?"

Kirill had on a hospital gown, but it was stuffed inside his jeans like a baggy, extra-long shirt. He was barefoot.

"Gabe! I'm supposed to be at Ochoa Imports. Mikhail is expecting me. Where's my van?"

He paid for the taxi. "First, how did you get out of the hospital?"

Kirill smiled.

"You walked out? Right. Are you okay?"

"Fine, Gabriel. The van?"

"Ah. Hauled away by the police. Looking for evidence. We

can get it back."

Kirill was not happy. "When?"

He shrugged. "Why don't you stay here? I'll call Mikhail and tell him that you aren't feeling well...."

"No! He'll think I'm drunk."

Which was undeniably true.

"Please, Gabriel. Take me to work."

"Maybe. Come inside first."

Kirill made it up two flights of stairs before he gave out of gas. "Stay here. I'll get some of Cory's clothes."

Cory and Kirill were both big guys but not shaped the same. Cory's shirt had been snug but fit Kirill well enough.

But the pants had been too tight in the waist so he had kept on the blood-stained ones. The boots had also been a no go.

Still, he had gotten Kirill into the Kia, and he was pulling into the parking area of Ochoa Imports on the Delaware River.

Mikhail walked out of the warehouse.

"Kirill?"

Kirill smiled at his brother. "You should see the other guy."

Mikhail was not amused.

He said, "He didn't get into a fight."

"No?"

So he explained about Pavel's bar and Penelope and the gunmen in the black SUV.

Mikhail took it all in without a word. He shook his head at this Bergeron creature who looked so harmless. And then he hugged his brother. "Idiot. You should learn to duck."

Kirill hugged him back. "I did! It was a ricochet."

Mikhail smiled and rubbed the side of his own head. "You just wanted a scar like mine."

Mikhail had been whacked in the head with a wrench by his brother-in-law, after he had caught Charlie embezzling.

Kirill smiled.

Mikhail said, "Mom?"

Kirill shook his head vigorously.

Mikhail nodded. "You need boots."

"Yeah?"

"I'll get some. You can't work."

"I can answer the phone."

Mikhail nodded and headed for the office inside the warehouse. He and Kirill followed slowly.

There were two shipping containers filled with big sacks of cocoa, and inside the warehouse, long rows of pallets piled with more 60 kilogram sacks of cocoa beans. The ones he saw were stenciled "Shipped from the Ivory Coast."

Kirill made it to the office and sat down and put his head back. Mikhail found a pair of boots and put them on his brother.

Kirill said, "Thanks, Mikhail. I'm sorry I can't do much. But I'll be stronger after I rest for a while."

Mikhail nodded and went back to work.

He sat beside Kirill. "You okay?"

"Sure."

"So I get that you've been pissed off because you lost your job."

Kirill just stared at the ceiling.

"But it seems like you were pissed with me in particular? Before?"

Kirill just lay there with his eyes closed.

"Why? I know we were never buddies, but I thought we were okay after your father's wedding?"

Kirill looked around. "He put Mikhail in charge here."

"Right? And you wanted to take over the business? I thought you hated office work, hated the business?"

"Maybe."

"So what's the problem, Kirill?"

"He should have offered it to me. I'm smarter than Mikhail. But you like Mikhail better, and you talked Dad into picking him."

It was absolutely true that he liked Mikhail better. "No, I like you fine, Kirill, and I never talked Danilo into anything."

"No?"

"No. Danilo and Anna and Mikhail came to see me...after Charlie embezzled all that money. Anna didn't want any part of running the business, and nobody seemed to think that you wanted the job so Mikhail was the only option. And he said he'd try.

Danilo made it plain he didn't think Mikhail could do it."

Kirill frowned. "Dad always puts Mikhail down."

"I've noticed that."

Kirill nodded. "It pisses me off."

What didn't? "So we're okay now?"

Kirill nodded. "Yeah. I had fun."

"With Penelope?"

"And with you. You're a bad ass with the Glock."

"Of course, I am. Really?"

"Yeah. Now shut up."

"Okay, but I haven't forgotten that I owe you a thousand bucks."

But Kirill's eyes were closed.

He walked out and said goodbye to Mikhail.

"Is he okay, Gabriel?"

"I think so. I'll go to the hospital and find out. He was supposed to be released today anyway. But I'll call you."

Mikhail nodded and went to check on his brother.

And he drove to the hospital and found Kirill's doctor. She was pissed, but she finally admitted that Kirill seemed to be doing okay when she'd examined him.

And then he had been presented with a bill for services rendered.

He had written a check on the spot, and the atmosphere had noticeably improved.

And then he had gone to work.

He figured that Kirill's van was totaled, but maybe not? He would get Stan to look at it and see if it was worth fixing. At the very least, Stan would get a kick out of all the bullet holes.

Wednesday
5:00 pm

He had called Mikhail, and Kirill was doing okay.
Which was great.
And so far, the brothers weren't fighting.
Which was also great.
And he had returned the Kia to Stan and gotten his Jeep.

But it had been two days, and Czerwinski hadn't found Penelope even with her fingerprints, her photo, and even her freaking DNA.

He was sitting on his sofa eating a pizza; a whole pizza. He didn't care. Cory would be home on Friday or Saturday, and he would either have to tell him what he'd been up to or give up on the case.

Or possibly both.

And he had no idea who had killed Phillip or tried to kill him. The only thing he hadn't done was talk to Jonathan Bergeron.

He dialed.

Lydia said, "Gabe? Any news? I'm sorry. How are you?"

"Fine. Good. Excellent."

She laughed. "You don't sound like it?"

"Well, it's been a lively week so far, but I'm no closer to finding Phillip's killer than I was the day he died. Well, a little bit. So I was wondering if I could see your father? I wouldn't stay long; I wouldn't want to tire him out. Is he up to visitors, Lydia?"

Silence.

"Lydia?"

"I'm here. I don't know, Gabriel. Let me speak to him."

"Where is he by the way?"

"Here. He lives with us, Gabriel. We certainly have the room in this pile."

"Right. Well, that's nice." Another bout of silence. "So could you go ask him?"

"I imagine he's asleep. He's better in the mornings."

"Right. So we lost Penelope and haven't found her again. Not yet anyway."

"You found her? When, Gabriel?"

"Sorry. I thought Reed would have heard."

"Reed is in New York and is focused on other pressing matters."

He made a note to call Max Nagy and ask how ole Reed was doing. And then he told Lydia about Kirill and Pavel's Bar and the gunmen and Penelope's daring escape.

"I'm so sorry, Gabriel! You could have been killed."

"I could, but I wasn't."

"I think you should stop. I can't have your death on my conscience. I'd rather not know what happened to Phillip."

"Thanks for that, but I'm not giving up just yet. This is for me now as much as it is for you. So will you ask Jonathan if I may speak to him?"

"I will. I'll ask him tomorrow at breakfast and call you."

"Do you think he'll agree?"

"Oh yes, Gabriel. And I want to help, but I'm not sure he's strong enough."

"You'll be there with me. And you can shoo me away if it's too much for him."

"You don't strike me as the type of person easily shooed."

He laughed. "No, but I can be. Let me know."

"Tomorrow."

He stopped gorging on pizza and put the rest in the refrigerator for breakfast.

He patted his belly. He should have been going to the gym every day that Cory had been gone.

Thursday
6:00 am

Something had disturbed his blissful slumber before his alarm had gone off. He wasn't sure what, but he couldn't get back to sleep.

He had turned the mattress and was trying to put what Kirill and Penelope had done to the other side out of his mind.

He got out of bed and padded to the kitchenette. It was very quiet or he might not have heard the little scraping noise coming from the door.

He tip-toed over and peered through the peep hole. He caught a glimpse of a shape moving out of view.

A gray shape?

He didn't have his Glock; Czerwinski hadn't returned it yet. He wasn't going to open the door unarmed.

He ran back to the bedroom and got his phone. Calling 911 for a gray shape might not get a rapid response?

And then someone banged on his door.

He froze.

When his brain kicked back in, he started searching for a weapon. He had never played baseball so he didn't have a bat. Well, not since high school.

He was about to grab the cast iron skillet Aunt Flo had given him, when he spotted Cory's weights.

He hefted a 20 pound dumbbell.

Another knock. "Mr. Bergeron?" He didn't know the voice. "Mr. Bergeron, sorry to bother you but it's Cordrey...the electrician.

I need to get inside your apartment, Sir? Won't take long. Mr. Bergeron?"

It was 6:30 am and the early bird got the worm and all that, but he may have been suspicious.

He had the chain on. He opened the door keeping the dumbbell out of view. "Why do you need to get in, Mr. Cordrey?"

Cordrey was in his gray coverall with his gray Phillies cap again.

Cordrey smiled at him. His sandy blond hair was sticking out of his cap. He had plump lips and smallish, gray eyes with translucent lashes and barely visible eyebrows. He looked about as dangerous as a teddy bear.

Except for the eyes. Maybe he was imagining it? But no way was Cordrey getting into his apartment.

"Just need to check the outlets in the kitchen, Sir. Won't take more than five minutes."

"Right. Sorry, but now is not a good time. My outlets are fine. Maybe you could check Mrs. Bruska's?"

Cordrey's plump face tightened up as much as it could. "Mrs. Bruska?"

"Across the hall, the rear apartment."

Cordrey shook his head. "I checked her outlets."

Which was interesting since Mrs. Bruska was not in residence. "Really? How did you get in?"

Cordrey was focused on him. "The building manager let me in."

"Really?"

Cordrey's face had lost what little color it had possessed. "Mr. Foley."

"Wait. You met him? When was this?"

He had never seen Mr. F. X. Foley and was beginning to think that he didn't exist.

"Last week."

"That's interesting. Mrs. Bruska and I have never seen him, and she's lived here for a decade."

Cordrey was pushing hard against the door, and just as Cordrey couldn't see the dumbbell in his hand, he couldn't see what, if anything, the electrician had in his.

He shook his head. "Sorry. You'll have to come back."

"I can't. I have another job, and I'm late for that."

"Do you have I.D.?"

Cordrey's full lips curled into a sweet smile. "Sure, but I'll have to take my coverall off to get it. Can't you just let me in, Mr. Bergeron? Please?"

And then a heavy tread could be heard ascending the stairs. Cordrey's head pulled back. He may have taken that opportunity to slam his door and bolt it.

And then somebody was banging on his door again.

He threw it open, dumbbell raised high and ready to smite Cordrey with a mighty blow.

But it was Czerwinski.

"Shit! Put that down! What's wrong with you, Bergeron?"

"Nothing! Sorry. Did you see a guy in a gray coverall?"

"Sure. He passed me heading down?"

He was looking at Czerwinski. He would have told Vonda the truth, but Czerwinski might think he was losing it...even after everything that had happened.

"Right. Well, he woke me up wanting to get into my apartment."

"And you decided to crush his skull for that?"

"I was just going to scare him." He tossed the dumbbell onto the sofa. "Come in, Detective. I'm making coffee. Have a seat."

Czerwinski sat but kept a wary eye on him.

When the coffee was brewing, he said, "Want a slice of pizza?"

Czerwinski shook his head. "I grabbed something on the way out the door."

He didn't know anything about Czerwinski. Well, he wasn't wearing a wedding ring, but that didn't mean he was unattached.

But the suits did. And the ties. This was the gray suit. Again.

"So you don't live with your mother, and you don't have a girlfriend."

Czerwinski glared at him. "Not that it's any business of yours, but I do have a girlfriend."

"And she lets you go to work in that suit?"

Which was mean. But he'd had a bad week, and he was cranky.

Czerwinski looked defensive. "What's wrong with it?"

"Do you throw it on the floor when you take it off...or let your dog bed down on it?"

Czerwinski turned red. "I don't have a dog."

He was about to suggest a cat or a herd of hamsters and then bring up the red ties, but he decided to be nice. "I'm sorry, Tad. Is that your name, by the way? Astrid said it was, but she could be wrong?"

"Astrid?"

"Do you really want to know?" Czerwinski shook his head.

He gave Czerwinski coffee and a toaster pastry; the last one. But only because he had been a very poor host. He joined Tad on the sofa. "So let's start over. Welcome to my humble home, Detective. How may I help the Philadelphia Police Department today?"

Czerwinski gobbled up the last pastry and chased it with black coffee. "There's nothing wrong with my suit."

He smiled his very best smile. "Of course not."

Czerwinski was stalling, and he had no idea why.

He sipped his coffee and let him find his way.

"My name is Tad...Tadeusz really."

"That's a lovely name." Tadeusz glared at him. "Sorry. That's a very masculine name...virtually oozing with testosterone. Go on."

"And I date lots of women."

"Right. You have 'babe-magnet' written all over you." Which wasn't as sarcastic as it sounded.

Tadeusz glared some more. "You want to get smacked?"

"Nope. Sorry. Again. I've gotten it out of my system. Have you found out anything about Penelope?"

Tadeusz closed his big, brown eyes and rested his black curls on the back of the sofa. Babe-magnet wasn't far off.

"No."

He waited, but Tad seemed done. "And?"

"We put out the fingerprints and the photo; first statewide and then national. Then we went international."

"And you got nothing back."

Tad nodded. "The woman is a ghost."

"Nope. She's a Russian spy. Well, to be clear, she's a spy of Russian descent. I think she's self-employed and doesn't actually work for Mother Russia."

"Whatever."

Tad was down. "We're going to solve this, Tad."

But the detective was shaking his head.

"Yes, we are. We found Penelope once, and we'll do it again."

"You found her."

"There is no 'u' in team."

Tad almost smiled. He finished his coffee, and smoothed his jacket surreptitiously. Tad had something to share.

"Yesterday. It was late, but I was still at my desk."

He didn't make a snarky comment.

"And these two guys came in. They had badges and looked legit."

"What kind of badges?"

"Homeland Security."

"And?"

"They wanted to know why I was looking for Penelope Black. And I told them she was a witness or maybe a suspect in a homicide."

"And they said?"

"As little as possible. Something about her fingerprints being connected to an ongoing investigation. No details. They wanted to know where I got the photo and what evidence I had against her. I was pissed at that point and wouldn't tell them. And they just smiled at me and went to talk to my boss."

"And your boss made you tell?"

"No. My boss hates all Feds."

He remained silent and receptive because Tad had more to

relate.

"And they split after demanding that we contact them before taking any action against Black. Or Stanko or whatever her name is."

"I think it's Chernova, but that's not important. What else?"

Tad looked him in the eye. "One of the guys...."

"Yes? What?"

"Well, after they left, I happened to look at the sketches...."

"Shit, Czerwinski! One of them was Monroe?"

Tad nodded, looking so forlorn and downcast that he wanted to hug him...after he kicked him in the ass.

"I'm sorry, Gabe."

"That's okay." It wasn't. Not at all.

Tad said, "I guess I never thought he was real."

"He is."

Tad nodded. "And just as smirky as you said."

"Right. Wait. Did you call Homeland Security about Monroe and his partner?"

"Not Monroe. Give me a little credit. He was Goodwin, and his partner was Wolfe. And Homeland Security denied all knowledge and denied being interested in Black or having any info about her."

"Of course, they did. Which might even be true. I don't know who Monroe works for. He might be free-lance like Penelope."

Tad nodded.

"So how did he react when you told him that the victim was Phillip Bergeron? Was he surprised?"

Tad nodded some more. "I think so. He definitely wanted to know what I had against her. That wasn't fake."

"Did he tell you anything?"

Tad shook his head. "Any ideas?"

"One." He went to the laundry alcove and grabbed the iron. "I can't stand it any longer. Take off your jacket."

"Why?"

"I have to iron your jacket." He plugged the iron in.

He was looking at the pants, but Tad said, "I'm not taking

my pants off."

"I could avert my eyes? No? Okay. But let me iron the jacket. Please?"

Tad handed over the jacket. "It isn't that bad, Bergeron."

It was, but he didn't say anything. He ironed the most egregious wrinkles and felt better.

Tad put his jacket on. "Thanks. I guess. So the case?"

He should give Tad a tie. He focused. "I have one last idea. I want to drive out to Berwyn to talk to Jonathan Bergeron."

Tad's skeptical look was above his baseline expression. "How old is he?"

"He's in his seventies."

"And he's sick?"

"Yes. But he wasn't always a senior citizen or sick, Detective, and some events cast long shadows. And we don't really know how sick he is."

Tad smiled at him. "Is that so? So Jonathan strung up his son and hired those two guys to blow you away?"

"I hope not."

"You're serious."

"Yes."

"Berwyn?"

"Yes. Probably tomorrow. I can drive?"

But Tad shook his head. "I have other cases, Bergeron."

"Right. Well, can I get my gun back?" But Tad smiled at him. "I'm a good shot, Czerwinski, and I know how to handle the Glock."

Tad nodded. "I thought the Russian guy must have done some of the damage to the SUV and the perps, but that was all you, wasn't it?'

"You don't believe it?"

"All the bullets were from a Glock, and the other guy had a Markarov. You'll get it back soon."

And Tad headed for the door. "And thanks for pressing my jacket."

"Get your suits dry-cleaned, Detective."

Tad smiled his killer smile. "Will do. Later, Bergeron."

Thursday
9:00 am

He had rushed to take a shower and hadn't been too late. More importantly, he had been in his cubicle when Jennifer arrived.

He pretended to be looking at his computer as he called the number for F. X. Foley. He got a robot voicemail message just like every other time.

"This is Gabriel Bergeron. Your tenant. In 4A. On Arch Street. Did you send an electrician to my apartment? And if so, what's wrong with the place. And if not, we need to talk about building security. Call me. Gabriel Bergeron."

Which was a total waste of recording time.

He called Max Nagy as he scrolled through his email.

And after being on hold long enough to discard the junk and to read and reply to everything else in his inbox, Max picked up.

"What?"

"Good morning, Max. How are you today. Going to be another hot one. How is Stephanie? And how did you ever get her to marry you?"

Max and Stephanie were very much the frog and the princess.

Max snorted. "I was very, very lucky, and don't think I don't know it. But I'm busy?"

"Of course, any rumors about Reed Gibson?"

"How did you know?"

"Know what?"

"That something was up with Gibson?"

"Just a hunch. So?"

"So, you didn't hear this from me, but it seems that Gibson is having legal and financial problems."

"Specify, Max."

"No idea. Just rumors that all is not well. Which may turn out to be overblown. I mean he could sell that place in Berwyn and pay off the national debt."

"Right. Thanks, Max."

"Not going to share with your buddy Max?"

"Not yet. It was just a hunch."

"Call me when it's more than that. Okay?"

"Sure, Max."

And he went to work with willing hands and heart. Until break time when he got two calls.

The first was from Lydia. "I spoke to Dad, and he would like to talk to you, but I'm afraid today isn't one of his good days. Maybe tomorrow, Gabriel?"

"Sure. Thanks, Lydia. You'll call me?"

"I will."

Which was disappointing.

And then Cory called. "Hi, Gabe."

"You aren't coming home."

"I am. But not until Sunday."

"Is Sunday a sure thing, Poirier?"

"Yes, Gabe. But if something should go wrong, which it won't, you could come here?"

"Here where? Nova Scotia?"

"Yes. Well?"

"Well, sure."

Shit! He had never been allowed to be anywhere near Cory while he was on a case. "But won't you get into trouble? With Danielle?"

"No."

"And why is that, Special Agent? Use your words."

"Because Danielle might be mulling over the idea of letting

you consult on certain cases. The bizarre, strange, weird ones."

He looked at his phone. It was his phone, and the voice certainly sounded like Cory's, but this had to be an elaborate prank.

"Right. I can hear Bornheimer laughing in the background, Poirier."

"This is not a joke."

"Sure. Right. We'll talk when you get home."

"This is real, Gabe."

"I'm looking forward to seeing you on Sunday, Mr. Poirier."

"And I you."

And Cory was gone. He wasn't going to think about this. It wasn't real. It couldn't be.

He went back to work.

Friday
9:00 am

He hadn't heard back from Mr. F. X. Foley, who might or might not exist. He hadn't seen Cordrey, who might or might not be an electrician.

He also hadn't heard from Lydia, whose father might or might not be sick.

So except for Cordrey not being around, things weren't going too well.

But it was the weekend, and he might see Cory so he shouldn't complain.

He was thinking about going for a run when his phone rang. An unknown caller wanted a moment of his time. And probably his identity and bank account information. But still.

"Hello?"

"Nosy bastard."

"Who is this? People call me that all the time so you need supply some additional information...."

"Will you just shut up!"

"Penelope?"

"Who else would it be?"

"Almost anyone else I've ever spoken to."

"I should just hang up."

"No! Please don't do that. Are you okay?" She sounded sloshed or possibly ill? "Where are you?"

"Wouldn't you like to know? You and that Kirill. Bastard took advantage of me."

He wanted to say that no one had taken advantage of Penelope Chernova since she was three. Well, four tops. Whenever she got her permanent teeth.

"Kirill really likes you." If Kirill remembered her?

"He does? I like him too. We really had fun."

"Yeah, my mattress will never be the same."

Which sent her into a paroxysm of glee that almost ended her. "Take a breath, Penelope, and tell me how you are."

She stopped cackling. "How do you think I am! You've screwed up everything, Bergeron. My fingerprints and photo are out there. I'm screwed; my career is screwed. I hate you. Nosy bastard."

They had come full circle. "Does Billy know where you are?"

"Wouldn't you like to know!"

"No, I don't care." Well, he did; very much. "But Billy's worried about you."

"He is?"

"Of course, he is. At least, call him, Penelope."

"I'll think about it. Is Dr. Stanko there?"

"Joe? No idea."

"Bastard."

"Right. I didn't like him very much. His smile is fake."

Penelope said, "Only intelligent thing that's ever come out of your mouth."

"So, Penelope, about Phillip...."

"Shut up about Phillip."

And she started blubbering. Which went on for some time but segued into the hiccups.

"Drink a glass of water."

She snarled. "That doesn't work!"

"Right. And Phillip?"

More crying which sounded real but petered out eventually. He was glad there was no video; Penelope was probably not looking too attractive by now.

"I'm sorry about Phillip, Penelope. Did you really like him?"

"Yes. It wouldn't have lasted, but it was good. It started out as a business transaction, but then it changed."

"Right. He liked you too. He told his sister, Camille."

"Is that bullshit, Bergeron?"

"No. You could ask her yourself."

"You went to the funeral."

"I did. It was nice...for a funeral. Were you there? Lurking somewhere?"

"Yes."

"So who killed him, Penelope?"

"I don't know, Bergeron."

"But you have a very good idea."

She laughed. "He was handsome and fun and knew how to show a girl a very good time, but he wasn't too bright."

"No?"

"No."

And then the silence stretched out so long that he thought she was gone.

"He didn't think about the consequences."

"But you do?"

"Yeah."

"But you want the guy who killed Phillip to pay."

"Yeah. If I had any cash or anyway to make some, I would hire some putz to take out that smiling bastard. I'd do it myself but I hate guns."

"So instead, you're going to tell me?"

More silence.

"Go see Uncle Bergeron."

"I don't have an Uncle Bergeron, Penelope."

"Jonathan Bergeron. Your cousin or whatever the Hell he is."

"Okay. I should go see Jonathan Bergeron and talk to him about what?"

"Ask him about David."

And this time she really was gone.

He called Czerwinski, and the detective answered him.

"What?"

Nobody had phone manners any more.

"You have to come with me to Berwyn to question Jonathan Bergeron."

"No, I don't."

"You do, because Penelope just called me and told me to ask him about David."

"Who the Hell is David?"

"It would be my guess that David is the one who was being blackmailed by Phillip Bergeron."

Friday Noon

He had called Lydia and told her that he and Detective Czerwinski needed to see her father urgently.

And she had been reluctant and distant and noncommittal. Which seemed strange since Jonathan didn't seem to be at death's door?

But he had gotten in his Jeep and headed out of the city anyway without waiting for permission or for Czerwinski to come with him.

And now he was almost to the house.

His phone rang. "Hello, Detective. Nice of you to call. Are you coming, Czerwinski? By any chance?"

"Yeah. Don't do anything until I get there, Bergeron."

And Tad was gone. He was going to sit Tad down and school him in phone etiquette. It would be nice to know how far out Czerwinski was.

And he needed to teach him how to properly knot a tie.

He sighed. He pulled into the driveway and parked. The Jeep still looked tacky next to Schönbrunn Palace, but he wasn't going to let it bother him.

He knocked on the door; three times.

He waited. He knocked again.

The door itself was a slab of iron-bound oak that would thwart a Viking horde, but the stain-glass sidelights didn't look so tough.

Not that he was going to smash Lydia's windows.

The door swung open, and Nordic Frost was glaring at him. "Gabriel Bergeron. I'm here to see Mrs. Gibson. I called."

Nordic Frost shook her head, but he saw Lydia crossing the entrance hall. "It's all right, Britta."

Britta was itching to defend the castle from this obviously unwelcome guest. "Are you sure, Mrs. Gibson?"

Lydia smiled. "Yes, Britta. Let Gabe in. And a Detective Czerwinski may be coming."

Britta said, "Should I call Mr. Gibson?"

Lydia shook her head. "Come in, Gabe. I told Dad that you were coming, but this has to be a very short visit."

Lydia really didn't want him talking to Jonathan, but he couldn't figure out why not?

Lydia started up the stairs, and he caught up to her. She turned right at the top, and they were strolling toward the west wing when somebody started beating on the front door.

Britta spun on her heel and opened the door.

But it wasn't Tad.

Mr. Cordrey strode in. Without his coverall, cap, or tool belt, but with a large, black pistol made yet more sinister by a long, black silencer. And with a frenzied look in his gray eyes.

Cordrey shoved the pistol into Britta's face. "You're coming with me! Now!"

Britta didn't flinch or say a word.

"Where is Gabriel Bergeron?"

Britta's eyes tracked up and locked onto the mistress of the house and one Gabriel Bergeron.

Cordrey pointed the pistol at him and smiled. "Good. All of you together."

And then with admirable sang-froid, Britta punched Cordrey in the face. And ran.

Cordrey was wearing a suit but no amount of tailoring could conceal his basic pear shape. He had probably never been in a gym and likewise had never been punched in the nose.

Britta's aim had been perfect, and Cordrey was bleeding all over his white shirt and silk tie.

But Cordrey recovered and loosed a volley toward Britta,

and she went down. Cordrey was stalking over to finish her off.

He grabbed a vase and hurled it, flowers and all, at Cordrey. His aim was almost as good as Britta's.

It would have made Cory proud to see the vase clip Cordrey's blond head before smashing into the wall and raining ceramic shards and water all over him.

And lilacs.

Cordrey shrieked and flailed. His squeal became an alto screech; a composition scored for badly-tuned piccolo and broken clarinet.

He grabbed Lydia, and they ran as Cordrey started up the stairs firing at them.

Cordrey had also never been to a gun range.

He had no idea where they were going, but Lydia seemed to be certain of their course. They made it around a corner and turned left before Cordrey reached the top of the stairs.

"Where are we going?"

"Dad's suite!"

Lydia ran down the hall and turned right into a short hallway and sprinted to the solid looking door at the end.

Which was all well and good, but they had passed a perfectly good set of stairs, which probably led to a perfectly good exit.

But she was slamming the door almost before he got inside the suite. She bolted the door and took a breath.

"We'll be safe here."

He scurried around. The main room was a bedroom, and in the center of a large bed lay a frail man with snow white hair; probably an antique. The bed, not the man. Though he was no spring chicken.

There was a sitting room and library on the right along with a kitchenette; a large bathroom with a walk in shower on the left.

There were no other doors.

"Shit."

Lydia said, "What's wrong? We'll call the police...."

The frail man said, "What is it, Lydia?"

She shot over to his side and took his hand. "Nothing,

Dad."

Dad smiled, and the origins of Lydia's cool smile were obvious. "The truth, Lydia. This is Gabriel? I assume?"

"Yes. A man is here, but he can't get into this room, Dad."

The oak door was as thick as the door to a castle keep. Which was good. It had an antique lock but also a deadbolt so he didn't think Cordrey could batter it down.

But he could set fire to the house.

And there was a glass transom above the door.

"Shit squared." Lydia managed to raise a disparaging eyebrow. "He can break the glass and shoot us!"

She considered. "Well, I suppose he could...but we can go into the study?"

He tried calling Czerwinski, but he had one bar.

She said, "Service is spotty out here...especially inside the house."

"Right. Try your cellphone, Lydia."

She shook her head. "It's downstairs, but Dad has a land line."

"Great. Call 911."

And she tried. "There's no dial tone."

"Shit cubed." He thought Jonathan smiled. "Okay. Has Cordrey ever been in here? Would he know where Jonathan's room is?"

"No. How would he?"

He didn't know, but he was getting a trapped feeling.

He looked at Jonathan. "This isn't exactly how I imagined our first meeting, Sir, but you wouldn't have a gun tucked away in a drawer?" A head shake. "Pepper spray? A stun gun? A bow and arrow? A sword?"

Jonathan was definitely smiling. "I have a letter opener, but it isn't very sharp."

They were all going to die.

He wanted to open the door and see if Cordrey had found Jonathan's room, but that didn't seem wise.

But the antique lock had a keyhole large enough for a chatelaine's key. He knelt and peeped. The short hallway looked clear.

Of course, Cordrey could have flattened himself against the wall, just waiting for someone to open the door.

Lydia whispered in his ear. "Do you see him?"

He gritted his teeth and didn't flinch or flail. He had to live up to the stiff-upper-lip standards of this branch of his family.

"No."

"You aren't going to open the door, are you?"

"No."

He kept staring. He thought he heard something. And then Cordrey came into view. He was methodically opening each door along the long hallway and searching each room.

He would probably start on this hallway next.

"He's searching the rooms along the main hall."

Lydia was two inches away breathing in his left ear. "But he'll find us."

"He will." He looked at Jonathan. "Can you get him into the study?"

She nodded. "Yes. He has a wheelchair. What are you going to do?"

"I'm going to go out there and lure Cordrey away...preferably outdoors."

"Is that a good idea?"

"Sure. Absolutely. He's a terrible shot. Couldn't hit the broadside of a barn."

Which was true, but in a narrow hallway, he didn't have to be very good.

He stood up and unlocked the deadbolt slowly and silently. He peeped through the keyhole one last time.

And then another voice whispered in his right ear. "Take this, Gabriel."

Jonathan had gotten himself out of bed and was offering him a silver candlestick.

He took it. Jonathan said, "Be careful."

He smiled at his cousin. Well, he was his first cousin, once removed. "Will do. Hunker down in the study."

Jonathan smiled and may have winked at him. "Will do."

Lydia guided her father away from the door, which he opened one millimeter at a time until he was sure Cordrey wasn't lurking just outside.

He stepped out and closed the door. He heard the deadbolt slide home.

He ran to the intersection of the hallways gripping the heavy candlestick; it had a nice heft and would do some serious damage.

Cordrey was just finishing the rooms along the main hall, and was backing out of what looked like a linen closet.

He covered the distance to the stairs in two strides. He grabbed the newel post and swung his body around. He paused just long enough to deliberately smack the post with the candlestick.

Cordrey spun.

Cordrey spotted him

Cordrey smiled and made a triumphant, screech like an owl drunk with blood lust.

He ran down the stairs to the sound of thump, thud, thump, thud as the pistol spat bullets in his general direction. The last thump was followed by the sound of glass shattering and tinkling down.

It occurred to him that he should have asked Lydia for the location of the nearest exit.

He was on the first floor running down another gleaming hallway. Who waxed all these floors?

He was coming to a door. If it was locked, he was up a malodorous creek without a paddle.

It swung open.

He was in a kitchen which was the size of his apartment. There was one other door. He sprinted across.

The door was locked, but the deadbolt didn't require a key. The door opened into a mud room with boots in a row. The mud room widened into a glassed-in porch which led to a greenhouse.

He ran between the raised beds heading for the far end.

He heard a noise behind him and ducked out of instinct. An instant later came a series of thumps, and the glass wall ahead of him shattered into a hundred singing shards.

Which made looking for a door unnecessary.

He smashed through the empty frame and ran as fast as he could.

He was in the middle of Reed's rose garden.

Roses did not provide much cover. He decided that running in a straight line was not a viable survival tactic. He may have tripped and fallen and damaged a few bushes as he zigged and zagged.

He saw his Jeep. Which wouldn't offer any refuge. Next to it was a metallic blue Mercedes which was surely Cordrey's.

But next to that was a faded red, Ford SUV with dirty windows. It was empty.

What were the chances that Czerwinski drove such a vehicle?

He was tired of rose hopping; he ran for the SUV. He heard a thump and then the driver side window of his Jeep shattered into a thousand ice chips. He hit the dirt and crawled behind and under the Jeep.

He could see a pair of legs approaching.

He was surprised to learn that through everything he had kept a grip on the candlestick. The legs were still coming.

The legs stopped and assessed the situation. The legs tried to tip-toe along the side of the Jeep.

He waited until the legs were almost to the rear of the vehicle before he lunged. He smashed the silver candlestick down on the foot that belonged to the legs that connected to Cordrey's pain centers.

Cordrey screamed and fell down, but didn't lose his grip on the pistol.

He ran for the red SUV.

Cordrey was on the ground still firing.

"Drop the weapon! Do it now!"

He peeped out. Czerwinski had the drop on Cordrey, but the guy was shaking his head.

"Drop it! Or I will shoot you!"

Czerwinski was holding the gun with both hands, arms outstretched. Cordrey was on the ground...with tears in his eyes.

Cordrey screamed, firing as he raised the pistol toward the detective. Czerwinski fired twice.

The discharges were thunder-loud after the thumps of the silenced pistol.

Cordrey dropped the pistol and slumped. Czerwinski ran forward and kicked the gun away. "Bergeron?"

"Here."

"You okay?"

"Yeah."

"Get the gun."

"Right." He looked at Cordrey. "Is he dead?"

Czerwinski leaned over and felt for a pulse. "No. Not yet."

Cordrey was bleeding a lot.

"What happened? Who is this? Anybody else going to start shooting at us?"

He said, "No. He's the only bad guy. I'll tell you what I know, but first you need to find Britta. She might still be alive."

"Who?"

"Maid. Blonde. Nordic. Cordrey shot her after she punched him in the nose. She's inside. In the entrance hall."

Czerwinski said, "Call for an ambulance."

"Right. I'll try." He had three bars now. He dialed 911 and told the lady that he needed an ambulance for two gunshot victims and explained about Detective Czerwinski being on the scene.

He was tired; very, very tired. He sat down beside Cordrey. He should probably try to stop the bleeding?

He thought he should do that. He grabbed an old sweatshirt out of the Jeep.

Cordrey had two holes in his torso: one was high, just below his shoulder, the other was midway down on the right.

The lower one looked more serious even though both were bleeding. He applied pressure to the abdominal one.

Cordrey groaned, and his eyes flickered open. Cordrey focused on him. "Bergeron?"

"Yes, Cordrey." The guy had tried to kill him; probably several times. "The ambulance is on the way."

"I'm dying?"

"No. You'll be fine."

"I don't think so." Cordrey was staring at him. "Why were you so hard to kill?"

He shrugged.

"And you just wouldn't stop asking questions."

He should leave the guy alone, but he might never know if he didn't ask.

"You came here to kill me? And Jonathan?"

He nodded and coughed and screamed in pain. "I had to. The guys I hired wouldn't come. They were scared. Of you."

"Why did you have to kill us? Jonathan is an old man and sick, Cordrey, and I don't know anything. Really. That isn't your real name, is it?"

A little smile formed on Cordrey's plump lips. "No."

"So what is your name?"

Cordrey lay there, but then he said, "Bart Stoker."

"And what's your beef with Jonathan? And Phillip?"

Cordrey's eyes were closed. "Dead men tell no tales."

"Phillip knew something? Which Jonathan also knows?"

"Jonathan."

"What about him?" And then he remembered what Penelope had said, "Who is David?"

Cordrey squeezed his eyes shut and then seemed to relax.

"Stoker? Stay with me, Bart! I can hear the ambulance." Which he could.

But it was the police. The officers rolled out of a white SUV with their weapons drawn, freaked by all the blood on Bart and on him.

"Hands over your head! Now!"

He followed instructions, and they cuffed him and left him kneeling on the ground as the ambulance pulled up.

He told them all about Czerwinski and Britta, and they went in and got acquainted. And nobody shot anybody.

And after a while, Czerwinski came out and made them uncuff him. Britta was brought out on a gurney, conscious, calm, and composed.

He said, "Czerwinski? The guy said his name was Bart

Stoker, but that's all he'd say. Wait. Have you told Lydia it's safe to come out?"

Czerwinski looked at him; his hands were red and sticky with Britta's cold, Nordic blood. "Kinda busy, Bergeron."

"Right. Okay. I'll do that then?"

Czerwinski nodded. He was talking to the officers.

He retraced his steps to Jonathan's suite. Lydia was peering out from behind the door; she had the matching, silver candlestick clutched tightly in her hand.

"Gabe! What's happened? Are you all right? Is that your blood?"

"No, Lydia."

Jonathan's voice whispered, "Lydia? Where are you?"

Lydia turned and went back to the study.

He said, "Everything is fine. The gunmen, Bart Stoker, was shot and disarmed. It's safe now."

Jonathan nodded, but his face was flushed, and his breathing was ragged. And his lips were a funny color; a bluish shade that lips shouldn't be.

Lydia said, "Help me get him back into bed."

And they did.

She gave Jonathan a pill. "Try to calm down, Dad." She smiled and stroked his white hair. "The excitement is over now."

Jonathan tried to smile as he nodded, and then he closed his eyes.

This was obviously not the time to ask questions even if it might be the only chance he'd ever get.

Lydia said, "I think you should go, Gabe."

He nodded. "Right. I think so too."

And then a deep, booming voice, which reminded him of Bornheimer's voice but two octaves lower, rumbled behind him.

"Mrs. Gibson! Are you all right? And Mr. Jonathan?"

Lydia said, "Yes, we are. Thank you."

The guy was refrigerator shaped...one with double doors. He sported the chest, arms, and shoulders of a professional football player who had been fired because he'd killed too many of the other players...in practice.

He was even bigger than Dale or Roy.

Lydia said, "I'm glad you're back, Hand. Could you show Gabe out?"

And she turned back to her father.

He looked up at the guy. "Hand?" His eyes may have dropped and scanned from right to left. Hand's hands were monumental...just like the rest of him. Presumably.

Hand gave him a look, and he trotted out of the bedroom and down the hall with Hand behind him. If he stopped suddenly, Hand might stomp him into the carpet without noticing.

He didn't feel safe until he was out the front door.

"I'm Gabriel Bergeron, Mrs. Gibson's cousin."

Hand just stood there.

"Are you Mrs. Gibson's bodyguard?" Hand just stared. "I wish you'd been here an hour ago."

Which might be construed as criticism of Hand's job performance.

"Not that you probably didn't have a good reason to be out of the house."

Hand growled at him, jaw clenched, dark eyes flashing. A vein was throbbing in his temple.

He took three steps back and spun around.

The ambulances were gone. Czerwinski was gone, but his red SUV was still there.

A couple of white SUVs were blocking his Jeep. They had "Tredyffrin Township Police" emblazoned on their doors.

Two officers were looking at him. They had medium blue shirts and black pants with a medium blue stripe down the outside seam.

He tried smiling at them. "Where is Detective Czerwinski?"

The younger glanced at the older. The older said, "Ask the lieutenant."

"Okay. Where is he?"

The older cop shrugged. "He doesn't check in with me." The younger cop smiled.

He was bruised and rose scratched and had been shot at. Repeatedly. He got a notebook from the Jeep.

He walked up to the officers until he could have tapped them on the chest with his pen. He recorded their names and numbers. "Thanks for your help, Officer Blanchard. You too, Officer McCullough. I'll be sure to tell your lieutenant...and your captain...just how helpful you've been."

Officer Blanchard glared at him but didn't punch him in the face.

"And now if you could move your vehicle just a foot or so, I'll be on my way?"

Young Officer McCullough said, "Who are you exactly?"

"Nobody." He gave them his very best smile. "Well, I'm Mrs. Gibson's cousin, and Reed James Farley Gibson, III, and I are the very best of friends."

Which impressed them more than they were willing to admit.

He sat in his Jeep for a good five minutes as McCullough argued with Blanchard. Eventually, McCullough ignored his partner's counsel and moved his SUV. Which appeared to vex Blanchard no end.

McCullough stuck his head through the shattered Jeep window. The officer had cornflower blue eyes. "The cop from Philly went with the ambulance...with the shooter."

"Thank you, Officer McCullough. You have a swell day."

And he drove home with the wind whistling through his hair. He played "Ride of the Valkyries" at full volume and tried to go with it.

Sunday
2:00 pm

Cory had gotten home to his condo a little after 9:00 am to find him waiting, and they had enjoyed getting reacquainted.

Really enjoyed.

But he was too exhausted now to do more than call in an order for food; Italian.

Cory smiled at him. "So what have you been up to?"

"Moi? Nothing much." He had thought about what to tell Cory, and he thought that a slow release of the pertinent details might be best.

"I did meet three, long-lost cousins; well four actually."

Cory rotated his noble head to stare at him. "You did? Three or four, Bergeron?"

Cory didn't need to know that Phillip was gone. "Four. Three second cousins and one first cousin, once removed; the first cousin is Jonathan. Nephew of my grandfather, Andrew."

"How?"

"Well, I imagine they were conceived in the usual way."

"Bergeron."

"You mean how did I meet them? They found me. They came to Aunt Flo's house...to the bed and breakfast."

"Which you are totally fine with now?"

"Totally, Dude."

"So tell me about them."

And he did. All the information that Cory really needed to know at this point.

"And how about you, Special Agent? Tell me about your case. And why you went to Halifax?"

And Cory told him a tale of an Egyptian necklace, a gold, bejeweled necklace, supposedly given by one Akhenaten to one Nefertiti.

He raised an eyebrow and tried to look as skeptical as Czerwinski.

Cory said, "I know. From the photos we were given, the style and workmanship look authentic. It appears to be gold. But we aren't even sure that it was stolen."

"Insurance scam?"

"Possible."

"So you don't know where it is?"

"We might."

He frowned at Cory. "You'd be very cross with me if I told you a story as confused as this."

Cory smiled and stroked his face. "We do have two guys in custody."

"Because?"

"They broke into the Boston residence of a very wealthy individual."

"Who is going to remain anonymous?"

"Until he isn't."

"What?"

"We are negotiating with the thieves for the return of the necklace." He stretched his gorgeous muscles. "Well, Brunetti is."

"So the owner is more interested in getting the necklace back than jailing the thieves?"

"It's more complicated than that."

He shook his head and leaped gracefully out of bed. "I'm taking a shower. Don't tell me any more about this until you can put together a cogent narrative, Corentin."

Cory was looking at him. "Where did you get all the scratches?"

"These? I fell into a rose bush. Well, maybe it was a couple of rose bushes. But I'm fine." He gave Cory a double biceps pose. "See?"

"Gabe."

"No, it's the truth. You know how clumsy I am."

"I know how much you hate being called clumsy, Bergeron."

"Do not."

And he ran for the shower.

And Cory joined him. Which was nice.

And Cory told him more bits and pieces about his case.

He had called Czerwinski half a dozen times on Saturday and left messages and gotten zero response. The officers at the 24th District Headquarters were less than helpful.

But he hadn't called Czerwinski today to find out what the Hell was going on with Bart and their case. Not yet.

He was beginning to fear that Czerwinski was cutting him out now that the main culprit had been caught.

He didn't even know if Bart Stoker was still alive.

Cory was staring at him.

"What?"

Cory said, "I don't know, but something is up with you."

"Poppycock and balderdash."

Cory said, "You weren't serious about getting a puppy?"

"A puppy?" His brain kicked in a half second later. "No, not if you don't want to?" What was he saying? He didn't want a puppy.

"I don't think so, Gabe."

"Okay."

"Okay?" Cory was staring at him funny.

It was fortunate that Cory had been distracted by the arrival of their food. He was very careful not to mention anything dog related for the rest of the day, and Cory hadn't mentioned it again. Which was good.

But he hadn't had a chance to call the perfidious Tadeusz Czerwinski.

Tuesday 10:00 am

He had seethed Monday, and had been so angry by mid-afternoon that he had told Baldacci and Carla and Jennifer just how betrayed he felt. In great detail.

And after they had offered what cold comfort they could, he had whined to Paul Hearne and Chatterjee.

He thought Paul had been outraged on his behalf, but he didn't appear capable of much more than a mild outrage.

Chatterjee had shown zero sympathy.

And today he was working up a fine, righteous fury again. He might as well stop pretending to work.

He spun around his chair, but Carla and Baldacci were ignoring him. Which he understood. They were tired of hearing what a snake Czerwinski was.

But Paul was heading his way. "Gabe?"

"Yes, Paul." Paul's face looked grayer than usual. He got out of his chair. "Have a seat."

Paul smiled. "Thanks. But I'm fine." He patted his belly.

"No, sit down. I insist."

Paul smiled and sat and didn't say anything.

"Was there something, Paul?"

"Yes." Paul smiled. "I think you should go there."

"Where?"

"To his office. Czerwinski's."

"You do?"

Paul nodded his gray, fuzzy head. "After all the work you

did on the case. You were shot at twice, Gabe. He shouldn't treat you like this."

"No! He shouldn't." And then he remembered Paul's contribution. "After all WE did, Paul."

Paul smiled. "You should talk to him. Or to his boss."

"You're absolutely right! I should. I will!"

And he marched into Jennifer's office. He may have banged on her desk. "I need a few hours off, Jennifer! Right now!"

Jennifer glared at him. "Because I think you've been treated unfairly, Bergeron, I'm going to overlook what sounds like a demand and grant your request."

"Right! Thanks, Jennifer. Sorry. But Czerwinski...."

Jennifer rolled her eyes. "Don't tell me, Bergeron. Tell him."

"Right. You're right as always, Jennifer, and I am truly lucky to have you as a boss. Truly lucky...."

"Get out of my office, Bergeron." She looked up from her screen. "And never, ever bang on my desk again."

"Of course, Jennifer. Never again."

And he turned to go, but Baldacci was blocking his way. "What is it, Harry?"

But then, over Baldacci's shoulder, he spotted Czerwinski. Smirking at him.

Czerwinski was saved from being assaulted only because Baldacci tackled him as he launched himself toward the detective.

And because Baldacci was currently sitting on his back.

"Get off me, Harry! Right now!"

Czerwinski crouched down by his head. "Want to take a swing at me, Bergeron?" More smirking. "And after I came to get you so you can meet David."

"What?"

Paul said, "The guy Penelope told you to mention to Jonathan, Gabe."

He almost snarled at Paul. He gritted his teeth. "I remember. Thanks, Paul."

Paul smiled at him, but this smile wasn't the least bit dim or unfocused. Paul Hearne was amused by him. And maybe had been all along? And then Paul winked at him.

"Okay. You can get off me, Baldacci."

Which Baldacci did.

He got to his feet gracefully. He glared at Baldacci. "You need to lose weight."

Baldacci smiled at him. In fact, the whole office was smiling at him; especially Czerwinski. And Jennifer.

Well, she was smiling at Czerwinski mainly.

He hated them all.

Czerwinski said, "Coming?"

"Maybe. Where are we going?"

"The 'Oxley for Senate' campaign headquarters."

And Czerwinski sauntered to the elevator.

He may have followed.

Czerwinski's red SUV was parked in front. He got in. "Two things: is this Oxley connected to Oxley International?"

"Mr. Oxley is the son of the founder."

"Really? And is Bart Stoker alive?"

Czerwinski shook his head as she pulled into traffic. "No. He made it to the hospital. Crashed in the ER."

"Sorry, Czerwinski." The detective shrugged a macho, death-is-my-business shrug. "Did you question him? On the way to the hospital?"

Czerwinski nodded. "He admitted that he killed Phillip Bergeron. Even told me how hard it was to hold him and tie the sheet and then to raise him off the floor."

"And?"

"And that was it. Not a word about David. Nothing else except that Phillip was a smiling bastard and a blackmailer."

"And he was blackmailing Stoker?"

Czerwinski laughed. "I don't think so. The guy was squeaky clean until he went insane."

"Then who?"

"I have a suspicion." Czerwinski stopped smiling. "But I doubt I'll ever be able to prove it." Czerwinski winked at him. "Even with your help."

"Like I'd help you."

Czerwinski was still laughing when he parked in a no-parking zone on Market Street.

The building was twenty stories or so; the first five stories were all glass. A pharmacy occupied one corner of the ground floor, but the other corner had big banners proclaiming "Oxley for Senate."

There was a police officer guarding the door. Czerwinski nodded at him and went inside. The place was either just getting set up or was being cleared out.

Rows of barren desks marched across the space but there wasn't much else except a couple of tables with stacks of fliers and some folding chairs.

Dust motes floated in the shafts of sunlight coming through the glass walls.

Czerwinski marched to the back where there were a half dozen, private offices.

He entered the first one.

There was an air mattress on the floor and clothes, mostly dirty, scattered around. The desk was covered with take-out containers and electronic stuff. And boxes of ammo.

"What is this, Tad?"

Czerwinski said, "This is where Bart Stoker has been living and plotting to kill people for the last two months."

"Why? Did he work for this Oxley?"

Czerwinski nodded. "Yeah. C. David Oxley is a congressman, representing a district near Harrisburg."

"David?"

Czerwinski smirked again. "David."

"And Stoker's job?"

"Mr. Stoker had been Oxley's chief of staff."

"But wasn't currently?"

Tad was smirking again. "According to Mr. Oxley's wife. Stoker was selected to run the senate campaign at the end of last year, but he was put on leave a few months ago. Also according to Mrs. Oxley."

"But we don't believe her?"

Tad shook his head.

"So what is the electronic gear for?"

Tad smiled. "That was to bug your apartment."

"Say again?"

"He bugged your apartment. We also found bugs in the row house on Savin Street where Phillip was crashing."

"You never said."

Tad nodded. "Sorry. The bugs from Savin didn't lead anywhere."

"Wait. How do you know that my apartment was bugged?"

"The techs found them...yesterday. Stoker had drilled through the wall from the hallway and slipped the bugs through the holes. Never had to get into your apartment. And they were tiny. You wouldn't have noticed them unless you climbed a ladder and really looked."

"Shit! I saw him in my building...a month ago."

"And he's heard everything you've said since then."

"So he heard me tell Kirill about Penelope and heard me questioning her. And he heard me repeat the name David when she called me."

Tad nodded. "Smart little bastard. Insane but clever."

"He was planning on killing all of us; Lydia, Jonathan, me, you...and Britta."

"Yeah."

"So he did it for Oxley?"

Tad really smiled. "That is the million dollar question. He's coming here by the way."

"Oxley?"

"And the wife. They want to 'help' with the investigation."

"You don't believe it?"

"Never trust a politician. Give me a murderer or a bank robber any day."

He smiled at Tad. "That's very cynical, Tadeusz."

Tuesday
11:00 am

The officer guarding the door stuck his head in. "Detective? Some people to see you?"

Tad said, "Let them in."

And C. David Oxley and his good wife entered with a trumpet flourish and a drum roll. Well, not really.

But they did strike a pose as if waiting for the flashing of cameras to cease. Two stocky, young men were behind them; their faces set in semi-permanent scowls. A young lady dressed all in black entered and stood next to the scowlers.

David Oxley might be fifty. He was almost Cory's height and well-built. He had a handsome face barely touched by time.

But the electric blue eyes were his salient feature. That is, until he smiled, and then it was a toss-up.

He may have forgotten how to breathe for just a bit. Shave off a decade or two, and Oxley must have been extraordinary.

He looked at Tad. Did Tad see it? Feel it?

But Tad was smiling an ordinary smile as he shook Oxley's hand. "I'm Detective Czerwinski. Thank you for coming, Congressman."

Oxley smiled again, including him in the smile, and he soaked it in like a desert flower in the cool rain.

Oxley said, "Glad to help, Detective. If I can."

And then he noticed Mrs. Oxley. She was studying the effect David was having. There was just the trace of a smirk on her face.

She was younger than David by a good bit and beautiful. Her auburn hair was parted in the middle and fell sleekly around her ears. She was wearing a navy dress. Her earrings were silver filigree with royal blue beads dangling below and matched her necklace. She was shod with silver heels laced with gossamer straps.

But she had gone a bit too heavy with the eye makeup, and her lashes were straining under the weight of the black gunk.

Oxley said, "And this is my beautiful wife, Isla."

Tad liked Isla, and Isla clocked all of Tad's assets. They smiled and shook hands.

And then Isla turned to him.

She wasn't sure about him. He could feel the analysis as the cross hairs locked in, and the gray eyes swept over him.

He should have worn his best suit, but it probably wouldn't have helped.

"It's nice to meet you, Mrs. Oxley. I'm Gabriel Bergeron."

Isla didn't react at all, but David's face went as stony as if he had run into Medusa.

She shook his hand. "And you too, Mr. Bergeron. Are you with the police?"

"No. But I have a connection to the case."

She was willing him to say more, but he just smiled at her.

Oxley was also staring at him. He had summoned a semi-smile which seemed to be his default state. They shook hands. Oxley's grip was strong, but he matched it.

Tad said, "What can you tell me about Bart Stoker?"

Oxley ditched the semi-smile for a serious, grave demeanor. Isla focused on David.

Oxley said, "It's very sad. He was such a bright, young man. Did he really attack Mrs. Gibson, Detective?"

"I'm afraid so. He broke into her home and shot her maid with the intention of killing everyone there. Any idea why he would have done that, Congressman?"

"I don't know of any reason, Detective, except that he wasn't well and hadn't been so for some months."

Czerwinski said, "Not well how?"

Isla said, "He had a breakdown, Detective." She glanced at the closest table. "Why don't we sit down?"

Czerwinski unfolded a metal chair for her and dusted it with the arm of his suit. Which wouldn't hurt the suit.

Isla smiled at Tad and managed to aim the cleavage at his face as she sat.

"Thank you, Detective." Tad sat next to her. "Bart was incredibly bright, but the strain of work became too much for him...was it three months ago, David?"

He and David were sitting across the table from Isla and smiling Tad.

David fielded the ball. "A bit more, Dear. And I suggested he take a leave of absence...with pay, of course. He had been my chief of staff for years until I assigned him to head the committee that was exploring a possible Senate run."

Isla said, "But it became clear that it was all too much for him."

He said, "How did it become clear, Mrs. Oxley?"

Isla looked at David and then turned to speak to Czerwinski. "This is confidential, Detective. We don't want this to leak out."

She patted poor Tad's hand and gave him a look that said he was the hottest man she had ever met, and she wanted to ravish him on top of the stacks of campaign literature.

Tad gave her a besotted smile. "I'll do my best to see that it's kept confidential, Mrs. Oxley. What are we talking about?"

Isla said, "We were rethinking the idea of a senate run...."

David said, "But we have since decided to go ahead."

He said, "And when did this rethinking take place?"

Isla gave him side eye. "Four months ago."

"And Stoker freaked out?"

Isla whispered into Tad's ear, which had turned an interesting shade of red. Well, she didn't really whisper, but she was really close.

"He broke down and cried. And then he ranted about forces that were working to destroy David."

David said, "Evil forces."

Isla nodded and patted Tad's hand again. Tad's ears were the color of Rudolph's nose.

He said, "And that's when you put him on leave?"

Isla nodded.

David said, "He was just devastated. He had worked so hard on all the ground work, Mr. Bergeron."

"And when is the last time you saw him?"

Tad managed, "Or communicated with him in any way?"

David and Isla had a brief telepathic exchange before David said, "I spoke to him on the phone in June...probably four weeks ago. Just to check in."

He said, "And what did he say? Did he mention blackmail to you?"

A longer telepathic exchange. David said, "Blackmail? Nothing like that. But he was still obsessed with the campaign. He tried to talk me into putting him in charge again. I don't understand where blackmail comes into the picture?"

Tad said, "It seems he thought there was a blackmail plot, and he was trying to stop it."

Isla said, "But who was being blackmailed? Not us?"

Tad nodded. "It's a theory we're exploring, Mrs. Oxley."

She smiled at Tad. "No one is blackmailing us, Detective. I'm afraid that was another of poor Bart's delusions.."

David said, "Because there's nothing scandalous that could be used against us, Detective. We've led very ordinary lives."

A big smile offensive.

He said, "Right. Did you ever work for your father's company, Mr. Oxley?"

David stopped smiling. "For a year or so. After I got out of law school. Why?"

"No reason. So Stoker...Bart was sure about the blackmail, and we have other evidence to support the idea, Mr. Oxley."

David smiled and then patted his hand. "What evidence, Mr. Bergeron? It was all in Bart's mind." He put on his solemn face. "I blame myself for not checking on him. I knew he was struggling with his demons. He needed help, and I wasn't there for him."

David shook his head; silver locks and electric blue eyes flashing in the sunlight pouring through the windows. And then David's knee bumped into his and didn't move away.

He stared at Mr. C. David Oxley. "What demons, Sir?"

"Bart had some problems growing up. He mentioned a few things over the years that he worked for me. But I thought he was over them."

"Psychological problems?"

David nodded and rested a hand on his thigh.

Tad said, "Was there anyone close to him? On your staff or this campaign organization?"

Isla stood up. "Kim can get you a list." The young lady detached herself from the scowling young men and moved forward.

Isla smiled at Kim. "I'm sorry, Dear. I should have introduced you. Kim Munson is our chief of staff. This is Detective Czerwinski."

Kim was as animated and cheerful as a Doric column chiseled from black granite.

Isla said, "Get a list together, Kim. And I suppose you'll want to talk to them?" Tad nodded. "Please help the detective."

David was still sitting. "Anything he needs, Kim."

Isla turned to go, but Czerwinski said, "Just a few more questions."

She stopped but she was having a problem smiling at Tad now.

Tad said, "Did you know a Phillip Bergeron? Congressman? Mrs. Oxley?"

David shook his head. "No, I didn't. But I meet so many people, Detective."

Isla said, "Nor I." She looked at the Bergeron in the room. "Are you related to this Phillip, Mr. Bergeron?"

"My second cousin. Stoker murdered him in early June."

He glanced from her to David as he spoke, and he was almost certain that this was no shocker to the congressman. But Isla? He thought she might have been blindsided, but he wasn't certain.

Even so Isla recovered first. "Are you sure?"

Tad said, "He confessed before he died, Mrs. Oxley."

She was shaking her head. "Poor Bart. And I'm so sorry about your cousin, Mr. Bergeron. Did you help the detective in discovering who killed your cousin?"

"You could say that." David's hand was still on his thigh. "Do either of you know Reed Gibson? Or his wife, Lydia?"

David gave him a smile meant to rock his world, but he rode it out.

"No. I've heard of Mr. Gibson, of course. Isla?"

"No, I don't know them?"

Czerwinski said, "Lydia Gibson is the sister of Phillip Bergeron."

Isla said, "Are you saying that Bart killed her brother and was trying to kill Mrs. Gibson?"

Czerwinski nodded.

David stood up. "I think we're late, Isla. Kim is signaling that we need to go."

Kim didn't miss a beat. "Yes, Congressman, we do."

He said, "One last question, Congressman. Bart was also trying to kill Lydia's father, Jonathan Bergeron. Do you know him?"

David had known it was coming. He did his best to smile. "I don't recall the name, but I meet so many people."

Isla said, "We really do have to go now, Detective."

How many muscles did it take to smile? Isla used the bare minimum.

But David was smiling again; he leaned over. "I'm sorry I couldn't be more help, Gabriel."

And David ran a hand along his shoulder and stroked the nape of his neck. "If there's ever anything you need?"

He dropped a card on the table.

Isla had turned back and was staring at them. "David."

And David scurried away to rejoin his wife, and the entourage departed.

Except for Kim. She shook Tad's hand.

Tad said, "Did you know Stoker?"

"I worked with him for a few months until he was assigned to the senate campaign, but we weren't close. I'll get a list together and email it to you, Detective."

And Kim had nothing further to add, and no tears to shed for Bart Stoker. She departed with the same blank expression she had maintained from the start.

Tad sat down at the table. "Shit."

He sat next to Tad. "It could have gone better."

"Yeah. Ole David's hiding something, and he isn't going to give it up."

"Nope." He smiled at Tad. "So think you have a shot with Isla?"

Tad blushed again. "What? She's a married woman, Bergeron."

"She is, but she's willing to do some damage to her wedding vows for you, Young Tad."

"You're crazy, Bergeron. Really? She was just trying to snow me...us.?"

"That was one reason for the attention she lavished on you."

Tad shook his head. "Think we're ever going to find out what is really going on?"

"I'd say the chances are nil unless you can prove that Phillip called one of them, and even then. Or unless Jonathan Bergeron knows something?"

Tad nodded. "We've already looked at Phillip's phone calls and emails, but I can check it again. And I'll call the daughter."

"And you'll let me know?"

Tad winked at him. "Roger that. Let's get out of here, Gabe. The dust is getting in my throat."

And they walked out into the roar of traffic and the July heat.

Tad had dropped him off at GB&H. He had stood in the lobby looking at the card that C. David Oxley had given him.

C. David Oxley had come on to him.

And Isla Oxley had known it was happening.

Thursday
4:00 pm

He was finishing one last project before his weekend. Carla and Baldacci were in the breakroom doing something naughty.

Well, they were fully clothed, but there was way to much giggling going on.

Tad had called him after the David and Isla show.

"I called the daughter."

"Right. Lydia. And?"

"I got the husband."

"Reed James Farley Gibson, III. And?"

Tad said, "No go. He informed me that Jonathan was much to ill to 'suffer interrogation' and that he and his wife 'would fight any attempt to compel him to do so with every resource at their disposal' and something about 'unconscionable badgering' of a dying man. You know he's the senior partner at Vance & Gibson?"

"Yeah. And can move mountains and is on retainer to God."

Tad said, "So unless you have an idea, I think it ends here."

"I've got nothing. But we caught Phillip's killer."

"We did."

"It was fun working with you, Czerwinski."

Tad laughed. "It had its moments. Though I'll deny saying that, Bergeron."

And Tad had hung up and probably turned to other cases.

He had briefly considered storming the Hapsburg palace, but Hand would bend him into a pretzel shape, and Reed might use his broken flesh as compost for the roses.

So he was taken aback to get a call from Cousin Lydia.
"Hello?"
"Gabriel, it's Lydia. How are you?"
"Fine as frog's hair. And you?"
"What?"
"Sorry, it's an expression that Aunt Flo uses. I'm fine. How may I be of assistance?"

A longish pause. "I don't know how to say this, Gabriel."
"Start at the beginning and keep on to the end."
She was not amused. "My father...."
"Jonathan. Yes, I remember."
"He wants to see Florence Barnes. Is that possible?"
"What? Sure. I guess. Aunt Flo did express an interest in seeing him, but I don't know. To be clear, you want Aunt Flo to come to Schönbrunn...to your house in Berwyn?"
"Yes. Dad can't travel. And I don't think this is a good idea, but he's insisting."
"I can ask her. But if she comes, I come. And I'm not waiting in the car with the window cracked like an incontinent poodle."

A slight snuffling sound that might have been suppressed laughter.
"Of course. But there is one thing that I have to insist upon."
"Which is?"
"That detective can't come. And I want your word that you won't mention Phillip or Bart Stoker or anything connected with them. Dad can't be upset. He can't."
"All right. I know he's sick, and I don't want to upset him. Okay. I'll talk to Aunt Flo and get back to you."
"Please let me know as soon as you can. Tomorrow if possible."

He called Aunt Flo. She had a cellphone, but she hardly ever carried it with her; the landline was the best bet.

Ute answered. "Hello, Ute. Is Aunt Flo nearby? If not, ask her to call me."

A loud thunk as the phone was dropped from a great height.

He waited. And then he heard laughter and strange voices and a dog barking. Had Ute talked Aunt Flo into taking pets?

But then he heard voices coming closer.

"Gabriel?"

"Aunt Flo, you need to keep your cellphone upon your person at all times."

She laughed. "I don't think so, Dear."

"Really? Well, they can be a pain at times. In any case, I have news."

"Something more about this Congressman Oxley?"

He had brought Aunt Flo up to speed about David and Isla and even Kim. "Nope. Jonathan Bergeron has intimated that he wouldn't be averse to having you call upon him at his residence at your earliest convenience. Any interest?"

She laughed again. "Was he quite as formal as that, Gabriel?"

"He wasn't anything. Lydia invited you. And me. I am temporarily not persona non grata."

"When, Dear?"

"I think it needs to be very soon."

"I can't drive, Dear, and Ezmeralda will be busy for the next few weeks at least."

"I will come and get you. How about tomorrow?"

"This is very sudden, Gabriel."

"I know. Sorry. I could come Sunday, but I have clients coming in on Monday. Think about it and call me back when you've decided."

She said, "No. I may never get this chance again. Tomorrow will be fine."

And he called Lydia and told her to expect the Barnes party on the morrow.

Friday
11:00 am

He had called Cory and told him not to expect him at the condo and had driven to Aunt Flo's house after work.

And he had told Aunt Flo everything he had learned or suspected about C. David Oxley and his lady wife, Isla, on the journey north.

And now they were pulling into the Gibson estate in Aunt Flo's black Lincoln Continental which was very nice to drive if you didn't mind that it had the gas mileage of an Abrams battle tank.

But it did look much more suitable than his canary yellow Jeep; especially with the shattered window. Stan kept saying he'd fix it soon.

"See. I told you. Schönbrunn Palace. And the rose gardens are spectacular. They're Reed's pride and joy apparently."

"They are lovely, Gabriel." She surveyed the whole scene. "But why would anyone ever need so many rooms?"

"No idea. Maybe it started out only semi-grand, and they just kept adding wings?"

Aunt Flo was just sitting there.

"Are we ready to go in? Assuming they'll let us in."

She nodded. "I don't remember Jonathan at all."

"It's been a year or two, Aunt Flo." If his math was right, it had been sixty years.

She nodded and opened the door. He grabbed the briefcase and got out.

He took her arm. "Come on, Aunt Flo. 'Once more unto the

breach, dear friends, once more.'"

She smiled at him. "Thank you for doing this, Gabriel."

"I'd be a knave and a varlet and a jackanapes if I didn't."

She laughed. "You're very Shakespearean today, Dear."

"The Bard has a line for any occasion." He raised the lion's head knocker and let it smack the door.

He looked at Aunt Flo. "If they haven't fed Hand, I want you to run back to the car. I'll throw my body in front of him which should slow him down long enough for you to get away."

Aunt Flo shook her head. "Gabriel. Stop joking. Who is Hand?"

And the door opened to reveal the largest man he had met in the flesh. He smiled at Aunt Flo. "This is Hand."

He thought she was suitably impressed.

He smiled up at Hand trying not to gaze into his nostrils. "This is my great-aunt, Florence Barnes. We were invited."

Hand stopped glowering and offered a hairy paw the size of a baseball mitt to Aunt Flo.

"Pleased to meet you, Mrs. Barnes."

Aunt Flo was braver than he was and entrusted her hand to Hand's hand.

"It's very nice to meet you, Mr. Hand. I take it you've met my nephew?"

Hand and Aunt Flo looked at him and found him wanting. He may have winked at Aunt Flo.

Hand said, "This way, Mrs. Barnes. Mr. Jonathan is expecting you."

And they followed Hand's heavy tread to Jonathan's suite to find the entire Gibson family assembled.

Lydia and Reed were sitting at Jonathan's bedside. Their son, Jack, was pacing, and Olivia was sitting on the bed smiling at Jonathan.

After the introductions, Jack, who had made only fleeting eye contact with the strangers, asked to be excused and departed. His sister, Olivia, continued to sit on the bed.

Aunt Flo had the briefcase. "I brought some photos, Jonathan, that I thought you might like to see?"

Jonathan said, "I would. I have some photos too. A few. Can you get them, Olivia?"

Olivia smiled. "Of course, Granddad."

Reed said, "I'm sorry, but I'm expecting some calls I can't miss." He smiled at Lydia.

Aunt Flo said, "Your roses are lovely, Mr. Gibson."

He nodded and left almost as quickly as his son.

Aunt Flo turned to Jonathan. "Your grandchildren are very handsome."

Jonathan nodded. "I may be biased, but I think so." He smiled at Lydia. "And Phillip's children are too."

Lydia looked worried.

"It's all right, Lydia. I'm fine. You don't have to watch over me."

Lydia patted her father's arm.

Jonathan was in his mid-seventies, but he looked frail; more frail than Aunt Flo who was a decade older.

Lydia said, "Would you like some coffee, Mrs. Barnes? Or tea?"

Aunt Flo said, "Tea, Dear. But don't go to any bother."

"No bother at all."

And Lydia went off as Olivia came back with two albums. "Are these the right ones, Granddad?"

"Yes, Olivia. Now you can go play tennis with your friends."

"No, I can stay."

He smiled at his granddaughter. "Of course. But go have some fun."

And Olivia smiled and disappeared.

Aunt Flo showed Jonathan the wedding photo of Andrew and Natalie.

He smiled. "Just look at us. Mother is so young; she was Ava Stanton. And look at me. I was twelve I think."

Aunt Flo said, "I was twenty-three."

Jonathan said, "Miss Sadie was a wonderful person, Florence."

Aunt Flo nodded. "She was. I think of her every day."

Jonathan said, "You look like her." He smiled. "Uncle Andrew looks a bit grim for his wedding day, doesn't he? But he wasn't. I remember him laughing and dancing with Aunt Natalie."

Aunt Flo shook her head. "I don't remember."

"Do you remember me at all, Florence?"

"Yes. A little. I'm afraid I was totally consumed with my own plans...."

Jonathan said, "You were going to Cuba! To become a revolutionary! Uncle Andrew told me."

Lydia came back and served tea. It was very nice tea in a very nice china set but no petits fours were offered.

Jonathan said, "After my mother died, I came to live with Uncle Andrew and Aunt Natalie. Mother died the same year that your mother, Leanne, was born, Gabriel." Jonathan smiled. "Your mother was such a beautiful child. If a bit willful."

He didn't think his mother had ever mentioned Cousin Jonathan. But he had been so young when she died, and maybe he hadn't paid attention.

They looked at photos of Jonathan's parents, Samuel and Ava, and of Jonathan with his wife.

"That's Fionagh, and of course, Lydia and Camille. And Phillip."

Phillip was a baby in Fionagh's arms.

Lydia was watching Jonathan.

But he just nodded. "Miss Sadie was very proud of you, Florence." Jonathan smiled and the pallor was less evident. "She wouldn't hear a word spoken against you."

He said, "Who was speaking words against Aunt Flo?"

Jonathan frowned. "Uncle Andrew."

"What did he say?"

Jonathan was lost in the memory for a second. "Nothing really." He smiled at Aunt Flo. "He was more worried about an American girl being on her own in Cuba...with all those nasty communists."

Aunt Flo said, "I had a wonderful life in Cuba, Jonathan." She smiled, "And I was a communist myself...for a while."

Jonathan shook his head. "I don't think Uncle Andrew

would have approved, Florence. Not that you would have asked for his approval. He was concerned. Well, Natalie was very worried about her little sister, and Andrew couldn't bear for anything to upset his Natalie. He loved her very much. As she did him."

Aunt Flo smiled. "I'm glad to hear that, Jonathan. About Natalie and Andrew. I can't say that I really remember him...except for the photo." She shook her head. "I'm not sure how I feel about my life in Cuba. I made some wonderful friends and had two husbands...I loved both of them...in different ways. But I wasn't here when my mother needed me. And I was wrong about the politics. Completely."

He said, "But you were so young when you went there, Aunt Flo."

"I was. But I should have listened to Mother and to Natalie."

Jonathan said, "We all make mistakes, Florence. Some of us don't have the rashness of youth to blame." He smiled. "But your letters were treasured by Miss Sadie. And Aunt Natalie."

Aunt Flo closed her eyes as tears ran down her cheeks. "They got them? All of them?"

Jonathan shook his head. "I don't know about all of them, but there must have been a half dozen or so? Over the years. Miss Sadie was so happy when she got the one about your marriage to...Zamora? I think that was the name?"

"Juan Carlos Zamora. He was an amazing man."

Jonathan nodded. "That's what Miss Sadie and Aunt Natalie said! If you married him. You told Natalie that you would never marry anyone."

Aunt Flo laughed. "I was so sure of everything!"

Jonathan said, "And there was the letter about Mr. Zamora's death. Which was a bit cryptic as I recall?"

"I had to be careful what I said, Jonathan."

"About what exactly, Florence?"

"About the manner of his death."

Jonathan looked shocked. "Was he...he wasn't murdered?"

She nodded. "Assassinated by indirection. He was sent on a mission to Angola, into a situation where his death was almost certain."

"Sent by whom?"

She said, "By his enemies...in the Dirección de Inteligencia."

It was a miracle that Danilo Ochoa was still alive...given that he lived next door to Aunt Flo.

Jonathan looked confused so he said, "The Cuban version of the KGB, Jonathan."

Jonathan looked scandalized and intrigued all at the same time. "He was a spy?"

"He was Major Zamora; I guess you could say he was a spy master, as well as a guerrilla fighter."

Jonathan smiled. "And you were married a second time...to an artist?"

Aunt Flo said, "You have a remarkable memory Jonathan. To Antonio Cabrera."

Jonathan said, "Whenever I visited Uncle Andrew, he and Miss Sadie would tell me about your adventures. Is the house still the same?"

"There have been a few changes. I have some photos."

And they looked at pictures of the rooms and the river; pictures Ute had taken for the B&B ads.

Jonathan said, "I would like to see it again, but I don't think I will."

Lydia got to her feet. "Maybe that's enough, Dad? You look tired."

"I am a bit. But perhaps Florence would like to see the rose gardens before she goes?"

Aunt Flo wasn't as pushy as he was. "She would. Very much. I think?"

Aunt Flo smiled at him. "Just a peek. If it isn't too much trouble, Lydia?"

"Of course not. Reed will grumble but he loves showing off his roses."

Friday Noon

And cold-blooded Reed did frown but mostly at the sight of Gabriel Bergeron. Did Reed think he was going to present a bill for services rendered in the matter of finding Phillip's killer?

But then Mr. Gibson saw how knowledgeable and impressed Aunt Flo was with his thousands of roses and waxed almost lyrical.

He liked roses, but he had seen a lot of them when he was running from Bart, and his eyes may have glazed over after the first thousand.

And then something grabbed him and snatched him back.

"Shit!" A mighty hand had a joint crushing grip on his shoulder. "What the Hell, Hand?"

Hand put a finger to his lips and hauled him into the house like a Tyrannosaurus with a fresh kill.

Hand let go. "Mr. Jonathan wants to see you."

"Right. Okay. I'll get Aunt Flo."

Hand shook his head glaring at him; the glare amplified by the dark eyes, the black beard and shaggy hair. He poked him in the chest hard enough to make him take a step back. "He wants to see you."

Which was clear enough. He resisted the urge to ask why.

Hand conveyed him up a back stairway and into Jonathan's room.

Jonathan said, "Thank you, Hand."

And Hand smiled. It was a scary smile, but it was a smile.

Hand departed.

Jonathan said, "Please sit down, Gabriel."

"Sure. Of course."

He waited but Jonathan didn't say anything. He picked up the photo of young Jonathan with his wife and children.

"Phillip looked like you." Young Jonathan had been more handsome than Phillip.

Jonathan shook his head. "Such a long time ago. I want to talk to you about David Oxley."

"Right. So you and C. David Oxley were good friends when he worked at Oxley International? Really good friends?"

Jonathan smiled at him. "Lydia said you were clever."

"How did it happen? You were married?"

Jonathan shook his head. "Fionagh and I were divorced by the time I met David. He came to work in the legal department of his father's company. We had offices across the hall from one another. He was fifteen years younger than me, but we became friends."

"And then more than friends."

"Yes, Gabriel." Jonathan frowned. "I tried to fight the feelings I had for him. I didn't want to admit it even to myself, but Charlton David Oxley was just so damned handsome. And the attraction was incredible. At least, it was for me, and I think it was for David too."

"Yeah, attraction can be a bitch."

Jonathan said, "Lydia told me that you have someone?"

He pulled out his phone and selected a random photo showing Cory looking gorgeous as he did ninety-nine point nine percent of the time.

"This is Special Agent Corentin Georges Poirier of the FBI."

Jonathan smiled. "He is very handsome. Are you happy together, Gabriel?"

"Ecstatic. Well, mostly. When he's home. He goes off on these undercover missions."

Jonathan said, "David and I couldn't be open about the relationship, of course. Even if he hadn't been married."

Jonathan was looking tired, but he had to ask. "So what did you tell Phillip about David?"

Jonathan closed his eyes and when he opened them, tears spilled out. "Almost nothing, but so much more than I should have. I was sick...sicker than I am now...and I don't know what I was thinking. I wanted to confess to someone I suppose. I'm not even sure I knew it was Phillip I was talking to."

"Jonathan?"

"I told him about the affair. I told him that David had been married to his first wife, Jīngyí. She was a lovely girl, and I've always felt guilty about that. David told me that they had an arrangement, and she had her own lovers and didn't care what he did. I wanted to believe him, but I knew better."

"And Phillip wanted to use what you'd told him?"

"I don't know, Gabriel. I loved my son, but he would always take the easy road. He hated working at Oxley, but he was outraged when they fired him. Fired him for good reason. He came to me and demanded that I call David and force the company to rehire him."

"But you wouldn't do that?"

"No. I hadn't spoken to David since we stopped seeing each other."

"When was that?"

"In 1989."

"But you saw each other every day at the office?"

Jonathan shook his head. "His father transferred him to a factory he was setting up in France." Jonathan looked at him. "No. I did speak to him one more time before he left. I warned him about a reporter who questioned me."

Jonathan looked very tired now, but he had to ask. "What reporter? And what did he want to know?"

"I don't remember his name. He was asking about Jīngyí's death. And about my relationship with David. I've always thought he suspected us."

Which was very interesting. "And? Did he question David? And what happened to David's wife?"

"I never heard from the reporter again. And Jīngyí's death

was ruled an accident."

"But it wasn't?"

Jonathan shook his head. "I don't know, Gabriel. But David's father had plans for his son, and David was very ambitious. And probably still is. Being a congressman might be just a stepping stone."

"So Jìngyí found out about you and David? And David killed her?"

"No, I don't think David would have done that. He loved her...in his own way."

"So did Phillip call David? Or his wife, Isla? Or Stoker?"

But Jonathan shook his head. "I don't know. I called David's office after Stoker came here and tried to kill us. Someone told me he was unavailable and hung up. I don't know what I would have said to David anyway. I'm sure he would have denied knowing anything about blackmail or Stoker or Phillip."

He closed his eyes. "I'm sorry, Gabriel, but I'm very tired. I had to tell someone. I don't think David killed my son, but if he was involved, I don't want him to get away with it."

"No, of course you don't. I'll do my best to find out, Jonathan."

But Jonathan's eyes were closed, and he left him sleeping.

He was trying to rejoin Aunt Flo and Reed still strolling through fields of roses when Lydia waved at him.

Her face was far from serene. "You talked to him...about David Oxley."

He nodded. "He wanted to tell me, Lydia. I didn't question him."

"I know."

They were walking side by side. "He doesn't know that I know about him and David."

"How did you find out?"

She looked at Reed. "I had such a crush on David Oxley." She smiled. "I was seventeen, and he was twenty-four and the handsomest man I had ever seen. I made excuses to visit Dad at work just to catch a glimpse of David."

"He's still very handsome."

She nodded. "I didn't know about the affair when it was happening, but I noticed little things. And there were comments my mother made though she never came out and told me. It must have been ten years after the affair that it suddenly crystallized into realization."

"Right. I know what you mean." Why was she telling him this?

She said, "Did David have anything to do with Phillip's death?"

"Probably, but I don't know for sure. Yet."

She turned to him. "Please don't tell anyone about Dad and Oxley."

"I won't. If you don't want me to."

"Please, Gabriel. I don't care if he gets away with it. I'm sorry, but I don't know how my children and Phillip's would react...or how their friends would treat them...if they knew about their grandfather."

Was it that shameful to her? But he nodded. "I won't tell anyone, Lydia."

He wasn't going to tell her that the grand-kids would probably be a lot more accepting than she was.

Loyalty to her mother would always make it harder for her.

She was looking at Reed gesticulating as he pointed out a rose bush to Aunt Flo. "I'd like you to have this, Gabriel."

It was an envelope; an ordinary, business envelope sans gold leaf or embossed crests. Inside was another tan slip of paper with the requisite account and bank numbers in magnetic ink.

But the amount in the little white box was larger. Others might not call it a princely sum, but it was near enough for Gabriel Bergeron.

"This is too much, Lydia. I can't take this. Really."

She gave him a serene smile unruffled by such pecuniary matters. "I'm going to rescue your poor aunt, Gabriel. It's time for lunch anyway."

Saturday 10:00 am

And she had smiled benignly at Reed and invited them all to a luncheon spread worthy of her residence.

Aunt Flo had dozed on the way home to Snow Hill, and he hadn't shared what Jonathan had told him.

And now he was finishing up the breakfast dishes, and Ezmeralda was staring at him. "What? Aren't the dishes clean enough?"

She inspected them and shrugged. Which meant that they were operating room sterile.

She started putting them away. "Did Florence have a nice visit with this Jonathan?"

"She did. He told her that her mother got her letters from Cuba and treasured them. And that her mother was proud of her. And she liked the roses. But it was a long day for her."

Ezmeralda smiled at the dishes. And then she left them and climbed the stairs.

He put the last dish away and considered his options. He wanted to go to the condo and be with Cory, and he had no idea what to do about C. David Oxley. If anything?

He ran up the stairs and knocked on Aunt Flo's parlor door. "Aunt Flo?"

"Come in, Gabriel."

Ezmeralda was sitting next to Aunt Flo. "Am I interrupting? I can come back?"

"No, Gabriel. Sit and tell me what Jonathan told you in

private."

He smiled his very best smile. "So you noticed Hand's snatch and grab?"

She laughed. "It's hard for someone so large to be stealthy."

"Try impossible. Right. I wasn't keeping it from you. I thought you were too tired on the way home."

And he related Jonathan's cri de coeur to them. He had promised Lydia, but Aunt Flo and Ezmeralda knew how to keep secrets; better than he did if it came to it.

"So I don't see a way forward?"

Aunt Flo said, "Unless Detective Czerwinski can prove that Phillip contacted the Oxley's and threatened them directly. And even then, Gabriel, he's a congressman. It won't be easy."

"No. But did Phillip even talk to the Oxley's? Maybe he called Oxley's office and got transferred to Stoker?"

Aunt Flo said, "But Stoker wouldn't have assumed that a voice on the phone was telling the truth about an affair and a suspicious death that happened thirty years earlier."

"No. But would he have gone to David? Or to Isla?"

Ezmeralda said, "To the wife. She is the one in charge. This David is just the pretty face."

Aunt Flo nodded. "And perhaps David confessed to her at some point? You think he's bisexual?"

"Maybe. But I could have a date any time I wanted one."

Aunt Flo smiled. "You're very handsome, Gabriel. But is he that open about his desires with every attractive man he meets? If so, surely his life is a house of cards?"

"Right. So Isla is losing control of him?"

Aunt Flo nodded. "Perhaps it's only a matter of time before the truth comes out."

"Maybe yes, maybe no."

"What are you thinking, Gabriel?"

"Nothing."

"Gabriel."

"That I might call Charlton David. No! Not for a date. To get him away from Isla and question him."

Ezmeralda said, "If this wife had Phillip killed, she would

do the same to you."

"She could try." Aunt Flo looked upset. "But I won't do anything without telling you first."

Aunt Flo said, "And Cory."

"Right. And Cory."

That would be an interesting conversation. But maybe, just maybe, it would be a good idea to have an FBI agent along when he put the screws to ole Charlton David?"

"Right. Definitely Cory too."

Aunt Flo nodded.

And then he may have produced Lydia's check and handed it to Aunt Flo. "So should I send it back?"

Ezmeralda snorted; even Aunt Flo made a rude noise. "No, indeed, Gabriel. How many times have you been shot at?"

Which was true.

Aunt Flo said, "And they can well afford it."

Which was probably also true. He put he check away and felt a warm glow in the wallet region.

Ezmeralda said, "And what about Ute and Annika?"

His ears may have pricked up.

Aunt Flo said, "I know you're curious about them."

"Not really."

"Gabriel."

"A little. They're from East Germany, aren't they?"

Aunt Flo smiled. "There is only one Germany now, Dear, but their parents lived most of their lives in Karl-Marx-Stadt."

"I know."

Aunt Flo said, "You really shouldn't have been prowling around their house, Gabriel. Ute would have reacted badly to that."

Ezmeralda said, "She would have punched you in the face."

"Really? I know I shouldn't have done it. Sorry, You found the photos on your computer? I thought I had erased them?"

"Not well enough."

Ezmeralda said, "We met Annika's father in 1985."

Aunt Flo said, "Helmut Graf was sent to offer training in the latest techniques and equipment. To the Dirección de Inteligencia."

"Sent where? Cuba? So he was a spy too? An East German spy?"

Aunt Flo nodded. "He was a member of the Stasi; the State Security Service. The *Staatssicherheitsdienst*. And so was Ute's father, Manfred. They were friends and comrades."

Aunt Flo smiled at Ezmeralda.

"What?"

"Ezmeralda liked Helmut."

Ezmeralda snorted, but she looked a little flushed. "He was nothing special."

But Aunt Flo smiled again. "With the reunification of Germany in 1990, the Stasi was disbanded, but Helmut had seen it coming. Two years later, he was able to move his family and Manfred's to Niederkrüchten near the Dutch border."

"Right. And they didn't advertise the face that they had been members of this Stasi?"

"No, Dear. It was hard for them. Too hard for Ute's father, Manfred."

"What happened to him?"

But Aunt Flo shook her head. "I'm sure Ute wouldn't want me to talk about that. Please don't ask her about her father, Gabriel. Ever."

"Okay. I won't."

Ezmeralda said, "But her mother, Brigitte, was a figure skater; a champion in East Germany and internationally. She was a beautiful woman."

"Yeah. I saw the photos. And the medals."

Aunt Flo said, "We kept in contact with Helmut for years...until he passed away in 2002, and then we lost touch with Ute and Annika."

He said, "Until they came to New York six years ago?"

Aunt Flo smiled at him. "Yes, Dear. Now you know about them, and you aren't going to bother them or be suspicious of them."

"No, Aunt Flo. Thank you for telling me."

And he sat there. He should get on the road and get back to Cory for what was left of the weekend.

"So why didn't you tell me before?"

Aunt Flo looked at him. It wasn't a loving look.

"You seemed to think that we had taken Ute and Annika into our lives without being certain about them."

Ezmeralda said, "We would never do this, Gabriel."

"Right. I know."

Aunt Flo said, "But do you? I'm not senile yet, and Ezmeralda certainly isn't."

Ezmeralda shook her head vigorously.

"Right. I'm very sorry. I was just worried about you, but it won't happen again."

He gave them his very best smile. He had hurt their feelings by implying that they were past it. Which they weren't.

He would do better.

And he wasn't even going to think about what had happened to Manfred Wetzig in 1990.

Sunday
2:00 pm

Cory was glaring at him. "You couldn't just forget about this?"

He nodded. "I could try."

He had told Cory everything. Well, he had glossed over Bart's hit-men trying to gun them down on Arch Street, and the whole running through the rose garden, bullet-dodging part.

And Cory was still pissed.

"But because of your training, I came through it without a scratch. That should make you happy?"

This was obviously not the case.

He and Cory had been lounging on the sofa in Cory's condo in D.C. on 23rd Street NW. He had told Cory part of the story when he'd gotten to the condo yesterday.

But he'd just floated the idea of calling C. David Oxley and arranging a "date" so they could question him.

Cory was shaking his head. He had let his brick red hair grow long, and his locks were thrashing like flames in a wild fire.

"No! I am not going rogue and interrogate a sitting congressman! Danielle would fire me so fast, I'd be on the sidewalk outside the Hoover Building before I knew what was happening."

"Right. Well, we certainly don't want that to happen."

Cory's glare intensified. "No, we don't. And you are not doing this by yourself."

"No. Of course not. But it wouldn't really be dangerous. I

could meet him in a public place?"

More head shaking.

"You could come with me but stay outside?"

Cory said, "Are you determined to do this?"

"Not determined. Per se. I mean it would be good if Jonathan knew who was ultimately behind his son's death."

Cory shook his head.

"And he was my second cousin. He sort of brought it on himself. But still."

Cory grabbed his shoulders and pulled him close. "If I agree to calling Oxley, I want your word of honor that you won't go anywhere without me along."

"I promise."

Cory's big, blue eyes were skeptical. Had he told him about Czerwinski's eyes being slightly crooked?

"What are you thinking about?"

"Me? Nothing pertinent. So?"

"Call him. But he isn't going to break down and confess, Gabe. It doesn't work that way."

Maybe yes, maybe no.

He called Charlton David Oxley. "Hi, it's Gabe Bergeron."

"Gabe! I was wondering if I'd hear from you."

"You doubted yourself, David?"

He laughed. "Well, I'm a lot older than you."

"Not that much. I was hoping we could get together?"

"I'd like that very much, Gabe. I really would."

"But?"

"I'm not sure when I'll be back in Philadelphia."

"Where are you? D.C.?"

"Yes."

"So am I."

"Great. Then how about tomorrow? In the afternoon? I could call you when I can break free. There's a condo where we can meet."

"Sounds great, David."

Cory was glowering. "So you have a date?"

"Not a date. No matter what he thinks. Tomorrow afternoon

at a condo in the city. He'll call me."

Cory said, "This is a bad idea, Gabe."

Which could be true. "It will be okay. You can come with me and hang around outside the door."

"Won't I be a little obvious, Bergeron?"

"We'll work it out. And I'll take the Glock." Which he had finally gotten back from Czerwinski. "Not that I'll need it to handle Oxley."

Monday
10:00 am

He had called Jennifer and begged to have the day off and sworn a mighty oath that he wouldn't ask for time off again for years. She had snorted and agreed.

And Cory had asked Bornheimer to cover for him.

But Cory was deeply unhappy.

"It's going to be okay."

And then Cory's phone played "Va, pensiero" from Verdi's *Nabucco*. "Poirier?"

And Cory mostly listened. He tried to interject a few protestations before giving up.

"What does Brunetti want?"

"She wants me in Baltimore within the hour."

"Why?"

Cory shook his head. "She got a tip that an art dealer there has information about my case."

"The Nefertiti necklace case?" He nodded. "Well, you have to go."

Cory got very close. "If Oxley calls, you will reschedule this assignation for another day."

"Or you will be very cross with me? Don't worry. I promise that I won't go anywhere until you can go with me. You don't have to worry. You can focus one hundred percent on finding Nefertiti's necklace. If it really was hers."

"I mean it, Gabe."

"I know you do, and I'm not fibbing. Hit the road, Special

Agent. If you find it, can I see it?"

"If you're very good." Cory winked at him and was out the door.

He was going to be good. Very good.

Maybe Cory would be back before David called. Of course, it wasn't impossible that David wouldn't call. If Isla found out.

He went into the kitchen and made coffee.

He was about to start on a new book when the doorbell rang.

He looked through the peep hole.

And what to his wondering eye should appear but Charlton David Oxley. Sans reindeer.

"Shit." He looked again.

He strapped on the Glock and donned a jacket.

The bell sounded again. He put on the chain and opened the door.

David smiled at him, electric blue eyes radiating in the ultraviolet. "Surprise."

"David? What are you doing here?"

"I had a cancellation, and I took a chance. May I come in, Gabe?"

The hallway looked clear.

"How did you know where to find me?"

"Poirier's boss gave me the address."

"She did? Which boss?"

David smiled again. "Nadia Brunetti. We've known each other for years."

Which was almost certainly the purest bullshit, but David had gone to a lot of trouble to find him, and he had to know why.

He unchained the door.

"Please come in. Wait. How did you know that Cory wasn't here?"

David was smiling at him when the door burst open, and Hand grabbed him and held him tight.

David was closing the door. "We watched him leave."

"Put me down! Help!"

Hand had one arm locked around his chest; he clamped a

paw over his mouth. He kicked and tried to bite Hand, but it had zero effect.

David pulled out a syringe, jammed it into his arm, and injected a colorless liquid.

Hand toted him like he was a fractious child into the living room and dropped him onto the sofa. He tried to reach the Glock, but Hand grabbed it first.

He didn't feel right.

"What do you want?"

David sat down next to him. "How much have you told Poirier?"

"Nothing. He doesn't like it when I play detective."

David laughed. "I wonder why."

He wanted to punch David, but his smiling face was blurry.

David said, "It doesn't matter. I can't take a chance. He'll have to go." David was looking at him. "How are you feeling, Gabe?"

"Woozy."

David smiled. "I am sorry. I was hoping we could be together...at least once...before it became necessary to get rid of you."

Where was Hand? "Hand?"

"He works for me. He's quite impressive, isn't he?"

Hand was in the kitchen making a lot of noise, but he couldn't seem to summon the energy to turn his head.

And then Hand was in front of him. He was holding a shiny thing. A tool?

David said, "And you're sure Jonathan is dead? And no one will suspect it was murder?"

Hand flexed his enormous hands. "Dead."

"You didn't break his neck or something obvious?"

"No. His heart stopped."

"Good. He didn't suffer?" Hand shook his head. "Good. How much longer?"

Hand was holding something else, but his brain was well past the point of decoding any visual input.

"A few minutes."

He said, "Why?"

David smiled. "I suppose it all began with Jīngyí." He shook his head. "My first wife. I think I loved her, Gabe. She was lovely. Truly beautiful. But fragile. Too fragile as it turned out."

He tried to ask how Jīngyí had died, but he couldn't do it.

David said, "And then Phillip came to see me and knew everything about my wife and the reporter too. Poor Jīngyí had been gone so many years, and I was sure I was safe. And then the dread came rushing back."

David patted his face. "Phillip pretended he wanted to be with me too, and I sent my security away before I realized who he was." He laughed. "I've learned not to trust a Bergeron no matter how handsome he is."

David got up. "It took me a few weeks to convince Stoker that Phillip was evil and had to go."

David passed through his field of vision a few times. The field seemed to be narrowing and getting darker.

David said something like, "...don't smell anything...."

And then David was directly in front of him and very close. "Goodbye, Gabe."

And he thought David kissed him.

Monday Noon

He wasn't dead.

Well, he couldn't see anything, but that was probably because his eyes were shut.

He tried to fix that, but he couldn't seem to do it.

Where was he?

He was lying on his back on something hard and cold. His fingers seemed to be working at least. Tile? He was in the kitchen? Or one of the bathrooms? If he was still in the condo?

He really needed to open his eyes.

But first he was going to be sick. He rolled and vomited onto the tile floor...wherever it was.

He lay flat again and worked on that eye-opening thing.

Well, they were open, but they weren't focused.

He rubbed them.

He was in the condo's kitchen. Hand or somebody had pulled the gas range away from the wall. Which seemed like a strange thing to do?

He rolled over...away from the vomit...and got himself on his elbows. His legs were still too weak to make crawling, much less standing, possible.

And then he saw an oblong shape taped to the kitchen window. He elbowed closer. Two strips of duct tape were holding it fast.

It had wires and lumps and some pieces that looked like they might have come from a cellphone.

He mulled that over for a bit.

"Shit. Shit! SHIT!"

He elbowed out of the kitchen and down the hall to the door. He managed to get the door open and shimmied around it like a beached walrus.

He was in the hallway. "Help! Help!" Cory had two neighbors, but he didn't think either was home.

Cory. Shit!

He called Cory.

And Cory answered. "Cory! You're alive! Look, if you see an enormous man with a black beard, shoot him and ask questions later."

"Gabe? What the Hell are you talking about?"

"You are in danger. David wants to kill you. And Hand is his henchman. Did I tell you about Hand? Doesn't matter. He's seven feet tall and can juggle refrigerators. And he has black hair and a beard. Watch out for him. And come home. When you get a chance."

Cory was saying something, but he was too close to the freaking bomb. "Can't talk. Shoot Hand and come home. Shoot David too, if convenient."

And then he punched the elevator button. He crawled out of the elevator on the ground floor and dialed 911.

"I need help! I think there's a bomb in my apartment! Call the FBI...Danielle Elkins. And send the fire department! And the bomb squad! And the police!"

The gentleman inquired as to his location. His tongue was thick but he got the address out. He further inquired about the appearance of the bomb.

"Wires. Lumps of explosive stuff. A cellphone."

He thought the cellphone detail pushed his credibility over the goal line.

He was still resting next to the elevator when he saw policemen approaching.

He was very tired, but he said, "Eleventh floor. The door is open. In the kitchen. You'll see it. If you go in, but you probably shouldn't do that."

And then he took a time-out.

"Bergeron? Gabriel?"

The voice wasn't Cory's. He wasn't sure he was up to conversing, but somebody shook him hard and slapped him..

"What?"

He opened his eyes, and Nadia Brunetti was gazing at him. He was on a gurney in an ambulance, and she was sitting beside him.

"Gabriel, can you hear me?"

"Sure. Where is Cory?"

"He's on his way."

"He's in danger. David wants to kill him."

Brunetti focused her dark eyes upon him. She had an narrow, elliptical face framed with long black hair. In an alternate universe in which she was a smidgen less menacing, she would be pretty. Or at least attractive.

"David?"

"Congressman Charlton David Oxley. Do you know him?"

She didn't react at all. And then she leaned over him. "Don't make any accusations like that, Gabriel. To anyone."

"Okay. Why?"

"Oxley has many friends in Washington, and any loose talk could rebound to hurt the person talking."

"Right."

She tried to smile. She leaned closer again and stared into his eyes. "Careers have been ruined by a lot less than that, Gabriel. Careers in the FBI."

"So I could get Cory into trouble?"

She nodded.

"But he tried to kill me? Just now. He drugged me and planted a bomb in Cory's condo."

She shook her head. "I believe you, Gabriel, but if anyone asks...the D.C. police or anyone...say that you don't remember what happened. The FBI will take over this case, and we'll sort it all out later. Do you understand me, Gabriel?"

"Sure. Wait. Do you know about Oxley's affair and the death of his first wife? And that his chief of staff murdered my second cousin?"

Her eyes may have widened. She shook her head. "What the Hell have you gotten into this time, Bergeron?"

"I'd say it wasn't my fault." He gave her his very best, devil-may-care smile. "But nobody ever believes me. Except this time, Stoker really did start it."

"Stoker?"

"Oxley's chief of staff. Former. Do you know Oxley?"

"I've met the congressman."

"Why did Cory go to Baltimore?"

"We got a call...about his current case. No more questions, Bergeron."

And she got out of the ambulance.

The paramedics wanted to take him to get checked out, but he refused and got off the gurney.

He was sitting on a bench when Cory arrived.

Cory hugged him until he was sure his ribs were going to shatter and impale his lungs.

"Are you okay, Gabe?"

"Fine. Well, I have this awful taste in my mouth, and my stomach isn't right, and I'm still a little woozy, but otherwise okay. How are you? Did you spot Hand?" He looked around for anyone in earshot. "Or CDO?"

Cory smiled at him. "CDO? Why are you using his initials, Doofus?"

"Go find Brunetti and talk to her."

Cory was looking at him. "She's here?"

"She is."

And Cory went on a badge-flashing frenzy and talked to everybody from the bomb squad guys to the first officers on the scene.

And now he was talking to Brunetti. Well, he was mostly listening.

"Shit." He hauled out his phone and called Lydia.

She answered. "Gabe? How nice to hear from you."

Which was taking sang-froid to a whole new level if her father was lying dead in his bed.

"Is Jonathan.... How is Jonathan?"

"He's fine. He was so happy to get reacquainted with Ms. Barnes. They were speaking on the phone just now."

"I'm glad to hear that."

"Was there something in particular, Gabe?"

"This may sound odd."

She laughed.

"Is Hand around?"

"How did you know? He left yesterday...without notice. But he wrote a nice letter to Dad saying how he'd enjoyed working for us. He just said that he had to move on."

"How long had he been with you?"

"Only three months. I thought we were lucky to get him after Marcus left suddenly, but now he's gone too, and we'll have to start all over and find someone new."

"Right. Sorry. Thanks, Lydia."

And he hung up. Which was very interesting...the Marcus leaving and the Hand popping up part.

He was putting his phone away when he felt something in his pocket.

He pulled out a slip of paper.

It read, "Sorry. I needed the money. Hand."

It was in cursive, and the penmanship was lovely.

He was staring at it when Cory came back.

Cory said, "The bomb was fake, Gabe. And somebody messed with the gas connection to the range without actually releasing more than a trace of gas into the apartment."

"Right. I'm not surprised."

Cory shook his head. "Explain that before I punch you hard."

He showed Cory the note. "So?"

"So I think Hand agreed to do some very bad things for CDO because he needed the money. But he didn't really want to do those very bad things."

Cory said, "And one of those bad things was to blow up our condo?"

"Yeah. And to kill you. And to kill Jonathan. Who is alive. I think that Jonathan's murder was probably the bridge too far."

Cory said, "And so Hand faked it."

"Long enough to get his large hands on the cash David promised him."

"So where the Hell is he? And Oxley?"

He shrugged. "Can we go back inside? I need to brush my teeth."

Friday
8:00 am
4 Days Later

Cory was looking at him. "What are you going to do today?"

He wanted to ask if there was any news about David, but Cory would be cross with him.

"Putter around. Regrout the master bath. Bake a soufflé. Stuff. And you?"

Cory smiled. "I'm wrapping up the Egyptian case."

He had recovered the Nefertiti necklace in Baltimore so there had been a tip, and Brunetti hadn't been fibbing.

"So the gold and jewels are real, but it's a reproduction?"

Cory shrugged. "The jury's still out. One idea is that it's an Italian piece...or French...from the Napoleonic period. What are the chances that it's really Nefertiti's necklace?"

"Slim to none? But presumably she had jewelry?"

Cory wasn't really paying attention to him. "Of course. She was the wife of the Pharaoh of Egypt." He was reading a text message. "Have to go, Gabe. Bornheimer's downstairs."

"Right. Have fun."

And Cory waltzed out. Well, he bounded like the man of action he was.

Leaving him to his own devices.

He made sure Cory was really gone and then he placed a call. Brunetti had not specifically forbade him from making discreet inquiries. She may have thought she had, but he disagreed.

A female voice said, "Munson."

"Kim? This is Gabriel Bergeron. I need to speak to Mrs. Oxley."

Silence. "Kim? Do you remember me? I was with Detective Czerwinski. We spoke to the congressman and Mrs. Oxley. And you."

"I remember. She's busy."

"Busy? Doing what? Worrying about the congressman? Detective Czerwinski and I have some information about him."

"Hold on."

And she was gone for three minutes and forty-three seconds which seemed a lot longer.

"Bergeron?"

"Still here."

She snorted. "She can give you ten minutes. At noon. Where are you?"

"In D.C."

A sigh equal parts boredom and exhaustion. "Where in D.C.?"

"At my condo." It still felt weird to say that. "On...." He stopped before he blurted out the address. "In the city. But I don't...."

Kim interrupted. "Hold on." She was gone a few seconds. "Give me the address."

"No, I don't think so. I'll meet her in a public place."

Kim sighed. "All right."

And she gave him the address of a restaurant and was gone. He had to amuse himself until noon. How hard was it to bake a soufflé? Or petits fours?

The restaurant was a swanky place but dark. The people across the room were just shapes in the gloom, and the ghoulish waiter found him unexceptional.

He ordered coffee anyway.

And a half hour later, Isla Oxley arrived. Well, the outliers of her party arrived. The two, stocky, scowling young men surrounded him but assessed his threat level as being minimal.

It was just as well they didn't check and find the Glock.

One of them spoke into a microphone thingee, and Kim

Munson entered. She tried to survey the scene. Night vision goggles would be necessary for an actual survey, but she peered into the foul and filthy air.

And then Isla entered accompanied by a third stocky, scowler.

Isla smiled at him and allowed Scowler #3 to pull out her chair. ""Hello, Gabriel."

"Isla."

Scowler #3 glared at him for using her first name and then chased the waiter away.

She said, "I was surprised to hear from you."

"I have a few, unanswered questions."

She looked at Kim. "Questions? I thought you had some information for me."

"About David? No, I'm sorry. Have you heard from him?"

"Not since Monday morning. He left the house...he seemed in good spirits. I've told the FBI all of this, Gabriel."

"And you didn't know what he had on the agenda?"

She shook her head. She looked a bit like his cousin Lydia; the shape of the face and the perfect features. But if Lydia was cool and urbane beneath the facade, Isla's face surged with anger, resentment, laced with a touch of Weltschmerz?

"No. What did he do, Gabriel? The FBI agents were uncommunicative...even for them."

"He wanted to kill me. And Jonathan." He didn't bother explaining who Jonathan was.

She looked at Kim and jerked her head.

Kim marched the three scowlers into the gloom.

"I'm sorry, Gabriel. I had no idea."

"But you aren't surprised."

She laughed. "I've lived with David too long to be surprised by much. At least, I thought that until the last four months."

"What changed?"

"His father died, and David began to shake off the constraints his father had imposed. And the structure. It was he who convinced David that a senate run in 2022 was premature."

"Because too many damaging things might come to light?"

"David's father didn't share his reasons with me, Gabriel. But David never gave up the idea, and after his father died, he restarted the campaign. And he began having meetings with poor Bart again."

"Why poor Bart?"

"Bart suffered from paranoid schizophrenia. He had to drop out of college in his sophomore year, but he got better. And he seemed fine when he was first hired, but the stress of the job was too much."

"And David decided to exploit his illness?"

She closed her eyes. "I don't know that, but it's not impossible."

"You know about his first wife?"

She shook her head. "Almost nothing. David never spoke of her."

Which might or might not be true.

She smiled. "I know her name was Jīngyí, and that she was lovely. David kept some pictures of her, but he thought I didn't know.

"Did he love her?"

Her smiled faded. "A better question might be did David ever love anyone?"

"'Did'? Past tense?"

She shrugged. "I've answered your questions, Gabriel. Tell me what David did."

He gave her a condensed version. "Do you know Hand?"

She shook her head. "And David left with this Hand? Who was deceiving him? Did Hand kill him, Gabriel? I deserve to know."

"I don't know, Isla. I'd tell you if I did. If the FBI knows, they aren't sharing with me."

"Or with Special Agent Poirier?"

"Not even with him."

She shook her head. "I need to know if David is alive...."

"You don't feel safe?" She shrugged again. "David wants to get rid of people who know his secrets. Do you know any secrets, Isla?"

"Not really." Kim materialized and whispered in her ear. Isla nodded. "I have to go, Gabriel."

She stood up, and the scowlers closed up around her.

"So if David is gone, what happens to his seat in Congress?"

Isla smiled. "The party may ask me to step in for the rest of his term."

She had already assumed the mantle and the trappings.

"And after that. You'll run for his seat yourself?"

But Isla ignored the question and departed.

Kim said, "Don't bother calling again, Bergeron."

And he was left in the gloaming with a cold cup of coffee and a pissed off waiter.

Tuesday
7:00 am

He was sitting on his sofa minding his own business. He was eating a toaster pastry; it was brown sugar-cinnamon and his last one. He needed to go grocery shopping. Really.

He had a hankering for more bagels. And gherkins.

His phone chimed.

He sighed. It wasn't like he hadn't expected a call or a visit after he had gotten the word from Cory the night before..

Tad Czerwinski said, "Bastard!"

"Sorry?"

"What the Hell, Bergeron. I know you know what happened to him. So don't even try to bullshit me!" Tad was using his angry voice.

"I'm very sorry."

"You should be! Now spill! How long has the FBI had the body? And how did he die?"

"I don't know how he died. They aren't telling me anything, Tad."

Tad said multiple bad words in some novel combinations. "Get your ass down here right now, Bergeron."

"Down where, Tad?"

"Whitaker Avenue."

And there was a thud. He believed that Tad had thrown his phone across whatever room he was in. He went to the bathroom, knotted his tie, put on his jacket, and locked the Glock in Cory's gun safe.

He found a parking spot across from the Egyptian mortuary temple that housed the headquarters of the 24th and 25th Districts.

He entered and was told to take a seat.

He waited. He called Baldacci. "Harry. Turn on my computer and put some papers on my desk and get out my coffee mug."

Baldacci sniffed. "And why would I do that?"

"Because you're my best bud. And I might tell you about my visit with the police when I get in."

Baldacci said, "Shit, Bergeron. Czerwinski? Okay."

He waited some more and then was conveyed by a gimlet-eyed officer to an interrogation room. The guy fondled his cuffs before leaving him.

And after a lot longer than was necessary, Tad stomped in.

He sat and glared; his lower eye, the right one, was looking particularly skeptical this morning.

But otherwise, Tad was looking rather spiffy. "You look nice. Is that a new gray suit? Love the tie."

It was burgundy, black, and gray and was of a suitable width and even knotted properly.

"Wait. You have a new girlfriend?" A less happy explanation could be that Tad had moved back in with his mother, but he wasn't going to believe that of Tad.

"What? Forget my suit!"

"And the tie?"

"And forget the freaking tie too." But a fleeting smile graced Tad's crooked face. "Tell me."

"Any chance of getting some coffee?"

"No!"

"Right. So I'm assuming that you know that the body of C. David Oxley was found floating in the Potomac?"

Tad gritted his teeth. "Lexi saw it on the news and called me!"

"I should have called. Wait. Lexi?"

"Bergeron!"

"Okay. I was told not to talk about this by a very scary FBI lady."

Tad shook his head. "Cory's boss?"

"Not even. The boss of Cory's boss."

"Why?"

"She said because he was a congressman and that made it complicated."

"Simplify it for me, Bergeron, or I'll arrest you for something."

"She said that talking about Oxley could have a negative impact on a career...a FBI career. So Cory and I agreed that talking too much was verboten."

Tad leaned across the table. "You can tell me something, Gabe."

"Right. Oxley was murdered no matter what the FBI eventually says."

"And?"

"And Bart Stoker was more a guided missile than a loose cannon."

"So it was Oxley?"

"I can neither confirm nor deny that at this time."

"Bergeron, I'm going to strangle you with my new tie."

"Don't do that. Yes."

Tad said, "It was Oxley."

He nodded as noncommittally as was possible.

"So Stoker killed Phillip for Oxley. I thought it might have been Isla."

"Me too. But no."

"And how do you know this?"

"Oxley may have told me."

"Dammit, Bergeron. Why didn't you call me? I would have arrested the bastard no matter how big a shit-storm it set off."

He was sure Tad would have tried.

"I couldn't. I was under the weather due to the fact that Oxley was arranging for me to be blown into tiny bits at the time."

"What? How and when?"

He shook his head. "I can't say. Except that Oxley visited my condo in D.C., and it wasn't a social call."

He didn't want to tell Tad about Jonathan. He had promised

Lydia. "Maybe in a few months I can meet you at CoffeeXtra and tell you more, but for right now, my lips are sealed."

Tad got to his feet and paced in the little room like a tiger held in a tiny cage too long.

"You know the main points, Tad."

"But there's a lot more, and this is my case!"

"Au contraire, this is the FBI's case now."

More pacing.

"The guy who committed murder and the guy who put him up to it are dead. The only guys left are the two guys who tried to shoot me and Penelope and Kirill."

"Golczewski caught them. Total idiots."

"Well, then your case is closed. Right?"

Tad sat down and a little smile played across his asymmetric but pleasing face.

"What?"

"Nothing."

But it was so not nothing. "Tadeusz Czerwinski."

Tadeusz was grinning at him. "I shouldn't tell you this."

He smiled his very best smile at Tad. "But you're going to."

"I got a call."

"Right. I often get calls myself."

"From a Ms. Amato who was asking about Oxley. She heard about his death...on the news...just like I did."

"I'm sorry about that. Truly. My bad. And what did Ms. Amato have to say for herself?"

"She was upset and wasn't very clear."

Tad was being very mean. He folded his arms and glared at Tad.

Tad smiled again. "But she just came in, and I was going to question her."

"Please, Tad. Please."

"Only if...after the dust settles, and I mean a month tops....you'll tell me everything you know?"

"I promise."

Tad was looking moderately skeptical. "A month, Bergeron. Or I'll make up something and arrest you."

"No need for threats, Young Tad. I am a man of my word. Where's Ms. Amato?"

And Tad left only to return a minute later with a middle-aged, Chinese lady. Tad got her seated.

"I'm Detective Czerwinski, and this is Bergeron."

Ms. Amato nodded. "Thank you for seeing me, Detectives."

Tad didn't correct her. "What can we do for you, Ms. Amato?"

He smiled. "I'm Gabriel or Gabe, Ms. Amato."

She smiled or she took a shot at it. "I'm Xué."

It sounded something like "Sh-way" but not really

Her hair was still black, but her round face was lined. She had dark eyes and a wide nose. She was dressed in a emerald green, business suit.

"I read that David Oxley's body was found in the Potomac River?"

Tad looked at him. "Yes, Ma'am, that's right. The FBI hasn't released the cause of death yet."

She nodded. "But he is dead?"

"Yes. What is your interest in the congressman?"

Her face was blank. "I need to be sure that he's really dead."

"And why is that?"

"Because I hate him. He killed my younger sister."

Tad said, "Who was your sister, Ms. Amato?"

She said, "Her name was Zhāng Jìngyí, and she was Oxley's first wife. She was a beautiful, sensitive girl."

She pulled out her phone and showed them a photo of young, Chinese girl wearing a floppy hat, half turned away, but smiling shyly at the camera. She had been lovely. She didn't look much like Xué.

Xué said, "Jìngyí should never have married that monster."

He said, "When was this? And what happened to your sister, Ms. Amato?" He wasn't going to try her first name.

She put her phone down on the table. "It was 1987. Jìngyí was eighteen. I don't know how she met Oxley. I was older and had married Anthony, and we had been living in Chicago for a few years."

"But you met him?"

"Yes. Him and his father. Anthony and I went to the wedding. It was clear that Oxley's father was a racist and had nothing but contempt for Jìngyí. And he was disgusted with his son for marrying her. I think that the marriage might have been the first time Oxley had ever defied him. And he hated Jìngyí for that too. But my mother couldn't see it. Or wouldn't see it."

"And what happened?"

Xué stared down at the image of her sister. "Jìngyí and I were never close. I tell myself it was the age difference. But Anthony and I returned to Chicago, to the university where we both worked. And then my mother, our mother died, barely a month after the wedding."

"Was Oxley involved somehow?"

"No, Gabriel. My mother had been very ill for years. But her passing meant Jìngyí was alone. I tried to keep in touch with her, but she didn't seem to want to make the effort."

Tears had filled her eyes and were slipping down her cheeks one by one.

"And what happened to Jìngyí?"

"She died. The Oxley's claimed it was an accident, but I never believed it."

Tad said, "And what did you think happened to your sister?"

"I think...I think she killed herself. But she was driven to it by that man, by David Oxley."

He said, "Why do you think that, Ms. Amato?"

"She sent me a letter...before she died."

She had the letter but it was in Chinese.

"Did she say that she was going to commit suicide?"

Xué shook her head. "No. But she said that Oxley had been unfaithful to her. That she hadn't been able to tell me. That she couldn't bear for anyone to know."

He looked at Tad. "Did she say who he was having the affair with?"

Xué shook her head. "No." She stopped talking and stared

at the table. "But she said it was a man."

Jīngyí hadn't revealed Jonathan's name, which was why Xué hadn't reacted when Tad had introduced him.

She said, "I wanted to tell the world what Oxley had done to my sister, but he had lawyers and wealth, and my dear Anthony talked me out of it. Or tried to."

"What did you do?"

"Oxley was up for some appointment in the state government. In Harrisburg. And I spoke to a reporter who had written articles...exposé articles. He seemed interested and said he would get back to me. But he was killed in a car accident."

"And you suspect Oxley of being behind that too?"

"Him or his father."

Tad said, "What was the reporter's name?"

"Rob Barr. He had been a correspondent in the Vietnam War and had seen death and bloodshed. I warned him that Oxley might be dangerous, but he told me he wasn't afraid of some wannabe politician."

Tad said, "And where did it happen? In Philadelphia?"

Xué nodded.

He said, "Why have you come, Ms. Amato? What do you want us to do?"

She shook her head. "I don't know. If he's really dead, I don't suppose there is anything?"

He thought he was, but he hadn't seen David's body.

But she wasn't looking at him. She was staring at the photo of her younger sister.

She said, "水落石出. (Shuǐluò shíchū.)"

"I'm sorry?"

She shook her head. "Just something my mother used to say...'waters ebb, rocks emerge' is the literal meaning. I guess 'the truth will out' is the closest English equivalent."

"The truth about your sister's death?"

"And the truth about Oxley. But will it, Gabriel? I wonder. My mother's saying hasn't come true to far. No one knows what he did to Jīngyí. What a monster he was. I'm sure there's more; more crimes he committed. I would just like the truth to come out."

Tad said, "We'll look into it, Mrs. Amato, but it's been over thirty years."

She nodded. "I know. But he must have done other things. What about Oxley's campaign director, this Bart Stoker? That's your case, Detective?"

"It is, and I'll look into what you've told me."

She shook her head. "But Oxley is dead."

Tad didn't say anything, and Xué got to her feet. "Thank you for listening to me. I wanted to tell someone...even after all these years."

And she walked out.

Tad looked at him. He gave him his very best smile. "That was interesting."

Tad said, "So is that what Phillip thought he could blackmail Oxley with? This affair? Or the death of this reporter? Or both?"

He shrugged.

"Bergeron."

"I don't know."

Tad said, "How would Phillip have found out about all this?"

He sat there.

Tad said, "I want to know, Gabe. Call me."

"I will." But he wasn't sure what he'd tell him? He could just tell him the truth? Tad deserved it.

And then Tad held out his hand. "Thanks for your help, Gabe."

"Sure. Any time. And I will call you."

Tad was looking moderately skeptical again as he showed him out of the building.

He had rushed to work and told Baldacci that Czerwinski had caught the two guys from the drive-by shooting. Which Baldacci didn't totally buy.

But he couldn't tell him about Congressman David. Or about Xué Amato and her sister.

Or about Jonathan.

Wednesday Noon

After work, he had driven out to talk to Zack Bergeron and his brothers, Phil Jr. and Jacob.

But there had been a for sale sign in front of an empty house. It appeared that Kelly and Haruki had made the jump to California.

He hadn't been looking forward to lying to Zack about Phillip. The best story he'd come up with was that Bart had been a paranoid schizophrenic. Which was true. And that he had become fixated upon Phillip believing that Phillip was out to destroy Oxley when all he wanted was his job back at Oxley International.

He had driven home feeling relieved and guilty at the same time.

And this morning, he had been besieged as soon as he had stepped off the elevator at Garst, Bauer & Hartman.

Baldacci and Carla and everyone in the office knew that Bart Stoker had been the chief of staff for Congressman David Oxley. Besides being a murderer.

And they knew that the congressman's body had been found in the Potomac. From Paul. Who was apparently a news junkie.

He had answered their questions with single words and grunts and barefaced lies.

They hadn't been satisfied, but they had given up after Jennifer had scowled ferociously and ordered them back to work.

And now he was in CoffeeXtra wanting coffee and banana bread. Which he got from Billy.

Billy had reappeared for good after Stoker's death, but Billy was looking particularly disheveled. And forlorn. It was a steambath outside. Well, it was August so he could see why Billy might forsake his suits for shorts and a tank top.

But his fur was on display. As were his big, brown eyes.

"How are you?"

Billy shrugged.

"No Penelope?"

Billy glared at him, the eyes suddenly not so sad. "One call since you almost got her shot."

"That wasn't my fault, Billy!"

Billy shook his head. "Dude."

"I met somebody taller than you." Billy ignored him. "But he was about five times as wide. He had black hair too."

Billy ignored him.

"You should give Martin a raise."

Billy nodded. "I did." And then he went into the kitchen.

He turned to find a table, and Baldacci waved at him. He and Carla and Jennifer and Paul and Dhruva were sharing a table.

He smiled his very best smile and joined them.

Baldacci said, "We aren't going to ask any more questions, Gabe."

"Thank you, Harry."

Carla said, "Even though you insisted on telling us the first half of the story." She was staring at him. "This is an FBI thing now, isn't it?"

"No. There's just nothing to tell."

He took a too-large bite of banana bread and was chewing like a grazing ruminant when Penelope walked through the front door.

And behind her was Monroe.

He promptly choked and would surely have died if Carla hadn't Heimliched him savagely.

When he stopped coughing, he looked up, and Billy was hugging his mother. Which was nice.

Carla said, "Is that Penelope?"

"In the flesh." And they all studied her like she was Jimmy

Hoffa with the Loch Ness Monster on a leash.

But Monroe was sitting at a table across the room gazing at him.

Jennifer said, "Who is the guy staring at you, Gabe?"

Paul smiled. "That's Monroe, isn't it, Gabe?"

"It is."

There was a sharp, theatrical intake of breath.

Carla said, "He's hot." Baldacci looked like she'd stabbed him in the chest with a boning knife. Again.

Carla patted his face. "He is, but he's no you."

Which was plainly true. He liked Baldacci, but he would never be Monroe. Well, maybe in a thousand years when somebody's entire genetic code could be rewritten?

Monroe was wearing a dark gray suit that hung elegantly from his lanky frame. His silver-gray hair was perfect, and his angular, Cubist face was set in a cheery half-smile. He looked quite genial if you ignored the cold, alien eyes.

Baldacci said, "What are you going to do, Gabe?"

He took a deep breath and almost started coughing again. He squared his shoulders and marched over to Monroe's table.

Monroe was smiling at him. He was one scary, handsome, sexy, fascinating, scary package. But he wasn't attracted to him.

"Sit down, Gabriel. If you like?"

"If I like!"

Monroe smiled some more, and his little gray eyes twinkled with evil delight. "I was going to leave, but I was afraid you'd think I was avoiding you."

"You are! And the whole FBI too."

"No, Gabriel. The FBI knows where I am. Some of the time. You've had an exciting few months, haven't you?"

He sat down and leaned across the table. "You almost got me and Cory blown up in our own condo. Well, it's Cory's really."

Monroe smiled and shook his head. "I'm innocent of all wrong doing."

"Are not!"

"What do you think I did? Exactly?"

"You led Lydia Gibson to me, and that was the first step

that led to all the other shit."

Monroe's smiled dimmed. "I intended to lead Lydia to you, but she was so very slow to take the bait that I changed my mind."

"No! You wanted me to meet Jonathan Bergeron." He lowered his voice to a whisper. "And to investigate you know who!"

"Congressman Oxley?"

He hissed at Monroe. "Yes!"

"Why would I want that? And how could I possibly have foreseen that your meeting with Lydia would lead to his downfall? Which didn't interest me in the least."

"Bullshit!"

"No, Gabriel. I had no interest in Oxley."

"Why not?"

"Because no one paid me to take an interest. If I had been involved, I can assure you that the body count would have been much lower."

He shook his head. "That sounds good, but you're lying. You asked me about Andrew and sent Lydia my way. Why would you do that if not because of Oxley?"

"So I ask one question about your dead grandfather six months ago and give Lydia a slight nudge, and then I sit back confident that things will inevitably go my way? Just how clairvoyant do you think I am?"

He shook his head. "You were in the background pulling strings and cackling."

Monroe laughed at him and patted the top of his head. He batted the hand away. Monroe gave him a look meant to flash freeze his blood from aorta to capillaries, but he wasn't intimidated. Not one bit.

He suppressed a shiver.

"You used Penelope. To manipulate events."

Monroe sighed. "This is none of your business, but I don't see that it will do any harm now. I was interested in Reed Gibson. Not David Oxley."

"What?"

"Reed Gibson, Lydia's husband? Tall, arrogant fellow? For

reasons which were never stated, it was critical that I scuttle his career and impugn his reputation, and I thought you might be useful in gathering intell."

"I wouldn't have done that!"

"Not if you knew why I wanted the information. But then the prevailing winds shifted, and it became vital that I save him. Which was a bit of bother, but I did get paid double. So there's that."

"But he's having difficulties now?"

"Which will soon go away as if by magic."

And Monroe smiled like a Cheshire cat.

He didn't know what to believe. "Wait. What about Penelope and Phillip?"

"Penelope was a very bad girl. Which she often is, but this time it almost got her killed."

"She wanted to blackmail Oxley?"

Monroe shook his head. "No, Gabriel. She seduced stupid Phillip so he would steal research from Oxley International."

"Right. I knew that much, but he didn't get paid?"

"The buyer backed out when Oxley discovered the theft right away."

"And David Oxley?"

"The story that Penelope tells...which I think is true in this one case...is that she and Phillip were in bed in post-coital languor, and a piece about David Oxley and a possible senate run appeared on the newscast they were watching. And Phillip bragged to her that he could bring Oxley down with a phone call."

"And she got the whole story out of him?"

"During the commercial break."

"And she talked him into blackmailing Oxley?"

Monroe considered. "She swears she didn't."

"Phillip needed the money or thought he did."

"In any case, Phillip met Oxley, and Phillip died as a result, and Penelope has been hiding out since then."

Monroe was looking at him. "What happened to Oxley, Gabriel?"

He smiled his very best smile. "I have no idea."

Monroe laughed and laughed. "How did you get this old and not learn how to lie?"

"I can lie! I can lie with the best of them, Monroe. If that's your real name. My friends call me Machiavelli."

Monroe said, "If you have friends, and you obviously do, you aren't Machiavelli, Gabriel."

"But why do you care? You weren't interested in Oxley. Or so you say."

"I wasn't, and I'm not. Just curious. We're alike in that respect."

"We're nothing alike." Monroe was making leaving motions. "Wait. So why are you here? Now?"

"I brought Penelope home." And Monroe was striding away.

"Will I see you again?"

"Do you want to?"

"No." He didn't trust Monroe one little bit. "No offense."

"None taken."

And Monroe was out the door and gone. And out of his life forever.

Probably.

He rejoined his friends. It occurred to him that planting Hand inside the Gibson household would have been a perfect way to spy upon Reed.

But he would never know. He sat at the table and finished off his coffee.

Jennifer said, "Are you all right, Gabe?"

"Yes. But my head hurts. I don't know what to believe? He says he had nothing to do with Phillip's murder and all the rest."

Baldacci said, "And you don't believe him?"

"His story sounds reasonable."

Carla said, "But he's a born liar."

"Exactly."

Jennifer said, "We should get back to the office."

And they did. He was sitting at his desk in his cubicle. He was going to stop thinking about Monroe and Penelope and Brunetti. And Hand.

He wasn't a detective, and he was going to forswear all detective work in future.

He had new clients coming in, and he was sure that they were going to be a delight. He was happy as an accountant, and that was what he was going to be for the rest of his life.

Probably.

Made in the USA
Middletown, DE
05 July 2021